I'LL BRING YOU BUTTERCUPS

Part 2

When Tom and Andrew volunteer to fight for King and Empire so too do Alice and Julia as VAD nurses on the Western front. All find trials that will test them to the limit. For all, passion and hope must be tempered by heartbreak and sorrow...

Those who survive the torment of the trenches return to their homeland as very different people. For Alice it is a reluctant return as one of the aristocratic Sutton family... Will she find peace and fulfilment once again?

This book is the concluding sequel in the *I'll Bring You Buttercups* saga.

I'LL BRING YOU BUTTERCUPS

Part 2

I'LL BRING YOU BUTTERCUPS
(Part 2)

by

Elizabeth Elgin

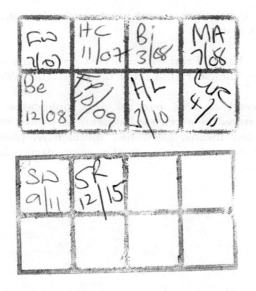

Magna Large Print Books
Long Preston, North Yorkshire,
England.

British Library Cataloguing in Publication Data.

Elgin, Elizabeth
I'll bring you buttercups (part 2).

A catalogue record for this book is
available from the British Library

ISBN 0-7505-0809-4

First published in Great Britain by HarperCollins Publishers,
1993

Published in Large Print August 1995 by arrangement with
HarperCollins Publishers Ltd., and the copyright holder.

Magna Large Print is an imprint of
Library Magna Books Ltd.
Printed and bound in Great Britain by
T.J. Press (Padstow) Ltd., Cornwall, PL28 8RW.

To my father Herbert Wardley
whose book this is

1

1915

Helen smiled, her eyes following the darting, diving bird that circled the stable block: a swallow—the first of summer. She was always glad when the little birds arrived to build beneath the stables eaves: swallows brought luck with them, Jinny Dobb said. The year the swallows *didn't* nest at Rowangarth would not be a good one, she said, for the Suttons. And the same with the rooks—if ever they deserted the rookery, took off to build elsewhere, then ill would befall Rowangarth.

There were many, of course, who thought Jin a little peculiar. She had 'feelings'; read tea-leaves with uncanny accuracy. But then her mother had been the same; a witch, some had gone so far as to say.

'Tommy-rot,' she chided herself, lifting her face to the June sun, closing her eyes for that first-swallow wish, not to be wasted. She was always careful with wishes; never asked for something so highly improbable that it could never be; would never be so foolish as to wish that on the first of July there would be a great, blazing miracle and the war would end. Better to wish that all those she loved would come safely home from the war. She would settle for that: for Robert, in France now; for Andrew, at a base hospital, Julia thought—and please God he was; and for Nathan, so very like Giles.

Poor Giles, Helen frowned, who had learned to live with pointed enquiries about when he would enlist, and the raised eyebrows that one so young was still a civilian.

'No!' She shook such thoughts from her head and surrendered to the peace of the garden and the birdsong that never failed to soothe her. She was glad it was summer. Bad news seemed never quite so bad when the sun shone; it was less awful on a day such as this to think back on what had happened these last six months.

The winter had not been a good one, there was no denying it. Last Christmas, when everyone hoped to be celebrating peace, they'd all been caught unawares. No one had dreamed the war could strike so close to home; at nearby Whitby and Scarborough. London, maybe, or even the south coast towns—but not two northern fishing ports. Their bombardment from the sea had been vicious; had lasted for more than half an hour before the enemy ships disappeared, without challenge, into the winter mists of the North Sea.

And after that, the zeppelins. They came, as everyone had feared, silently out of the night, leaving death and destruction behind them, and ghosting away, sinister in the moonlight. It was as if, Judge Mounteagle said, the Kaiser had issued a warning.

Don't sit there so smugly, you Britishers, with your seas all around you. You are not inviolate. We can reach you any time we want, by sea and air. And they could, she shivered, despite guns and searchlights around all the cities.

There were good things, though, she smiled, remembering the march on Parliament. Fifteen thousand women asking —nay, *demanding*—the right to work in factories, on farms, or anywhere they were needed. It had pleased Anne Lavinia who, immediately after Christmas, joined the First Aid Nursing Yeomanry, swearing hand on heart she was fifty next birthday, and most put out to find even then she was too old to go to France to drive a motor. Now she had settled for teaching young women to drive, declaring that some were so empty-headed they hadn't the brains to be in charge of a wheelbarrow, let alone an ambulance. Most of them she had sent packing, telling them to come back when they were serious about the war and not merely taken with getting into uniform.

Yet how senseless and futile this war had become, Helen sighed, especially on so beautiful a June day, which had started so well with letters from France and India arriving by the same post. One from Cecilia, one from Robert—a good omen indeed.

Yet there had been the poison gas. How bestial. Men poisoning men; sending over waves of the noxious substance so that British troops had collapsed, half blinded, fighting to breathe. The rats had known, though; had been seen leaving the German trenches in their hundreds. They'd smelled it, and been warned. Such clever rats, to save themselves...

Then the sinking of the *Lusitania* within sight of land. That great ship had gone down in minutes. *Stay where you are, Cecilia. Even if you have to wait out the war—stay. What is a year—two years even—if at the end of it you are together again?*

Yet why, she frowned—determined to put the world, if not to rights, then into some semblance of order in her mind—were men plotting in Russia? Those who called themselves Bolsheviks, arrested in Odessa for treason. It had worried her greatly, she remembered, until Anne Lavinia snorted, 'Nonsense! Don't worry your head about Russia. Nothing like that could happen here, thank God.' Or it wouldn't, she'd sniffed, once they had the sense to give women the vote. But even so, Helen pondered, there was something in the wind, or why had Gallipoli happened? It should have been a short, sharp bombardment from naval guns, quickly over and placing the Dardanelles under British control; yet it had turned into a tragic failure. Each day now, more and more lives were lost: she dreaded opening the newspaper.

The action at Gallipoli was intended to open up a shorter seaway to Russia, the Judge supposed—but why to Russia? And were those men in Odessa really so important? Weren't we taking them a little too seriously? Were they our problem?

Yet in spite of it all, today the world had not gone quite to the brink of madness. Today, the swallows had returned bringing wishes with them, so that she *knew* everything would be all right. One day, the war would end and those she loved would come safely home and—

'Mother! You must come—*at once!*' Julia called, running across the grass. 'Will Stubbs is beside himself and wants me to find Giles.'

'Giles is at York—had you forgotten? But why is William upset?'

'You may well ask! Just come, will you, and tell those men to be off!' Impatiently she took her mother's hand. 'Cheeky as you please and without so much as a by-your-leave! Two horses they want, and won't take no for an answer. Tell them they can't do it!'

They found Will Stubbs protesting loudly; telling the men to be on their way before he called the constable.

'What is going on?' Helen demanded. 'Why the commotion, William?' Three men in khaki spun round to face her. Two wore the stripes of a sergeant, the third was an officer. 'My daughter says you intend taking two of my horses. Perhaps you will tell me on whose authority?'

'Ma'am. I am veterinary officer to the Third Battalion, Royal Artillery, quartered at Creesby. This,' he stressed, offering a document to her, 'is my authority. The army needs horses urgently and I am empowered to take them. You'll be paid a fair price.'

'Even when I have no wish to sell?'

'Even so. Your coachmen tells me you have four horses.'

'That is so.' Helen lifted her chin. 'Two geldings, a mare in foal, and a pony—all of which we need.'

'Then I am sorry, ma'am. I require the geldings. A rider will come tomorrow to take them away. I'll be obliged if you will make sure they have first been fed and watered. I must remind you we are at war and—'

'Oh, be *quiet!*' Julia's anger seethed over. 'We know all about the war without reminders from you! My husband is at the Front, and my brother. What more do you want?'

'Tomorrow morning, ma'am. Please have the animals ready,' said the young man quietly. 'You will be given a receipt for them and will hear from the Paymaster's office in due course.'

Helen opened her mouth to protest, then closed it, traplike. 'Come, Julia,' was all she said, before turning abruptly and walking away.

'They can't do this!' Julia raged when they were out of earshot. 'How are we to manage?'

'As best we can, I fear. Buy more carriage horses if we can get them,' Helen said flatly, 'and use the pony and the governess cart, meantime.'

'*If* we can get horses! I'd heard those men were around. They're even taking farm horses. It's monstrous. You must complain, Mother!'

'Not I. They are within their rights.

They hide behind the Defence of the Realm Act and do exactly as they please. And if the surrender of two horses will shorten this war by even one day, then they are welcome to them!' Helen swept up the steps and into the house. 'And tomorrow, Julia—when the men come again—leave it to Giles and William. Don't interfere.'

'Very well, but I don't know how you can accept it all so calmly. What next will they take from us? The house?'

'If they want to, they can even do that, though I hope they will not.'

Take Rowangarth? Take her lovely old house. John's house? That would be most cruel of all. Please—they would not take her home, would they?

'Are you all right?' Julia guided her mother to a chair, settling a cushion at her head. 'Shall I ring for tea?'

'Thank you. I would like that. And don't worry—I'm all right...'

But, oh, sometimes—just sometimes —she was so very afraid.

Andrew read the letter through twice, folded it carefully, then placed it in his pocket.

Julia was well, he smiled fondly, though her letters were alternately sad or glad, according to her mood. She missed him, wanted him, as he missed and wanted her.

Was there any news yet about leave? And if so, when would he get it? Where, when he did, she demanded, would they spend it? Longings poured out on paper; yearnings between every line. His Julia was exquisite. She walked the wards beside him, stood at his side, and brought sanity to a world gone mad. She was his reason for staying alive; for breathing out and breathing in, even.

Today he had needed her letter. Today he had looked upon savagely broken bodies; seen more young lives viciously ended. Many had died without protest, like the gentle snuffing out of a candle flame; others had fought death, crying out their right to live.

It was obscene they should die in such filth; in lice-infested uniforms caked with stinking mud. Many had no chance. There were not enough doctors or nurses; though to expect a woman to brave the dangers of the clearing-stations so near the front line couldn't even be thought about. There, medical orderlies and stretcher-bearers patched up the wounded before sending them to the hospital behind the lines or despatching them to Blighty.

A hospital in Blighty. Home, though wounded, to a clean bed in a clean ward and soft-voiced nurses to tell them it was all right; that they were out of the fighting for as long as it took their wounds to heal. Well worth, some said, all the pain and horror they had endured.

Yesterday, north of Hooge, a battle had raged. Infantrymen had gone over the top of the trenches to crawl stealthily—the better or the worse for a mug of rum—through barbed-wire entanglements and into No Man's Land, to surprise the enemy in the trenches opposite; to throw in grenades, spatter the communication walks with gunfire, take prisoners. If they were lucky, that was. If the enemy had not seen their coming: though God help them if they had.

That was why, in the small hours of a silent morning, the stretcher-bearers crawled the cold wastes of No Man's Land to bring back wounded under cover of darkness. Brave men all, taking with them a priest to comfort the dying, give absolution to the dead.

And afterwards, the counting of discs. He disliked even touching them. Corpse tickets, the men derisively called them; the red identity disc taken from the body of a soldier so his death might be recorded officially; the green disc that was buried with him.

When morning came, he held eighteen lives in his right hand; eighteen red discs to slip into his pocket and give to the adjutant when he returned to the field hospital. Eighteen telegrams; eighteen grieving homes. How long could he stand it; how long before he stepped over the thin line that divided compassion and cynicism and learned to accept what he could not change?

He closed his eyes, hearing Julia's voice, feeling the small breath of her whispering close to his ear. He wanted her now; needed the softness and comfort of her. How could he have come here; how could he not have come here? And why did the six months of their parting seem like six lifetimes, six glimpses into eternity?

'Julia.' Her name was like a blessing. He must close his mind to this day. Soon he would be back at the field hospital, would open the door of the small room that was his own; where Julia's photograph stood beside his bed and there was no stench of death. For two days he would be on stand-down; time to sleep, to eat, to clean himself before going back to the forward dressing-station. That was the pattern of his life now. Two days on duty without sleep or food; two days away from it.

Now he knew what hell was made of.

That morning, the army had taken the horses and doubtless it was the last anyone at Rowangarth would see of them. Horses were essential to the war—more so than motors. They heaved loads, pulled guns, munitions carts, even ambulances. Before very much longer, the Government would realise the need to build more and more motors but, until that happened, no horse hereabouts was safe from the covetous eye of the veterinary officer. It all went to show, William said, that horses were of far more use. Stinking, spewing motors needed fuel poured into them; a horse, at a pinch, could find its food at roadsides and in hedgerows. Horses didn't break down; were living creatures, warm and faithful to man, Will declared not three hours ago as the army rider had cantered off with never so much as a word of remorse. All it had taken was a signature on a receipt, Alice told Tom as they stood now in the thickening of Brattocks Wood, arms entwined.

She seemed to exist, now, for their next meeting. A lot of what was of consequence in her life seemed to have happened in Brattocks, this last year. She wondered if it was here that one day Tom would tell her the time was right for him to go.

'Will Stubbs isn't best pleased,' Alice murmured. 'Says what's the use of a coachman without horses? There'll be nothing to keep him here once the mare has foaled. Be gone to the army, he reckons, before the back end. He'll have to, if he wants to get with horses. Wouldn't be any use him going for a marksman; couldn't hit a pig in a passage, not Will...'

'To every man his own,' Tom said comfortably. 'I could take a snipe on the wing, but I'd not be a lot of use with a carriage and pair. 'Sides, I'd look right daft in one of those top hats.'

'Be serious, Tom.' He always made light of it; never gave a yes or a no to anything she mentioned about the army. 'Don't know what's got into you these days.'

'That's because you think I've forgotten your birthday!'

'Tom, love...' He'd remembered. She smiled, lifting her lips to his. Nineteen in two days' time, yet still two years to go before they could wed—if Reuben persisted with his stubbornness and Tom insisted, still, that it wasn't right to marry, then go to war. 'Tell me how we're going to wait—if you still want to marry me, that is?'

'You know I want to,' he said fiercely, his arms tightening around her. 'But we have no house, even if Reuben was to say yes tomorrow.'

'We'd find somewhere...'

'Then have me leave you—is that it? You fancy being a widow, maybe with a bairn?

Where'd you go then? Who'd take you in but the workhouse?'

'So you're still set on going?' He didn't want her, that was the truth of it. 'You'll go for a soldier, and forget me?'

'Aye. Likely I will. It's got to be faced, sooner or later. The war could go on for years yet. But as for forgetting you, Alice...'

'You will! An' all because of this war!' She pushed away from him. Everything had been all right till war came. 'What's happening to us, Tom?'

'Nothing's happening, you silly lass,' he said softly, eyes tender. 'And just to prove it, you shall have your birthday present now. Close your eyes and hold out your hand.'

It was a small, square box, satin-covered. She looked at it, bewildered, then murmured, 'Must I wait, or can I look at it now?'

'Open it, bonny lass—see if you like what's inside.'

It was a ring; a flowerlike cluster of tiny pearls, glowing dully against a velvet bed. She looked at it for a long time, unbelieving, then whispered, 'For me? Does it mean we're engaged, official...?' Her cheeks burned, her eyes filled with lovely tears.

'Engaged, official,' he said, tilting her

chin. 'Is my buttercup girl happy? Will it fit, do you think?'

'You'd best try. Left hand, is it?'

'Left hand. We'd best do it proper.'

He slipped the little circlet on to her third finger and she gasped with delight that it fitted so perfectly, holding up her hand, loving him so much it was impossible to describe.

'There now, Alice Hawthorn; that ring says I *won't* forget you. Not ever.'

'Can I tell them, Tom—say you're my fiancé?'

'Aye. Tell them. And when they ask when we'll be wed, tell them as soon as maybe; just as soon as this war will allow—that Tom Dwerryhouse wishes it could be tomorrow. I'd have liked it to be diamonds, Alice: maybe one day, perhaps...'

'Don't you dare. Buttercup girls don't wear diamonds.'

'Nor yearn for orchids, Alice?'

'Never orchids.' She smiled tremulously into his eyes, so suddenly happy it was like a burst of sunlight inside her. 'Kiss me, Tom—please?'

The meeting of their lips was warm and gentle; a wondering kiss; a kiss of commitment.

'I love you,' he said, his voice rough with wanting. 'I love you so much it's near unbearable...'

'I know.' Her voice was little more than a whisper as she sank down on the soft summer grass, holding up a hand to him, begging him silently with her eyes.

'You're sure?' he said, dropping to his knees beside her.

'Very sure, only I don't know how. Show me, Tom?'

'You know I'll be careful.'

'Yes, my darling; I know...'

Alice knew from the urgency of the footsteps, the slamming of heels along the passage, that Julia would any moment fling open the sewing-room door.

'Hawthorn!' Her cheeks were bright pink, her eyes shone. 'I've told Mother and now I must tell you! It's all so wonderful! No leave, he said. Don't ever begin to hope—yet listen to this!' She unfolded the letter, reading breathlessly.

I think perhaps I might tell you, even though nothing is certain, that somewhere before the end of the year there may be good news. Married men can now be considered for ten days' leave. Names go to Brigade HQ—if taken alphabetically, I'm just about half-way.

Please, my love, don't build your hopes too high—nothing in this war is certain—but even I am beginning to hope we might spend our first anniversary together...

'Hawthorn! Just imagine! To see him, touch him...' Her voice whispered into a sob. 'Dare I hope? He wouldn't say it if there wasn't a chance, would he?'

'He wouldn't, miss. The doctor's a cautious one. It's my belief there's something in the wind or he'd never have written that. And I'm right pleased for you. Funny, isn't it, but luck breeds luck, they say.' Smiling, Alice held up her left hand. 'Go on, Miss Julia—have a wish on it. Everyone else has.' Carefully she pulled off the ring, dropping it in the outstretched palm. 'Slip it on your finger, then close your eyes and wish.'

'Engaged! You never breathed a word!' Impulsively, she kissed Alice's cheek. 'When will you be married? Has Reuben said yes at last? Oh, my word! Tom hasn't enlisted, has he?'

'I didn't say anything because I didn't know. Took the ring out of his pocket all of a sudden. And no, he hasn't volunteered, thank God, yet he will, I know it. There won't be a wedding, though,' she sighed. 'I'm only nineteen, or will be—'

'On Sunday,' Julia finished. 'I haven't forgotten. But tell me about the ring?'

'We-e-e-ll, I was going on at Tom, I suppose, worrying about him going to the war—so I think he sprang it on me before he'd intended.'

'Well, you're half-way there now. Does it feel strange, wearing a ring? I was very conscious of mine. I went left-handed, sort of, till I got used to it...'

'Don't think I'll ever get used to it, miss,' Alice smiled shyly. 'I'm sort of —*floating*...'

'I know the feeling. Scattering rose petals from a lovely pink cloud. Aren't we lucky? Must fly, though. Got to write to Andrew at once! I'll tell him about you and Dwerryhouse and I'm so happy for you, I truly am. I'll wish and wish you'll soon be married, because being married—you know what I mean—is the most wonderful, *wonderful* thing...'

'Yes,' Alice whispered as the door banged and footsteps danced down the stairs. 'I know exactly what you mean, miss.'

She had hardly slept last night for thinking about it; had stared at herself in the mirror, wondering if it showed, if in some way she had changed because of it. But Alice in the mirror had stared back, unchanged except for eyes that held a secret.

Last night had been so good. A gentle giving and taking, too soon over; as if after that first careless soaring they had realised the enormity of it. She had wanted to stay in his arms; to cling to him to prolong the moment, but he had left her, abruptly.

Yet it had been so wonderful, their first fleeting loving. It bound him to her and her to him. Neither of them spoke on the walk home, thighs touching, hands too tightly clasped as though now they must always be close. Bemused, almost, they walked to the edge of the wood.

'Sweetheart...' As if, suddenly, she were fragile china, he helped her over the stile. 'What came over us?'

'Nothing that wasn't right and proper. Nothing save love, Tom...'

'And was it...?'

'It was good, if that's what you're asking, and it'll get better with every time.'

'No!' She felt the tightening of his hand on hers. 'There won't be another time. Tonight we were lucky and I managed—well, I left you before any harm was done. But no more till we're married, Alice. Another time I could lose control and you'd fall for a baby.'

'And would that be so bad?' She had wanted him, then, to take her again, but he'd touched her cheek gently and told her to be away.

'I'll stay here—watch you to the door.

27

And Alice, love...' He kissed her again. 'I do love you.'

He'd said it sadly, she thought; said it sort of yearning, as if he really meant it wouldn't happen again—or as if he regretted, already, what had been between them.

But there *would* be another time, she argued fiercely, and if making a child together was a means to an end, then so be it. It would be a love child to bind them ever closer. And if that happened, she thought, laying her lips to the cluster of pearls on her finger, then Reuben would *have* to say yes!

2

Cook was not best pleased. Neither wedded nor bedded, much less a mother, she'd been near overcome to learn that the three nephews she looked upon as sons and to whom would go her worldly goods when her time ran out, had been sent to the Front. All in the same regiment, too, which was downright foolish of the army when she brought to mind what had happened to Jinny Dobb's nephews. Killed, both of them, by the same shellburst, and Jin still a mite peculiar because of it.

'Pah!' She vented her dismay on the bread dough she was kneading: lifting, punching it, slapping, banging it, because that wasn't all by any manner of means. She'd been upset by what she had read in the paper this morning: that nice young Mr Churchill banished to be Chancellor of the Duchy of Lancaster; no sort of a position for a man who'd been First Lord of the Admiralty.

But someone had to be blamed for Gallipoli, she sighed, for they'd never get over the shame of it. She closed her eyes tightly because it hurt to think of the young men who'd come all the way from Australia and New Zealand to die for a far-away King: she'd wager a week's wages that if their womenfolk had known they were going to breathe their last on the soil of a heathen country like Turkey, they'd never have let them come!

'That's going to be a grand baking of bread, Mrs Shaw, the way you're knocking it about,' Tilda observed.

'Is it now?' Cook puffed. 'And less of your sarcasm, miss, or I'll knock you about an' all!'

Tilda smiled, not the least put out. Nothing could upset her now she was in love, deeply, for all time in love; and with the most handsome, eligible bachelor

29

in the world. He was brave, an' all, in France with the Grenadier Guards and even though she knew he wouldn't be allowed within miles of the fighting, to her he was a hero.

She smiled dreamily at the mantelshelf from which His Royal Highness, David, Prince of Wales smiled down from a silver-plated frame, and reaffirmed her devotion with a sensual pouting of her lips.

'And another thing,' Cook flung to no one in particular, 'what's to be done about the dinner party—food being what it is?'

'You'll manage,' Mary soothed. 'You always do. We're well into the shooting season, so the meat shortage won't bother us. It's only to be a small party; it'll run to a partridge apiece—and there's no one like you when it comes to cooking game-birds.'

'We-e-ll...' Only ten at table; family and close friends to mark Miss Julia's first anniversary; the date not certain, mind, on account of them not knowing exactly when the doctor would be arriving—if Miss Julia and the doctor decided to spend his leave at Rowangarth, that was.

Just a main course and pudding, her ladyship had said it was to be, on account of them having to follow the King's example and eat frugally. Eat a third less, the Government was asking everyone: two potatoes instead of three, and smaller helpings of meat. Her ladyship was being frugal, all right. Only bacon and eggs, now, at breakfast; sometimes not even bacon— and less toast in the rack, for bread could no longer be wasted. Cook thought sadly about her precious, squirrelled-away sugar. Half a hundredweight she'd laid in just before it all started, yet most of it was gone now. Food was getting more and more expensive, which wasn't right nor decent when the wife of a soldier was hard put to manage on what the army paid her man.

Mind, the grocer in Holdenby was fair. Rowangarth still gave him their weekly order and hadn't changed to the big shop in Creesby like some had done in the hope of getting a bit more of things in short supply.

'Maister says he's sorry,' said the lad who delivered their order only that morning. 'He's sent what he could of what you asked for—'cept the sugar. Getting real short of sugar, and no chance of getting any more till next month.'

Two pounds! Two pounds of sugar for a household of nine, and what about the margarine? Who'd have thought to see margarine in Rowangarth's groceries! But use it she must, because butter was so scarce it would be going the way of sugar before long; ceasing to exist, almost.

Sighing, she returned her thoughts to the cooking of the partridge. She couldn't roast them in butter, nothing was more certain. Folk kept what little they could get to be eaten on Sundays.

'Red wine,' she murmured. Yet however the dratted birds turned out, they'd be a lot more palatable than the food the poor lads at the Front were getting. Iron rations, when they were in the trenches, she'd heard. Cold tinned stew and biscuits hard enough to crack your teeth, though they ate better by all accounts when they went behind the lines for a break from being shot at.

The trenches would be getting muddy, now that winter was almost here, and there would be no warm beds in the dugouts. Tommies slept on their feet, though if they had any sense they didn't sleep at all, folk said.

She looked round her clean, well-ordered kitchen and counted her blessings. Then she shaped the bread dough into tins for its first rising, all the time trying to think up a pudding that was careful on sugar. It was her duty, after all, to do her best and not grumble, for the sake of the lads at the Front and particularly for her nephews now in mortal danger. And for Sir Robert, too, and Doctor Andrew and the Reverend Nathan. She almost added Mr

Elliot, then decided against it on account of what happened in Brattocks for which she would never forgive him and him not being at the Front, neither. Can-lad to some high-ranking army man at the War Office, so talk had it and like as not spending every night at his mam's new house in Chelsea in a comfortable bed.

'Miss Julia had a letter this morning. You should have seen her face,' Bess announced, back from checking the upstairs fires. 'From the doctor, I think it was.'

Bess had taken great care over the building-up of the breakfast-room fire: raking it, laying on just enough coal, then painstakingly brushing the hearth; but she still heard nothing worth carrying below stairs.

'She's hoping, now that the doctor's been given official leave, that he'll get it for their anniversary,' Alice said, wishing she and Tom were married and living in Keeper's Cottage as if the war had never been. 'She asked me,' she confided, 'to get her blue out and give it a sponge and press.'

'The one she was wed in,' Bess smiled.

'Yes—it was the one she was wearing when he proposed,' Alice added for good measure, not wanting them to think her uppity because she'd once gone to London with Miss Julia. 'When they used to meet in secret in Hyde Park—with me walking behind, of course,' she added.

'Wonder where they'll spend their honeymoon?' Tilda slid her eyes to the mantel. 'Because it'll be like another honeymoon, won't it, them being apart for so long.'

'In London, would you think, or here at Rowangarth?' Mary ventured.

'I think she'll go to London to meet him,' Alice nodded, 'so they'll have to spend one night there at least—probably at the doctor's place.' Miss Sutton's house was small; no room for them at Montpelier Mews. 'Reckon they'll come home to Rowangarth once the doctor's seen to it that everything's all right at Little Britain. Ooh, but it's exciting for Miss Julia, isn't it?'

'Her'll be dreaming about it all the time,' Tilda sighed.

'Well, I hope that nothing goes wrong. Those high-ups out there can do peculiar things at times,' Mary warned primly.

'Ha! Those high-up officers don't know the first thing about it,' Cook grunted, 'on account of them all being in London, sending their orders willy-nilly to them that's doing the fighting.'

'Not *all* of them,' Tilda sniffed. Oh my word, no. Wasn't her lovely David there—it was Matilda-dear and David, in her imaginings—and didn't he know all about it? Probably on the waiting-list for leave himself, and right at the bottom on account of him having a German name no one could pronounce.

'Well, *all* of you are on war work one way or another, so you'd best be about your business,' Cook pronounced. 'The likes of us also serve, don't forget.' *They also serve.* She liked the phrase, even if she could never quite get it right; because not everybody could march off to war, thanks be. 'Now then, young Alice, are you sewing or working this morning?'

'Miss Clitherow says I'm to help down here, if I'm needed. There's nothing in the sewing-room that won't wait.'

Which made her very glad, because if Tom should call at the kitchen door with the hare Cook had asked for she would see him and that, to her love-starved heart, meant a whole lot more than the peace and quiet of the sewing-room.

Oh, Lordy, she sighed inside her, but how she wished they could be wed.

There were two letters of importance next morning, and both from the Western Front. Julia's was brief. Andrew was counting the days to his leave, which could well be at exactly the right time for their anniversary; she was to take good care of herself and he loved her. But more important even than that was the date at the top of the sheet. *Saturday 13 November 1915*. The letter had taken only four days to get to her, which meant that as little as four days ago he was alive and well and loving her and today he was alive and well and loving her! He *must* be! And when this war was over, she would never let him out of her sight again. *When* it was over; when the killing had stopped and no one need live in dread of the knock on the door and the small envelope the telegraph boy held in his hand.

'He's well; he loves me,' she smiled through her tears. 'What news from Robert?'

'Ssh!' Helen held up a finger for silence, her eyes not leaving the page, her cheeks flushed.

'Listen to this, both of you—just *listen.*' Briefly dabbing her eyes, taking a deep, shuddering breath, she gasped, 'Oh, no, I can't! My eyes—so silly of me. I keep wanting to weep. You read it, Julia; read it out aloud then I'll know I'm not dreaming.' She thrust the letter into her daughter's hands. 'Go on! Hurry! The bit that starts *Do you remember...*'

'Do you remember the night of Julia's wedding—oh, *yes*, Mother, I do *so* remember it...'

'Go *on!*'

'...*of Julia's wedding when you and I wished Cecilia a happy birthday, then spoke of where you hoped the army would send me? I can't actually write it in a letter for reasons of security, but your totally impossible wish is about to come true! I simply don't believe it! Dearest Mother, you are a witch...* A witch?' Julia frowned. 'How come?'

'It was after the wedding and neither Robert nor I could sleep. So we went downstairs for a drink, to wish you both luck,' Helen beamed. 'And I—well, I said I hoped that he and Cecilia could be as happy and that I'd wish and pray that the army would post him to India instead of France: he was waiting his call-up at that time, if you remember.

'And my impossible wish is about to come true, he says. He can only be referring to India. They're probably sending him to the Afghan border, I shouldn't wonder. The army does have a garrison there. But if it's true—don't you see? They'll be able to be married!'

'I don't believe it!' Julia cried. 'How lucky can a family get? First Andrew's leave, and now this!'

'Someone must have the luck,' Giles said softly. 'Why shouldn't Rowangarth have its share? But this is what you wanted, isn't it, Mother—all your children married? So are

37

you going to witch a wife on me too?'

'I shall if you don't hurry and find one for yourself.' She held her hands to her burning cheeks. 'And they say miracles don't happen!'

'Might I look?' Giles held out his hand for the letter, carrying it to the window, squinting at the postmark. 'This was posted a week ago. For all we know Robert could be on his way home now.'

'But will he get leave?' Helen murmured. 'They might tell the battalion to pack up and send them lock, stock and barrel to India on the next ship available.'

She wouldn't mind were it to happen that way. She wanted to see him, for however short a time, but the fact that he was being sent away from the fighting in France and back to the woman he loved was all she could ask.

'I rather think he'll be home,' Giles smiled. 'They'll need special kit—shorts, and all that sort of thing. It's hot in India, remember.'

'You could be right, Giles. He might come to Aldershot.'

'Or even York,' Giles teased. 'That's where he reported when he enlisted. Would York suit you? And had you thought that he just *might* arrive on the same day as Andrew?'

'Don't!' Helen closed her eyes and held up a hand. 'It's all too much!' She mustn't be greedy: Robert was being posted to India and the woman he'd thought never to see again and—'Oh, my goodness! I must write and let Cecilia know—carefully, of course—just hint, sort of, so she can share the excitement...'

'Mother! Robert will have written to her. By the time your letter reaches her, he might already be there.'

'I know, Julia. I'm being foolish, aren't I? All this is just a little too much to take in. I think I'll wrap up warm and take a turn round the garden...'

'I'll come with you.' Giles rose to his feet.

'No,' Julia mouthed, reaching for his arm. 'Idiot!' she grinned when the door had closed and they were alone. 'Oh, it's easy to see why you aren't married. You've got so much to learn about women.'

'Learn?'

'Yes, you soft old thing. She's going out for a little cry. Leave her be...'

'Cry? But I haven't seen her so happy for a long time.'

'Of course. That's why she needs to weep—can't you understand?'

'No. No, I can't at all...'

'Oh, Giles Sutton—how I pity the girl you'll marry! And,' she whispered, cupping his face in her hands, 'How very lucky she'll be...'

'I don't know what's going on upstairs,' remarked Alice to Tom as they walked carefully in the darkness to the place they called their courting corner, 'but this afternoon, when we were having our sewing circle—for comforts for the Front, I mean—you could fairly feel the excitement.'

'That'll be Miss Julia, I suppose.' Tom unbuttoned his overcoat, wrapping Alice into it as she snuggled against him. 'With the doctor coming on leave, I reckon.'

'No. It was her ladyship an' all. All sort of happy, she was, and smiling and—oh, I just couldn't put a finger on it. But milady's got a secret, if you ask me.'

'She's got a gentleman?' Tom frowned.

'No, she has *not,* and don't you go putting it around that she has. But there's something in the wind, mark my words if there isn't. Could hardly thread her needle, her hands were shaking so much. "Be a dear," she said to Bess, "and do it for me. My eyes are getting old." *Old?* Not her!'

'Then what?' He kissed the tip of her nose; such a pretty nose. Tip-tilted and cheeky, sort of. A kissable nose.

'Couldn't say. But what I do know is that Bess is likely giving notice.'

'An' why is the silly lass doing that? Her and Davie are courting strong, if what I hear is to be believed.'

'Aye, but Davie is out of his time, now, and Mr Catchpole says he's welcome to stay in the bothy, but if he wants promotion he'll have to look elsewhere. Rowangarth don't want no more time-served gardeners—leastways not till things get back to normal. So Davie said, "Right. I'll go for a soldier afore they conscript me." And he means it. Told Bess, and now she's vowing that if he goes she's going, too.'

'I can understand it. Sooner or later they'll bring in conscription and that'll be that. No choosing where we'll go.'

'*We?*' A shiver that was nothing to do with the November cold sliced through Alice.

'We. Davie, Will Stubs—and me. Will's going an' all. Says he'll see to it they don't put him in the infantry. Wants to be with horses when he goes. And me—'

'You want to be a marksman because you're a good shot,' Alice whispered, stiff-lipped. 'So the three of you'll volunteer.' Alice pulled away from the circle of his arms. 'You've been talking—all of you. You're all of you going before they make conscription into law...'

'No, lovey. Not *going*. Just talking it over between us.'

'I see.' There was a terrible shaking inside her; a feeling that if she let herself, she could be sick. 'You're like Bess, aren't you? Can't wait to be off...'

'No, Alice. We've been talking, I'll admit it. Can't blame us for that—not for talking; a bloke has to think things out. But we aren't going to rush off and grab the King's shilling if that's what you're bothered about. I'll tell you, I promise I will, before I make up my mind about anything. I give you my word, bonny lass. So give us a kiss and tell us what Bess aims to do. Going to set the world alight, is she?'

'Bess only said *if*. If Davie goes. They're building a munitions factory at Leeds. It'll be making shells—the army's terrible short of shells, it seems. And it's respectable now for women to work in factories—married women, an' all. There's good money in munitions; better than in service.'

'Maybe so. But I hope you won't do anything like that if I should decide the time is right for me to go, Alice.'

'Are you asking, Tom?'

'I'd like to think,' he said, choosing his words carefully, 'that if I went for a soldier I could think of you here, with her ladyship, and Reuben on hand to look after you. I wouldn't want you to go into a munitions factory, lass. Those shells can blow up. There's been some nasty accidents, you know that as well as I do: women blinded, or their hands blown off—or worse.

'And they go yellow, those women who make shells—can't blame folk for calling them canaries. Something in the powder, it is. No amount of money is worth going *yellow* for.'

'Happen not. But they'd give Bess a badge to wear. She'd be in a starred occupation. She says she'd rather have a star to wear than be sent white feathers.'

'Folk don't send white feathers to women, daftie.'

'No, but there'll be some busybody sending 'em soon to Mr Giles.'

'And to me too, Alice.'

'No, Tom. *No!* You aren't a conchie. You'll go when the time is right—you've always said so. But Mr Giles says he won't go; not to kill, any road. And he don't care, he told me, if folk do call him a conchie. And it's a free country, I suppose...'

'No love, it *isn't*. Not any more,' Tom murmured, pulling her closer. 'Soon there'll be a choice; fight or go to prison, because that's what'll happen to objectors before so very much longer.'

'Poor Mr Giles,' Alice whispered. 'He's a good man, Tom.'

'He is. You know it and I know it—but tell that to the recruiting sergeant next time he's around, and see what *he* says. But we're wasting good courting time. Here we are, putting the world to rights, and not a kiss between us. Tell me you love me,' he demanded.

'I love you, Tom Dwerryhouse, and I want us to be wed. I want you and me to be married so much that I don't care if I've fallen for a baby...'

'You haven't—and Alice, there's got to be no more of *that* between us. We've got to wait. I don't want to walk down the aisle with a shotgun at my back. I want us married decent.'

'Well, I just want us to be married,' she murmured mutinously, 'and I'm giving you fair warning, Tom. I don't care how I get you!'

'We'll be wed when there's a house for us to live in,' he muttered, stubborn to the end, 'and I don't have a war hanging over me. I'll not marry you, then leave you for a widow.'

'The doctor wed Miss Julia. Are you saying he shouldn't have?'

'I'm saying it's his business—his and hers. And anyway, they're both of them better heeled than you or me. You haven't any kin of your own to go to if you were left with a bairn, Alice. Miss Julia has her family around her—aye, and money of her own too.'

'And she's counting the days to them being together again,' Alice whispered, lips close. 'She's so happy, you wouldn't believe it.'

'And you've got me here every day, so why aren't you happy too, Alice Hawthorn?'

'I am happy, only I want us to be wed, Tom; I want to belong.'

'And I say we'll be wed when the time is right and now isn't the time! So let's not fratch and fight over it. I love you. I've bought you a ring for all to see my intentions, but we won't be wed—happen because I love you too much.'

'All right,' she murmured. 'I'm only saying I love you and want you—you can't blame me for that, can you?' She inched closer, whispering her lips across his cheek, teasing him with soft little kisses until she felt the hardening of his body against hers.

'Kiss me,' she murmured, huskily. 'Kiss me and touch me and hold me...'

She lifted his hand to the rounding of her breast, searching with her mouth for his.

Eve had done it with an apple, the Bible

said. It had been the same between men and women since ever the world began, so where was the harm in it? She closed her eyes, knowing it was wrong even to think such things. And hadn't Adam and Eve lost Eden because of it?

'Sorry, sweetheart,' she whispered. 'Forgive me?'

3

Julia unfastened the button at her waist, letting her petticoat slide to her feet. Since Andrew demanded she should throw away her corsets, life had become unbelievably comfortable. Now her breasts were where nature intended them to be, and not pushed in and up by harsh, uncomfortable bones.

Unfastening her supporters, she gazed dispassionately at her body in the mirror. For the young and daring, tight bust bodices were out of fashion. Now 'supporters' were all the rage—a brassière, the French called the new undergarment; but by whatever name, it gave such freedom she wondered why something so clever and chic hadn't been thought of long ago.

The light from the peach-shaded lamps

touched her naked image. Strange, she thought, that the exchanging of wedding vows should make the hitherto unacceptable into something completely respectable, and the unthinkable into an act of wifely duty, with the generous blessing and complete approval of the Church and society. In short, wasn't sleeping with Andrew an utter delight?

And soon, now, she would hear from him. By letter, would it be, saying he was on his way, or a telegram asking her to meet him at the lodgings in Little Britain? Or would it be a telephone call? Would the phone ring and would she pick it up to hear, 'Darling, I'm at Holdenby ...'

Yet if she could choose, it would be to meet him in London at the station: to savour the excitement, the anticipation; to watch his train arriving, wonder which compartment door would open and...

She laughed with delight as she pulled her nightgown over her head—her sensible, winter-warm, sleeping-alone nightgown—then placed the guard over the fire. She hurried into bed, impatient to close her eyes and be near to him, for this was a time for counting days and dreaming dreams; to wonder where they would meet, what they would say.

Would it be with a chaste kiss of greeting; a sharing of glances that said, *I want you?* Would she run the length of the platform to him, throwing herself into his arms? People kissed in public now. Lovers apart for a whole year cared not a jot for convention. Even skirts were shorter. Now the human race had discovered ankles, she giggled, hugging the hot bottle to her.

Skirts. When she met Andrew, should she wear the hobble skirt—that *daft* skirt, he'd called it. If she did, though, Hawthorn would have to take it up at least three inches, for it wasn't just ankles that were in fashion. In Leeds, a week ago, Miss Clitherow had seen a lady police constable wearing a skirt no more than four inches below her knee: showing her calves, would you believe?

She switched off her bedside light, then burrowed into the feathers of the mattress to dream again of loving and being loved; of sleeping in her husband's arms and the joy of awakening to find him beside her still.

'I love you, Andrew MacMalcolm.' She ached all over, just wanting him; longed for his caress and the wonder of their coupling. She hoped that this time they might make a child, but at this moment of her terrible need of him, she would settle just for being loved.

God. She closed her eyes. *Thank you for Andrew. Keep him safe for me? Don't let anything awful happen to him.*

Yet awful things did happen, every minute of every day and night. It wasn't fair, really, to ask God to choose, because German women were praying now, exactly as she was and for much the same thing.

Best she should send her love to her man instead, send it in great, warm waves; a love so strong that nothing could harm him because of it.

'I want you so much, my darling,' she murmured, as sleep took her.

She awoke to a crisp, cold morning and the first frost of the year. It sparkled the lawn below her window and touched the bare branches of the trees in Brattocks Wood. Mornings such as this gave way to wintry sunshine, she smiled, flicking over the date on her writing-desk calendar. One day nearer.

She took her sponge-bag and hurried to the bathroom, eager to start the day. Perhaps today she would know when he would come and how it would be. Soon they would be together again. She was so happy. Not *too* happy; she dare not be that. Too-happy people made the gods jealous. And today she *must* remember to write to Sparrow; ask her to light fires at the lodging, make sure the bed was well aired. *Why* couldn't she get beds out of her mind!

She slid home the bolt then turned on the taps. Quickly now. She must not be in the bath when the telephone rang! Dear, sweet heaven, how happy she was. Crazily, stupidly happy—and be damned to jealous gods!

Alice could not get Giles Sutton out of her mind. Since it happened she had been upset—aye, and angry, too. This morning it had been—and all because of that Morgan sliding down to the kitchen; gazing at Cook with big, begging eyes, and generally being a nuisance underfoot.

'Take that animal back to where it belongs,' Mrs Shaw ordered. 'Animals in kitchens isn't sanitary!' How Alice wished she'd told Tilda to take him away instead.

'In you go, you bad dog. Sit on your blanket and wait.'

She had found the library door open, the room empty, and had crossed to the hearth to make sure there was water in the drinking bowl. That was when she saw it: no one could miss it, no one was intended to miss it. A garish poster, spread out on the desk, exactly like the one she had seen in Creesby.

THERE ARE THREE TYPES OF MEN
THOSE WHO HEAR THE CALL, AND OBEY
THOSE WHO DELAY
AND THE OTHERS...
TO WHICH DO YOU BELONG?

She could still remember her shudder of revulsion; how she had wanted to tear down that poster because it was aimed at Tom and Davie and Will. Now someone had sent one to Mr Giles!

'Hawthorn!' He was standing in the doorway. 'What are you doing?'

'I came to bring Morgan back. You let him get out, Mr Giles.'

'I'm sorry. Thank you.' His face was ashen, his knuckles stood out white in clenched fists.

'That's all right.' She stood there waiting, stubbornly, angrily, standing her ground. 'And, sir—you'd better tell me who sent that. Or didn't they put a name to it?'

'No name. There never is.'

'What do you mean, *never is?* You've had one before? Why you? Nobody's sent anything like that to Tom!'

'Nor will they. That poster is aimed at shaming men to enlist. Dwerryhouse will go before so very much longer, but they know I won't: God knows I've said so often enough. I asked for it, I suppose...'

'It isn't right. It's not fair!' She snatched up the poster, twisting it into a ball, flinging it on the fire. 'There now—the best place for it! This is a free country and don't let them make you do anything your conscience don't approve of. I know Tom will go, but I'd give anything for him not to—I'll tell you that for nothing!'

'Bless you, Hawthorn. But you won't breathe a word about this, will you? Julia is so happy, my mother too. I don't want anything to spoil it for them. Not a word to a soul?'

'Not one word, sir. I promise.'

'Good. Then while you're about it, you'd better do the same with these.' Cheeks blazing an unnatural red now, he opened a drawer and took out an envelope, shaking it so the contents floated to the desk-top. 'Burn these too...'

'Mister Giles—*no!*' Horrified, Alice gathered up the feathers: three white feathers. 'When did these come?'

'Two days ago.'

'Then you should have told me! You can't keep a thing like that to yourself: not white feathers!'

There'd been a man at Creesby who'd hanged himself from a tree; they'd found three white feathers in his hand when they cut him down. Sad that whoever sent them hadn't bothered to find out he was dying

52

of consumption! Some cat of a woman, she supposed. White feathers weren't a man's way of doing things.

'There now—that's them over and done with!' The acrid stink of their burning filled the room, and she opened the window the sooner to be rid of it. 'I'll come for Morgan this afternoon before it starts getting dark, and don't you fret none till then. No one knows but you and me—and her who sent them,' she added darkly.

She worried about it all morning. Who would do such a thing? Who hated Rowangarth so much?

Mrs Clementina? she'd asked herself, then immediately dismissed the thought. Mrs Sutton had sons in uniform, one of them at the Front. She couldn't have sent that vicious poster, nor any of her ladyship's friends, either. But a young man like Mr Giles who stood by what he believed was fair game to the stupid lot who hung on to every word that Baroness Orczy woman said; she who preached that it was glorious a man should die for his country; who openly encouraged women to do their duty and persuade every man they knew to enlist, or award them the Order of the White Feather, present them with the badge of cowardice.

Women of England, she cried at recruiting meetings. *Do your duty! Send your men*

53

today to join our glorious army!

Glorious, Alice fumed. What had been glorious about Artois and Loos and the slaughter at Gallipoli? And Mr Giles wasn't a coward; he didn't deserve three white feathers! Giles Sutton knew what being a conscientious objector was all about. It took a special courage to stand up and be counted.

All at once, her anger spent, Alice felt helpless and bewildered. What was the use of this war, she demanded, and how was she to bear it when Tom went?

Because the afternoon was so sunny and the sky still amazingly light for November, Helen decided that tea would be taken in the conservatory, probably for the last time this year, she thought, relaxing in the unaccustomed warmth, thinking that this could be mistaken for a day in spring. She looked up, smiling, as Mary brought in the afternoon post.

Helen's heart thumped with excitement now, each time the postman pedalled down the drive, anticipation adding to the joy of opening a letter, maybe to discover at last whether it would be Robert or Andrew who would arrive first.

All her children would be at Rowangarth again, even if only for a short time, she thought. She was the luckiest of women.

54

Soon Andrew and Julia would be together and Robert on his way back to Cecilia. And who but knew, Helen thought; this time next year they might not only be married but Cecilia might well be pregnant.

She cleared her head of such thoughts. She must not wish for such things when already she'd had more than her fair share of good luck. Grandchildren—grandsons— would come in their own good time.

'Well now, what have we here?' She thumbed through the letters, not noticing the look of apprehension on her son's face. 'Two for me, one for Julia and one for you, Giles, from York,' she smiled, recognising the agent's flowing script.

'I'll read it later.' He set it aside, relieved that no one had sent another poster—or three white feathers.

'Julia's is from Andrew.' Helen held out the letter as the door burst open.

'Mary says there's one for me from France,' Julia cried. 'Probably Andrew knows when he'll be arriving by now.'

Her cheeks were flushed, her eyes shone. She had never, Helen thought, seen her daughter so beautiful. Such happiness was good to see, but then, she'd always known that Andrew was right for her daughter from the moment he'd looked at her with John's eyes. It had been as if—

'No! Oh, *No!* I don't believe it! They

can't do this!' Julia's voice rose shrilly, trembling on the edge of tears. 'Read it! Go on, read that,' she cried, thrusting the letter into her mother's hand. 'He isn't coming! They've stopped his leave...'

She wrenched open the door, running out and down the stone steps, head down across the grass, making for Brattocks Wood.

'Sis! Wait!' At once, Giles made to follow. 'I'll go to her.'

'No.' Helen laid a hand on his arm. 'Leave her. There's nothing you can do; nothing anyone can do,' she whispered bitterly, opening the letter.

The writing on the single sheet was small and crabbed as if each word had been distasteful to write. It was dated the fifteenth day of November.

My dearest,

I am writing this because to send a telegram and throw such news at you suddenly and starkly would be unforgivable.

I was told this morning that my leave pass is withdrawn for the time being. No explanation was given though none was needed. We are worked to a standstill, almost, and still the wounded flood in. I think the powers that be have only now realised that neither I—nor any doctor or nurse—can be spared...

'The poor child,' Helen whispered. 'How could they be so cruel? She was so happy, so looking forward to it.' She folded the sheet into four, unwilling to read on. 'I find it very easy to dislike those lunatics at Sarajevo who caused all this.'

'It wasn't them especially.' Giles took her hand, holding it tightly. 'Europe was ready for war long before then. It was like a time bomb ticking away, and we thought to ignore it. The assassination was the excuse they'd been waiting for. Try not to be bitter. It won't help Julia.'

'No. Nothing will help her. Though when Robert comes home, she's going to feel it even more, knowing he'll soon be with Cecilia.'

'I realise that, but we must let her come to terms with it in her own way and her own time. We can't intrude, Mother. We must just be there when she asks for our help.'

'Nevertheless, it is my instinct to shield her, comfort her.' Helen glanced apprehensively across the lawn and to the cloud that all at once blocked out the sun, making it November again. 'It'll be dark soon. Perhaps you should go and find her. I don't like her being in the wood in the half light—so many poachers about now. I don't want her mistaken for a trespasser.'

'Don't worry. The keepers know the law. They would call a warning first. But I'll find her. I think I know where she'll be.'

He found her beneath the tallest tree in the wood, leaning against it, hugging herself tightly, her eyes closed and dry of tears. Above her, rooks cawed and flapped as they settled to roost for the night.

'Sis? Come inside,' he said gently. 'It's getting dark...'

'You should always let them know,' she said, dully. 'Always tell the rooks—good things and bad—did you know that, Giles?'

Her eyes remained tightly closed as if she were unwilling to open them on so cruel a world. 'I was counting the days, the hours.' Her voice was harsh with pain. 'I want him so much it's like a terrible ache inside me. What am I to do?'

'Dearest girl.' He held wide his arms and she went to him, her face a mask of torment, giving way to her grief; weeping with great, tearing sobs.

He held her gently, making small, soothing sounds, stroking her hair, not speaking. It was a long time before her tears were spent and she let go a shuddering sigh of surrender.

'I'm cold,' she whispered. 'Let's go home, Giles.'

Alice knew Julia would come. News of any

kind found its way to the sewing-room sooner or later. It was why she waited now, putting the finishing stitches to the tiny nightgown some soldier's wife would be glad of. And though she wanted to marry Tom so much that she could weep for need of him, she knew he had been right. It would be downright foolish of them to marry. Miss Julia knew it now, only too well. Crying her eyes out, like as not, and only this morning her so excited: jumping every time the telephone rang, waiting for the postman, and all the time a far-away dreaming in her eyes.

Alice switched off her thoughts with a snap. Not for the sewing-maid to put dreamings of a honeymoon nightdress and big, sinful double beds into Miss Julia's mind, though if she wasn't thinking exactly that, then there was something very wrong with her, Alice sighed.

This morning her courses had come, right on time as they always did, and she'd been relieved, she had to admit, that their one snatched loving hadn't got the child she'd thought would bind Tom to her. Their bairns, when they had them, she sighed, would be properly got; made in wedlock in Keeper's Cottage and born into a world at peace, she conceded soberly. Tom was always right.

She broke off the thread, laying the

baby gown in the sewing-circle hamper, wondering if she should knock on Miss Julia's door and see if she wanted anything. A bit of sympathy never hurt anybody, and a glass of warm milk might help.

'Hawthorn?' The door opened quietly. 'I saw the light.'

'Come in, do, miss, and sit you down. I thought you'd come...'

'I'm glad you're here. I don't want to talk about it, though. I shall start weeping again if we do.'

Her voice was flat, her face slablike. But the gentry didn't parade their grief, Alice knew, glad she'd had the sense to take the blue dress from behind the door and hang it out of sight in the wardrobe.

'I went to Brattocks, though.' Julia leaned back in the chair, eyes closed. 'I told the rooks that—'

'Hush, now. No use going on about it,' Alice interrupted in a most unservantlike way. 'You did right, just the same, telling those birds.'

'Superstition, Hawthorn, for all that. What Luke Parkin would say if he found out, I don't know.'

'Well, the reverend isn't going to find out, is he? I shan't tell, nor them birds, neither. Know how to keep a secret, they rooks, and now that you've told them—trusted them, like—they'll make it come right for you,' Alice rushed on, eager to stall fresh tears. 'Your bad news came by letter, so it's the postman you'll have to be watching out for now.'

'You think so?' Julia's eyes opened wide, her shoulders straightened. 'There might be some good news in a letter, you mean?'

'Jin Dobb reckons that's the way it usually goes, and I'm not inclined to argue with her. Mind, my aunt Bella swore by the bees,' Alice added, steering the conversation into safer channels. 'Daft as a brush, her; stood by that hive and the bees all busy and taking not one blind bit of notice of her. Have served her right if she'd got herself stung,' she added with relish, for she had never liked Aunt Bella. 'But you and me'll stick with the rooks, miss, and if you'll pardon me, I'd try to get some sleep now if I were you. And no more weeping? Think I'd best see you into bed with some hot milk, then find some witch hazel for them eyes...'

'You're right.' Julia rose to her feet, glad for someone else to make the decisions, tell her what to do. Dear, kind Hawthorn, who had shared her dreams and hopes right from the start; who'd sent the policeman flying that night in Hyde Park. 'Do you know something, Hawthorn? If I'd had a sister, she'd have been just like you.'

'Oh, *miss!*' Sister, indeed! To the gentry?

'She would. One I could share secrets with and who'd always be there, as you are, when I needed her. If we asked the rooks, do you think they could do something about it?'

'Away with your bother, Miss Julia! There's no way at all I could be sister to you. So get yourself undressed and I'll see to that drink.' Yes, and one of Miss Clitherow's herbals an' all, to help the lass sleep. 'And then we'll see to them puffy eyes.'

'And not one tear while my back's turned—not *one,*' she added sternly, 'or the sight of you will frighten the horses. The rooks'll put it right,' she crossed her fingers behind her back. 'I promise they will.'

Agnes Clitherow's herbal tablet did its work. Julia slept late and Helen gave orders that her daughter should not be disturbed with the usual early-morning tray of tea.

'I think I won't have breakfast—just coffee here in my room. Mr Giles will make do with tea and toast in the library,' Helen murmured, arranging her pillows, drawing her shawl around her shoulders. 'And will you tell Mary I won't be receiving this morning. No explanations, tell her. She's just to take cards, Bess...'

Helen did not feel like callers today; didn't want to have to admit, when asked for news of Andrew's impending arrival, that he wouldn't be coming on leave after all.

'Not at home to *anyone*, milady?' Bess murmured.

'Well, to Lady Tessa and Mrs Lane, of course. Mary will know who.' And to Pendenys, she supposed. 'Mrs Mac-Malcolm is still upset, Bess. Best she shouldn't have to face callers—not for a couple of days.'

Bess understood; wasn't best pleased herself with the war and Davie getting himself all in a bother about being conscripted if he wasn't sharpish about enlisting.

'I'll tell Mary, milady,' she murmured. 'Not unless it's urgent, you mean?'

'Urgent?' Helen gasped.

'Why yes, milady. Like a telegram message from Sir Robert, saying he's on his way,' she smiled impishly.

Robert. But of course. 'Only if it's that kind of urgent.' Helen returned the smile and Bess bobbed a curtsey, as she always did first thing in the morning and last thing at night, then closed the door behind her.

Robert. The army was giving him a second chance: if the foolish boy didn't

63

carry off his Cecilia and marry her as soon as maybe, then he wasn't his father's son! Robert happy at last, she sighed contentedly, and Andrew's leave was only postponed. Who knew but that he wouldn't make it home for Christmas, she thought, putting her world to rights. What better time to have his leave? They'd all be glad, then, for this setback. And thinking about Christmas, why shouldn't Julia go to London and do some shopping? Not that there would be a lot to offer, so bad were the shortages becoming, but it would take her daughter's mind off things, and there was little risk of air-raids now that winter was setting in. The judge said only recently that a zeppelin had no chance of finding London in winter, what with the chimney smoke that rose in a great thick blanket over it, and the terrible fogs, too. London in November was the safest place imaginable, and Anne Lavinia's booming common sense would soon put paid to Julia's unhappiness. It was a splendid idea. Soon, when her daughter was a little less upset, she would put it to her.

Smiling, she took the carefully folded morning paper and dropped it to the floor beside her bed. She would read it, of course—it was her bounden duty to do so. But later. The newspapers made such depressing reading that, just for once, she might be forgiven for putting off the evil hour. Later she would read the sad list of deaths; of young men killed in action or died of wounds or missing at sea; read it as she always did whilst offering a prayer for wasted young lives and for those left behind to mourn. But not just yet. Later, perhaps...

It was ten o'clock exactly, the housekeeper was to remember, when Bess burst into her sitting-room, because she had only then checked her fob-watch with the ponderous booming of the grandfather cloth in the great hall.

'Bess! That is *not* the way to enter a room,' she remonstrated, rising from her desk, tilting her chin to its usual angle. 'How many times have I—'

'Ma'am! Oh, come *please!* Mary don't know what to do with it. Standing there, she is, and refusing to take it in to her ladyship. The telegram, I mean,' the housemaid supplied in answer to the unspoken questioning of the housekeeper's eyebrows. "I'm not taking this to her ladyship," she said to me. "I *won't,* not for anything!"'

'And why ever not?' Agnes Clitherow smoothed her skirts, making for the door.

'Milady's been expecting one hourly, almost, from Sir Robert—what on earth has come over the girl?'

'The sixpence, that's what...'

'The *sixpence?*' The housekeeper's annoyance was real. Never would Bess Thompson train up into a parlourmaid, she clucked inside her. Indeed, what could be the matter with Mary, who knew how to conduct herself, that she seemed to be so mesmerised by the arrival of a telegram?

'Mary offered it, and he wouldn't take it!'

It was then the housekeeper remembered. A sixpenny piece. Kept in readiness in a small china pot on the hall table, to be given as a tip to any telegraph boy who came on his red Post Office cycle from Creesby. Usually, Rowangarth telegrams or registered deliveries were snatched up at once, for the sixpenny tip represented half a day's wages, almost, and was spat upon for luck before being pocketed. Most folk tipped only a penny—if at all. And the stupid lad had refused it?

'You're sure?'

'Sure. He said nothing. Just clapped the thing into her hand, and when Mary told him to wait he turned tail and was down the steps afore she could hand him his tip. And he didn't even ask if there was a reply. They always ask if there's a reply...'

Agnes Clitherow bumped into a wide-eyed Mary at the turn in the passageway.

'Ma'am—take it in, will you?'

'This is no way to act, Mary!' She gazed archly at the small envelope deposited in her hand without so much as a by-your-leave. 'What has got into you? Did the boy say anything?'

'No, and he didn't need to. Didn't wait for his tip. Didn't you know they never take a tip when—' She stood there, shaking.

'When *what*, girl?'

'You know what I mean, ma'am.'

Death telegrams, those boys called them. Unlucky to take a tip for one of those. Like robbing the dead, they said.

'Good gracious!' There was nothing else for it. She must take it in herself, then give Mary and Bess the talking-to of their lives for acting no better than foolish peasants in a gentleman's household. 'Such nonsense! I shall speak to the pair of you later!' was her parting broadside as she sailed to the winter-parlour door.

Hesitating for only a second before opening it, taking a quick calming breath before walking up to the desk at which Helen Sutton sat, she offered the envelope without so much as a word.

'Thank you,' Helen smiled. 'This is probably from Sir Robert, asking to be met at Holdenby. Oh, dear—and we are still without carriage horses...'

She took the pearl-handled slitter, opening the wretched thing so very daintily, the housekeeper thought, smiling as she did it.

The slitter fell to the floor; the small piece of paper fluttered to join it. Helen Sutton's head fell on her hands on the desk-top with a moan so soft it was little more than the letting go of her indrawn breath.

Her face was chalk-white, her head, when the housekeeper took it in her hands, lolled heavily, then fell again with a soft thud.

'Milady!' In two steps she had crossed the room and was pulling furiously on the bell. Then she returned to the desk, calling, 'Help me!' to Bess and Mary, who had been hovering outside the door because they'd known, hadn't they?

'Water and smelling salts,' she hissed. 'Then fetch Miss Julia and Mr Giles! Oh, milady, open your eyes, do,' she pleaded, supporting her as best she was able, rubbing the cold hands furiously.

It was Mary who, having recovered her wits, helped the housekeeper to carry her to the sofa, pushing her head between her knees and all the time begging her to open her eyes.

'I told you, didn't I?' Bess muttered, thrusting the bottle into Agnes Clitherow's hands.

'Be quiet!' she snapped, waving the bottle to and fro, sighing with relief as Helen Sutton's eyes fluttered open.

'Another sniff, milady? Just one more, then a sip of water? And do as I bid you,' she flung at Bess, who disappeared in a flurry of skirts, running as if her life depended on it.

'Mother! Darling—what is it?' Helen was still bemused when Julia arrived. 'Bess said you fainted.'

'A telegram...' Helen murmured, eyes closed.

'Here, miss.' Mary had retrieved it from the floor. 'I'm sorry, but I think—'

The message was addressed merely to Sutton, Rowangarth, Holdenby. Its message was terse to the point of cruelty.

Regret to inform you that Lieutenant Sir Robt Sutton reported missing believed killed at sea on 17 Nov 1915. Letter follows.

The words swam before Julia's eyes. She had to read them again before the jumble of words formed themselves into any sort of meaning.

'Read this!' She thrust the telegram into her brother's hand as he entered the room, then wrapped her mother in her arms, rocking her, kissing her, trying to say the words her lips could not form.

'That troopship,' Giles whispered. 'In the paper, this morning—men coming home. Torpedoes...'

'Damn them! *Damn them!*' Julia's voice, when at last she found it, was harsh with pain. 'Oh Mother, not Robert?' Please, not her brother?

Helen rose slowly to her feet, swaying. Giles gathered her to him, holding her tightly.

'Water, Miss Clitherow,' she murmured. 'If you please...'

'Will you telephone for Doctor James please, Mary?' Julia's voice sounded strange and strained. 'Tell him it's urgent. Then ring the vicar. You know the numbers?'

'Yes, miss. What about Mrs Lane and Lady Tessa? Will I tell them an' all?' Friends. A woman needed her friends about her when her son's been taken.

'Just the doctor and the vicar, Mary. The others later, if her ladyship wants them...'

'I would like,' Helen whispered, 'to go to my room. Will you help me, please?'

70

'Put an arm around my neck.' Giles scooped her up as if she were no weight at all. 'Julia and I will stay with you...'

'Missing, didn't that telegram say?' Tilda murmured. They were sitting around the kitchen table, stunned by the news. 'Missing means there's a chance, doesn't it? Happen Sir Robert could have been picked up.'

'And happen he hasn't,' Cook wailed, bursting into fresh tears. 'Didn't you read what the paper said this morning?'

No survivors, that's what. Hit twice. *Two* torpedoes. Men coming home on leave. It had happened three days ago, but the Government had held back the news till all the telegrams had been sent. If there had been survivors, they'd have known...

'What is her ladyship to do?' Agnes Clitherow whispered. 'She was lying there when I went in, her face like chalk and holding on to Miss Julia's hand as if she was afraid to let it go. Staring at the ceiling, her lips moving yet not saying a word. Like she were praying...

First her husband and now her son. And him going back to India to his young fiancée and her ladyship so pleased about it. There's no justice in this world...'

The doorbell rang. It clanged and echoed

through the house, sending Mary jumping to her feet.

'I'll come, too,' the housekeeper said. Milady was in no fit state to receive—only those who were close. Agnes Clitherow knew how to deal with unwelcome callers.

Edward and Clementina Sutton stood on the doorstep, he white-faced, she lips pursed.

'We telephoned, Clitherow,' Clementina accused. 'The exchange said there was no answer.'

'Mrs MacMalcolm instructed me to remove the receiver.' It pleased the housekeeper to supply the information.

'How is she?' Edward asked, softly. 'Just a minute—if she's up to seeing us? Just to let her know we've been...'

'Will you be kind enough to take a seat, sir, madam? Mrs MacMalcolm is with her ladyship. I'll tell her you are here. Perhaps she'll be asleep. Doctor James has only just left. He gave her a draught...'

'If she's asleep, we'll call later,' Edward said gently.

'Yes, sir. Thank you, sir.'

Agnes Clitherow walked stiff-backed up the stairs, swallowing hard. Less than an hour since that telegram arrived, yet that woman from Pendenys Place already in black from head to foot.

Like a carrion crow...

4

'I'm sure they will understand, Miss Clitherow. No one at all.' Helen Sutton sat straight-backed at her desk, her face white, eyes red-rimmed from weeping. 'No Pendenys; not Letty or Tessa, even. Ask Mary to take cards—tell them tomorrow, perhaps.'

'Doctor James said you were to stay in bed.' The housekeeper offered the small glass. 'You ought to be resting. Why don't you take the sleeping-draught he left you?'

'Because there is something I must do. And I thank you for your kindness, Miss Clitherow. Everyone is so good, but just for today, I don't want anyone...'

So short a time ago she had felt such happiness that Robert would soon be with the woman he loved; now she knew they would never meet again and that it was she who must write the letter to break Cecilia's heart.

'I'll see you aren't disturbed, milady, and if there's anything I can't deal with, I'll ask Mrs MacMalcolm to see to it. I'll go now; tell Mr Edward...'

'Thank you.' Helen gazed at the photographs on her desk: the one of her son, the other of the woman he would have married. How was she to find the words? How did she tell someone that the man she loved was dead? How had it been, five years ago, when John was killed? She couldn't remember; hadn't wanted to. She'd shut out the world that day.

'Oh, Cecilia Jamilla Kahn.' She took the photograph in gentle hands. 'I understand, my dear. I do so understand.'

'Her ladyship is not to be disturbed today.' Agnes Clitherow gazed at each in turn. 'Not for *anyone*,' she stressed.

'The poor soul.' Mrs Shaw's eyes were red and puffy. 'I'd shut myself away for ever if it had happened to me. Isn't there any hope? Missing, didn't the telegram say?'

'Missing, believed killed. The survivors have been listed in the morning papers— less than twenty. Sir Robert's name isn't one of them. That is why no one must disturb Lady Helen. She is writing to Miss Kahn—a terrible thing to have to do....'

'But won't the army have told her?' Tilda frowned. 'She was his young lady.'

'A fiancée doesn't count. Only the next of kin is told.'

'Her ladyship set great store by that

74

wedding,' Cook sniffed. 'Wanted nothing more than to see them married.'

'And grandchildren. She wanted children to follow on,' Mary added. 'It's going to be up to Mister Giles, now, and him not in the least interested.'

'I hope you aren't inferring...' The housekeeper left her remark hanging in mid-air.

'Course I'm not! It's just that he's—well —*bookish*. But he'll have to look sharp and get himself wed, now.'

'No one *has* to do anything, Mary, though we shall all be pleased when he finds a nice young bride.'

'But if he doesn't, then what's going to happen to the title?' Tilda demanded. 'There's been a Sir at Rowangarth for hundreds of years.'

'And please God there always will be.' Tilda, thought Agnes Clitherow testily, had an uncanny way of putting her finger on things; of demanding, in all innocence, an answer to the question they had all been longing to ask. 'And I suppose—officially—that Mr Giles is already *Sir* Giles. But for delicacy's sake—her ladyship being in such terrible shock, I mean—we'd all best leave it for the time being.'

'But what,' Tilda persisted, 'if he doesn't have bairns?'

'Then the title sidesteps,' Cook clucked distastefully, 'to Pendenys. And if you don't mind, I want no talk in my kitchen about Sir Robert's title ending up at the Place!'

'Amen to that,' whispered the housekeeper as she climbed the twisting staircase that led to the great hall, though for Mr Edward to have it would be right and proper, him being born a Sutton, and the late Sir John's brother. But *Lady* Clementina—the Ironmaster's daughter? Oh, my word, no. And worse than that, even, was where the baronetcy would end up. Imagine it? Sir Elliot Sutton—and his doting mama just squirming with delight, should she live to see it.

Well, there'd be no shortage of Sutton heirs in *that* direction, she thought, lips pursed. It wouldn't surprise her if there weren't a few already—hedge children and by-blows, of course. Elliot Sutton had been bailed out of fatherhood more than once by his mother's money! It was the best-known secret in the Riding.

The housekeeper's cheeks pinked at such unladylike thoughts—and at a time when the house was in mourning! *Again.* Her ladyship in black once more; for a year, this time, and Mrs MacMalcolm and Mr Giles for six months and, oh! she was in such a state that she'd forgotten to tell them downstairs to dress soberly and wear black armbands until such time as advised differently. And to remind them there was to be no gossiping in the village; that, if asked, they should say her ladyship was bearing up as well as could be expected.

She sighed deeply, retracing her steps. Best she should tell them and, anyway, Cook would have the kettle on the boil soon. It might be a comfort to take a cup of tea in the kitchen. There might even be cherry scones, she thought sadly. Cook always seemed to know when to bake cherry scones...

Helen gazed at the envelope. She had written and rewritten the letter inside it, but had found no way to blunt Cecilia's pain. She had hoped never to use those envelopes again, nor the black-edged matching notepaper, left over from the time of John's death. Now John's son was dead, too.

'Is there anything special you want from Creesby?' The door opened quietly and Giles stood there, uncertainly. 'Shall I—post the letter?'

'If you will. And I think I shall go upstairs now, and lie on my bed. I didn't sleep last night.'

'Will you be all right alone? Julia has gone out. Walking, she said...'

'To the top of the Pike, I suppose.' Julia always went there when she was very happy—or very sad. 'I'll be all right. I'd rather be alone, truth known.'

She offered her cheek for her son's kiss, then turned, unspeaking to walk unsteadily up the stairs; past the Sutton men of long ago—those who had fought against the Armada, the Roundheads. She stopped to gaze at the one so like Robert; at Gilbert Sutton who had fought at Balaclava. And all of them had come home to Rowangarth, save her son.

She closed her eyes, gripping the banister rail, walking like a woman suddenly old. At the half-landing she turned and looked down to see Giles watching her, his eyes wide with concern.

'Off you go. I'm all right—just in need of sleep, that's all. We'll have tea in the conservatory when you get back.'

Dear Giles, whose conscience must be heavier, even, than his heart. Brave Giles, because it took a man of courage to refuse to fight.

She smiled down to reassure him. Only Giles left now. Giles, who must give a son to Rowangarth...

Elliot Sutton replaced the earpiece of the telephone on his desk and smiled. Not a smile of pleasure, for even he found no joy in the death of any soldier, much less his cousin. He disliked the war intensely, baulked at taking orders and observing rules and regulations; liked still less the ever-present threat of the front line because, sooner or later, he would have to go there.

His smile was more one of mockery, of derision even, that Robert Sutton should have come home to England to get himself killed when he could have stayed safely in India. Little brother Albert had had more sense. Not for anything would he come home to enlist for, like himself, Albert thought nothing of the glory of dying in a stinking trench or choking slowly on mustard gas. Just to think of it made him shudder.

But that was life. Sorry you copped it up on the way home, Robert, old man. Elliot sent his thoughts winging. Not even killed in action, he thought. What a way to go, dammit. A soldier drowned at sea.

They wouldn't get Elliot Sutton so easily, though. He would stay at the War Office as long as he could, and be damned to France and Belgium—foreign countries, both. Mind, he didn't like kowtowing to a penniless aristocrat with one pip more on his shoulders. He didn't mind people at home knowing that all of the fighting he'd seen was from a window in Whitehall.

What he *did* mind about was going home to Pendenys in a coffin. No death or glory for Elliot Sutton.

For the first time in his life he was glad he had more than his fair share of Mary Anne Pendennis's blood in his veins. Mary Anne had been a survivor, and so would he be. Sorry, cousin Robert. Bad luck, and all that...

Sighing, he took pen and paper and prepared to write, as his mother had just ordered him to, to his aunt Helen; to tell her how shocked and heartbroken he was. Best do it now. He aimed to be at the theatre in less than an hour. Better get it over with.

Tongue-in-cheek, he began to write.

'I'd never have thought—not even with a war on—that I'd be wearing black again,' Julia whispered. 'Somehow, it was going to happen to other people, not to me, Hawthorn. Do you suppose you can find a button for this dress?'

'How's her ladyship today?' Alice murmured, emptying the contents of the button-box on to the table-top, searching carefully through all the black ones.

'Not so good. She's just written to Cecilia; not a very nice thing to have to do.'

'I'm sorry, miss.' There didn't seem

anything else to say.

'Sorry? I still can't believe it. Robert was—well—always *away*, somehow. Away at school, or in India. He was like a shadowy person: not as real to me as Giles. Then he came home to enlist when he could have stayed with Cecilia and I saw him differently. He loved her very much, and all at once we understood each other.'

'Life's awful, isn't it, miss? It's wrong for two people in love never to see each other again...' Tears filled her eyes then trickled down her cheeks.

'Don't cry, Hawthorn. Please don't cry.'

'I can't help it. It isn't just Sir Robert and his young lady I'm upset about—it's me and Tom and you and the doctor. It isn't fair. I hate this war. It's going to take Tom from me and I'll have to stand by and see it happen.'

'I know. When Andrew walked away from me, slammed the compartment door, I wanted to scream, *"No!"*, but I stood there and smiled. I stood there and watched him go when I ought to have lain down in front of that engine to stop it leaving.'

'They'd have carted you away to the lock-up.'

'Maybe so, but I'd have made my protest, wouldn't I? Now I feel it's partly my fault that I'm looking for a black button that's missing from a black frock; because no one has tried to stop this war! And there's my mother, trying to be brave when they've killed her son! She doesn't want Giles to go, you know. She'd support him, stand by him, if he refused to enlist.'

'But he *will* go. They all will. It's getting so they're afraid not to.'

'Not Giles. I think he'd go to prison first. They can call him coward and conchie, but he won't kill—not my brother.'

'Then I pity him with all my heart, miss.' Alice did; especially since the white feathers. 'And you'd best leave the frock. I'll see to it.'

'Black! How I dislike it!' Julia laid the full-skirted dress over the chair arm. 'And it's miles too long! I wish I didn't feel so guilty, Hawthorn. I'm glad, would you believe, that I'm wearing black for Robert and not for Andrew. I'm trying to feel sorry for my mother and Cecilia—and I *am* sorry—yet all the while I'm grateful it wasn't Andrew's name on that telegram. I thought my world had ended when his leave was cancelled, thought nothing worse could happen. Yet now I keep saying thank you to God for letting Andrew live. What is this war doing to us?'

'I don't know. I'd give ten years of my life, though, for it to end, *soon*, before

Tom has to go. And I'm really sorry for her ladyship and for that poor lady in India. How long before she gets the letter—telling her, I mean?'

'About a month. Mother's hoping it won't arrive until after Christmas, but it will. Bad news always travels fast, don't they say? Oh, look! There's Giles and your Tom.' Julia drew aside the lace curtain. 'Wonder where they're going?'

'They're making for Brattocks. Happen to see Reuben; happen to talk keeping business.'

Alice stood there, her eyes on Tom's back, loving him with her eyes, willing him to turn and see her. But he did not. Whatever it was they were talking about didn't allow for waving to a young lady in a sewing-room window. Poachers they'd be on about. Poachers, without a doubt.

'So you're all set on it, Dwerryhouse?' Giles dug his hands deep into his pockets, hunching his shoulders against the cold. 'Davie, William and yourself?'

'Well, sir. Davie's out of his time, so it seems sensible he should go, and now that the mare has foaled—and her ladyship not being able to replace the geldings the army took away—'

'There's a terrible shortage of good carriage horses,' Giles frowned. 'We've

83

been trying to match a pair—you'll tell William that, won't you?'

'Will appreciates the position, sir.' Was he to call him Sir Giles, Tom pondered, or maybe, with Sir Robert only being *believed* killed...? 'But he says a coachman without horses to see to—well, he reckons he might as well enlist.'

'And you, Dwerryhouse?'

'Same for me. I'm a good shot—that's what I'd be best at. If I wait till conscription comes I'll have no say in the matter.'

'You're off to Creesby then, to join up?'

'If it's all right with you, sir. We're asking for a couple of hours off. Now seems as good a time as any—and after what happened to Sir Robert...'

'So when will you be going?'

'Tomorrow. If we walk to the station we can get the nine o'clock train. We'll be there and back by noon, I shouldn't wonder. And, sir—if happen you could keep it quiet?'

'The young ladies?' Giles smiled.

'Aye. They'll not be pleased.'

Giles Sutton watched the keeper walk away, gun over his arm. Then he turned abruptly, whistling to the spaniel.

'Come on, Morgan.' He bent to fondle the silky head. 'It's getting dark. Let's go home...'

'What on earth is going on all of a sudden?' Mrs Shaw demanded of Alice when she came in by the back door. 'Is everybody going mad around here? Bess says Davie's been to volunteer, so she's giving notice. Away to Leeds to make shells, and Mary offering to go with her.'

'Why Mary?' Alice asked dully, holding her hands to the fire.

'Gone all patriotic. She's got a brother in the navy, remember; him that's mine-sweeping in the Channel. And what's to do with you, lass? You and Tom been having words?' She gazed pointedly at Alice's pale, tear-stained face. 'Been having a weep, have you?'

'Weeping, yes; words, no. Tom's volunteered, an' all.'

'So you'll be going next?' Cook frowned.

'That I won't,' Alice flung. 'What has this war done for me, 'cept take my man? And you're right. Everybody *is* going mad, but me. Because Alice Hawthorn isn't going to work in no factory. There'll have to be someone here to help take care of Rowangarth. They've got Tom now; they shan't have me!'

She hugged her arms around her chest. She felt so cold, even here in the warmth of the kitchen. She ached all over too, and there was a pain exactly where her heart should have been. The way ahead looked bleak and threatening as a winter that never ends.

'You're feeling sorry for yourself, that's what,' Cook pronounced comfortably, arranging the hot coals with the poker, making a bed for the kettle. 'What about poor Miss Julia? Her's all alone in her room and today's her wedding anniversary. And no one but me seems to have remembered.'

'And I'd forgotten, too. Taken up with my own miseries, I suppose. Poor Miss Julia—and her wanting him with her like he should have been, if his leave hadn't been denied him.'

'Then how about if I set a tray and you take it to her, Alice? She'll not be asleep, be sure of that. Just a pot of tea and happen a piece of sponge cake—and you giving her a bit of sympathy, like. Might help the lass to feel a bit better.'

'I'll do that.' Alice took off her coat and hat, patting her hair into order. 'And you're a good soul to remember her. My, but it seems half a lifetime ago, that wedding; and last year Sir Robert newly home and all of us so happy.'

'That's the way it is, lass.' Cook placed a bright red cosy over the little teapot. 'But remember that it'll all pass, given time. Nothing lasts—neither good times nor bad. So off you go. You and her are close. Stay with her for a while; she'll be glad of a bit of company.'

Alice tapped on the bedroom door, softly, in case Miss Julia was asleep, but it was opened at once.

'Hawthorn! I've been hoping you'd come.'

'Do you want a bit of company while you drink it?' Alice set the tray on the dressing-table. 'Cook sent it on account of it—' She stopped, not knowing what to say.

'Of it being our first anniversary and I'd hoped we'd spend it together?' Her cheeks were flushed, her eyes bright, though dry of tears.

'Something like that.' Alice closed the door. 'And will I make up your fire?—it's all but out.'

'No thanks. We've got to save coal, you know. Tell me why you've been crying, Hawthorn?'

'On account of Tom.' No use denying it.

'Enlisting, you mean? I'd heard. There'll be no one left at Rowangarth, before so very much longer. Only Reuben and Catchpole.'

'There'll be Sir Giles.' It was *Sir* Giles now. Lady Helen had as good as said so.

'Ask Sir Giles if he can spare me a minute, will you, Mary?' she'd said. 'He'll see to things.'

'No. He'll be gone, too. He volunteered today, along with Tom and Davie and Will Stubbs. Only he went to York to do it.'

'But he said he'd never take life! Did he say why he did it?' Those white feathers! Damn the stupid woman who sent them!

'No reason given. All he said was that he could enlist without blotting his copybook. They're in great need of doctors and nurses, he said—anyone to help care for the wounded.'

'So he's going to be an orderly?' Medical orderlies didn't fire guns. It was a fair solution, Alice thought.

'No—he's volunteered before conscription comes, he said, so he can have some say in where he goes and what he does. Today, he volunteered for a stretcher-bearer.'

'But, *miss!* Doesn't he know that's just about the daftest, most dangerous thing he could go and do? They send stretcher-bearers into No Man's Land to bring back the wounded and dying as can't help themselves. There'll be barbed wire and minefields to contend with and the German machine-gunners sat there waiting...'

Her cheeks flushed pink at her eloquence —and her stupidity, she thought bitterly

—at saying such things which could only worry his poor sister. She had spoken out of turn, an' all, but it had to be said. '*Why* didn't he settle for being an orderly? What's he trying to do—get himself killed? Hasn't her ladyship suffered enough already?'

'That's what I said, more or less, but it's done now. And he admitted it wasn't the best of times to have sprung it on Mother. But what choice does a man have when his brother has been killed—and someone has sent him three white feathers?'

'He told you, then? He told me an' all, a while back,' Alice choked. 'There's some folk making it impossible to draw breath even, if you aren't in khaki! When does he think they'll send for him?'

'He explained about Robert, so they agreed to defer call-up until the New Year. That should give him time to do what's got to be done here. Did Tom say when he'd be going?'

'No, but he thinks pretty soon. I reckon he'll be gone before Christmas. It's an awful world, isn't it, to be young in?'

'Terrible, Hawthorn. Yet tonight, when I should be miserable, I'm not. And if I tell you something, you won't breathe it to a soul? I wouldn't want it to get back to Mother, you see.' She opened her jewel case and drew out a letter. 'Read this, will you?'

'You're sure?'

'Quite sure. And anyway, you are entitled to see it. You said it was the postman I must watch out for,' she urged. 'You said it would come by letter, and it did. Look—written on the back of the envelope. *Do not open until 20 November.* It came yesterday...'

Alice unfolded the single sheet of paper. The handwriting on it was firm and dependable, somehow; just like the doctor.

My dearest love...

'You know, miss, I've never had a letter from Tom.'

'You will have, before so very much longer. Your life will come to revolve around letters,' Julia whispered. 'But go on...'

My dearest love,

I write this in the hope that you'll be able to read it on our first anniversary. It makes me sad you'll be alone when you do, and when we shall meet again, it is hard to say. The situation here is near chaos and all leave but the most urgent or compassionate is suspended. This I accept, and although I have not heard from you since, I know your disappointment is every bit as great as my own.

Yet there is a silver lining to our cloud.

I was to have left here early on 17th November to arrive at Le Havre for the overnight crossing by troop transport to Southampton. I know now, that if my leave had not been cancelled, I would have been aboard a trooper which was torpedoed mid-Channel with a terrible loss of life.

Now I am certain I shall survive this war and come safely home to you, one day. With such prodigious good luck, my darling, nothing can harm me. Your love has kept me safe. What happened was meant to be.

I love you with all my heart.

Andrew.

'Oh...' It was all Alice could say.

'Oh, indeed. Andrew will only now have heard about Robert. When he wrote that letter he had no way of knowing my brother was aboard that troopship. Imagine—*two* of them killed at sea? That's why Mother mustn't be told yet about Andrew. And that is why I can't be sad Andrew isn't with me today. If his leave had gone ahead, I'd be a widow now.'

'It's a funny thing, isn't it—Fate, I mean.' Alice ran her tongue around suddenly dry lips.

'Funny, capricious, a chance in a million; whatever you call it, Andrew wasn't meant to come home. I'm so lucky, Hawthorn.'

'But Sir Robert and his young lady—they aren't lucky.'

'No, poor loves—not in this life, anyway. But I *know* Andrew will come home to me now.'

'And you'll wait, miss, and be content?'

'Wait? That I won't! Oh, no! I've decided. *I* am going to *him!*'

'But how?' Alice wanted to smile. It sounded just like Polly Oliver in the song they'd sung at school; Polly, who'd dressed as a soldier to follow her love.

'Simple! There are too many wounded and too few to care for them. I shall drive an ambulance. Aunt Sutton will help me. She's in the First Aid Nursing Yeomanry—she'll put in a good word for me. I don't know why I didn't think of it before.'

'And you'd do that, just to be near the doctor?'

'No—I'd be doing it to help my country and those poor wounded troops, out there and—'

'Truth or dare, Miss Julia,' Alice said, looking her straight in the eyes.

'Oh, all right! I want to be near Andrew, truth known, but if I can do something useful at the same time, then so much the better. I'd at least be on the same continent, if not in the same country. Just think—one day I might look up and see him standing there.'

'And you might spend the whole war just missing each other by hours. Or you might even be sent to the Eastern front, where the Russians are fighting. You'd have to go where they sent you, remember.'

'That's a risk I shall have to take.'

'And her ladyship? She'll be alone. Had you thought of that?'

'Yes, I had.' Julia's face was all at once grave. 'But I know that when I tell her she'll give me her blessing, for all that. She and Pa were very much in love. She'll understand.'

'Then I'll come with you! If Bess and Mary can make shells, then I can go to France!'

'You will? You'll come, Hawthorn? You'd have to learn to drive first, but Aunt Sutton will help, I'm sure she will.'

'Drive, miss—oh, no; not me!' Alice held her hands to her blazing cheeks. 'I couldn't control one of them contraptions, but I could be a nurse, now couldn't I? I'm young and strong and I'm not afraid of hard work.'

'There'd be some terrible sights,' Julia warned.

'Happen. But if you can stick it, Miss Julia, then so can I. Though if I gave in my notice I don't know where I could call home—with me not having any parents. I suppose I could stay with Reuben if ever I got leave...'

'You could. Or you could keep your room at Rowangarth. Well, you did once say that Rowangarth was the only real home you'd ever had. But we'll worry about that later. What is important—and I'll bet you haven't so much as thought about it—is that you aren't twenty-one yet. Men have to be nineteen before they can be sent to the Front and women twenty-one. And you won't be *twenty* till June.'

'Damn!' All her life, it seemed to Alice, her age had been against her. 'Well, I'll just have to add a bit on, won't I? I don't suppose they'll ask for my birth certificate.'

'I don't suppose they will.' Julia held out her hand. 'So is it a bargain, then? Shall we shake on it? After Christmas, we're going to France?'

'But we can't just pack up and go, miss. It might take time.'

'I'd thought of that. I shall go to London and see Aunt Sutton. She'll help us, I know she will. In the New Year it shall be, Hawthorn; when Mother has had a little more time to adjust to Robert's death.'

'Seems as good a time as any.' Tom would have gone by then.

'And meantime, we mustn't say a word

to anyone about it or Reuben will stop you going and Andrew will think up a dozen different ways to keep me at home. The New Year? 1916?'

'The New Year!' Alice grasped Julia's hand and held it firmly. 'It won't be a bed of roses, but we'll manage somehow.'

She didn't want Tom to go to war, but all at once his going didn't seem quite so awful. And, like Miss Julia said, who was to know that, somewhere in France, just around the next corner, they might not meet? She was still a little uncertain, and afraid, too, if she let herself think too much about it, but being afraid and doing something about it was better than staying at home worrying—if someone didn't discover how old she really was...

She glanced in the dressing-table mirror. It was her nose, truth known. It made her look even younger.

'You think we'll get there, miss?'

'We can try our damnedest. Maybe I can't be with Andrew, but at least I can be nearer, without the Channel between us. And just think, we might even be able to be together just for a few hours.

'There's nothing to keep me here, and Mother herself said my first duty is to my husband, though duty doesn't come into it, really. I want him, Hawthorn. I've *got* at least to try...'

'Then I'm coming with you.' Alice tilted her chin, breathing slowly, deeply, though it did nothing to stop the shaking inside her.

Alice Hawthorn—going to France? Oh, my word...

5

The seventh of December, the Tuesday on which Tom was to report to the army at Richmond, was a date and day written deep on Alice's heart. Tomorrow, when they met, would be their last goodnight, their last kiss. Already William and Davie had gone, and Bess and Mary had left Rowangarth for shared lodgings in Leeds and the hard work—and good wages—of the munitions factory.

Her sweet, safe world was falling apart, Alice mourned. All she held dear, had believed would outlast time itself, was slipping away from her. And how soon would it be, she fretted, before she and Miss Julia were gone too—if their schemes came to anything, that was; if Reuben didn't find out and forbid her to go.

But she would worry about that when Tuesday had been and gone. Tonight, being with Tom was all that mattered, when soon she would be living in a world so bleak, so loveless and empty, that she would die of heartache unless she was able to go nursing with Miss Julia. And if cousin Reuben put paid to it she would never speak to him again. Not as long as she lived!

She switched off the light and drew back the curtains. There was no moon tonight, no stars. She could hardly pick out the bulk of the bothy, shadowy against the skyline. Not a glimmer of light showed from Tom's window, as if he were gone already.

She swished the curtains together again, wondering if Sir Giles had told her ladyship about the letter. It had come on the same day as Tom's calling-up notice, and he'd told her about it, Alice frowned, just as he'd told her about the white feathers.

'I'm to report to Kingsford Camp on the fourteenth of January, Hawthorn—near Salisbury...'

'Then best you tell her ladyship as soon as maybe, sir,' she had warned. 'At least give her time to get used to it.'

But as yet he'd said nothing. Giles Sutton was too kindly for his own good; too mindful of the feelings of others. She hoped the war would deal gently with him, but she doubted it, for war took account of no man's feelings. She raised her eyes to the ceiling.

'What were you about, God, to let it happen? Just what, will you tell me?'

Julia met her brother's gaze, held it, then nodded her head in a movement which meant, *Now!* Then her eyes narrowed with a challenge that said, *If you don't, then I will!*

'Mother,' Giles cleared his throat noisily.

'What is it?' Helen smiled, laying aside the sock she was knitting, offering her full attention. 'Tell me?'

'I'm sorry, dearest, truly I am,' he said softly. 'I was trying to keep it until after Christmas, but it's best you should know. I volunteered, you see. Did it on the same day as Dwerryhouse and the others. They said, though, that I could have deferment, because of Robert...'

'But he's to go in January,' Julia supplied. 'On the fourteenth.'

For a moment there was a silence so complete it seemed to stretch out, crystal clear and cold, into forever.

'I knew something was upsetting you.' Gently Helen spoke. 'I wish you'd told me at the time, though. It might have helped to share the worry.'

'Say you understand?' Julia begged. 'I know you don't want him to go—who

98

in her right mind would?—but it had to come...'

'Yes, and I accept it, even though I shall never know how we came to let this war happen,' Helen sighed bitterly. 'And I admire your courage, Giles. I realise how painful it must have been for you.'

'Not so bad, really, once my mind was made up. The worst bit was getting the feathers. That's why I volunteered. Someone sent me three white feathers, you see.'

There! It had been said. Now she knew she had a coward for a son.

'Oh, my dear!' Helen held wide her arms and he went to her, kneeling at her feet, laying his head on her lap as he had done when a small boy. And she bent to kiss him as she had kissed him when he'd awakened from a bad dream and called out for her in the night.

'You aren't both ashamed of me?'

'No, we aren't! And, darling—can you bear any more? There's worse to come.' Julia's eyes, dark with pleading, gazed into her mother's.

'More, child? Oh, well...'

'Mother, I am *not* a child. I'm a married woman,' Julia said, her voice indulgent. 'And that, really, is what it's all about. I want to go too. I know I'm being selfish,' she rushed on, 'and that my duty is here with you, especially after—'

She stopped, wishing she had drawn breath, thought more carefully, not about what she wanted to say, but the way she should have said it.

'It's all right,' Helen prompted. 'And before you say any more, you know I have always insisted that your duty—if duty we must talk about—is to Andrew and not to me.'

'Thank you for understanding—especially now,' Julia smiled sadly. 'But I want to be nearer to Andrew. If he were given a few days away from duty, then I'd be able to go to him. I'd do anything just to see him. I love him so much, you see, that I have no pride left.'

'Pride, Julia MacMalcolm? What has pride to do with loving?' Helen's voice was gentle with remembering. 'And I do understand. I loved your pa in just such a way.'

'Then it's all right? You don't mind?'

'No, it *isn't* all right and I *do* mind. No mother wants to see her children walk headlong into danger, but I accept that you are both adults and I respect your wishes. I shall be grey-haired with worry by the time it's over and you are both—Andrew, too—back safely at home. But you shall go with my blessing—and my love.'

And if she could, she would make a

bargain here and now with the Almighty; pledging what remained of her life for the safety of theirs. She would do it gladly, if only to be with John again.

'Dearest milady—will I give you an answer to something you have asked me more times than I can remember?' Giles rose to his feet, looking down at her with love. 'Why I haven't married, that is. Well, I'll tell you now. It is because Pa found you first, and if I look for ever, I shall never find another woman who could hold half a candle to you.'

'Stuff and nonsense, flatterer!' Helen jumped to her feet. 'Oh, let's try not to be sad! Let's try to pretend there is no war out there.' For wasn't this Rowangarth, and didn't her beloved house have walls so thick and comforting that nothing could penetrate them unless she chose to let it? And when her children were gone—dear heaven, how would she bear it?—John's house would share her loneliness and comfort her with its warmth. 'And I think we'll ring for a tray of tea.'

Such a comforter. Sutton Premier Tea, picked less than a year ago. The last Robert would ever grow.

'Run down and ask Cook—there's a dear girl.'

It had come, the night she had dreaded

since they realised the war was not to be a six-month skirmish. Alice stood quite still, accustoming her eyes to the darkness, then walked carefully across the lawn to the wild garden and the stile.

'Tom?' She stood, head tilted, listening for his answering whistle.

He was out there, waiting—for the last time until it was all over. She wanted this night to be special, to remember every word, every laugh, every kiss; but she would not, because already she was shaking and cold inside and there was a tightness in her throat that was really a hard ball of tears, waiting to be shed.

She called his name again, then saw his outline with its wide-open arms; its safe, protecting arms.

'Bonny lass!' He was gathering her close, whispering his lips across her cheek to her waiting, wanting mouth.

'Hold me,' she whispered. 'I'm cold. Let's go to the corner.' To the warm place, sheltered from the wind that blew from the east; warmed by the boiler fire on the other side of the wall. And private, because no one had bothered, lately, to cut back the bushes that grew beside it.

'We aren't going to talk about the war tonight,' Tom said firmly, 'nor about me going in the morning. I'll be away long before anyone's awake, and I don't want any goodbyes—nothing like that. You understand, Alice Hawthorn?'

They had agreed more than a week ago that that was how it would be. No talk of undying love, of being faithful, of the pain of wanting. Those things they took for granted; no sense wasting good breath saying over again something they had known since the day they first met.

Does this creature belong to you?

No, but he's with me. He belongs to Mr Giles...

No one had even heard of Sarajevo that day.

'It was not so far from here that we met—remember? You called Morgan a daft dog.'

'And so he was, the spoiled creature. You'll have to look after him when Sir Giles goes—see he gets his walks. Not in the wood, though.'

There would be more poachers in Brattocks than ever, once they knew there was only one elderly keeper to keep an eye on their goings-on. And not only poachers. Elliot Sutton might think to use the woodland path again when next he visited Rowangarth.

'Penny for them, or are they worth more?' Alice smiled.

'Much more. Far more than you can afford to pay,' he lied. 'I wouldn't take a hundred sovereigns for them.'

'And I haven't got that much to offer.'

'Then I might just 'change them for a kiss.'

'About me, were they?' she laughed, teasing him with her lips.

'About a bonny lass with big brown eyes and the sweetest nose ever; about the lass I'm going to marry...'

'When, Tom? Soon, will it be?' Their teasing was over, and wanting took her, twisting her insides, setting every small pulse throbbing out her need of him.

'As soon as we can, Alice; just as soon. Happen, if ever they gave me leave, we might persuade Reuben to change his mind. I did read, somewhere, that if all else failed you could ask the Courts for permission.'

'I could never do that. Courts cost money and, anyway, eighteen months will soon pass. They say there's a time and a place for everything and our time will come, Tom. I've accepted it, now. And no matter what happens meantime, you and me will have our day.'

'You think so.' He closed his eyes, wanting her.

'Course I do. I told the rooks about us. They'll see to it that we'll be wed. And tomorrow, when you're—' She stopped, confused. 'Tomorrow, when me and Morgan are passing by, I shall tell them you're up Richmond way, and that they're to take care of you.' She snuggled closer, thrusting her hands into his jacket pockets. 'And they'll—ooooh! What have you got in there?' She pulled out her hand as if it had been bitten. 'A mouse?'

'That'll teach you to go in your man's pockets—especially if he's a gamekeeper, Tom grinned. 'Now hold out your hand, because I want you to wish on it.'

'N-no,' she said, dubiously. It was dark and she couldn't properly see. She held out a probing finger and touched the soft fur that lay on his palm.

'It's all right. Only a rabbit's foot. They're lucky, if someone gives one to you. Reuben said I'd better take one along with me. He gave one to Will and Davie, an' all; said we'll be all right with one of these in our pocket. Now take it in your hand and wish, like I told you.'

She took it, stroking it with her forefinger, wishing with all her might for him to come home safely. Then she laid it gently back in his hand, wrapping his fingers over it.

'There now,' she sighed, 'between the rabbits and the rooks, you'll do all right. One day, we'll be together again.'

'You seem so sure, sweetheart.' His voice was touched with sadness, for she didn't know the half of what would face him after this night.

'I'm sure, Tom. Very sure. Our turn will come. But oh, I don't want you to leave me. I want us to stay here, all night.'

Stay for ever, arms entwined, bodies close; stay until they petrified into stone, like the figures in the garden at Rowangarth. And a hundred years on, people would stop a while and gaze at them and wonder who they were. Then those people would pass on, because in a hundred years from now it wouldn't matter anyway.

'Say you'll never love anyone else, Tom?'

'I love you, bonny lass. There couldn't be anyone else for me. And when I'm away and missing you and wanting you near me, I shall picture you beside the stile at the edge of Brattocks. And it'll be a summer's day, in my dreamings. There'll be sunshine and new, gentle leaves, and you'll have buttercups in your hair...'

She sat alone in her room that night, dry-eyed and numb, thinking back to their parting and how she had wanted to weep and cling to him and beg him, on her knees if she had to, not to go. Yet she had sent him to war with her head held high and, though he couldn't see it in the darkness, with a smile on her lips.

Now she wanted to throw herself on her bed, to weep into her pillow, beat it with angry fists, but that wouldn't do. She must stay awake until she saw a light in his window. At five, Tom would be leaving to walk across the fields to the station and the milk train that left a little before six. And she would be there at the bothy gate to surprise him; to walk with him, her hand in his, saying all the things they should have said and hadn't, and all the time watching the sky lighten to the east over the Pike.

The room was cold and she wrapped her shawl around her, pacing the room slowly, softly, that she might keep awake. Her eyelids felt heavy; her eyes pricked as if they were full of dust. She clucked impatiently. The room was too bright. Reaching for the matches, she lit the candle that stood beside her bed then, snapping off the light, she pulled her chair to the window to wait.

She had not meant to fall asleep and when, next morning, Tom looked up at her window as he closed the bothy gate, there was only a flickering of candlelight to bless him on his way.

'So long, my lovely lass,' he whispered. 'Take care of yourself.'

For the first time since his childhood his eyes filled with tears. He was glad she was not there to see them.

Christmas was a quiet one that year. Rowangarth was in mourning again, so it had to be. No one said, 'Happy Christmas.' Even those in Holdenby village lucky enough to have sons and husbands at home didn't go about with smiling faces, for there was little to be glad about.

On the Western Front, the intense cold had done nothing to slow down the fighting; casualty lists in the morning papers were so upsetting Cook declared, that if things got any worse she would refuse to open another newspaper till peace came.

Food was becoming harder to get. Sugar and margarine had to be queued for now, and the shopkeepers had had neither sight nor smell of a keg of butter since the summer. Food, Cook said, ought to be on official ration, then everyone would get fair shares and a soldier's wife have her entitlement at a price she could afford to pay.

Now, like Julia's, Alice's days were regulated by the thrice daily knock of the postman. Every day she wrote to Tom; most days there was a letter from him. Yesterday's letter had made her laugh.

Imagine, he wrote, *today I learned how to load a rifle and clean it.*

Ha! Trying to tell Tom about guns. As

daft, almost, as trying to teach Mrs Shaw to boil an egg.

Yet when they had made a soldier of him, what then? France, would it be, and the trenches? Tom had no say in his destiny now. For as long as the war lasted, he was a name and number: he had ceased to be a person—a real person—the day he signed his name at the recruiting office in Creesby.

Alice gave her full attention to the letter she was writing, the special Christmas Day letter, telling him how much she loved him, how much she longed to see him. And she told him how things were changing now, with all Rowangarth's young men gone and Bess and Mary doing war work in a factory in Leeds.

They had visited, not long ago; each of them wearing the new, shorter coats and smart hats and gloves of softest leather. Very prosperous, they'd looked, except that their fingernails were beginning to turn yellow and the whites of their eyes the colour of saffron, Cook said. And who, Tilda demanded when they had left to catch the motor bus back to Leeds, was going to fall in love with a girl who'd gone a peculiar shade of yellow and looked like her cousin Maud who'd once been so badly with jaundice she'd all but died of it?

'That'll be all from you, miss,' Cook

retorted sharply. Tilda Tewk was getting a mite above herself now she'd been promoted to housemaid and Jinny Dobb brought in to do the kitchen work. Though Jin was glad of it, since there was no one in the bothy now for her to look after.

But Cook was fast losing patience with the war. She'd be dead and in her grave, she lamented, before both sides tired of it and filled in their trenches and took themselves back to homes they ought never to have left in the first place! She had brooded deeply and long in church that morning, the beauty of the Christmas gospel and the joy of carols lost to her. Mrs Shaw was becoming increasingly annoyed with a God who could, in her opinion, have stopped the fighting with the lifting of a finger.

Peace on earth, goodwill to men—whatever had happened to it?

Alice was glad that Christmas Day was almost over. It hadn't seemed right, sitting well-fed on roast pheasant when Tom and Davie and Will had dined off bully-beef and biscuits, like as not. The lads in the trenches fared even worse, she brooded, taking the long, heavy pins from her hair and letting it fall over her shoulders.

Yesterday, a letter had arrived from Tom and she had resisted the temptation to tear open the envelope, slipping it beneath her pillow to be saved for Christmas morning. And on this Christmas morning he missed her, loved her, wanted her. She closed her eyes and it was as if he were saying the words. It had helped make the day bearable.

Now she would clean her teeth and brush her hair as if this had been an ordinary day. Then she would get into bed, relieved it was over, because there was no Christmas Day at the Front: men still fought and were killed. Wars didn't seem to stop just because a baby had been born and laid in a manger.

She drew back the curtains, gazing into a star-bright night, looking for the Christmas star—the one the Kings had followed to the stable.

It was there now, brighter than the rest, throbbing with light. Smiling, she reached for her Bible and opened it at the special place. St Luke, Chapter Two. It was still her favourite story and the buttercups were still there—all but the one she kept in her locket. They were no longer golden, but a reminder, still, of the first days of their loving.

Please take care of Tom? Alice raised her eyes to the star. *Don't let him be killed? Let him come home safely? Please? And let me see him—soon?*

111

Warmly wrapped, Alice watched the spaniel lumber off, nose down, yelping and snuffling in search of some new, adventurous scent. She lifted her face to the pale, winter sun. This was a clear day, a rare day; a day too good to be wasted thinking about war.

The morning had been sharply cold, the grass sparkling with silver hoar. Beyond the trees, the distant hilltops were white with snow that had fallen over a week ago and would lie unmelted until a spring wind blew from the south. Now it glistened under a cold sun, softening the craggy pike into beauty.

Alice walked carefully. The woodland paths were slippery from melted frost, though the sky was still brightly blue; a dazzling backcloth for the dark, winter-bare trees.

Trees were miracles, Tom said. You had to believe in God, he insisted, when you looked at a tree.

Tom. He sprang so easily to her thoughts. Always on her mind, in her heart. Loving him, missing him, wanting him always. She was incomplete without him. Even Brattocks Wood was different, now the chance delight of meeting him was gone.

Where are you, Tom? Are you wishing, like

me, that the year to come will see an end to the war?

She pulled her muffler around her ears and over her mouth and nose. It was colder in Brattocks with the small warmth of the sun screened out by the undergrowth. And darker, too.

She called for Morgan and he came at once, skidding to a clumsy halt in the mud; yelping, whining, looking up with pleading eyes.

What had he found? Some creature, hurt and afraid, perhaps, cowering beneath a bush? She stood still, breath indrawn, eyes sliding from left to right. A poacher, maybe? Some man with a family to feed, seeking a game-bird for the pot?

The spaniel yelped again, running forwards, stopping, looking back.

Was he asking her to follow him? Did he want her to forsake the depths of the wood for Reuben's cottage, for that was where he was heading. And why was he standing on the doorstep, tail wagging, barking to be let in?

Alice began to run. Was Reuben ill, had a fall maybe? Oh, good dog, Morgan, to know it!

She knocked on the door, lifting the latch, calling his name.

'It's Alice. Are you all right? Where are you, Reuben?'

The dog pushed past her impatiently, throwing himself at the kitchen door, bounding inside. Then he set up such a barking that she was afraid, almost, to step inside.

'Well now—look who's here...'

Reuben was standing, back to the fire, puffing on his pipe. At his feet was a litter of—goodness gracious! A kitbag, a steel helmet, a knapsack! And, leaning in the corner, a rifle and—

'Hullo, bonny lass.'

Not Tom—it couldn't be! That stranger in khaki, holding wide his arms, it couldn't be him!

'Sweetheart!' He gathered her to him, and she wrapped her arms around his neck, laughing, crying, searching—eyes closed—for his lips. He smelled of new cloth; cloth rough beneath her fingertips.

'Say it's you?' She mustn't open her eyes for fear he would vanish. 'What are you doing here?'

'Come to see my girl. I was leaving all this kit with Reuben before I came looking for you. And before you ask it, they haven't given me leave. This is by way of being a two-hour detour.'

Two hours? Half a lifetime! She laughed out loud because she didn't believe any of it. These weren't Tom's arms around her nor Tom's lips on hers. It was all a dream.

She had wanted him so much that he'd appeared out of the air and could just as easily vanish again.

'It *is* you?'

'It's me. I have to be in York at five, so let's hope the three-thirty from Holdenby is still running, or I'll be in trouble.'

'But how did you manage it?' She still had difficulty breathing; was still fearful her dream would end.

'My platoon sergeant—not a bad sort, really. I told him, when we could see Pendenys's tower, that my girl wasn't far away from there. Asked him if there was any chance of a stop-off. Didn't think he'd let me...'

'That was good of him, Tom.'

'Aye. Takes all sorts to make an army, I suppose. Anyway, he called to the driver to stop and told me that if I wasn't on that platform at York at five o'clock, he'd come looking for me himself and the angels would weep for me when he found me—or words to the same meaning,' Tom grinned.

'But how did you get here?'

'Made a beeline across the fields from the Great North Road—no trouble at all. Didn't expect you to walk in on me, though I'm glad you did. Saved a lot of time finding you. I'll have to be on my way in half an hour.'

'Walking to the station, are you?'

'Can't think of any other way to get there.' His cheeks were flushed from the warmth of the fire, his eyes bright with teasing.

'Then I'm coming with you. She'll let me, won't she, Reuben?' Miss Clitherow couldn't say no, could she? 'I'll run and ask her...'

'Don't you be running anywhere. I'll make it all right with that housekeeper woman—and Cook an' all. You stop yourself here, lass, and make Tom a slice of toast and dripping and a sup of tea, and I'll take that daft dog back for you—tell Sir Giles. Though that creature isn't so daft, come to think of it. He knew Tom was here...'

'He did—and you're a love, Reuben!' Alice kissed his cheek warmly. 'But what if she says it isn't all right?'

'I shouldn't worry overmuch about that,' he nodded. 'By that time you'll be well on your way to Holdenby. And if she gives you a telling-off when you get back—well, it'll have been worth it, to my way of thinking. So how about you seeing to that tea, and let's all drink it in front of the fire. It'll be a cold walk to the station, in spite of the sun.'

'And a cold walk back for Alice. It'll be getting dark an' all,' Tom frowned. 'Can't

116

say I like the idea of her coming back alone. Happen you'd best not come, sweetheart. Don't want anything happening to you.'

'I'll run like mad, Tom. I'll soon be back.'

'And just gone three, I'll set out to meet her; she'll be all right,' Reuben offered, comfortably. 'She'll not come to any harm.'

'That's settled, then!' Laughing, Alice set the teapot to warm. 'Oh, I don't believe any of this—I *don't!*'

Alice eyed Tom dubiously. He looked, she thought, like a packhorse, a beast of burden, weighed down with knapsack, kitbag, mess tins, groundsheet and ammunition pouches. But the one piece of his infantryman's equipment that worried her was the bag which contained his gas helmet. She'd seen pictures of those sinister-looking things that turned soldiers into monsters.

'Those gas helmets, Tom.' She looked with distaste at the bag, swinging as he walked. 'If they're really any good, why do men get gassed?'

'Because they don't get them on quick enough! Four seconds, it should take. They show us how. I can do it in three, so stop your worrying!'

'I love you, Tom.' There didn't seem

anything else to say. 'I love you for tramping all that way just to be with me for a couple of hours.'

'I'd have come a lot further for a couple of *minutes*. You're my girl, aren't you?'

'I'm your girl, Tom. There'll never be anyone but you. We belong, remember?'

'So you'll think on about that when the train goes? You won't spoil that pretty face crying? I couldn't bear it if you cried...'

'I won't weep.' She wouldn't. Tom was going to be all right.

'Not if I tell you that I think we'll soon be in France?'

'Not even if—' She stopped, smiling. 'Kiss me and I'll tell you something.'

She closed her eyes and lifted her mouth to his. And as their lips met such love of her raged through him that he wanted to take her in his arms and never, ever let them part him from her.

'So tell me, lass?' he said, linking her arm in his; walking on again.

'Well, there are two things, really. They happened to me and Miss Julia both. She hasn't told her ladyship and I oughtn't to be telling you. But remember that the doctor was to come on leave and didn't? Well, she got a letter about a week after. He said if his leave hadn't been cancelled he'd have been on that troopship that was sunk in the Channel.'

'The one Sir Robert was on?' Tom let out his breath in a whistle.

'The one. There'd have been two of them. It'd have been past bearing. Miss Julia said she would never complain again. Said it had been down to Fate, his leave being stopped; a sure sign he'd see the war out. She told me that now, when she wants him something unbearable, she reads that letter and is thankful...'

'And you, Alice?'

'It happened almost the same. I wished on the Christmas star; I always have, since I can remember. I know you aren't supposed to tell wishes, but it doesn't matter, now, because mine came true. I wished you'd come back to me—for me to see you, soon.'

And she told him everything, exactly as it had been, from her cheek in wanting to see him, right to the minute she had pushed open Reuben's front door.

'So you see, Tom,' she finished breathlessly, 'you being there was better than a sign—more like a miracle.'

'I reckon it was,' Tom conceded gravely, 'when you consider that the regiment is being moved by train from Richmond to Aldershot in two days' time. I was picked for the advance party—just a few of us sent by motor to York station, then to travel overnight to get the billets ready and the cookhouse set up. Suppose if it doesn't qualify for a miracle, then it's a real bit of luck the driver took the route he did.'

'And don't forget that the sergeant let you off for a couple of hours. It was meant to be, Tom. You and the doctor; you'll both be all right. I know it.'

'Bonny, *bonny* lass. Do you know what a joy you are to me?'

'I do,' she smiled. 'And you won't worry overmuch, will you? What with those old rooks in Brattocks and that Christmas star, we shall end up together in Keeper's, just see if we don't. And you've still got that rabbit's foot, haven't you?'

'Still got it. Safe in my pocket.'

'Well, then...' Now, she thought, was the time to tell him. This winter-bright day when they were so happy was when she should share her secret. But would he want her to go to France, lie about her age? Would he want his girl in a ward full of soldiers?'

'A penny for them, lass?'

'They're worth more'n a penny.' She swallowed hard. Now was *exactly* the time to tell him, and she couldn't! 'I—I'll take a kiss for them instead.' She reached up on tiptoe, closing her eyes as she always did when they kissed, then sighed, 'If you must know I—I was wondering what it would be

120

like, you and me wed...'

For shame, Alice Hawthorn! You never meant to tell him! Not for a moment did you, for fear he'd forbid you to go; demand your word on it that you wouldn't!

'Were you, now?' He smiled, and her heart did a somersault. 'Take my word for it, it'll be wonderful—I promise it will—and well worth all the waiting. Now let's get a move on or I'll miss that train!'

'I love you, Tom,' she whispered hurrying after him. *And I promise,* she vowed silently, *that for the rest of my life I'll never lie to you or deceive you again. But I need to do something to help win the war, and what you don't know about you can't worry over...* And weren't some lies—the white ones, and some deceits—the allowable ones, justified? She and Miss Julia were going to France, and nothing must stand in their way. Not even a promise to Tom.

The sun was still shining; the sky still baby blue when the signal at the end of the platform fell with a thud and a rattle.

'Train's coming,' Alice whispered.

'Aye—and no tears, mind?'

'No tears.' Rooks and rabbits and Christmas stars would keep him safe.

'Kiss me, then, and say so-long.' He gathered her to him and his lips were hard on hers. 'I love you. Wait for me?'

'For as long as it takes...'

Her lips found his again. She wanted to cling to him and never let him go, but the stationmaster was calling to them to stand back.

'York!' he shouted. 'Next stop, York!'

Tom picked up his kit, throwing it piece by piece into the compartment. Then he pulled the door shut with a terrible finality, leaning through the open window for a last, brief kiss.

'I love you,' he whispered. 'Take care on the way home.'

'I will, and I love you. Look after yourself. I love you, love you...'

She stood there, waving, until the train had rounded the bend. She was still standing there when it was gone from her sight and all she could hear of it was a far-away hoot as it entered the long tunnel, half a mile down the track.

When shall I see you again, Tom? How long...?

But he would come back to her. He was coming home safe and sound and however long it took it didn't matter!

Head down, she began to run. Reuben would have set out already to meet her and she mustn't be late. And goodness only knew what Miss Clitherow would say when she got back; taking the best part of an afternoon off without so much as a by-your-leave!

But Tom *would* be all right. Her love would keep him safe—and the Christmas wish and the rabbit's foot and the rooks.

So why was she weeping? Why the great, choking sobs and tears that tasted salt on her lips? *Why?*

6

1916

Helen could no longer bring herself to read what she had come to look upon as the death column, for now it was no longer a column but a page—*pages*—of wasted lives. Young men killed in action; husbands, brothers, fathers, sons. When Robert died, she had determined never to read it again, though she would still pray each night for all the lost souls, and that their women might find the courage to accept what they were powerless to change. But read it in the papers she would not. Soon, when the Military Service bill became law, there would be even more men called to the colours and even more killing and maiming and blinding.

Yesterday saw the bill passed in Parliament. Mr Asquith had had his way, and now every unmarried man between nineteen and thirty would be called to fight. After all the conjecture, conscription was a fact and, in years to come, when the war was nothing but a bitter memory, it would be considered unthinkable—something to be ashamed of, in fact—never to have fought.

Now, in just one week, her second son was going to war, and after him, her daughter: Rowangarth would be a sad, lonely place. If she let it; if she gave in to self-pity and shut herself off from everything; if she wept and bemoaned her loss and wore her black until the autumn...

It was the fault, she thought almost angrily, of the old Queen. Victoria had made mourning fashionable, a religion almost. She it was who refused consolation after the death of her Consort; had taken to widow's weeds with maudlin pleasure. And thereafter, her subjects had done the same. Public mourning became a way of life.

But Queen Victoria was long gone, and her son too, Helen thought with sudden defiance. Now her grandson was King, and the Empire the old woman had once ruled over like a distant, doting mother had taken on a fight to the

124

death. The Empire, Britain—Holdenby and Rowangarth too—were at war, and there could be no time for public mourning. Grief must become a private thing, not something to be paraded and wallowed in! Helen's elder son had given his life—had been killed—for his country, and enough was enough! There was work, *war* work, to be done, wood to be brought in to eke out the coal; the green and perfect lawns around Rowangarth to be ploughed up and planted with potatoes. And there were people to be comforted and the elderly who couldn't queue for food to be fed.

'Julia!' she said so loudly, so decisively, that her daughter jumped visibly. 'I am going to find war work!'

'But, dearest, you already do your bit.' Julia laid down her pen. 'Perhaps when you come out of mourning—'

'I am out of mourning—public mourning, that is!' She felt quite light-headed, but it had to be said. 'Don't you realise that bereaved women are making munitions, heaving coal, working as railway porters? They have to, because the widow's pension that the army pays won't feed and clothe their children! They can't wear black and retire from living, so how dare I?

'Oh, I shall never forgive this war for taking Robert.' She paused, taking a long, trembling breath. 'But that is between me and my son. It is private. Wearing mourning, cutting myself off, won't lessen my despair, nor bring him back. So I shall visit Pendenys. I shall put on some stout shoes and walk there, across the fields.'

'But why must you?'

'Because we have no coachman and no horses. The exercise will do me good and it isn't far. And there is something I must learn to do for the war effort—you must teach me to harness the pony into the cart. I must be able to drive myself about.'

'But I can drive you to Uncle Edward's. You only need ask.'

'And when you are gone, Julia? Do I stay within these four walls? Or maybe I should learn to ride a bicycle?'

'Mother! You simply can't do that!'

'*Can't?* I see. It's too undignified for a middle-aged lady to be seen pedalling along the roads?'

'It would be a great deal more undig-nified were you to fall off,' Julia chuckled. 'I don't suppose it's any use suggesting you buy a motor?' It made sense. Alone at Rowangarth, her mother would be virtually isolated. 'Aunt Sutton wouldn't be without hers.'

'No motors here,' Helen said flatly.

'Very well. I'll see to the pony and drive you to Pendenys.'

'No! I shall drive myself there. I'll take

126

the back lane—it's very quiet. I'm not entirely helpless!'

'Just so long as you'll be all right. You're sure, now?'

'I am *not* sure.' Briefly, Helen's defiance flagged. 'But we are at war and it is time I too joined in—*really* joined in. It is everyone's fight, and the sooner I learn to manage the pony and cart, the better!'

'But you've never driven yourself. Are you sure you can cope?'

'I'm sure. Or I will be, by the time I get back. Now be off with you, *please...*'

'Milady!' gasped Pendenys's butler, eyes wide.

'Good morning,' Helen smiled brightly. 'Be so kind as to have someone see to my pony.'

'Of course. At once.' He held wide the door. 'I will inform Mrs Sutton you are here.'

'Please don't bother.' Helen hurried past him. Clemmy was always in the morning-room between ten and eleven—her at-home time—and if it was unforgivable to walk in on her unannounced, then so be it. There was so much to be done that Helen no longer had any time for niceties. Tomorrow, heaven only knew how she would feel; in a week's time, when Giles left for Salisbury, she might even feel suicidal; but today she was angry with the war and intended to do something about it.

'Clemmy!' Hands outstretched, she greeted her brother-in-law's wife. 'Forgive me for arriving unannounced, but I need your help.'

'My dear!' Clementina's mouth sagged open. The very last person she had expected was Helen, a stickler for etiquette, and her in mourning until November! 'My help?'

'Yes, indeed. There comes a time, I told myself not an hour ago, when enough is enough!'

'But you should have telephoned. I'd have come at once, if you needed me.'

'I thank you, Clemmy, but all at once I am weary of wearing mourning and have become very angry with the war. I intend to find more to occupy me. I shall do war work.'

'*War* work?' Agitated, Clementina settled her caller in a chair. 'But you are in mourning.'

'I am.' Helen's voice faltered only slightly. 'But that is between Robert and myself and will not end when I come out of my black in the autumn. I believe there is a hospital you work for. I, too, would like to offer my help.'

'But, Helen, it is not the place for a

lady.' Denniston House, did she mean? 'And I don't exactly work there. I organise events and gatherings and raise money for comforts for the wounded there. But I couldn't *work* at Denniston House.'

'Why not, pray?' Helen nodded her thanks for the cup of tea Clementina had shakily poured. 'Is it a fever hospital—an isolation hospital?'

'No, but it is full of wounded—in all kinds of distress. Some of them quite awful to look at, I believe. Burns, you know. And some of them with no arms, no legs. Many have lost their sight...'

'Then that makes me all the more determined! I can read to the blind soldiers or write their letters. Perhaps those who can't see will be glad of a chat. So will you telephone the matron. Clementina? You know her. Will you ask her if I can be a hospital visitor?'

'Very well—since you seem set on it. But I hope you know what you are doing,' Clementina sighed, wondering what had come over Helen that she must visit wards which were quite awful. And she'd heard that the smell could be quite terrible at times. 'Have you given any consideration to what people will think what they might say?'

'If helping the wounded causes comment, then I'd be most surprised. But I care little what anyone thinks or says, Clemmy. Suddenly, I decided to do something about the state I was in, and I know that Robert would approve. That is good enough for me. Giles will soon be leaving, and Julia intends to take up driving. I shall be alone with my thoughts then, you see, and it simply wouldn't do. You *will* help me?'

'Completely out of character,' Clementina said to her husband when Helen had left. 'Visiting at Denniston House, I mean. It isn't even a proper hospital—just a house the army took over.'

'It's Blighty to a lot of wounded men, Clemmy. And I think it admirable that Helen wants to help.'

'Well, I *don't*,' she sniffed. 'In fact, I think it a little—*eccentric* to want to expose herself to such terrible sights.'

'Those terrible sights were whole men before they went to war, my dear.'

'Take her side—you usually do!' No use complaining to Edward about Helen-who-could-do-no-wrong! Yet to Clementina's way of thinking, her sister-in-law was acting most peculiarly; a woman who, because of her birth, could get away with anything. Let the daughter of an Ironmaster do the same, and she was reverting to type! Clogs to clogs in three generations, people would say!

Life was very unfair!

'Don't see me off—please?' Giles Sutton had asked his mother. 'Just give me a hug and a kiss and wave to me from the door, just as you did when Robert and I were going back to school.'

'Very well, if that's the way you want it.'

He was right, of course. Partings had never been her strongest suit, though it wouldn't be a parting—not quite yet. Giles would be given leave when his training was over. He wouldn't—couldn't—be sent to France until the summer at least. And by summer the war might well be over, because in spite of all the money being wasted on developing tanks, she had great faith that once the inventors and engineers could make them work properly, those lumbering monsters could prove to be the turning point of the war—and Mr Churchill thought so too!

Now that time had come. Giles's case stood on the top step, and Julia was leading the pony and trap through the stableyard archway. Helen distanced herself from it; stood apart and watched as she would watch actors on a stage. And she would stand there, smiling and waving until they were out of sight, exactly as she had done when the boys were little and John had driven them to the railway station in his latest, newest motor, their school trunks strapped on the back. Nothing to get upset about, she insisted; she had done this before many times: only then she had known they would always come home to her.

'Giles was in splendid spirits when I saw him off,' Julia smiled as they sat that evening in the winter-parlour. 'He seemed very confident, as if he knew he'd do all right. He's sure he'll get leave before they send him to France—if they send him, that is.'

'But I thought...' Helen frowned. Of course Giles would go to France. 'Where else are stretcher-bearers needed?'

'In every army hospital in these islands and at railway stations meeting hospital trains and on hospital ships,' Julia supplied, recognising her mother's need for comfort. 'Nurses don't carry big heavy men around, you know.'

'Perhaps not...' Helen lapsed into silence, remembering their last minutes together.

'You are not to worry, dearest...' He'd always called her dearest, even as a small boy. 'I know I shall be all right. I'm not worried—truly.' He had cupped her face in his hands and gently kissed her closed eyelids. 'I'm more worried about Morgan.

You'll see he's looked after, won't you?'

'Morgan!' Helen gasped now. 'Oh dear —I'd quite forgotten the poor animal. He'll be all alone in the library. Has he been fed, do you think?'

'He's fed at midday—Giles will have seen to it before he went. And he has biscuits morning and night.' Julia jumped to her feet. 'I'd better ask Hawthorn. She usually takes him out. Giles probably arranged it all with her.'

'Hawthorn mustn't take him out at night—not in the dark, alone,' Helen warned.

'All right. If that's what you want. But Morgan is devoted to her. She'll be safe enough with him. Look at the way he went for Elliot: I do so wish I'd seen it!'

'Julia! For shame! It was a dreadful experience for the poor girl!'

'I know. But I still wish I'd seen Elliot getting his comeuppance, especially when Dwerryhouse blacked his eye!'

'It all seems a long time ago,' Helen sighed. Robert was safe in India then, and Giles seeing to the books in the library. And Julia, of course, newly, blissfully in love.

'Those days will come back again—well, almost,' Julia said softly. 'Now you're not to get upset. Giles said you weren't to.'

'I won't.' Tonight, she would include

Giles especially in her prayers, then leave it all to God. 'Off you go and see if the animal is all right. Maybe someone should let him out for a few minutes...'

'Hawthorn and I will take him out. And afterwards, maybe, I'll bring him back here. He'll like it, sprawled in front of the fire, and he's quite well-behaved these days.'

'It's all right, miss,' Alice said. They stood in the shelter of the stableyard gates as the spaniel sniffed and snuffled into every corner, searching for his master. 'Cook will save him kitchen scraps like always and a drop of gravy, and I'll see to his biscuits and his airings. I promised Mr Giles he'd be all right. And I told him I wouldn't stray out of sound of the house at night, so tell her ladyship there isn't any need for her to worry about me—you neither, Miss Julia.'

'I'm not. I'm here because I particularly want to see you and there hasn't been a minute, today, with Giles going off. Have you heard from Tom yet?'

'Not a word.' Not for nearly a week, which could only mean he was on his way to France.

'I'm sorry, Hawthorn. Keep writing to him, though. Your letters will catch up with him eventually. Letters are important to a soldier—especially when he's—'

'At the Front,' Alice finished.

'Well...yes. Look, have you thought any more about taking up nursing?'

'Times like this, miss, when there's no word from Tom, I think of little else.'

'Then did you know that women are allowed to drive ambulances in France, now? It was in the paper. Just a small piece and mother didn't see it, thank goodness.' Her mother hardly ever picked up a newspaper, these days. 'It's the First Aid Nursing Yeomanry—that's what Aunt Sutton is in. She'd help me, I know she would. I realise it isn't possible to rush off and leave mother just yet, but I want to go to London as soon as I can; ask Aunt Sutton to put feelers out for me—to go to France, that is.' Nowhere but France. 'Are you still game to come along?'

'Be a nurse? That I am! If they don't go poking and prying too much...'

'Then leave it all to me. *Morgan!*' She placed her fingers in her mouth and sent out a piercing whistle. 'Come here, you silly dog! Come here *at once!*'

'Go to London? Why not? I thought you might have gone there before Christmas...'

'I thought about it, Mother, but I—'

'But you didn't, because of Robert?'

'Something like that. I'd like to go,

though—fairly soon if that's all right with you?'

'Of course it is. I intend to be very busily occupied. There is the sewing-circle and the sock-knitting, and the elderly to call on. And I start my visiting at Denniston House on Monday.'

Julia closed her eyes, lulled by the insistent clacking of the train wheels, thinking how easy it had been to get away. Once, she could hardly have left the house without a chaperon or a maid to walk with her. Now, chaperons were a thing of those past gentler days and there were fewer maids to accompany young women like her; there'd be fewer still at Rowangarth if Hawthorn managed to get away.

She looked at the watch on her lapel. The train would be late arriving at King's Cross: held up by a troop train and a hospital train, both of which were given priority. She hoped to be able to get a taxi. London was a city of dimmed lights and unlit shop windows now, and to leave her cases at the station and walk to Montpelier Mews didn't bear thinking about. Because of the war, motor buses were few and far between at night, and the army's need of horses had severely cut back the trams. Nor could Aunt Sutton be expected to meet her with the motor. Petrol was hard to come by for civilians, and what could be had cost ten shillings a gallon.

But she would manage. She would have to. Crossing London unaided was nothing compared to going alone to France. A long time ago she had accepted that the life she had known—the safeness and gentleness of it—was gone for ever. Best she should accept it.

Five o'clock, she sighed. She wouldn't be in London until seven at the very earliest. Three hours late...

'That was the best cup of tea I've had in ages, Figgis,' Julia smiled at the elderly servant. 'Now I feel human again.'

'You're sure you don't want a meal?' Anne Lavinia Sutton offered. 'There's soup, if you do, and cold meat.'

'Thanks, Aunt, but Cook packed me sandwiches and apples for the train. It was a hot drink I was in need of. Such a journey!'

'Thought you'd changed your mind; decided not to come. But I might have known you would. It's really all about getting to France, isn't it? Is it the wounded you are thinking about, or is it yourself?' she demanded. 'Are you sure you're not rushing willy-nilly to get to your husband by any means at all; acting like a lovesick milkmaid, are you?'

137

'No, I'm not! How could you think such a thing?' Her aunt didn't change. Blunt to the point of rudeness still. 'I'm not being selfish. I'm just sick of waiting about, wishing the war was over. I want to roll up my sleeves and help. Everyone is helping, though—' she looked directly into her aunt's eyes—'if I were to meet up with Andrew, it would be a wonderful bonus. And you can't blame me for wanting that?'

'Good! A bit of sense at last! And you want me to help you?'

'Please, Aunt? Mother knows about it, so you needn't worry. I don't think she wants me to go, but she understands that I need to. And I'd thought that since women can drive ambulances now, in France, maybe you could use your influence to get me in?'

'Be a Fanny, you mean?'

'If that's what they're called—yes. I saw in the newspaper that women of the First Aid Nursing Yeomanry have been driving in France since the New Year. I would like to go too.'

'Just like that, eh? Your Aunt Sutton snaps her fingers and makes it all right? Put another piece of coal on the fire—*one* piece. Coal's worse to come by in London than petrol! And what do you say to a sniff of brandy? Getting a bit short on supplies now. Should have stocked up more, but who'd ever have thought it would come to this?' she said sadly. 'I ache for France, you know. Wish I were young and strong like you. Nothing would have stopped me going.'

'And I want to go too, but for different reasons,' Julia murmured, selecting a piece of coal, positioning it carefully. 'You know I can drive quite well. With a few more lessons I'd be good at it. And you said you teach women to drive—why can't I be one of them?'

'You could, like a shot, if I thought it'd do any good. But there are more drivers than ambulances, and that's a sad fact. Motor ambulances are in short supply as yet. Thank the good Lord for horses. At least there's no shortage of them. But women don't drive horse-drawn ambulances; they just don't. You'll have to take your turn. There's a long queue of young women waiting for an ambulance. If you want to get out there, you'd do better to be a nurse. Far better you go for the Voluntary Aid Detachment. The VAD is crying out for nurses—or couldn't you stand the sight of blood?'

'Seems I don't have a lot of choice, and I'm not put off by blood,' she shrugged. 'I just want to help. Hawthorn wants to be a nurse; we could go together. I thought being a driver would get me there more quickly, that's all.'

'Oh, dearie me—if it's getting there quickly you're after, then I'm afraid...' The elderly woman offered a brandy glass. 'Sip it slowly. Lord knows when there'll be any more of the good stuff. World gone mad,' she murmured, nose in glass.

'What do you mean, afraid?' Agitated, Julia jumped to her feet. 'Red tape, do you mean?'

'I mean that Julia Sutton can't clap her pretty hands and demand to be in France the moment she thinks fit. You'll first have to do probation in a hospital here at home, and there'll be nursing and first-aid exams to be taken *and passed* before you can even begin to think of an overseas posting.'

'I see, Aunt,' she murmured, her eyes all at once grave. 'Forgive me, but Julia *Sutton* is no more, nor is the world she lived in and thought would last for ever. But Julia MacMalcolm is altogether a different person. And it's sad that we can't go at once, but we'll have to accept it. The sooner we get started, the sooner we'll be there, I suppose. So when can we begin, and where? Oh, and there's a complication: Hawthorn isn't twenty-one.'

'How old? Twenty?'

'She will be, in June. But it would only be a small deceit—a white lie. And perhaps they won't even bother to ask...?'

'They'll *ask* all right, but if she tells them she's old enough—adds a year on—I very much doubt they'll check up on her, especially if she's given good references. You'll both of you need a character reference, you realise that? I could give one to Hawthorn—say that in my opinion she would make a splendid VAD nurse. Or your mama could do it...'

'No! I'm sure Hawthorn would be pleased to have you, Aunt, though I suppose family wouldn't count in my case. I'd have to ask Judge Mounteagle, I suppose.' She gave a little laugh. 'Imagine having to ask someone to vouch for me—a Sutton.'

'Your cousin Elliot is a Sutton.' Anne Lavinia pulled down the corners of her mouth, 'and I wouldn't give him a good name for all the horses in the Camargue!'

'Then you'll back Hawthorn up—say she's old enough?'

'The dickens I will! But I won't go out of my way to say that she *isn't!*'

'Bless you. That's settled then!' Julia raised her glass. 'Let's drink to us being nurses—and an end to the war!' Oh, *please,* a speedy end to it, and the troops safely home.

'Amen to that. And I think that tonight we might just spare another lump or two for the fire. Now, where shall you begin your training? Here, in London, or shall you ask Clementina to get you into that hospital of hers? I don't suppose it matters much where you start.'

'Suppose not. What matters, really, is where we end up. And it isn't Aunt Clemmy's hospital, it's her pet charity. She organises things for it. It's called Denniston House, and Mother visits there. She started last Monday and she reads to the blind soldiers and writes letters for them.

'Mother actually helps at first hand. Aunt Clemmy won't step inside the place if she can help it; wouldn't be seen dead there. Oh, dear! That was a terrible thing to have said. Me and my silly mouth. So sorry...'

'Hm. That's one thing you'll have to learn to keep a check on—that sudden Sutton temper of ours. You're going to have to learn what it's like to put your tongue in your cheek and take orders. And you'll have to mind what you say to sick and wounded men. If you don't, Julia, you won't pass your exams, and you can say goodbye to nursing and France for ever.'

'I know that, but I have been a much better person since I met Andrew and I'll try, I really will. Word of a Sutton.'

'Of course you will.' In a rare demonstration of affection, Anne Sutton hugged her niece to her. 'I *know* you will. It's just that it's going to take you a little longer than you thought to get to that husband of yours.'

'By summer, do you think?'

'That's more like it. If all goes well, you could be there by July.'

'And how was London, Julia, my dear?'

'Different, Aunt Clemmy. Gloomy at night and getting drab, somehow. But you'll know that for yourself, having a house there now.'

No use telling her that London seemed drab because Andrew was no longer there. Only Mrs Sparrow, at the Little Britain lodgings, and only ghosts of past lovers in Hyde Park.

'London is—*different*,' Clementina Sutton acknowledged. It was less restrained in some ways, but socially—the socialising she had hoped to find when she bought the Cheyne Walk house—it was completely lacking. Everyone who was anyone was taken up, one way or another, with the war. Finding a husband, once the most important consideration in a girl's life, now took second place to war work: the licence it had given young ladies to do the most unimaginable things! Even

Julia, who'd said on the telephone that she intended to be a VAD nurse. Not content with marrying beneath her, she now seemed set on a course that could only end in disaster.

'I had a letter from Nathan,' Julia smiled. 'It was waiting for me when I got back from London. He's well, though busy. He seemed happy, too.'

'Happy I'm not sure about, but busy —yes, I can well imagine that. It surprises me how the working classes turn to God when they think they are in trouble.'

'So would I, Aunt. If I were in a foxhole,' Julia said with the candid gaze so like that of her mother, 'being shelled and machine-gunned. I'd sure as anything want God in there with me.'

'Tut!' Clementina forced a smile. 'But what was it you said on the telephone about nursing at Denniston House?'

'I believe you know the matron—will you ask her? We want to go nursing, you see, but we must first be probationers and take exams. Aunt Sutton wondered if it might not be best for us to go to one of the London hospitals and use Andrew's lodgings as a base. But after Robert—and with Giles not long gone away—I thought it would be kinder to Mother if we were to start our training hereabouts. The nearest military hospital is Denniston House, so could you ask the matron if she would take us—*please?*'

'But my dear child, I don't know the matron. We speak, of course, when there is some matter of charity to discuss, but I'm not at all sure if I could place myself under an obligation by asking a favour of her. And who, will you tell me, is *we?* Who else is going nursing with you?'

'Hawthorn, our sewing-maid. Her young man is on his way to the Front, she thinks. We both want to do our bit.'

'Hawthorn?' *That* one? The little innocent who had been the cause of so much upset. Hob-nobbing with her betters now. Was there no end to her impudence? And what was Helen thinking about to allow it? 'I see. And does your mama know about it? Has she consented to—'

'*Consented,* Aunt? I am of age and a married woman. I don't need parental approval for anything I do. But since you ask—no, Mother doesn't know that Hawthorn intends to be a nurse, but I'm sure she'll miss her when she goes.'

'Very well. I shall speak to the matron at Denniston House about you both.' Oh my word, yes! Tell her what a little troublemaker she'd be getting if she took in the servant. Or should she maybe just *hint?*

'Thank you, Aunt Clemmy.' Best not

mention Hawthorn's age. It would be just like her aunt to tell on her. 'It's really good of you.' She rose from her seat in the window, walking to the sofa-table, picking up Nathan's photograph. 'Doesn't he look handsome in his uniform? I hope he'll soon be sending a photograph to Rowangarth too. Aren't you so very proud of him?'

'I am proud of *both* my sons,' came the instant reply. 'And doubtless Nathan—Elliot, too—will be sending pictures of themselves to your mama. You know,' she looked down at her fingers, almost coyly, 'your uncle and I used to hope that one day you and Nathan—'

'Would marry?' Julia finished. 'I must say he's very dear to me, but we've always been more like brother and sister than cousins. Same with Giles. He and Nathan were almost like twins; born only weeks apart, as well you know. But I didn't even once think of Nathan as a husband. I like him too much—and, that's a stupid thing to say, though you know what I mean!

'But I've already taken up too much of your time. Can I telephone the matron and ask her if she will see us? Can I tell her that my aunt will vouch for us both? Can I, please?'

Put like that, Clementina thought wryly as she stood at the window, watching her niece pedal her bicycle most expertly up the carriage drive, what chance did she have to refuse?

And maybe, she thought, Julia would have been altogether too much of a tomboy for Nathan, and certainly little use as the wife of an Anglican vicar.

Perhaps, in the penniless doctor, she had found her true match?

7

Julia's brief apprehension about her future as a nurse was quickly gone. Not only was the matron at Denniston House kindly and sympathetic; she had also been trained at St Bartholomew's, where Andrew had worked. The coincidence was an omen, Julia decided, a good omen. She relaxed at once.

'Very well, young ladies,' smiled the white-haired woman who now had Julia's complete trust and affection, 'I think you might do well as probationers, though the matter does not entirely rest with me. You must now meet Sister Tutor. It is she who has the final say. Her standards are high and you will come to realise that being a VAD nurse is much, much more than a patriotic whim.'

'It demands complete dedication and can often be distressing. But it is rewarding. The sick and wounded in your care depend on you. Some even think of their nurses as angels. Can you live up to being angels, do you think? More important—can you convince Sister Carbrooke?'

She rose to her feet, holding out a hand to each in turn.

'I'll try my best, Matron,' said Julia breathlessly, 'and thank you.'

'Yes. Thank you, I'm sure.' Alice, overawed, bobbed a curtsey.

'That Sister Carbrooke's going to be an unholy terror,' she said flatly that night as she sat with Cook and Tilda at the kitchen table.

'Ward sisters is all the same.' Jinny Dobb poured hot milk into the cocoa jug. 'Best neither of you upset her or she'll make your lives a misery. Afore she's finished with you, she'll make you wish you'd never joined, and it'll be too late then.'

'No, Jin. Nothing is final till we've done our training. That's when we sign on, Matron told us.'

'Then be careful what you put your name to,' Tilda offered, obliged to warn them they could be signing themselves into white slavery if they weren't careful.

'It'll be all right. Nurses sign for a

year—a contract, sort of. When I've done that year, I sign on again if I want to. And if they want me,' she added dubiously.

'Can't say fairer than that.' The pair of them were set on going to France, Cook brooded, and a year might be all they could stand of it if what she'd heard was true. 'So when will you be going?'

'Don't rightly know. We got as far as filling in the forms.' Alice squirmed inside just to think about it—the date of her birth, that was—and how she had added on a year without so much as a blush. 'We had to give the names of two people who would vouch for our good character. In the end, it'll all depend on that, I suppose.'

'Referees, they're called,' Cook obliged. 'And who did you give, then?'

'Her ladyship, and Miss Sutton in London. Miss Julia gave Judge Mounteagle and Doctor James, him having brought her into the world.'

'You can't do better than a lady of title and a judge,' Jin said comfortably, 'and since it isn't likely you'd be daft enough to give names of folk as would say wicked things about you, I reckon you'll be all right. But best I take a look at your hand afore you go, Alice lass, to make sure you're forewarned.'

'Oooh...' Tilda beamed, for when Jin was in the mood and the 'fluence running, she would read any palm thrust at her.

'Next full moon.' Jin didn't hold with fortune-telling at any other time. 'I'll give you all a read, if you like.'

'Miss Julia as well,' Alice demanded.

'No. *Not* Miss Julia.' Palm reading and such-like was only for the lower orders as far as Jin was concerned. 'And you'd best not mention it in front of Miss Clitherow, neither, or I'll be out on me ear!' With her promotion from bothy to big house, Jin considered she had fallen on her feet. She ate better, despite the shortages, and looking after the gentry was easier than cooking for apprentice lads and washing their shirts and bedding, though God Himself knew she would forsake her life of ease this minute if things could be as they were and the killing ended. For how many of those apprentices would return to Rowangarth, no one knew, and of the lucky ones who did, none would be lads any longer. 'Ah, well. Best be off home. See you all in the morning,' she beamed, throwing her shawl over her head.

They did not ask her if she would be all right on the walk over, nor if she should take the candlelamp to light her way to the end almshouse—Reuben's house it should have been, thought Alice sadly.

'Careful how you go, Jin,' Cook called.

'She'll be all right.' Tilda carried the

150

empty cups to the sinkstone. 'That one can see in the dark, just like a cat.' Like a witch's cat...

...so you see, my darling. I am now committed. Nothing will stop my becoming a nurse—except my own stupidity, that is, and I intend not to fail. I didn't tell you before because I feared you would forbid it, but on seeing the wards today at Denniston House, I am prepared to risk your disapproval. Those soldiers are terribly wounded—some blinded—and I want very much to care for them. If all goes well, Hawthorn and I will report to the Barracks Hospital at York for two weeks' training and to be given our uniforms. Then we shall return to Denniston House for the rest of our probation.

Perhaps you never saw Denniston, but if you stood on Holdenby Pike, looking towards Pendenys, then a little to your right, you would see the place. It was empty and neglected when war started; now it holds fifty beds. Sleeping accommodation for nurses there is in short supply so Hawthorn and I will sleep at Rowangarth and bicycle to the hospital every day. I rather imagine that Aunt Clemmy arranged it for us, but it doesn't matter where we sleep.

'Please be proud of me, my love? I do

so want your approval. And isn't it good for a doctor's wife to be a nurse? Think what a help I shall be to you when the war is over and we are together again...

Julia laid down her pen and read carefully what she had written. She had decided not to tell Andrew about her intention to be an ambulance driver. She had thought then that she could be in France in a matter of weeks and present him with her *fait accompli*. But it hadn't turned out like that, and she knew she could not keep quiet about her nursing training for the next six months; nor did she want to.

Tonight, more than ever, I want you with me. I long to sleep in your arms, though the way I feel now, I would settle for a glimpse of your dear face—and perhaps just one kiss...

She would. She had no pride left now. She wanted him with a need that thrashed like a pain inside her. Even if he were to send a telegram forbidding it, nothing would change. She had no illusions about nursing now. The tight-lipped Sister Carbrooke had seen to that. The work would be hard and at times dangerous. So be it. It was the price she must pay to be nearer to Andrew, and besides, all at once, caring for the wounded was what she wanted to do; even had she never met Andrew, she would want it. A ward at Denniston House had been her road to Damascus. A young soldier, his eyes bandaged, had put out a hand as they passed and said, 'Nurse?' And Sister had gone to him and taken his searching hand in her own and said softly, 'What is it?'

Nothing to make a fuss about, but Sister's slab face had softened into gentleness even as she spoke, and that one small act of compassion had made her want to weep as she watched; had made her feel, in one blinding second, that to be a nurse was all she had ever wanted.

Goodnight, my dearest dear. I send you all my love—reach out and gather it to you. I want you so very, very much. God keep you safely.

Your Julia.

Jin Dobb was nobody's fool, thought Alice, as she hugged her bed warmer to her. Sister Carbrooke would indeed need to be watched.

'And how old are you, Miss Hawthorn?' Her gimlet eyes had met and challenged Alice's.

'Gone twenty. I'll be of age come June. It's me nose, Sister...'

Sister Tutor, they had come to realise before ever the tour of the hospital was half over, was a stickler for cleanliness and a strong believer in carbolic. Carbolic soap, carbolic disinfectant and Keating's carbolic powder for the banishing of fleas, she had stressed.

'Fleas. Some are covered with them when they come to us. Uniforms *alive* with them...'

'But, Sister—they come all the way from the trenches without—'

'Without being cleaned up? Ha! A dressing, if they're lucky, is all some of them get! They do what they can at the front,' she had acknowledged, loyal to her own, 'and I'll admit that conditions are improving out there. By summer there'll be more field hospitals—the wounded will get attention more quickly. That's where you'll both be going: if you satisfy me, that is, that you're up to it!'

'A *field* hospital, Sister?' Alice had frowned.

'Tents!' The reply had been derisive. 'Though I understand a lot of them will have been replaced by huts before another winter. Well, there's a limit to the number of houses they can requisition. Got to put the poor men somewhere...'

'You mean there are so many wounded they must put them in huts and *tents?*'

Julia's disbelief had been genuine.

'I mean just that! You won't just be fighting the enemy—and by that I mean near-hopeless conditions—but you'll have cold and damp to put up with, and likely as not you'll have to tramp the length of a field just to wash yourselves. Are you up to it? Can you stick it?'

'I don't know, Sister,' Julia had whispered. 'But my husband has stuck it for a long time. He can't complain, so why should I?'

She had thrown back the challenge in true Sutton manner, and Alice had been hard put to it not to cry, 'Good for you, Miss Julia!' But instead, she had thought of Tom, wounded and flea-ridden. Tom Dwerryhouse with a dressing—if he were lucky—on a shattered limb, beginning the long, painful journey back to England.

'How do you know all this, Sister?' she had whispered.

'Because I spent a year there.' Sister's eyes had all at once been far away. 'And when my year here is up, I hope to go back.'

'My young man is out there,' Alice had said to no one in particular, because really she was making the most solemn vow of her life.

Somehow she would get to France, get there in spite of her missing year and childlike nose. And when she did, she wouldn't complain about cold or damp or washing in a field, because every wounded soldier she helped nurse would have as much of her caring and compassion as if they were Tom, and she would fetch and carry and scrub and clean and try never to be afraid.

'Is he out there now?'

'Y-yes. In the West Yorkshires. And I'll do my best, Sister, 'cos I reckon if I do, then some other nurse is going to be good to my Tom, if ever he's...' Her voice had trailed into silence as she had fought the tears she dared not allow. Just imagine Sister Carbrooke making mincemeat of a weeping nurse! The thought had steadied her; banished all thoughts of self-indulgence. 'If ever he's in need of nursing,' she had finished quietly.

'Where are you, Tom?' she whispered now into the darkness of her room. 'Are you in France?'

Was he there, already being shelled and shot at; in a trench and unable to let her know? A man didn't take pencil and paper and write to his young lady, did he, not in a fox-hole? 'Keep him safe, God,' she pleaded, 'and make me a good nurse and oh, don't ever let them find out I'm not old enough to go to France...'

At the dressing-station forward from the rear trenches, Andrew MacMalcolm shrugged into his greatcoat, nodding to his relief. A few yards away waited the motor transport that would take him back to his bed and the sleep he had been praying for.

Sleep. It made life bearable. He struggled on, thinking of blessed sleep. It helped him ignore the stench of putrefying wounds; to shut out the misery. He had become a doctor because of the injustice of his parents' deaths, yet by contrast they had died in the comparative luxury of a clean bed and with a warm handclasp to help their first uneasy steps into death.

Yet, in this hell-hole, many died afraid and without dignity; died impaled on barbed wire out of reach of help.

...hanging on the old barbed wire...

Words from the marching song drummed in his ears. How could a Tommy bear to sing it? Had they become so immune to all this that to bleed slowly to death in No Man's Land was a relief?

'There are letters for you, Mac,' his relief called as he picked up his bag.

Letters from Julia, from Rowangarth where there was peace and safety and sanity. It was what he was fighting for.

Hands reached down and helped him into the back of the army lorry that would jolt him back to the base hospital and bed.

Yet he *wasn't* fighting for a faraway place in a faraway country; he was fighting, now, to stay alive—it was as simple as that. And he was here because Sarajevo had set alight the hatred of two nations, each for the other, and because Belgium had wanted to remain apart from the fight. And what now the price of their neutrality and the cavalier fashion in which the British Government had pledged to guarantee it. Broken young bodies and sleepless nights; men crying out to die; men crying out to live. Neutrality and hatred at war with each other, and the youth of Europe trapped in the middle of it.

He clenched tightly on his jaws. He was on stand-down now. He'd done his stint and now he could sleep, had earned sleep. He would take off his dirty, bloodstained clothes and fall naked into bed, with Julia's letters beneath his pillow where he could touch them for comfort; letters to read when finally he awoke.

Her name beat inside his head. When things became near unbearable, her name was the only prayer he knew; the only one he could say without bitterness.

He closed his eyes and she was beside him and the wind—and clean wind on the Pike—taking her hair, blowing it like a cloud about her.

'We're here, sir.' An orderly shook his arm. 'You dropped off...'

Back at the base hospital, almost four miles behind the front line; back to a bed and sleep and the defiant satisfaction of having survived another three days under fire. Three days nearer to Julia...

The world had become grey. A grey, grizzling sky, a grey sea—a sea forbidden to them by enemy submarines. So they had waited three days and two nights, sleeping in a dockside warehouse, eating food cooked in a field kitchen. It was the way it would be when finally he got to France, Tom Dwerryhouse reasoned; best accept it. And here on the dockside he was safe at least from shellbursts and sudden, whining bullets and machine-gunners with nervous fingers.

He hadn't minded the delay. They had finally left England at night on a frighteningly darkened ship; on a trooper painted grey to match the mood of every soldier on board. He had no idea where his regiment would be quartered, he only knew he wanted to be free of the load on his back. And he wanted to be able to write to Alice; bring her nearer. He ached to reach out and touch her. Alice was love and peace and a tip-tilted nose. Wherever she stood was home to him: waiting for her in Brattocks Wood and the lighted, leaded windows of Rowangarth glowing through the darkness. Alice was springtime and green things growing and soft, brown eyes; she was summer in his arms with buttercups in her hair. She was his. He had taken her, claimed her. Now he wanted this war to be over. It was none of his making and, truth known, he didn't want to fight for France—or was it Belgium? He didn't even want to fight for his King, though everyone said that was why he was here.

So why was he here, and burdened like a packhorse with kit; like the dozens and dozens of horses tied in the standings beyond the ammunition sheds—and with as little freedom of choice? He was fighting, he told himself firmly, for Alice. Fighting for the right to get back to her; to wed her and live with her in Keeper's Cottage and, when the time was proper, to have bairns with her—bonny little lasses and a lad to train into keeping, beside him.

He pulled his thoughts back to the greyness. The platoon sergeant was calling out an order and, dammit, he'd missed the half of it.

'...and I'm warning you—if there are any marks at all on that card, it'll be torn up.

You signs your name and you turns it over and writes the address on the other side. No secret marks or the Censor'll have you shot. And no crosses for kisses. Kisses ain't allowed, neither. When you've filled in your card, hand it to the corporal, and if you haven't a pencil about you, then hard luck, soldier!'

Tom read the card passed down the line to him. It was buff-coloured and, beneath the warning bawled out by the sergeant, several options were printed.

I am quite well
I have been admitted into hospital
I have received your letter dated...

Tom considered each of the eight printed lines gravely. Finally, he crossed them all through save the first and last. *I am quite well*, and *Letter follows at first opportunity.* Then he signed his name and number and rank after carefully printing Alice's name and address on the reverse side.

It would be a coldly worded, impersonal card to receive, but she would understand —be grateful, even—to get it.

'Stay safe, bonny lass,' he thought, passing the card back. 'This war can't last much longer...'

It couldn't. One big push, everybody was saying, was all it would take. One great battle on land and another at sea. Our navy was the finest in the world. Two good scraps and he'd be back at Rowangarth. Wars cost money and both sides wanted it over and done with now. Stood to sense, didn't it?

Alice. With luck she would have that card in three days, and maybe, when they got to wherever the faceless ones were sending them, letters from home would be waiting for them. Letters from Alice, who loved him...

The letter addressed to Mrs Julia Mac-Malcolm arrived by the first post. She knew what was inside it and hurried to the kitchen, ripping it open as she went.

'It's come, Hawthorn! Where's yours? What does it say?'

'Nothing for me. Nothing at all...' Miss Clitherow had sorted the post and shaken her head to Alice's unspoken enquiry. There had been nothing from Tom, and, even though everyone said no news was good news, it didn't help. There had been only two letters since their snatched goodbye; both hurriedly written notes, telling her he loved her, that he would always love her. Postmarked Aldershot, they bore no address, which meant he would soon be moving on. But since then, nothing had come for almost two weeks.

'When do you go, miss?'

'On Monday, the thirty-first. Report to the matron at ten o'clock, it says, and I'm to take only sufficient clothes for one week—underwear and stockings, they probably mean. Until we get our uniform, I suppose.' She read through the printed notice and the dates and remarks added by pen. 'And I'm to be prepared to take a medical examination, upon which, it says, depends my acceptance as a VAD probationer. Are you *sure* there wasn't one for you, Hawthorn?'

'Sure, miss. Nothing. Not from Tom nor the nursing.'

'Lordy! They've found out how old you are!'

'But who would tell them, miss? And I'm not too young to join, surely; just too young to go to France.'

'So you gave your wrong age, eh?' Cook demanded, button-mouthed, when Julia had left. 'What made you do a daft thing like that?'

Alice opened her mouth to protest and was silenced by Cook's raised finger.

'And no back answers, if you please. Don't be telling me it's none of my business and I shouldn't be listening, because this is *my* kitchen and whatever is said in it is *my* business!'

'I know, Mrs Shaw. And I'm sorry—for

what I nearly said,' Alice hastened, pink-cheeked. 'But you won't tell on me? Nobody else knows but Miss Julia. I want to get to Tom, see, and if Reuben got to hear about it he'd stop me, I know he would!'

'Bless you, lass, I'll say nowt. You must do what you think best. If it don't bother your conscience, then it don't bother mine. It's funny, though—your letter not arriving with Miss Julia's...'

'And nothing from Tom, either. This isn't my lucky day, is it?'

'There's always the twelve o'clock post. Cheer up, lass.'

'Didn't you say you wanted the pantry floor scrubbed, Mrs Shaw? I'll do it if you like.'

She could have scrubbed from end to end before Jin arrived at half-past. She felt like taking out her worry and frustration on someone or something—her anger at the war, too. Best it should be the pantry floor!

Alice watched for the postman from the sewing-room window: the midday post came to the back door because parcels came second delivery and the back door was the place for parcels. She was downstairs before the bell had stopped dancing on its spring, waiting for

Miss Clitherow to sort upstairs mail from below-stairs.

'Hm. Two for her ladyship, two for Mrs MacMalcolm and two for you.' The housekeeper's lips formed one of her rare smiles. 'What you've been waiting for, I think, Hawthorn. Take Miss Julia's, will you? I'll see to her ladyship's.'

'Ooh, thanks, Miss Clitherow.' Alice stared at the strange buff-coloured post-card. 'From Tom. Think it's from France. Go on—you can read it, miss.' She pushed the card into the housekeeper's hand. 'He's well, and a letter follows.' Tom had made the crossing safely. Not like Sir Robert. She sent up a prayer of thanks, then whisked away to find Julia. 'It's come, miss. A letter with the same writing on it as yours—and one from Tom!'

She handed over the pencilled card. She would have liked it to be in ink—more permanent, sort of—but a soldier couldn't cart around an ink bottle and pen, even if he carried most things else on his back.

'There'll be a letter from him soon,' Julia smiled. 'A proper one with an address for you to write to. He's as safe as he can be. Now open the other one and tell me what it says!'

'Same as yours, miss.' Quickly Alice read it through. 'We're going to York together, it seems...'

165

'Let's hope we can stay together, Hawthorn. Now, off you go and tell Mother about it. You know she'd like you to stay here, don't you, even though you'll be giving notice to Miss Clitherow?'

'Yes—but is it right, miss? Don't seem fair that her ladyship has to keep me and get nothing in return. I can just as easy go to Reuben's...'

'Do you want to?'

'Not really—oh, Reuben's a nice old gentleman and I'm fond of him, but he's got set in his ways since his wife died. If I can stay on here, I'd help out whenever I could and not be a nuisance...'

'That's settled, then. Mother wants you to stay. She's had enough upset in her life. Your staying would help. And besides, you promised Giles you'd keep an eye on Morgan!'

Alice laid down her pen and corked the ink bottle firmly. Another letter to Tom, but this one she would not send to the Richmond address. This she would hold in readiness because soon she would know his new address.

She had not mentioned going to York at the end of the month. Best say nothing until she'd passed her medical and been given her uniform. She would tell him, perhaps, when they were both settled at

Denniston House. He wouldn't worry so much when he knew she was with Miss Julia.

She placed her hands to her burning cheeks. Tom in France and Alice Hawthorn a nurse. And if all went well she might be out there near him, come summer. In July. Come buttercup time...

8

'Wouldn't you have thought,' said Alice as they walked through the early morning darkness towards the dim lights of the mess hall, 'they'd have built the nurses' quarters nearer the hospital?'

'I suppose the nurses' quarters were an afterthought.' Julia pulled her coat collar around her ears. 'When this place was built, nursing had still to become a respectable profession.'

'Then, not so very long ago, you and me couldn't have been nurses?' Alice gazed at the outline of the tall, gaunt army hospital.

'Goodness, no! Pity the sick before Miss Nightingale's time. In some hospitals, the night nursing was done by any slut of a woman. Sometimes a prostitute, even, would go in off the streets and offer to help, just to get shelter for the night. Nursing has come a long way since the days when anyone could set herself up as a nurse or midwife.'

'Now fancy that!' Miss Julia was very knowledgeable about such things—but then she would be, her being the wife of a doctor. 'So that's why we're so far away.' They were wet already from the cold, driving rain, and their shoes squelched with water. Without a doubt, the next two weeks were going to be very uncomfortable. 'Did you manage to get any hot water in the washroom, miss?'

'I didn't! We'll have to get there even earlier tomorrow. And I was so cold in the night I couldn't sleep.'

'At least we know where the mess hall is,' Alice gasped as they hurried to six o'clock breakfast and a mug of hot tea. 'And if we get a move on we can make our beds and still be at Sister Tutor's office for seven.'

The mess hall was as gaunt as the building that housed it, the brown-painted walls damp with condensation. They took their cutlery from a basket at the door, then found places at one of the long, bare tables.

'We're a bit late for the porridge,' smiled the nurse who followed them in. 'There'll only be bread and jam left. Take my advice and grab some margarine if you see any: it goes very quickly!'

They breakfasted on bread and jam and exquisitely hot tea, then ran, heads down, back to the nurses' quarters, hoping fervently that things might soon get better, for surely they couldn't get worse.

Their entry yesterday into hospital life had been by way of a door on which was painted, *Nurses. Strictly Private.* A wooden, well-scrubbed staircase led to the rooms and dormitories; the smallest, dreariest room—an attic with a small, grimy skylight—being given to Alice and Julia.

'Oh, my word.' Alice gazed in dismay. Against each wall stood a black iron bed on which lay folded blankets and sheets. Behind the door were two coat-pegs; the floor was as bare as the staircase.

'But where do we put our things?'

'In our case, miss, it seems; beneath our beds. At least there's a peg for our coats...'

'Spartan,' Julia muttered, all at once glad their stay here would be brief. 'And imagine them not letting us out at all?'

No young lady would be allowed to leave the hospital without permission for any reason whatsoever, Matron had read from her list of rules, then asked them if it was perfectly understood. They had murmured that it was.

'It's freezing in here!'

'It's to be expected. Attics are cold in winter and hot in summer,' Alice supplied, making a determined start on the beds. 'It won't be so bad, though. Think of the poor lads in the trenches. At least we aren't up to our ankles in water.'

'Trench-foot,' Julia said. 'Andrew says that's what they get, from having to keep wet boots on for days at a time. And I'm not complaining, Hawthorn, though I'll be glad when we've had our medical and can start being nurses. And I'm glad we're still together. It would be awful having to share with someone I didn't know.'

'There, now.' Alice smoothed the bedspread. 'Looks better already. Would you mind sitting on the other bed so I can see to this one? And don't forget we have to go for our pinafores.'

'Pinafores!' Julia wrinkled her nose. She had so wanted her uniform, instead of which they had been told to tie back their hair, roll up their sleeves and, for the time being, wear the red-cross armband which would be given them at the stores, together with long white aprons and heavy-duty pinafores—scrubbing aprons, Alice supposed they'd be. 'Oh dear, when do you think we'll get on the wards?'

'Tomorrow, happen. When we've had our medicals...'

'It's all a bit daunting, isn't it, when you think how unimportant we are here? Two new, untried VADs who don't even merit a uniform, it seems.'

'Unimportant.' All at once, Alice had missed Rowangarth and the warmth of the kitchen; missed Tilda with her love books, Miss Clitherow's straight back and button mouth, and Reuben and Mrs Shaw. 'We'll have to stick it out here, though, if we're ever to get to France.'

Her bottom lip had trembled with doubt, and she wished, just for a moment, to run like the wind, home to Rowangarth.

Then she thought about Tom and Doctor Andrew, and how dreadful this place must be for Miss Julia, who was used to the softest of beds and a fire in her bedroom, and who wouldn't know what to do with a scrubbing apron if she fell over one.

'Don't worry, miss. We'll be all right. Things are going to seem a lot better in the morning, just you see.'

So now they ran, eyes squinting against the rain, splashing through puddles to Sister Tutor's office.

'Trench-foot!' Julia gasped. 'That's what we'll get. My shoes are soaking!'

'They'll soon dry out if we stuff them

with newspaper,' Alice gasped over her shoulder, even though they didn't have a newspaper between them. 'Hurry, miss, do! It's nearly seven!'

'Where have you been?' Sister Tutor glared. 'Hawthorn and MacMalcolm, isn't it? You were told to see me immediately after breakfast, which in this hospital is one minute past seven a.m. You are five minutes late!'

'Yes, Sister.'

'Sorry, Sister.'

'Do you realise how precious the minutes are? I am here to teach nursing, not shepherd ewe-lambs who can't find their way from A to B on time. Do *not* be late again!'

'No, Sister.'

'Sorry, Sister.'

Julia fretted silently inside her; silently, because she learned quickly, and she had been warned never to say anything to Sister Tutor other than 'yes' or 'no' or 'sorry', and only to ask a question when given permission to ask it.

'Your medicals—best get them over with. Don't want you here if you aren't fit. Cut along to the lady doctor in Room 102. Wait until she has written your medical reports, then bring them back to me here at half-past ten. Do *not* read them!'

172

'She's going to be worse than Sister Carbrooke,' Julia muttered.

'At least she doesn't smell of carbolic.'

'There's a lot to learn in just two weeks,' Alice said soberly. 'It'll take longer than that just to find our way around this place.'

'But we'll learn it. If we don't...' Julia pulled a forefinger dramatically across her throat, then knocked firmly on the door of Room 102.

A voice bade them enter. Taking a deep breath, Julia stepped inside. Alice, as was her habit, followed behind.

They had passed their medical, Sister Tutor said, when she had studied the reports placed unread on her desk.

'But be that as it may,' she said severely, 'you have been here for all of a day and a half and done nothing at all. I therefore suggest that you report with your aprons to the staff nurse on Ward 3F. *Now!*'

'We've done it!' Julia exulted when they were out of earshot. 'We've passed! Now we can do some proper nursing!'

'And we'll feel a lot better once they give us our uniforms.'

'We'll get them,' Julia said confidently. 'We'll *earn* them. Do hurry, Hawthorn! Let's not upset Staff Nurse as well!'

Ward 3F was easy to find, Alice thought, once you realised that in the large, main building, all wards lay either side of a wide central corridor, and it was really only a matter of counting. She supposed that, given time, she would find her way around the huge hospital, just as once she had accustomed herself to the corridors and unexpected passageways at Rowangarth.

They walked slowly, peering through open doors into wards with long lines of beds. Everyone was busy; no one took the slightest notice of them.

'How many to each ward, do you think?'

'Dunno, miss. A lot...' A lot of beds; a lot of wounded soldiers.

The doors of Ward 3F were closed; there were no sounds of occupancy. Cautiously, Julia peeped inside.

'*Well!*' Alice jerked.

'Empty!' frowned Julia. Empty and echoing and unfriendly, somehow.

'She was having us on,' Alice said dubiously.

'I don't think so.' Julia stepped inside, taking in the high windows, the two-shades-of-green walls, the woodblock floor, urgently in need of cleaning. 'Sister Tutor wouldn't play jokes. Ward 3F. Report to Staff Nurse, she said.'

'You are quite right. Sister Tutor never jokes.'

'Staff Nurse?' They turned, eyes questioning.

'Staff Nurse Smith, and you are indeed in the right place. This is your ward, ladies, and I would like it cleaned. From top to bottom with the exception of the ceiling. That has already been done by men with ladders.'

'Clean it?' Julia squeaked.

'Clean it.

'From top to bottom?'

'What is your name?' Staff Nurse demanded.

'I'm Julia MacMalcolm—why?'

'Well, MacMalcolm, you and I will get on a great deal better if you stop repeating everything I say before it becomes an irritating habit! I want this ward cleaned in its entirety. Walls, beds, floor: I'm sorry the floor is in such a mess, but the men who cleaned the ceiling are responsible for that. Then, when you have finished, you will do the same to the sluice-room and to Ward Sister's office here beside the door.'

'But—but *how.*'

'I think she means what with,' Alice —who knew how—supplied.

'In the sluice-room are buckets and scrubbers and anything else you may need. In Ward Sister's office you will find a gas ring; you can heat your water on that.'

'But how long,' asked Julia, mesmerised, 'is it going to take?'

'You are here for twelve more days, I believe. I sincerely hope it will take less time than that! You will be wondering why such thoroughness?'

'Frankly—yes.'

'Well, MacMalcolm, I think you have the right to know. There may be some misinformed nurse who will tell you what you'll catch in doing it. But the plain truth is that we took in a lot of wounded from the fighting at Artois. Unfortunately, there were two typhoid cases amongst them.'

'Typhoid! And we've got to—'

'You don't *have* to do anything, Mac-Malcolm. You can put on your hat and coat and go back from whence you came, if you wish. There is no danger to yourselves. The entire ward has been fumigated and left to air for almost a month. In the circumstances, Matron feels that now is a good time to clean it thoroughly.

'We cannot know when the next influx of wounded will arrive. We would like it to be ready for occupation. Use washing soda in your water, and disinfectant—and I want everything cleaned. Every bed, locker—*every single thing.*'

'She can't mean it,' Julia wailed when they were alone in the vast, echoing room.

'She means it, all right!'

'But it's *yards* long, and the walls are really high!'

'There are step-ladders in yon' corner —we can use those. We'd best start on the walls first; do things methodical, like. Best push all the beds into the middle of the ward to give us elbow room, then we get on with it.'

'They're doing it on purpose,' Julia hissed, suddenly angry. 'We aren't going to learn anything about nursing here. They are seeing how much we can take—giving us a rough passage!'

'You mean, if we can take all they throw at us and don't complain, they'll send us on to Denniston House?'

'I'm sure that's what they're up to. I suppose things could get quite tricky in France and they want to be sure we're up to it. I'm angry, though. I came here thinking to learn about nursing, and it seems instead I'm to be taught to scrub and clean!'

'I learned to scrub and clean when I was thirteen, Miss Julia. I'm good at it—I'll show you how,' Alice said quietly.

'Oh, God! Hawthorn, I'm sorry! I truly am! I didn't mean...Forgive me?'

'It's all right, miss. I know you didn't mean it nastily, and I wasn't meaning to be pert. But if scrubbing is going to be our first step towards France, then scrub we will! So tie on your apron and let's get on with it, or we'll have to stay another week to finish the dratted hole and we don't want that, now do we?' She stared wide-eyed at the task ahead of them. 'Oh my word, no.' She lingered, her fingers on the cluster of pearls on her left hand, then reluctantly slipped it off. Strong disinfectant and washing soda would harm her precious ring; best she wore it around her neck. 'When we get our uniforms we won't be allowed to wear any jewellery at all, 'cept wedding rings.' She unfastened the chain at her neck, slipping the ring on to it to hang with Tom's locket and her mother's wedding ring.

'Let me look.' Julia opened the locket carefully. 'Who is this?'

'It's Tom, miss, when he was young. I'm hoping to have one of him in uniform soon, to put there.'

'And the flower—a buttercup?'

'Aye. He gave me buttercups the day he asked me to be his girl.' Alice's eyes filled with tears. 'I miss him. And I get so afraid...'

'I know, Hawthorn. I do so know.' Julia's voice was rough with emotion. 'Sometimes I think I'd do anything at all just to see Andrew: lie, cheat—anything.'

'Well, Miss Julia, lying and cheating might do very well,' Alice pulled the

178

back of her hand across her eyes, sniffing loudly, 'but in our present predicament there's only one thing is going to get us to France, and that's scrubbing.

'So let's hang up our white aprons—we aren't going to be doing any nursing in them yet a-while. This lot's going to take us days and days.' Alice knew about such things. 'The sooner we start, the sooner we'll be on our way to Denniston!'

'Hm. We'll have to watch out for Staff Nurse Smith, you know. I'll bet she can spot a speck of dust at twenty paces. Ooh! This apron smells *awful!*'

'That's because it's made of sacking, miss. Scrubbing aprons always are. And don't you worry none about Staff Nurse Smith. When we've finished this ward, she can poke and pry till she's blue in the face and she'll find nowt wrong with it!'

There followed a week the like of which Julia MacMalcolm wished never to live through again—or so she thought at the time: a week of hot, cruel water; of aching arms from reaching high to wash walls; of water, grey with dirt, trickling down her arms. And how she came to hate green; the pale, mawkish green of the upper half of the wall; the sombre olive of the lower.

Within two days her hands were red and swollen, her fingernails broken and pitted with dirt. Had it not been for Hawthorn's ability to tackle the work with sense and method, she'd have run home in tears Julia acknowledged, in her blacker moods. But as the week wore on, it lifted her heart a little to see other cracked and bleeding hands amongst the newcomers in the mess hall, all of them like herself; too stubborn to give in and ask for lotion to help make the aching soreness bearable.

'We'll see to all the walls first,' Alice had pronounced, sizing up the situation with the aplomb of one already well-versed in such matters. 'Then we'll do the lockers and wipe the bed-frames—and after that, the floors...'

The sluice-room they would leave until the end, her common sense decided, for that was where buckets were filled and emptied and, anyway, it was such a little room that half a day would see it finished.

'What would I have done without you, Hawthorn?' Now Julia obeyed orders without question. Now her hands were so swollen that she disliked even to look at them; her knees were bruised from kneeling. Even had her bed been soft, their attic warm and snug, still she would have lain awake contemplating her aching back, her sore knees, her throbbing hands. She had been ready, one night, to give up and go home humbled and disgraced, until

180

she thought of the letter she would have to write to Andrew.

...I gave up. After ten days it became so unbearable that I went home. Sorry, but I'm not cut out for nursing.

She could not, would not write that letter! Andrew could not give up; Alice's Tom couldn't pack his bags and buy a first-class ticket to Holdenby Halt! How *dare* she be so weak, so childish! She would go on until her back broke and her knees gave way. And come to think of it, why weren't Hawthorn's hands cracked and bleeding like her own, and her knees swollen?

Tears trickled down her cheeks, and she mopped them with her bed-sheet.

I want you, Andrew. I need you to kiss my hands better and tell me it will be all right. And, darling—I'm not going home. I won't give in...

Two days from the end of their cold, wet, hungry stay at the Barracks Hospital, Julia exulted, 'We've done it—it's all finished! Did you ever see such a difference!'

'Just the sluice-room floor to be scrubbed, then that's it,' Alice smiled, equally proud. Such shining windows, clean furniture and oh, how spotless a floor! 'Now, tell you what, miss; by way of a celebration, kind of, I'll finish off. I'm better at it than you.

Just rinse those poor hands under the tap and dab them dry. I reckon you deserve a rest.'

'You're a dear, Hawthorn. I couldn't have kept at it without you, I swear I couldn't.'

'You could, Miss Julia. You'd never have given up.'

'Then don't give up now, MacMalcolm,' said a voice behind them. Staff Nurse Smith, who walked with the stealth of a cat, had appeared again without warning. 'Fill your bucket and take your share of that floor! Hawthorn is not your servant now. Here you are equals, and I want to hear no more "Miss Julias". Is that clear?' she flung as she left in a rustle of starched indignation.

'Miss—I'm sorry,' Alice whispered. 'That was cruel and uncalled for. Don't let her upset you. She's annoyed 'cos we've made such a good job of it—*both* of us. She's poked and peeped and never once found anything wrong. So think on—we'll be leaving here on Friday.' It would be like getting out of the lock-up!

'Yes, we *have* made a good job of it, and up until now I've stood my corner. It's kind of you to offer, but I'll help finish it if you don't mind. If we get a move on, we'll be first in the supper queue!' On hands and knees they grinned at each other across the floor.

'First in the queue it is, Miss Julia!'

'She was right, you know. I hate to admit it, but for once Staff Nurse was right!' Julia pronounced as they scraped clean their rice-pudding dishes.

'Miss?'

'There you go again, Hawthorn—and there *I* go too. You mustn't call me Miss, or Miss Julia: we are both nurses—or will be, I hope. You must call me MacMalcolm, or Julia. I shall continue to use your surname if Denniston House demands it, but at all other times you are Alice—is that understood?'

'Oooh, miss, I couldn't. And even if I forced it out, what'll I call you when we're back at Rowangarth? Can you imagine Miss Clitherow standing for it? Can you, eh?'

'But it's different, now. We are nurses; it wouldn't be right for me to tell you what to do, now would it?'

'But you've never told me what to do, miss. Not ever. You and her ladyship both have always *asked* me to do things and thanked me for the doing of them. Not like that Mrs Clementina from the Place. Now she's a real martinet, that one. She's—oooops! Was forgetting she's your aunt. No disrespect, miss, I'm sure...'

'No. You've got it wrong. She's not a martinet; she's a bitch. Who else could have spawned Cousin Elliot? And as for poor Uncle Edward—it wouldn't surprise me if one day he didn't give her the slap she deserves. She's been asking for it for years!'

'Don't say things like that, miss! You know you shouldn't!'

'Not in front of the servants, you mean? Alice, can't you at least try? All right, I know we'll both forget sometimes, but it won't be long before we get it right. Say you'll try?'

'I'll try.'

'Good! Then let's get back to 3F and have a last look round. Sister Tutor is coming to check it, remember. Let's make sure we haven't missed anything.'

'Yes, an' we'd better tidy our hair and put on our armbands and white aprons.'

'Come on, then. There might even be some hot water in the wash-room. And the first thing I'll do when I get back to Rowangarth will be to run a bath—a *hot* bath—and wallow in it until the stink of carbolic is gone!'

'Me, too. Just *think* of it...' Just to think that in little more than a day they would be on the train to Holdenby and, if they were lucky, with Matron's recommendation that they were ready to start their training at

Denniston House...

'I've thought of nothing else, Hawthorn, for the past twelve days. And I shall never, *ever*, forget Ward 3F!'

Probationer Nurses MacMalcolm and Hawthorn stood stiff and straight in clean white pinafores, gazing, unblinking, at the wall opposite as Sister Tutor, followed by Staff Nurse Smith, entered Ward 3F, nodding to them in passing.

For what seemed an age—and was actually a full five minutes—Sister's forefinger searched and poked; her eyes slid to left and right and upwards and downwards. Then, without a word, she turned and walked the length of the echoing ward to where the pair stood, dry-mouthed and shaking.

'Let me see—today is...?'

'Wednesday, Sister,' Julia choked.

'And you leave on...?'

'Friday,' Alice whispered, bobbing a curtsey from sheer fright.

'Very well. I think you have time to wax and polish the floors and make up the beds. Apart from that, everything is satisfactory. Please draw mattresses and bedding from Stores, Staff Nurse.'

'And tomorrow, Sister,' Staff Nurse murmured, 'what are they to do, if you please?

'*Do?* They are to report after breakfast to Matron. She will sign requisitions for uniforms, doubtless, and when you are satisfied they are wearing them correctly, you will take them on a tour of the hospital and show them what the inside of a *real* ward is like. After which, you will give each a travel warrant to wherever she is going!'

For just a moment when they were alone, neither was able to speak. Then Julia gave out a great shout of laughter.

'We're in! *Uniforms,* she said!'

'Yes, and did you see Staff Nurse as they left? She smiled! She bloomin'-well *smiled.*'

Alice walked self-consciously down the kitchen stairs, pausing before she opened the door, savouring the moment of her homecoming.

'Cook! Oh, see who's here!' called Tilda. 'It's Alice back, and goodness, come and look at her!'

'Hullo, Mrs Shaw. I haven't missed teatime, have I?'

'Lass! Just look at you in that uniform. Our Alice, a nurse!'

Cook's eyes brimmed over with tears and, so overcome was she, that she sat down in the fireside rocker and, burying her face in her pinafore, sobbed as if her heart was ready to break.

'An angel, that's what, and thank God you're safely home, Alice!'

'But, Mrs Shaw, we've only been to York for two weeks,' Alice whispered, placing an arm around the trembling shoulders. 'And we're both to go to Denniston House for our training, so we won't be going away again for ages and ages. Don't cry over me—*please?*'

'I wasn't crying over you,' Cook sniffed, peering over the hem of her pinafore. 'It—it's because I should've baked some cherry scones. I would've, if I'd known. And if a body can't have a weep in her own kitchen when two young lasses come back from the war, then it's a poor carry-on!'

'But we haven't been to the war.'

Not yet, that was. Not until summer, when she was—well, twenty-one...

'Darling, it's so good to be back.' Julia sat at her mother's feet, gazing into the fire, a *real* fire, vowing that never again would she take one for granted.

'It's good to have you back, though I haven't been too lonely. Two weeks would soon pass, I told myself, and though I am still in black for Robert, Tessa and Letty have called—your aunt Clemmy, too. And I have made several visits to Denniston House. The bravery of those young men is incredible, Julia, and their nurses are devoted and hard-working. It made me proud that my daughter is going to be one of them.

'But goodness! How could I forget? There are letters for you. They all came yesterday. On my desk...'

'And all from Andrew,' Julia exulted, scanning the envelopes for the date below the Censor's stamp. 'Goodness! The last one was written only four days ago!' She thrust them into the deep pocket of her dress. 'I'll save them for later,' she smiled. 'When we've had tea, I'll take off this drab old dress and have a lovely long bath, if you don't mind, and read them then.

'Oh, Tilda, you don't know what a delight it will be to drink tea poured from a pot,' she laughed as the housemaid set down a tea tray.'

'A *teapot*, miss?' Tilda frowned.

'Yes, indeed. We've been getting our tea from an urn, Tilda. A great hissing thing that gave out the most incredible noises. What has Cook sent?'

'Brown bread and blackcurrant jam, Miss Julia. And she managed a slice of fruit cake—well, it's Christmas cake, really—and she says sorry there are no cherry scones; the oven wasn't right, you see. The coal shortage,' she explained, patiently. 'Cook banks the fire down with wood and slack now, in the afternoons. Affects the ovens...'

'I see. Thank Cook for her kind thought, won't you? I do understand. And blackcurrant jam is wonderful. I'll pour.'

Julia smiled, almost purring in the warmth of the blazing logs. 'I dreamed of drinking afternoon tea in the firelight. It was cold at the hospital—the stoves in the wards got the coal and coke.'

'And very right and proper, too. The wounded should get—Julia!' Helen stared, horrified, at her daughter's hands.

'Oh dear. They are a bit of a mess, aren't they? All the scrubbing, I'm afraid, but I'll soon have them healed; I'll have to. Can't do dressings with hands like these—wouldn't be allowed. I'll rub them with glycerine tonight, and in the morning I'll see Doctor James. He'll make me up a lotion for them.'

'But, child, they're so cracked and sore-looking. They must hurt terribly.

'Not a bit. They're fine. Hawthorns says once they've healed, they'll be all right; I'll have broken them in, sort of. I wasn't the only one there with bleeding hands. The soda and disinfectant in the scrubbing water did it.'

'You must have done a lot of scrubbing to get them in that state,' Helen frowned.

'Quite a bit,' Julia grinned, remembering Ward 3F with near affection and not a little pride. 'Hawthorn showed me how. And you're not to worry. At Denniston it'll be much easier.'

And oh, she exulted, tonight she would sleep in her soft, warm bed. Add to that a hot, scented bath and three letters from Andrew, and the world was all at once wonderful!

'Do you know, darling,' she murmured, 'as Hawthorn and I came down the drive there were snowdrops and aconites out. Drifts of white and gold.'

They had never before looked so beautiful, so welcoming. Soon it would be spring, and then, before they knew it, would come summer, and France...

Alice walked carefully, the small candle-lamp in one hand and the spaniel's lead in the other. So good to be back; to wrap the safeness of Rowangarth around her, sit in the warmth of the kitchen. And good to see that daft old dog, who had yelped and barked and rushed about with such excitement on seeing her that she'd felt obliged to take him for a walk. As far as Keeper's, that was. To Reuben's cottage and no further; tell him she was back; let him see her in her uniform before she took it off and set about making it fit. She would have all her work cut out to get both uniforms seen to in time for Monday.

To her right, Brattocks Wood stood dark and lonely; to her left, just over the stile, a light shone from Reuben's kitchen window. If only, when she pushed open the door, Tom could be there, just as he'd been that late December afternoon. It was her constant daydream, now. Just to think back to those two lovely hours set her longing for him.

'Tom, my love,' she whispered into the night, 'send me a letter, soon?'

Julia lay blissfully in the bath, scrubbing her fingernails until the ingrained dirt was gone, and with it the nightmare of Ward 3F. This was like old times again; as if she had never been away.

She closed her eyes, letting the water lap her shoulders, thinking back to Andrew's letter, written, unbelievably, only on Monday.

...and I find myself glad and sad you are to be a nurse; sad because my precious girl may have to face danger, but glad because a sea will no longer divide us. I awoke this morning to the sudden realisation that, if you came to France, I might, given luck, be able to telephone you. Just to hear your voice would balance out all else. We could even, with a small miracle, find we are sufficiently near each other to be able, briefly, to met. One minute would be heaven; one hour—oh, my darling, what could we do in an hour?

Julia laughed softly, placing her hands to her cheeks, wishing he wouldn't write such delightfully sinful letters; glad that he did.

She closed her eyes, hearing his voice. Soon she must step out of this warm luxury, towel herself and dry her hair, but now, her body soft and relaxed, she surrendered herself to the exquisite contemplation of one hour with Andrew. Sixty beautiful minutes; the two of them alone. In bed.

9

Last night, Jinny Dobb had told Alice's fortune, despite Cook's protest that telling fortunes on a Sunday wasn't right. To which Jin had snappily replied, without thought for Mrs Shaw's position, that the moon was right and, anyway, the better the day the better the deed!

So Cook folded her arms across her bosom without further comment, because only a fool would gainsay Jin when the 'fluence was on her.

'Sit under the light, lass.' Jin lifted Alice's hand. 'The right one is the way things are; the left hand the way it was meant to be. Sometimes they tally, other times they're in such conflict that—'

She rose abruptly to pull back the kitchen curtain. Over a puffy bank of silvered cloud, the moon shone high and bright and full.

'—such conflict, that sometimes there's no changing it.'

'So it isn't up to Fate? It isn't all cut and dried for us the day we're born?' Alice's suddenly dry mouth made little clicking sounds as she spoke. 'We can change things?'

'What's in your left hand is Fate—intended. Forewarned, you just might be able to change summat in t'other hand. Hush, now...'

She laid Alice's right hand on the tabletop, palm up, then gazed long at the other, brows meeting in a frown. Then she placed them side by side, running a forefinger lightly over the pads of her fingertips.

'You kept your teacup dregs? You know what to do?'

Unspeaking, Alice made three circles

with the cup she had just drunk from, upturning it into the saucer. Jin took it and shook out the drops left there, her mouth tightening as she did it. Then she turned the cup this way and that, shaking her head, closing her eyes, breathing loudly and deeply.

'Lay your hands on mine,' she said, at all once brisk and businesslike again, 'and look at me, lass, while I talk to you. Now then—there's a lot of nonsense in both hands, but young hands are bound to be frivolous, so it makes no matter. There are tears in your cup and tears in both hands, so you'll straighten your back and take what life throws at you.

'You'll know happiness and you'll have two bairns—one of each. The first will bring sadness, the second one joy. I saw a journey in your cup, though these days that's to be expected. Your going will be in hope, your coming back in sadness.'

Alice looked down at the table-top. No unhappiness, please? Surely Jin knew not to tell her about the bad bits?

'Look at me, Alice Hawthorn, and be thankful that you'll know good health and have a longer life than most, though you'll have a brush with death. Tell me—do you know about the walk through the wood?'

Alice shook her head.

'It's a so-to-speak wood, lass, and a

so-to-speak walk through it, if you get my meaning. Anyway, you'll walk through that wood three times and twice you'll take the long, sad path. And you'll come out first with a stick that's crooked and worthless and the second time with one that's weak and frail. But you'll find your straight, stout stave in the end if you've the courage to take that third walk, Alice, and the sense to listen to your heart...'

The wood, Jin wasn't meaning Brattocks. The wood she was talking about was Life. Alice frowned. And the so-to-speak sticks must be men, really. A bad one, a sickly one, and one that was straight and true. In the end, he would be—if she were brave enough...

'Think on about what I've told you, Alice. Happen now it makes no sense, but it will...' Jin stuck out her left palm. 'You seal it with silver. A threepenny-piece will suffice.'

Alice thrust her hand into the pocket of her apron—she'd known about the silver—and took out the shilling she had put there in readiness. Then she laid it on the waiting hand and folded her work-worn fingers over it. 'I thank you,' she said gravely.

'Now then, Mrs Shaw, how about you?' Jin challenged.

'Nay, I think not.' Not on a Sunday,

any road. 'Maybe I'll be obliged to you next time.' Next full moon, she calculated, wouldn't fall on a Sunday—this being a leap year.

'Me, Jin? Me Now!' Tilda had already seated herself at the table.

'All right, Miss Matilda—and what can I do for you? Is it a rich old man you want from me or a young, lusty one?'

'Both,' Tilda giggled, 'and in that order, if you don't mind!'

'I'll go upstairs now if I may, Mrs Shaw,' Alice whispered. 'I still have a few things to do before morning.'

She had, though really she wanted to think about what Jin had told her; to write it all down before she forgot the half of it.

'Aye, Alice. Away you go.'

Three men in the lass's life. Cook frowned. A nonsense, of course. There was only one man for her, and that was Tom Dwerryhouse: Jin should have known it. Walks through the wood indeed!

Don't you believe the half of it, Matilda Tewk. Jin Dobb's a peculiar one—always was and always will be!

'You'll take a sup of tea with us afore you go home, Jin?'

No matter what had disappeared from larders and store cupboards, at least Rowangarth had tea, Cook was forced to admit. Two chests of Sutton Premier had safely run the blockade and been delivered by the railway cart as they had been since ever she could remember. Their arrival had smacked of normality in a world gone mad.

Sighing deeply, she set the kettle to boil. She was so tired of this war. Everyone was. So very weary of the wretchedness of it; of food queues and the bleakness of having no hopes to an end of it. But mostly it was the partings, the woundings; the telegrams that brought death in terse, cruel sentences.

'I asked you both if you wanted tea,' she flung testily, but they didn't hear her.

Alice was up and dressed next morning long before she need have been, running her finger round the inside of her bone-stiff collar, wondering if she would ever get used to her uniform. In spite of alterations, the dress was still too long for her liking. A show of ankle meant nothing at all now, yet still a VAD's skirt must decorously tip the back of her flat-heeled shoes.

A long white apron and headdress lay carefully folded in one brown paper bag, her shining-clean ward shoes in another, lest they were splashed with mud on the ride to the hospital.

Last night they had checked the carbide lamps at the fronts of their bicycles, and fitted red-glassed candlelamps to the backs. Lady Helen had insisted on it, the road to Denniston House being little more than a lane.

Now, in less than two hours, they would report to Matron, and Alice wished she hadn't lain sleepless half the night worrying about it and about Jin's solemn prophecies. *Three* men? Tcha! Peculiar, Jin Dobb was! And why, Alice wondered, was her stomach making such noises? Was it hunger or apprehension, or a mixing of each?

She needed her breakfast. Porridge, it would be, eaten without sugar, and butterless toast with a scraping of jam—and be thankful for it, girl! Tom wouldn't be eating his breakfast in a warm kitchen!

'Mornin', nurse,' beamed Cook as Alice pushed open the kitchen door. 'Hurry and sit you down, so's we can make a start.'

Tilda and Jin were smiling, their eyes sliding to Alice's plate and Tom's letter.

'Go on, then. Get it opened!' Tilda laughed. 'Thinking he'd run off with a *mam'sel,* weren't you?'

'Course I wasn't!' She took her knife, carefully slitting open the envelope, shaking with relief.

'France. He's got there. And there's an address I can write to.'

'Where?' Tilda demanded.

'It doesn't say. Just a Field Post Office

198

number. But he'll try to let me know if he can. They've got to be careful what they write.' She folded the letter, slipping it in her pocket. 'I'll read it later,' she murmured as Jin, red-faced from the fire, spooned porridge into plates.

Now was the time to tell him; to let Tom know she was a nurse and to beg him, implore him as he loved her, not to write to Reuben and forbid her going to France.

I'm not meaning to deceive you, Tom. It's just that I want to help win the war—get you home sooner. And I want to be near you, my love...

But she couldn't tell him. Not yet.

'Denniston House,' said Julia, 'used to scare the wits out of me. Giles and Nathan always insisted that a witch lived there. They were never apart in those days, and I'd follow them around like a lost dog. They hated it—did their best to get rid of me.

'"We're going Denniston way", was all they'd have to say to send me running back home. There wasn't a witch—just an eccentric old woman.'

'I got a letter from Tom this morning,' Alice offered. 'He's got an address now. It's lovely countryside where he is, and some of the trees already greening up, he says. Well, they would be. It's warmer there. Doing bayonet drill and helping unload transports...'

'Doesn't sound as if he's in the trenches, does it? I got one, too. Mine didn't say anything at all! Stop, and I'll show you. It's Andrew's writing on the envelope, but look at what's inside!'

Alice withdrew the picture postcard, turning it over, frowning. 'Not a word on it...'

'I know. It's too dark to see, but it says "View of the River Meuse", on it, in French—and the postmark is Reims. That envelope hasn't been anywhere near the Censor. There's a French stamp on it—censored letters don't need stamps.'

'You think he bought that postcard and managed, somehow, to post it?'

'At Reims,' Julia nodded. 'He was probably there on army business, or something. It's his way of telling me where he is. I could never be sure before, and I know he shouldn't have done it—but I'm not going to tell anyone, and besides, I still don't know which regiment he's attached to. Tonight I'll have a good look at the map and see if I can pinpoint where he might be. But we'd better get a move on. Don't want to be late this morning, or Sister'll be furious. And had you realised, Alice, that just around that bend is about to begin the first day of the rest of our war? Exciting, isn't it?'

And one step, one day, nearer to Andrew.

'Where on earth have you been, Julia? I was just about to come and find you. I thought you must have fallen asleep.'

'Good job you didn't, or you'd have found me sitting on the edge of the bath, up to the ankles in cold water! We were run off our feet. They're so short-staffed, Mother. Two nurses in sick quarters with streaming colds, and one on compassionate leave—family bereavement.

'It was the heavy shoes, I think. My feet really hurt. But what has Cook sent up? I'm starving. All we had all day was a cup of tea, one sandwich, and a mug of soup, and taken on our feet, too. How nice to eat off trays tonight, just you and me.'

'There's cold meat and chutney and a pear for pudding. Catchpole says the late croppers are starting to ripen now. And just because today has been special for you, I thought we'd have a glass of wine. Now, tell me all about it!'

'Right from the start? Well, we reported to Sister Carbrooke—the junior nurses call her Sister Carbolic! She's a dragon. No "Welcome to the VAD" or anything. She just snorted, "You've come!", then told us how short-staffed they are.

'Because my hands aren't properly healed, I went on the convalescent ward—very few of the men need dressings there—and Hawthorn was sent to help out on the surgical ward. There isn't an operating room at Denniston. The ops are done at York, then sent to Denniston.

'I've got a lovely staff nurse. She's called Ruth Love and the men call her Ruthie behind her back. Before long, most of them will be going on leave, then back to their regiments, but some will be discharged. They are all so very cheerful. Hawthorn said that, even in her ward where some of them are really ill, they never grumble. She said it's because they've got Blighty wounds. Do you know what that is, Mother?'

'Sadly, Julia, I do.'

'Sorry. You work at Denniston, too.'

'If you can call it work,' she shrugged. 'I shall be there tomorrow. I might even be in your ward. Really, it's only doing what I can to help without getting in the way of the real nursing—things like just listening to someone who wants to talk, or reading the papers to a man who has lost his sight. And I write letters for them, too. I feel so fortunate, when I've been there. It makes me count my blessings.'

'Me, too. This morning, Nurse Love asked me to help a man to shave—his right arm was shattered. So I lathered his face—he said he enjoyed that bit—but when I tried to shave him his courage failed. He said he'd make a better job of it with his left hand! I was very relieved. That razor made me nervous.

'Mostly, though, I fetched and carried. Hot water for shaving; helping those who couldn't make it to the washroom; and I nearly died when Staff asked me to give a man a bath!'

'Oh, *dear...*' Helen murmured.

'Oh, it turned out all right, in the end. He was more embarrassed than me, I think. He'd lost a leg, above the knee, and couldn't manage on his own. I think it was the first proper bath he'd had since he was wounded, and he looked so embarrassed. I managed to hide my blushes though. Told him I had brothers of my own, and a husband too. I scrubbed his back, then left him to it. Staff thought it best, I suppose, to throw me in at the deep end, though I'll admit I felt a bit hot under the collar at first.'

'Goodness! I don't think your pa would have liked it if I'd been asked to do anything like that. Do you think Andrew—'

'Andrew's a *doctor!*' Julia laid down her

knife and fork with a clatter. 'Oh hell! I do want him.'

'I know, dear. I know.' Helen reached for her daughter's hand. 'And one morning, I promise you, we'll wake up to peace. One day it will be over. The judge says there's going to be a tremendous showdown before long, on land and at sea. It might be over sooner than any of us dare hope.'

'Then if Judge Mounteagle is right, there'll be a lot of casualties. We're bursting at the seams now, and it's just the same at York.'

She gazed into the fire, remembering Ward F, clean and empty and its long rows of waiting beds. Then she shut down her thoughts and arranged her lips into a smile. 'I'm going to be a good nurse, Mother. Andrew will be proud of me, one day.'

'He's proud of you already, I shouldn't wonder. And can I tell you my news now? I needed to tell you this morning, and you weren't there. Now that you are, I'm finding it difficult...'

'Giles? They haven't sent him to the Front?'

'No. As far as I know, he's fine. It's Cecilia. This afternoon, I had a letter.'

'So she knows? How did she take it?'

'Very bravely. She thanked me for writing and sent me her love, she said, in my distress; but I think that at the moment she is fighting it—trying to convince herself it will all come right. She goes to church every day to pray, she says, that Robert will be found. She's asking for a miracle, but her faith is so strong, she imagines...' Her voice trailed into helplessness.

'She thinks God will listen to her? And you, Mother; what do you think?'

'There'll be no miracle,' Helen said flatly. 'A woman knows if her son is alive. Robert is not. But I shall write every week to Cecilia. I have such fondness for her. I often think that, when the war is over, I'll go to India. I saw the tea garden—just after your pa and I were married. I should like to see it once more, and meet Cecilia.

'I hope her parents won't try to hustle her into a marriage. She's so brave. Each time she writes I find something more to like about her, yet she will never be my daughter now.'

'Darling, don't be sad.' Her mother was close to tears. 'Try not to think about it. I want your advice.' It was Julia's turn to take her mother's hand. 'Dearest, listen. When we were at the Military Hospital, I got a telling-off because Hawthorn called me Miss Julia. Staff Nurse as good as said it wasn't allowed. She said Hawthorn must call me Julia or MacMalcolm, and I agree with her, though here at Rowangarth it would be an embarrassment to her to try to change things. But if I call her Alice, you'll understand and not think she's being pushy?'

'I understand perfectly, though it might be below-stairs who will condemn Hawthorn, not me. I can't see Miss Clitherow allowing it, can you?' Helen smiled. 'I like the child. She's a good influence on you, and she's fond of you too. Don't worry. Things will even out, given time. Tell me, how was Hawthorn's first day?'

'She didn't say much on the way home. I think the ward she was on was a bit of a shock to her. Her Tom is in France. Seeing those awful wounds would upset her.'

'Poor little Hawthorn. She was so alone when she came to Rowangarth. Then Reuben took her under his wing and she met her young man. She was so happy, yet now she must feel it all slipping away from her. This war has much to answer for, and ordinary people like you and me—and Hawthorn and Cecilia, too—can do very little about it.'

'Don't be sad, Mother,' Julia raised her glass. 'Let's drink to those we love.'

'To our loved ones,' Helen murmured. 'And may God keep them safely...'

Alice signed her name to the letter, blotted it carefully, then sighed deeply, glad it was done. Tom knew now—or he would do before so very much longer. And how he would take it heaven only knew, because not only had she told him about being a nurse, but her pen had gone quite mad and she had found herself telling him everything. Now all she could do was hope he wouldn't write at once to Reuben, complaining about her foolishness in telling lies about her age.

She shrugged into her warm coat, then tied a scarf around her head. The moon was still bright; she needed no light tonight. She ran quickly towards Keeper's Cottage, knocking on the door, calling out as she entered.

Reuben was sitting beside the fire, reading yesterday's Sunday paper, passed on to him by Cook.

'Hullo, lass. I hoped you'd come. Sit you down. Morgan not with you?'

'I left him. He's in the winter parlour with her ladyship and Miss Julia, so I didn't bother. I can't stay long, Reuben.'

'Aye. Reckon you'll be tired, though I hope you'll stay long enough to tell me what's bothering you, because something *is*.'

'It is.' No use beating about the bush. 'There's something I've been keeping from Tom.'

'Then put it to rights. Write and tell him now.' As far as Reuben was concerned, the solution was as plain as the nose on your face.

'I have done. I've written him a letter and I want you to post it for me tomorrow. If I don't give it to you now, I'll lose courage and tear it up.'

'And what's in it that's so awful? Found another young man, have you?'

'Reuben—*no!* It's just that I hadn't told him about me being a nurse. I thought he wouldn't like it—that he'd forbid it.'

'But he can't forbid it. You're not wed to him yet.' Reuben folded the paper and dropped it to the floor. 'I can, though, because I'm your guardian. And I haven't, now have I—forbidden it, I mean?'

'No, you haven't.'

'Even though you didn't think to come and mention it to me at the time—as a courtesy, like?'

'I'm sorry. I should have.'

'Ar. So now we've straightened things out, why don't we have a sup of tea?'

Unspeaking, she filled the kettle and set it to boil. Then she took two large cups from the dresser, and the milk jug, and teaspoons from the drawer. Only when she had placed the teapot in the hearth to warm did she say, 'It isn't straightened out.'

'There's more?' He unhooked his reading spectacles, the better to see her.

'There is,' she nodded. 'My age.'

'You'll be twenty, come June—what is there to get het-up about in that?'

'Plenty. I told them I'd be twenty-one next, when I signed for nursing, and they didn't check up on me. I told them,' she rushed on, 'because Miss Julia's going to volunteer for abroad and I want to go too. But I've got to be twenty-one, and—'

'And Tom wouldn't like to think of his girl at the Front? I'm inclined to agree with him, an' all.'

'But I wouldn't be at the front line! They don't have hospitals full of wounded men right at the Front. And they wouldn't send a woman where it wasn't safe.'

'Not deliberately. But danger has a habit of turning up unexpected, like. They drop bombs from aeroplanes now, and the Kaiser has got that great gun—Big Bertha—that can send shells for miles and miles. How safe is safe, will you tell me?'

'You're going to say I can't go?' She didn't weep or pout. If she had, there'd have been an end to it and he'd have said she wasn't to go. But she looked up at him, her brown eyes so beseeching that instead he said nothing.

'You are, aren't you?' she insisted.

'Oh, dear. Do you know, lass, I used once to regret not having bairns of my own—but not any more. Sons go to war—even daughters go.'

'But not me; not Alice Hawthorn?' she whispered.

'It isn't up to me, Alice—not entirely. If the VAD people find out you aren't of age, then that'll be an end to it. They'll tell you to wait for another year, and no begging nor pleading is going to change it.'

'I suppose so,' she choked, like a child admitting to stealing jam.

'But you think you can get away with it?'

'I know I can. If they'd wanted proof of age, they'd have asked for it long since. They're desperate for nurses out there, and if I pass my exams they'll be satisfied enough. There are plenty of young men give a wrong age to get to the Front.'

'Aye, and their fathers should be taking their belts off to them, the daft young things—like I should be smacking your bottom now for telling lies to the Government. But I won't.' His face shaped itself into one of his rare smiles. 'You shall go, Alice lass, because I admire your spunk. If the nursing folk don't put a stop to it, then I won't either.'

'Reuben! Not even if Tom writes to you and tells you not to let me?'

'*Especially* if he tells me not to let you. The day is long gone when Reuben

210

Pickering took orders from younglings like Tom!'

'Oh, you lovely man! You *lovely* man!' She threw her arms around him, hugging him tightly. 'Thank you! And I'll be all right. Miss Julia and me'll stay together and I won't do anything to let you down. You'll be proud of me, I promise you will.'

'All right then,' he grunted, unwinding her clinging arms. 'Enough's enough. Let's be having that sup of tea shall us?'

She was, he thought, as he stood on his doorstep watching her go, a right little charmer. His own lass, had he had one, would have been just like Alice; every bit as sweet and thoughtful and wilful and bonny.

A right little bobby-dazzler, in fact...

10

It was all very well for Miss Julia, who'd had a head-start, so to speak, with regard to naked male bodies, her being reared with brothers and having the benefit, if only for a week, of a husband. On the other hand she, Alice, had learned about men from women; from whispered gigglings which ill-prepared her for what Julia took almost for granted. Now, however, after two weeks of bedpans and bed-bottles and rubbing male buttocks with ointment to prevent bed-sores, Alice's embarrassment was less acute.

By comparison, Julia's accomplishments were small: her energies had been focused on her feet coming to terms with her uncomfortable shoes; the healing of her hands; and the ability to manoeuvre patients into and out of a slippery bath with nonchalant ease.

'I feel happier now I know where Andrew is.' Julia, who had minutely examined maps of the Reims area, was as certain as she could be that about forty miles from there—somewhere around Verdun—was where she must hope to be sent when her overseas posting was approved. 'Imagine, if I were out there and he went to Reims again, there'd be a chance we could meet, even for just a little while.'

Oh, my darling, what could we do in an hour...

'Wish I knew where Tom was.' Alice pedalled harder to keep within earshot. 'Wouldn't it be grand, miss, if he's ended up in the doctor's part of the line? I've asked him—well, sort of...' She couldn't ask it outright. Soldiers were not allowed to say where they were, and their sweethearts should know better than to ask. 'I hinted, though.' She'd done it rather well, she thought.

I miss you, Tom, and I wish I could be with you. I wonder all the time where you are...

'He'll find a way. They mostly do.' Julia sighed her relief as they rounded the corner to see Rowangarth gate lodges ahead. 'And as long as we don't talk about it, it's all right.'

DON'T TALK! posters constantly reminded them. There were spies everywhere, sending messages back to Germany. Spies on motor buses and trains; spies dressed as nuns and dockyard workers, people said. Spies were the latest fad, and were talked about all the time. It made a change from those Russians shunting the length of the country and back again. Now women whiled away the long waits in sugar queues and margarine queues, embellishing the latest spy story.

'Do you suppose, miss, that we'll start proper duties tomorrow? Nights...?'

'I don't think so. I heard tell the nurses who had 'flu will be back on the wards, so we'll not be kept quite so busy.'

'We'll have to learn a lot, if we're to pass our exams.'

Alice longed for the chance to do some real nursing. On her first day in the surgical ward, a gangrenous wound had sickened her, made her want to turn away

213

from the sight and stench of it. But instead she had smiled gently into eyes uncannily like Tom's, lifting a dressing from the tray with tweezers, passing it to the nurse who was allowed to perform such tasks.

'We'll pass.' After two weeks, Julia needed to catch up with Alice. Both had learned the layout of the hospital and how best to cope with Sister's rapped commands. Now they were so used to the smell of carbolic they hardly noticed it. 'I'm hoping to get on one of the other wards tomorrow. Nurse Love is a dear, but the men in her ward can do most things for themselves. All I seem to have learned is how properly to make a bed, make hot drinks and serve meals.' And fill and empty baths, of course, and run errands until her feet ached and her ankles swelled. Yet whatever she did, however menial, would take her one day nearer to France. It was all, really, that mattered.

Monday morning was cold; a frosty beginning which pinked cheeks and a wind that brought tears to the eyes. Julia, tapping the weather glass in the hall, had watched the pointer tremble to 'Fair'.

'It'll be a good day.' She sniffed inelegantly. 'I wouldn't be surprised to see some sunshine. I hope Sister lets us work together today. Hey! What's going on?'

Outside Denniston House, all was activity, in the middle of which Nurse Love called orders, heaved kitbags, and shepherded men in hospital blue into motors and trucks.

'Staff!' Leaving their bicycles they ran up the gravelled drive. 'What is it? Can we help?'

'I'll say you can help! Imagine—they told me last night they wanted my ward cleared and cleaned. Look, just give me a hand, will you? The men are being transferred; most on leave, a few to another hospital. I'll explain later.

'Hawthorn—you are to work with Mac-Malcolm and me today. The 'flu nurses aren't fit for duty yet, Matron says. You know the ward, MacMalcolm. Give any help you can, and see that no one leaves anything behind. They're so eager to be off—can't blame them, I suppose. You, Hawthorn, will make sure that each has his leave pass and travel warrant, then you're to go with them to the station and make sure they can manage to get on their trains.

'Most of them are Jocks, so that'll be the best part of them on the Edinburgh train; the rest you'll have to see to as best you can. The driver will give you a hand, then bring you back here afterwards—is that understood?'

'Don't worry. I'll manage.' Oh, my goodness! More than thirty men, some on crutches, some with arms in slings, all carrying kit, to be despatched safely on their separate ways.

'Listen, *please!*' Ruth Love held up a hand for silence. 'Nurse Hawthorn and the driver will see you get your trains all right. Do exactly as she tells you and you'll be fine. Off you go, then. Goodbye, and good luck. Enjoy your leaves.'

' 'Bye, Nursie!'

'So long, Ruthie. Thanks a lot!'

To whistles and cheers, the driver slammed home the tail-board.

'See if you can find any Medical Corps lads on the station, Hawthorn—you just might be lucky. If not, get hold of porters to give you a hand. That lot are like kids let out of school, so don't take any nonsense. Let them know who's in charge.'

'Yes, Staff.' Alice took a deep gulp of air which did nothing at all to stop the giddiness inside her. Imagine! Nurse Hawthorn in charge of a lorry-load of walking wounded?

Oh, my goodness. If Tom could see her now!

'Clear and clean the ward?' Julia put on her apron and starched white cap. 'Why?'

'You might well ask! Be a dear, see if you can get me a slice of bread and a mug of tea? I've been hard at it since five this morning, with no help at all.

'And get something for yourself too,' she added. 'Heaven only knows when we'll find time to eat again! I'd best let Sister know they're all on their way—tell you later what it's about.'

Julia gazed around the ward. Beds lay unmade; locker doors hung open. In the kitchen, the VAD cooks could tell her nothing.

'They don't tell *us*. All I know is they wanted thirty-four breakfasts for six o'clock. Convalescent ward being emptied was all I was told. Is this for Ruth Love?' she demanded, cutting two thick slices. 'She likes the crusts cut off. Have some yourself, if you'd like. I tell you, it's mayhem in this place today, and nobody gives a thought to the cooks!'

'I promise from now on I will. And we'll soon know what's going on,' Julia shrugged, jamming the bread. 'They've got their reasons, I suppose.'

Eyes closed ecstatically, Ruth Love drank thirstily from her mug, then bit deeply into the bread. 'Aaah, that's better. Sorry to give you the run-around, MacMalcolm. Best tell you now what it's all about.

217

'I didn't know until late last night that they wanted the ward emptied. The clerk was at it into the small hours, writing out leave passes and warrants. There's heavy fighting at the Front; a lot of casualties too. Not just the usual wounded; Gerry's been using some new gas—Lord knows what it was. Pretty awful, though. Phosgene, Sister thinks. It burns out the lungs—they choke to death. That's why there's a panic on; the gas cases must have on-the-spot treatment, so most of the rest are being shipped on to Blighty.'

'I didn't know,' Julia whispered. 'There's been nothing in the papers about fighting...'

'Nor will there be, yet. They always seem to keep things back.'

'When did it start?' Her mouth had gone suddenly dry.

'About a week ago, I believe. York Military was on to Matron last night. They are being sent one hundred and fifty wounded without so much as a please or thank you. York can only cope with half, at the very most. The rest they've got to farm out anywhere they can.'

'There must have been very heavy fighting.' Julia recalled Ward 3F and the forty clean beds they had left behind them.

'There was—*is*; it's still going on. Could go on for weeks.'

'How much time do we have, Staff?'

'I'd like everything ready by noon. They're expecting the hospital train at York early afternoon, but you just can't tell. The lockers must be wiped out, the beds stripped and the waterproofs disinfected. Plenty of carbolic in the water. Then the floor will have to be done, but we'll manage that between us with mops. Did they issue you with a scrubbing apron?'

Did they indeed! Julia's cheeks blazed, just to remember.

'Damn!' she hissed. 'My hands are almost better. Not that I mind scrubbing, Staff,' she added hastily, 'but until my hands are healed, they won't let me near any real nursing.'

'I'll give you some rubber gloves. Go easy with them, mind. They're hard to get hold of.'

'What isn't? Bless you, Ruth—*sorry!*' Too late, she realised. Idiot that she was to use a superior's first name!

'That's all right. I don't mind, but be careful when Sister's around. My, but that was good!' She wiped a crumb from her mouth. 'Down to work, then! Beds first. Blankets folded, sheets and pillow-slips in the laundry basket. No rest for the wicked,' she smiled. 'We'll be casualties ourselves before the day is over.'

'Then bags I the bed nearest the big

window,' Julia laughed, all at once feeling affection for the red-haired, hazel-eyed nurse. 'Tell you what, though—I'd rather be here than in Alice's shoes. Wonder how she's coping with that lot?'

Probationer Nurse Hawthorn had coped very well, and now, on her way back to Denniston House, she felt the amazed satisfaction of a job well done.

'Thanks for your help,' she said shyly to the driver at her side. 'I couldn't have managed on my own.'

'Lucky for the pair of us there were all those medical lads around.' He offered a cigarette. 'Smoke?'

'No, thanks.' She watched, fascinated as, one hand on the wheel, he lit his own. Then, inhaling deeply and blowing out smoke through his nostrils, he said, 'Make you think, dunnit—all them stretcher-bearers and orderlies around? Waiting for a hospital train, if you ask me. Balloon must have gone up again at the Front. You'd have thought the bad weather would've kept things quiet.' He sighed loudly. It could only be a matter of time before he, too, would be sent to France. 'Got a boyfriend, Nurse?'

'I have.' *Nurse.* Alice glowed. She would never get used to the heady title. It lifted her at once from a servant to a somebody.

She gave him her brightest smile. 'He's at the Front, though I don't know where. With the West Yorkshires.'

'Infantry, aren't they?'

'Mm. Tom's got his marksman's badge, him being a gamekeeper.'

'Ar.' The driver lapsed into silence. If those Medical Corps lads were waiting for a hospital train, it meant only one thing. Wounded. So many wounded they couldn't cope with them over there. He hoped the little nurse's bloke wasn't among them.

Dipping into his pocket, he wrapped his fingers round the hag stone that lay there. Hag stones were lucky, and you needed all the luck you could get in this bloody war. 'Soon have you back,' he said.

Alice, still a little nervous about riding in motors, gave herself to thinking about the morning. Just as Nurse Love had said she might, she had found orderlies and stretcher-bearers on the station platform. Selecting one with two stripes on his arm, she had explained her predicament, then begged his help—just for a little while, she'd hastened to add. And the wonderful man had let go a whistle that hit the roof with a clatter than bawled, *'Aaghovereeeeere!'* In seconds, she'd had her pick of a dozen orderlies.

'Nah then—this little nurse 'ere has

221

thirty walking wounded and their kit to see on to trains and she needs a hand. Do as she bids you, and no old buck, mind!'

She had managed better than she could have hoped. People could be very nice. It was the war, perhaps, that had made them that way...

'My word. You know how to time it!' Julia teased when Alice returned to the ward. 'Just off to find some cocoa. What does this remind you of?' She removed her scrubbing apron, regarding the gloves with near affection. 'I'd have killed for a pair of these on Ward 3F.'

'Hullo, Hawthorn.' Ruth Love tied on a clean, white apron. 'Did you get them away all right?'

'Fine. I had plenty of help at the station. You were right; the Medical Corps lads were there. Hope our lot will manage. It's a long journey to Edinburgh.'

'They'll be all right. They're going home. They'll each help the other. I suppose you're wondering what this is all about, but all I can tell you is that we are filling the ward with non-surgical wounded—leastways, let's hope that's what they are. Matron told Sister they'll most likely have a medical officer with them, which will be just as well, since they're coming to us straight from the Front.

'You're both of you being thrown in at the deep end. You'll see some distressing sights—I know, because I've done a stint out there. But at least you're going to learn sooner than later if you've got the stomach for nursing.

'That's all I can tell you at the moment, except to ask you if you could stay just a little later tonight—only this once? If we could get them settled and perhaps fed, it would be a big help to the night staff. I know you'll be tired after so long a day—but would you?'

They said they would; it was what they were there for, after all. They both had men at the Front; it was the least they could do. And besides, they wanted to.

'Bless you. Now let's get that cocoa—and if we're lucky there'll be bread and jam too. And on your way back, pop into Stores and ask them if the bedshirts are ready. And give them this requisition. It's for rubber gloves and scissors for each of you. Look after them. You won't get any more.'

In the nurses' sitting-room where a jug of hot, milky cocoa waited, Ruth Love flopped into the nearest chair and eased off her shoes.

'If I fall asleep,' she whispered, 'don't wake me. Leave me to sleep and sleep, will you?—for a *week!*'

Matron hung up the telephone receiver with a sigh.

'York?' asked Sister Carbrooke.

'The traffic officer at York station. The first of our ambulances is on its way—about an hour, I think it'll be.'

'Right! I'll see to it.' Sister Tutor was not in the habit of using two words where one would suffice. She had already counted out brown paper sacks and clean bedshirts. Now was the time for sterilisers to be set to boil and dressings prepared and placed in covered trays.

And *why* were the two in sick quarters still unfit for duty—because clearly they were! But it was, she supposed, a case of a fit, reasonably healthy female throwing off influenza far more quickly than an overtired, overworked nurse who most times ate snatched meals and neglected her own health shamefully.

There would be the new probationers, of course, but small help they'd be! Willing, but not a lot of use. See what they'd make of this little lot, she pondered grimly.

'You there—MacMalcolm!' Sister strode into the empty, echoing convalescent ward. 'Can you sterilise instruments; lay out a tray?'

'Yes, Sister.' That, at least, Staff Nurse had found the time to teach her.

'Get on with it, then. And from now on, nurses will wear rubbers over aprons. and I don't want to see one wisp of hair beneath caps,' she said to no one in particular.

'Wear gloves and you—Hawthorn, isn't it? You'll be with me to do the sacks. The minute the first ambulance arrives we are all on stand-to until told otherwise.' And heaven only knew when stand-down would be, she thought as the door banged behind her. And heaven wouldn't tell!

'What did she mean—do the sacks?' Alice demanded of Nurse Love. Wouldn't you just know it, though? Of all the nurses here, Alice Hawthorn had landed herself with Sister Carbrooke.

'Brown paper sacks—for the men's things. They'll be coming to us wearing the uniforms they were wounded in. As soon as they start arriving, close your eyes and you could be at a dressing-station in France. No difference at all, except that it'll be much quieter—and safer—here.

'The wounded, if they are lucky, will have had a dressing placed on their wound—that'll be all. It's going to be exactly as if you were on active service, so learn well. You'll write the man's surname and his number, if you can get it, on the sack in black crayon. His boots, tunic, everything he is wearing, will go into that sack. Don't handle them any more than you need to—some will have lice and fleas on them.

'We can take out personal possessions—paybook, things like that—later. The whole lot will be heat sterilised first—get rid of the beasties. Leave on the man's identification. It will be hanging around his neck and, if he is wearing a wristwatch, leave that on too...'

She paused, took a deep breath, then continued in the same, even voice, as if she had said exactly the same words many times before.

'Then, when the patient has been examined, put him into a bedshirt and, if no one is there to carry him into the ward, put a blanket over him to keep him warm. He'll be in shock, most likely, and cold...'

'It's like that at the Front?' Julia whispered.

'No. As I said, it's much safer here. And at the Front, when they're brought in, there's a lot of blood about. At least when we get them, the bleeding should have stopped.'

Julia clenched hard on her jaws and said nothing. Alice asked, 'Where will I find Sister? She didn't tell me.'

'Stretchers are being taken into the stableyard. Go there when you hear the first ambulance arriving.'

'They'll be stripped in the stableyard—*outside!*' Julia gasped.

'Outside,' Ruth Love nodded. 'Just the way it would be in France. Only today it isn't snowing or raining and there'll be no shells whining over head. And remember what you were told about your caps. Fasten them tightly and tuck your hair well in, or you'll be covered in beasties too.'

They hadn't told them it would be like this, Julia thought dully as the first ambulance turned in at the gates. Thrown in at the deep end? Andrew lived all his life in the deep end and she hadn't realised, until now, how awful it must be.

'They're here,' she whispered. 'Best cut along to the stableyard, Alice love. And don't let old Carbolic frighten you. They do say that somewhere beneath that apron she really does have a heart. Good luck...'

'You too, Julia.' Pulling back her shoulders, tilting her chin, Alice went in search of Sister—and the deep end they had promised her.

They would always remember the date and the day and the time. Monday, the last but one day of February, and a nightmare from which there could be no awakening.

The first of the ambulances came slowly up the drive as two o'clock chimed out from the stableyard clock. It bore a red cross back and front and on either side. The driver squinted ahead for potholes; the smallest jolt could send red-hot knives through limbs throbbing with pain, and the four he carried had endured enough.

'Right, lads—Blighty!'

The stretcher-bearer jumped down, lifting the canvas flap. Sister Carbrooke swept Alice with her eyes as the first stretcher was gently laid on the stableyard cobbles. 'All right?'

'Yes, Sister—thank you.'

The soldier's eyes were swathed in bandages. His hand reached out, searching for reassurance.

'You're all right.' Briefly the elderly woman cupped the young face in her hands. Then she leaned closer, saying gently, 'I shall undress you now and put you into a bedshirt. Are you in pain?'

'Not a lot. I can't see though. Can't you take the bandages off?' There was panic in his voice. 'When will I be able to see?'

'The doctor who will examine you will know better than I. The first thing is to get you into a warm bed. Tell me your name.'

'Ward. Bill Ward.'

'And your number?'

Impatiently he gave it, cursing the darkness, stiffening his body as she took off his clothes.

Alice wrote quickly on the bag, then stuffed the uniform inside it. The soldier shook with cold and she was ready with a blanket.

'You know where to take him?'

The orderlies nodded and picked up the stretcher. Alice grasped the helpless, searching hand, squeezing it briefly before tucking it beneath the blanket.

The stableyard was filling with stretchers.

'Next?' called Sister.

'Over here!' called an orderly.

Sister walked calmly, ignoring the urgency of the summons. Alice followed with sack and blanket, glancing down, frowning.

The soldier's forehead was marked with a purple cross, and she lifted asking eyes to Sister's.

'That's because he's had morphia,' came the terse explanation. 'Help me, please?'

The soldier moaned incoherently, suspended in half sleep above his pain. His trousers had been almost cut away; his legs and lower abdomen were covered with dressings, held fast by dark, congealed blood.

'He's due another injection in half an hour.' Sister read the label pinned to his jacket.

As if she were handling a new-born child, she removed his tunic and shirt.

A land-mine, she frowned. She had seen

many such injuries before. An awful way to die. She lifted the identification disc at his throat, then read out the name and number punched on it.

'You can take him now. Please tell Nurse Love that Sister suggests his dressings aren't changed until after his next injection.'

Alice gathered up the bloodstained, mud-caked garments. She could find no boots. Perhaps someone down the line had taken them off.

Her stomach churned. Forty of them, hadn't they said? She wanted a drink of water; wanted to go home to Mrs Shaw's warm, safe kitchen.

'Go to Matron, Hawthorn,' Sister said quietly. 'Tell her I need help. Two nurses for a couple of hours, if she can spare them. And *walk!*' she said.

Out of sight of the stableyard, Alice picked up her skirts and ran. It was against accepted practice, but she did it instinctively, blindly, as if fleeing from danger.

She wanted not to go back. It was awful there. She had never imagined it could be like that. Not just the wounding, but the filth and degradation and, oh, God! Any one of those wounded could have been Tom!

She hurried into the wash-house, filling

her hands with clean, cold water, drinking greedily. Then she pulled her sleeve across her mouth, straightened her cap, and walked quickly back to Sister's side.

'Matron's sending two. And she says that if you want her to...'

'We'll manage.' A matron wasn't expected to nurse. She was there to teach, to command, to ensure the smooth running of the hospital and, sometimes, to bear the brunt of higher authority's stupidity.

The brief brightness of the afternoon was fading; a cold, snappy wind blew from the north-east.

'How many more?' Sister rose to her feet, hands in the small of her back.

'One of the drivers says we've got the lot now—for the time being. Says there are about a dozen more following in horse ambulances—the walking wounded.'

Sister stifled a sigh of relief. At least walking wounded would be in better shape—could help themselves a little. She made a small, satisfied sound as two nurses hurried into the yard, then did a quick count.

Twelve more to go. Twelve more paper sacks then maybe, just *maybe*, there would be time for a mug of hot tea before the next ambulance arrived.

Alice took the black crayon from her pocket. The sight of two more nurses comforted her, made her feel less alone. Surely, soon, it would be over, then she could lock the sacks in the outhouse and run and be sick in the lavatory pan.

The light was beginning to fade as the last of the stretcher cases was carried to convalescent ward. Without waiting, the orderlies returned the empty stretchers to the ambulances, then headed back to the station. No time to dilly-dally. Another hospital train expected, they said...

'Thank you, Nurses.' Matron, appearing in the yard, smiled gently. 'I will be in Nurse Love's ward if you need me, Sister. I want the medical officer to sign requisitions before he goes back to York.

'There is a pot of tea in the sitting-room—I suggest you all take a few minutes' break before the next ambulances get here...'

A dozen more men, Alice thought dully, and all of them dirty, tired, their hurriedly applied dressings starting to smell. God—don't let them do this to Tom!

Her hands were dirty and blackened with crayon dust; the parts of her apron not protected by the waterpoof she was wearing were wet and soiled. Across her right sleeve was a smear of blood; her starched cuffs would never be clean again.

'Are you all right?' asked a nurse.

'No.' Alice shook her head vehemently. 'Are you?'

'You'll get over it. First time it happened to me, I threw up...'

'Where was that?' Alice picked up the last of the paper sacks.

'In London, when I was doing my training. That first big bombing raid. Civilians, they were. You'll harden yourself to it...'

'Will I?' Would she ever? Did she want to be hard?

She turned the key in the outhouse door, then took off her soiled apron, rolling it into a ball, pushing it into a paper sack.

'If you don't scrub up quick, they'll have drunk all the tea,' the nurse said.

A mug of hot tea. Alice needed it; needed to wrap her numbed fingers around its warmth. She straightened her cap, pushing in her hair, wondering if she had caught any fleas.

Hot, sweet tea. She hurried to the nurses' sitting-room, fastening on a clean apron as she went.

Best she should forget about being sick. There simply wasn't time!

Cook was waiting up when they got back to Rowangarth, her hair in a long plait, her serviceable dressing-gown covering her nightdress.

'Here you are—goodness gracious! Half-past ten!' she chided fondly. 'Her ladyship is in bed. Will you go up, she says, and say goodnight, Miss Julia? I'll bring you up a tray.'

'Don't bother, Mrs Shaw. If you're making tea, I'll come down and have it with you.'

She didn't want her mother to see her; not like this. All she wanted, truth known, was to creep into bed and weep into her pillow.

'You look all-in, lass,' Cook said to Alice. 'Why did they keep you so late? Fifteen hours—it's over-long.'

'Wounded, Cook. Just dumped on us without so much as a by-your-leave. Nurse Love had to clear her ward—all her patients sent home. I went with them to York and got them on to their trains.

'Then the wounded came. Straight from France. All filthy with mud and their wounds—you should have seen them! There's a big battle going on, Verdun way.'

'Isn't that where Doctor Andrew is?' Cook made a sucking noise through her teeth.

'We think so—and maybe Tom, for all I know.'

Tears, held in check for so long, ran down her cheeks. She lifted her pinafore, buried her face in it—just as Cook always did—and wept.

'Poor bairn. There, there now.' Cook took her, held her. Nobbut a bit of a lass. It wasn't right. 'Come on, now. Dry your eyes. Mustn't let Miss Julia find you like this when she comes down.'

'Sorry.' Alice splashed her face with cold water, dabbing it dry on the roller-towel; taking a deep, shuddering breath, vowing that, no matter what, she mustn't ever allow herself to weep again; not until this war was over. Tears were a luxury no nurse could indulge herself in. 'I'm all right, now. I'm just tired. Will there be hot water for a bath?' Have a bath, Sister had told them, and wash your hair.

'Plenty. Enough for both of you. Now then, will I make some toast before I bank the fire down?'

'You're a good soul, Mrs Shaw. Thanks for all you've done for me.'

'Away with you! I'm proud of my nurses! Say goodnight to Miss Julia for me,' she smiled, pushing in the fire dampers. 'And don't sit up all night talking?'

'Tea?' Alice asked, when Julia returned. 'Cook says goodnight, by the way.'

'Please. A mug. Mother's all right. I didn't tell her too much. Don't want to worry her.'

'But she'll find out. Tomorrow is one of her visiting days!'

'I know. She's going to ring Matron first—doesn't want to get in the way. That isn't dripping toast, is it?'

'Mm. Cook left it for you.'

'Hasn't today been awful?' Eyes closed, Julia bit into the toast. 'I'm glad you were there; I couldn't have got through it if I hadn't known you were feeling just like me. Do you remember one of the first in—he had awful injuries.'

'The one with the morphia cross...?'

'That one. Ruth Love looked at his disc, and saw he was a Catholic. So she sent me to Matron to ask her to get the priest from Creesby. She says he might not live through the night. The medical officer who came with them said she wasn't to try to remove his dressings—just see he wasn't in any pain. It was awful. It's how Andrew has to live, day in, day out...'

'I know. I kept wanting to be sick. I couldn't stop thinking about Tom.'

'Andrew's at Verdun amongst all that fighting. That's where he is...'

'Where you *think* he is.' Where Tom might be. 'Today is over now. We did our best. And nothing will ever hurt us as badly as today. Remember that.'

They had survived their deep end. They were nurses now. She held out her hand

236

across the table and Julia took it in her own.

'Thanks, Alice. Thank you for understanding...'

11

Picardy, thought Tom Dwerryhouse, was a bonny area, not unlike the countryside he had left behind him; fresh and green, bursting eagerly into spring. At the lanesides, wild flowers budded and, in the thickly wooded distance, the land swelled into small hills to remind him of Holdenby Pike and Creesby Fell. Those hills, their platoon sergeant had been at pains to point out, were to be viewed with respect and not respected for their view! They were occupied—and never let them forget it—by an unseen enemy. Into those hills, the Kaiser's lot were entrenched, and behind those hidden dugouts, British intelligence gatherers reported, were batteries of enemy guns of all shapes and sizes, every one of them smugly safe—or so they thought, the sergeant added with a peevish smile and nodding of his head to indicate that he knew something his subordinates did not.

So, between those hills and our own

front line must be No Man's Land, Tom considered, though it wasn't at all like he'd been given to expect; what he had actually seen on films at the Picture Palace. No Man's Land should be pitted and scarred; stuck with gaunt, drunken tree stumps and shell-holes and mud. Sealed with coils of vicious wire, No Man's Land should be littered with abandoned guns and carts and dead, swollen horses. That had been his imagining of it, with men shivering in rat-ridden trenches either side of it. Until now, that was.

Thus Picardy, and the beautiful River Somme that wound through it had come as a surprise, a bonus; had even provided clean, dry billets in the shape of a row of empty houses a mile outside the town of Albert. Albert had been all but flattened, but by the whim or bad aim of the German artillery, the row of seven houses had escaped, though those who lived in them had long ago left.

Tom's billet had a sound roof, a kitchen range made good use of, a wash-house with a deep, wooden sink, and a mangle, left behind in the haste of leaving. No soldier could ask for more.

They had been playing at soldiers ever since their arrival in France; practising bayonet charges, yelling like banshees. It was essential to yell, the corporal stressed, and not until they did it as well as the Jocks would he be satisfied.

They learned to advance under cover of night, following tapes laid there to guide them, all orderly and neat and just as it would be when the time for the big offensive came, because come it would; one great land battle and a meeting of warships in the North Sea to decide once and for ever in favour of Britain and her allies. And that land battle could well be here, most thought, in the area of the Somme. It didn't take a lot of working out, or why the great dumps of hidden ammunition? His platoon had unloaded and carried shells for weeks now, and great stocks of tinned food and hard-tack rations—even fodder, for horses. Fatigues, they called it. It would have been boring had it not been so good to know how well-equipped and well-fed the army of the Somme was to be.

Yet, through that almost peaceful spring, he missed Alice as he had never thought possible. The letters she sent to Richmond had reached him now, and he'd arranged them in order of the postmarks, rationing them against such time as she got his new address. Her letters he read and read again. She was never far from his mind, his buttercup girl. He need only close his eyes to see her face, her smile. He'd been a fool not to insist they be wed. He'd have liked more than anything to have a memory of her dark head on the pillow next to his own, his arms cradling her close.

There was a day he remembered well; a day they played the soldier games the sergeant called manoeuvres. They had advanced through a wood to take an imaginary enemy—two corporals, truth known—by surprise and stealth, with no snapping of twigs or rustling of undergrowth.

Tom was bored by it. He knew better how it was done than most and had let his thoughts wander to another wood and a girl who walked in it. And if he whistled like once he used to, would that daft dog come lolloping up and would Alice be there at the turning of the path?

But that was another place. She wouldn't come, and the pain had gone deep. He'd wanted her so much in that Picardy wood that, when he opened the letter in which she told him she was a nurse, he hadn't thought to feel anything but pride; had even smiled indulgently at her fibbing about her age. She wanted to help win the war, she said; needed to be near him.

Don't forbid me, Tom? I miss you so much. I tell myself that to be in France, knowing that one day I might turn a corner and see you there, is worth all the risk...

Alice and Miss Julia both; each would care for the other. By June their probation would be over and they could volunteer for France.

He should have written telling her not to, but instead, because he wanted her till he ached of it, he told her that he loved her and was proud of her. And the sooner, he'd thought, they had their big battles and got this war over with, the sooner he could get her into his bed!

'I need to look at your map of the war miss.' Alice read Tom's letter yet again, and why Mr Nathan's brother was thought worthy of mention she couldn't for the life of her think. 'Tom's trying to tell me something. There's a bit about Mr Nathan's brother—at the Front...'

'Elliot? I don't believe it!'

'His *younger* brother! He saw Nathan Sutton's younger brother in the distance, he said. But he wouldn't say it like that. He'd say he'd seen Albert Sutton, now wouldn't he?'

'But Albert is in America—or he was ten days ago. Mother had a letter from him saying how sorry he was about Robert. Albert wouldn't be in France; his wife would see to that! But we'll look at the map when we get home. Something Tom said rings a bell...'

The war map was pinned to Julia's bedroom wall, a Union Jack pin stuck in it at Verdun, and now they searched the entire Western Front.

'Alice, look!' Julia's finger jabbed at the map. '*There,* for heaven's sake! Albert-in-the-distance! Tom must be somewhere near a town called Albert. It's in Picardy. *Miles* away from Andrew.' She took a Union Jack pin, sticking it firmly in Albert.

'Funny old name to give to a place,' Alice frowned.

'No, it's not like we say it. The French pronounce it *Ol-bare*. How clever of him. You lucky thing! It's all quiet there—well away from the fighting. Still, that's got tabs on two of them. Wish I could find where Nathan is. Last I heard was a postcard of the Eiffel Tower—living it up in Paris, the gay dog!'

'*Ol-bare,*' Alice said, red-cheeked with pleasure that Tom was on Julia's wall map—away from the fighting, too. 'Think I'll drop him a line to let him know we've twigged; tell him we're pleased he saw young Sutton. And I'd best write to his mother, too.'

'But be sure not to mention the actual *name*—can't be too careful...'

'I won't, miss. And I forgot—Jin washed and starched our aprons and cuffs. I'll iron them and put them to air.' Run off their feet they may be, but Sister expected nothing less than white, immaculately pressed aprons of her nurses.

'You don't have to, Alice. You don't work at Rowangarth now.'

'I still get bed and board, though. I don't like being beholden.'

'All right, if it makes you feel better. But mind you write to Tom, and thanks for doing my ironing.'

Nursing must be doing Julia good, thought Alice, or was it the letter she'd just had and the fact that the doctor was safe and well, in spite of the fighting? Four days ago, that had been. Or could it be that she believed more than ever that one day they would meet?

Please—let them not be sent to the *Eastern* Front.

Giles Sutton watched England fade into the distance, wondering when he would again see those cliffs. He had had a good leave, even though he'd seen precious little of Julia.

His mother, he thought, seemed in good spirits, though she could hide heartbreak with a smile better than anyone he knew. He had spent little time in the library, taking long walks instead, fastening a picture of Rowangarth in his mind to carry away with him. Soft old Morgan had hardly left his side; had rushed around like a creature demented, so pleased had he been to see him; colliding with chairs, sending rugs skittering across the floor.

'Dearest. It's good to be home.' He had folded his mother in his arms, loving the sweet, clean scent of her hair, the perfume that had been a part of her since ever he could remember.

'Am I a disappointment to you, Mother?' They had talked, one day, about Cecilia, and inevitably about children. 'Would you be happier if I were married and had children—a son—of my own?'

'I should be ecstatic, but you are not married, so I don't think about it any more. I used to, when first you went to the army. I wanted a grandson so much. I'd worry about it and worry about you, Giles, not falling in love. I wanted you to. Loving and being loved is so wonderful that I want you not to miss it.

'But will I tell you something? Not long ago, when I said goodnight to your pa, he seemed to be trying to tell me something from his photograph. So I put out the light and closed my eyes and listened. And he told me not to worry about you; that all my fears would amount to nothing. It was such a comfort.'

'Did you perhaps dream it, Mother?'

He had touched her cheek with gentle fingertips. 'Did you want it so much that it came to you as you slept?'

'It wasn't a dream.' She had said it softly, surely. 'You *will* come home, Giles. I know it.' She had been so sure, had waved him on his way with a smile.

He sent his thoughts high and wide. *I am leaving you and all I love most now. I shall think about you always. And if it brings you comfort, hold on tightly to your dream, Mother.*

His eyes blurred with tears and he dashed them impatiently away, reaching for a cigarette, then remembered that to smoke on the upper deck of a troopship at sea was forbidden.

But how could a wife be possible? Where, in this mad world, would he find that woman?

Helen, Edward and Catchpole stood on the terrace, watching as Ellen's husband ploughed up Rowangarth's lawns. The gardener looked on with mixed feelings: a little sadly, because a beautiful lawn was disappearing; yet gladly, because now that there was only himself left to see to things, an acre and a half less grass to cut in the summer pleased him greatly.

'Potatoes,' Helen said firmly, as if trying to convince herself that this was the right thing to do. 'You can't eat grass...'

'My father,' Edward Sutton murmured, 'will send down fire and brimstone. He was proud of this lawn—camomile, you know.'

Percy Catchpole brightened visibly. He remembered old Sir Gilbert; a right stickler he'd been. Mind, there had been ten gardeners in the old squire's day; things had changed since twelve-year-old Percy Catchpole had the bluest, numbest hands in the Riding from a winter spent scrubbing plant-pots in ice-cold water.

'I'm sorry, Edward, but growing food is more important.' People were going hungry now—especially the old who hadn't the backbone to stand long hours in food queues.

Catchpole, at a respectful distance, sucked on his empty pipe, watching the nodding plough-horses and the farmer who held them straight and true, wondering how he would manage to supervise the growing, as her ladyship had insisted.

But March was almost gone now, and they could look ahead to warmer days; light nights and happen an end, this year, to the fratching and fighting in France.

'What do you think then, Percy, to the extra hour?' Edward Sutton asked. 'Is it going to help?'

Catchpole snorted. Those dratted fools

in London who ordered that every clock in the land be put forward one hour must be out of their minds. Saving an hour of daylight, the Government said. And how, would someone tell him, did you save daylight when what you gained evenings you would lose mornings? According to the seasons, there were so many hours of daylight and darkness; juggling about with them was against nature.

The birds would take no notice of it all all, nor the beasts. Cows wouldn't like being milked earlier nor babies having their breast at the wrong time. An experiment, said the Government, yet one they'd be glad to forget about when all was chaos. It would never work, war or no war.

'Ha!' he snorted, by way of reply.

'You don't agree with it?'

' 'Tain't natural, Mr Edward.' Agitated, he sucked harder on his pipe. 'Might I be excused, milady? There's a lot to be done.'

'Aren't you just a little sad about it?' Edward demanded when they were alone. 'The lawns, I mean...'

'Of course I am. If it weren't Ellen's husband doing the ploughing, I couldn't bear it, in fact.'

Ellen, who had been parlourmaid at Rowangarth in the old days, was now married to one of Helen's tenant farmers.

She had returned, once, to help wait at table. Dear Ellen, who remembered John. Such unbelievably green lawns, ploughed over by anyone other than Ellen's husband it would have amounted to sacrilege.

'It's time for coffee,' she murmured, linking her arm in his. 'Come inside and have a cup with me. The house is so empty, now, it echoes. And I want to hear about my nephews, and about Clemmy too.'

'I would like that,' he smiled, seeing the appeal in her eyes. 'I would like that very much indeed.'

Even after all the years, it was always good to go home to Rowangarth.

Catchpole pushed his pipe in his pocket, hurrying back to the kitchen garden. Watching other folk work was all very well, but it didn't do. My, but Rowangarth was a lonely old place now. Sir Giles gone a week past, and even Miss Julia planning on getting into the war.

He clanged shut the iron gate of the kitchen garden, feeling the safety of the nine-feet-high walls. Once that gate was closed behind him, he felt the better for it. His plants didn't know there was a war going on; in a garden, nothing changed.

A robin sang out a challenge from atop the wall; in the corner by the asparagus bed, the first of the pear blossom was white and thick. Was it an omen? Would this year see an end to the madness?

'Now tell me, how is Clemmy?' Helen passed the sugar bowl, though she herself had long since ceased to use it.

'She is well—or I imagine she is. She telephoned two nights ago and I haven't heard since. In London, of course, trying to find wallpaper for the Cheyne Walk house and someone to paste it up for her. The house next door is empty; the bombing has made them move further out into the country. Clemmy says she hopes it won't be taken over as an army billet or for Belgian refugees.'

'And Nathan? Do you know where he is?' Helen refrained from commenting on her sister-in-law's selfishness. 'I had such a lovely letter from Albert a few weeks ago. He seems happy with his Amelia, though it is sad he has given up his British citizenship.'

'His wife wants it, I suppose, if only for the sake of any issue.'

'But I understood Amelia is—well—a little past childbearing.'

'She hopes, I believe,' Edward smiled. 'And Nathan was in Paris, not long ago, though from the tone of his letters, he's back at the Front now.'

'In the fighting? Andrew is at Verdun, you know—well, Julia thinks he is.'

'I can't be sure, but I think Nathan is nearer to Paris than that. He hasn't mentioned running into Andrew or anyone else he knows. But it's a big battlefield; a very long front line. To meet up with anyone he knew would be unlikely.'

'And Elliot,' Helen asked reluctantly, holding out her hand for his cup, chiding herself for her lack of charity towards Edward's eldest son.

'He's still in London,' Edward sighed. 'Still at the War Office, though for the life of me I haven't been able to discover what it is he does there.'

'Perhaps it's too secret even for you to be told,' Helen smiled. 'And since Clemmy is away, would you take pity on a lonely woman and stay to luncheon? Julia works from early morning until well past seven. When dinner is over she begs to be excused. She looks so exhausted, poor lamb, yet still she makes time to write to Andrew at least once a day.

'Reuben brought in a young rabbit, yesterday, and Mrs Shaw has such a way with them. Stuffed with thyme and parsley, cooked slowly then cunningly carved, you wouldn't know it from chicken. Do stay?'

'Helen—much as I love you, I ought to refuse. I think it is wrong, now, to eat other people's food. But to think of luncheon cooked by Mrs Shaw corrupts me. Yes, please—I'll stay.'

May had only just gone; the bonniest month in all the year, Cook said. It should have made them feel glad, that time of hawthorn blossom and bluebells and apple trees frothing pink. And in Brattocks Wood, arum and windflowers growing thickly and the wild garlic smelling something awful if you trod on it.

It gladdened Alice's heart to see the first buttercup, growing beside the stile at the edge of the wild garden, and she carefully picked it, laying it in her Bible to send to Tom when it was pressed.

So why, at the ending of that cuckoo-month, when they should have been glad that summer was just around the corner, had there been the most awesome of sea-battles to spoil it; a battle long overdue, mind. One good victory at sea, said the man in the street, and a trouncing at the Front was all we needed to see the Kaiser suing for peace.

So now they'd had their sea-fight, Cook thought, becoming more alarmed with every line she read. The Imperial fleet, said the morning paper, had sailed north from its bases in Bremen and Wilhelmshaven; the Royal Navy had upped anchor from

Scapa Flow and steamed to engage them. They met in the Skagerrak—somewhere near Denmark, Tilda said it was, after studying Miss Julia's wall map when she should have been making her bed; met and clashed, big guns blazing.

It seemed a pity, Catchpole said when he brought in the vegetables for Cook, that neither side seemed to have won; not *really* won. Each navy had lost more than a dozen ships, and more men than dare be counted. The Victory of the Skagerrak, the Germans called it; the Battle of Jutland, *our* battle honours, claimed the Admiralty, since the Kaiser's fleet had been first to break off firing and turn tail for home, and *our* ships had chased them most of the way back. Therein lay Britain's claim to victory—and the accepted fact that it would be a long time before the Kaiser's navy ventured out again, having been taught that sabre-rattling in seas considered to be ruled by Britannia was not to be tolerated.

It was the loss of His Majesty's ship *Indefatigable,* though, that finally sent Cook's head into her apron. More than a thousand crew, yet only six survivors. It was hardly to be believed.

'What about Mary's brother?' came Cooks' muffled cry. 'Poor, poor lad...'

'Mary's brother,' said Tilda who had

been left to get on with the breakfasts as best she could, 'is on a mine-sweeper in the Channel—hundreds of miles away,' she retorted scathingly, wishing she had a penny-piece for every tear Cook had wept into that apron.

She sighed deeply, casting a long, loving glance at David-above-the-mantel, and sent up a prayer of thanks he'd had the good sense to join the army.

'You're both to go to Matron's office at half-past ten,' Ruth Love announced when breakfast had been cleared and the medicine trolley done its rounds.

'You know what it'll be about,' Julia said, stacking plates and saucers. 'Wouldn't it be a marvellous birthday present for you, Alice, to know you'd passed with flying colours?'

'Don't even mention it.' Alice was apprehensive. Her handwriting was neat and even, but her spelling left much to the imagination; she would need to have done extra well in her practical examinations to balance things up.

'Why ever not? You're a good nurse and you don't get tired out, like I do.'

'I'm more used to it than you.' Alice worked no more hours at Denniston House than she had done when in service, though being a nurse was more upsetting than ever scrubbing and sewing had been.

'We'll both pass. It's been a good six months; you can't say differently. Remember that awful day when first we started—the forty wounded from Verdun? We managed, didn't we?'

Alice did not deny it; was even secretly proud that every one of those terribly injured soldiers had cheated death, even the boy with the purple cross. They'd be sending him back to civvie street for good soon, Alice thought, wondering if he'd ever discovered he'd been given the last rites. The sight of his wounds had made her want to be sick, Alice remembered. It had been a deep, deep end they'd been thrown into that day.

'Well, you're out of your teen-years now,' Julia smiled.

'*Quiet!*' Alice hissed. 'I'm supposed to be twenty-*one* today. If anyone found out it was my coming-of-age, they'd want to celebrate. I'd feel so ashamed...'

'What do you make of Nurse Love?' Julia asked, elbow-deep in suds: VAD probationers at Denniston did all the washing-up, except for pans. 'I mean, she's such a dear person and a marvellous nurse.' Ruth Love hated death; had fought it like a mad thing for the purple-crossed soldier. 'Yet there's a barrier there all the time. And she never talks about herself.'

'She once said she'd done a year in France.'

'I know about that. But what she's never told us is why she came back here when her year was up.'

'Sister came back, too...'

'So she did, but there's no mystery there. She got a compassionate posting because her mother was ill.'

'All right, that's fair enough. But what was Ruth's excuse? Is it so awful out there that she couldn't stand any more? Are we going to be afraid, Julia, if we find ourselves in the thick of it? Remember the day the wounded came? Ruth said it was just like that at the Front, 'cept there were no shells.'

'What is it?' Julia dried her hands, taking Alice by the shoulders, turning her round to face her. 'Don't you want to go now? When we've done our training and taken our exams, have you changed your mind?'

'No. Far from it.' Alice shrugged away the hands, reluctant to meet Julia's eyes. 'I want to go; I really do. But I'm no scholar and I mightn't have done well in the written papers. I couldn't bear it if you went without me. I'd die of shame.'

'Listen, you'll pass. I promise you will—word of a Sutton.'

'But you *aren't* a Sutton,' Alice said perversely.

'I was for nearly twenty-two years. And you'd better pass, because I'm not going alone. Chin up! If we hurry with these dishes there'll be time to tidy up for half-past. Please, Alice, cheer up?'

They were walking dry-mouthed across the hall, hands clenched at their sides, when they saw the notice, VOLUNTEER NURSES WANTED.

'Look—they're asking for nurses for France!' Julia pointed. 'Now wouldn't you say that's a coincidence? It's as if it's meant to be! Come on,' she urged. 'What more do you want?' She knocked on the door with more confidence than she felt, swallowing hard.

'Come!' called Matron.

Alice shuddered visibly; Julia crossed her fingers. 'Word of a Sutton...' she whispered as she pushed open the door.

They had done well, Matron said, holding out a hand to each, hoping they would continue with the Voluntary Aid Detachment. They would be most welcome to stay at Denniston House, she said—or did they want, perhaps, to try for a teaching hospital?

'Or had you considered—' she hesitated.

'Volunteering for France? Yes—both of us,' Julia smiled.

'Then think about it carefully, and if

you have any doubts at all, talk to me about them. You have both done well. I wouldn't like either of you to be lost to nursing.'

'We passed!' Julia closed the door, leaning against it because her knees were shaking. 'We did it—*you* did it, Alice! Won't Andrew be proud of us when he hears?'

Flushed with triumph, they read through the notice again. Suitable volunteers would be paid twenty pounds per annum, a monthly allowance towards the upkeep of uniform, and all travelling expenses. They would be required to serve for the period of one year, after which their contract could, if desired, be renewed.

'Look who signed whilst we were in Matron's office.'

'Sister and Staff Nurse. Both of them going!'

'Shall we, then? Oh, Ruth's all right, but if we sign does it mean we'll be going with Carbolic?'

'Sister's not half bad,' Alice defended, still giddy with relief. 'She's fair and she's a good nurse. Better the devil we know...'

Julia picked up the pencil that hung on a string beside the noticeboard and signed J.H.M MacMalcolm so firmly that the Mac in her name made a hole in the paper. 'Well?' she said, turning to Alice.

'Give it here!' Alice took the pencil and signed her name with such a flourish that anyone could have been forgiven for forgetting that a little less than five minutes ago she had been shaking like a jelly. 'What's Sister going to say—saddled with the pair of us?'

'Who cares?' Julia laughed triumphantly. She was on her way! What else mattered.

12

So much had happened, so quickly, since that morning in Matron's office. They'd had injections—cholera and typhus; repaired and cleaned their uniforms; written letters.

Don't write again until you hear from me...

Goodbye to Brattocks Wood, green-flushed with summer, the evening air sweet-smelling with honeysuckle and wild pink roses; goodbye to the wraith of a girl, wide-eyed with love. She had long gone, and the lover she met there. When they would meet again, and where, she did not know; that they would be different people when they did so was the only thing of which she was sure.

Tonight was Midsummer's Eve. Four days ago, Alice had left her girl-years behind her. By the time July came she would be on her way to France. Just to think of it sent a mixture of excitement and fear churning through her.

Julia MacMalcolm was less apprehensive; had travelled abroad many times. The crossing of the Channel held no fear for her, despite Robert's death. To her, the narrow, submarine-infested strip of water was the last hurdle; to Alice it was a terror to be endured.

Many other things had happened. Portugal had been drawn into the war, our ally now; married men had been called up for service, and six months of fighting at Verdun had ended in stalemate. There had been victories and defeats on both sides, yet the No Man's Land between them was little changed. The Pyrrhic victory both sides claimed had cost a million lives: British, German, French, Austrian. Sons, sweethearts, husbands, fathers. So high a reckoning for so few yards of blood-soaked earth.

Now, the Western Front had lapsed into an uneasy, waiting silence, most felt along the banks of a river in Picardy, did Alice but know it; a stillness waiting to explode into the fearful roar of a new battle.

Alice called Morgan to her side, walking

the length of the wood to the tallest tree. Above her head, rooks cawed lazily home to nest. Eyes closed, she whispered.

Black birds, it's Alice here—Nurse Haw-thorn—sewing-maid as used to be to her ladyship. I'm going to France with Miss Julia and Sister Carbrooke and Ruth Love. We're all sticking together.

Heaven only knows what's to be the end of it, but I want to go, to be near Tom. You'll remember Tom—he was keeper here—and I'd like you to know about us, just to keep things straight. I won't be coming this way for a while, but look kindly on Rowangarth and, whatever you do, don't fly away.

The day the rooks left Rowangarth woods would be a sad one. Folks hereabouts knew that if they ceased to nest in Brattocks Wood, nothing but grief for the Suttons would follow. Mind, it had never happened; not in more than three hundred years, but it was what folk believed.

Goodbye, then. I'm going to see Reuben now...

'Come in and sit you down,' the elderly keeper smiled. 'The kettle's on the boil—I hoped you'd come afore you went.'

'Hoped? You knew I would!'

The windows and doors were open wide to the summer evening; tobacco smoke mixing with night scents and the smell of burning logs sent an ache of sadness through her.

'I've left everything straight and in order, Reuben. I'm taking Tom's locket and Mam's ring with me; all else doesn't amount to a lot. I've written your name on my trunk.'

'Good heavens to Murgatroyd! What on earth's got into you, lass?'

'Nothing that isn't right and sensible,' she retorted severely. 'And my bank book is at the bottom of the trunk. There's four pounds fifteen shillings in it.' She laughed suddenly. 'Didn't know I was a lady of means, did you?'

'I pray you'll be all right, Alice.' He touched her cheek in a rare gesture of affection. 'You'll be aiming to end up near Tom, I shouldn't wonder?'

'Aye, and Miss Julia wants to get near the doctor. We've had a look at the war map and the only solution is to get a hospital in Paris, half-way between the two of them.'

'Gay Paree,' Reuben frowned. 'You'll have to watch your p's and q's if you end up there.'

'It'll be nearer the Front, Sister says—but not too near,' she hastened.

'That hard-faced Sister woman—you'll both be with her?' Reuben felt greatly relieved.

'Yes, and with Nurse Love an' all. And Sister isn't hard-faced, really. If I was in trouble, I'd rather she were beside me than most I could think of. But promise you won't worry about me? I'll be with Miss Julia and it's likely we'll be staying together. I'd be better pleased if you'd keep an eye on Morgan.'

Affectionately she prodded the spaniel with the toe of her shoe. He snuffled softly in his sleep, then went back to his dreaming.

'I'll see to him. Now then, let's be having that sup of tea, shall us? It'll be a long time afore we have another, I shouldn't wonder?'

'It could be as long as a year,' she said, sad again. 'We sign on for a twelve-month, though we'll get home leave after that, I think.'

She hugged Reuben tightly when she left, patting his back, kissing his cheek.

'I'll not say goodbye,' she smiled, snapping on Morgan's lead. 'Just so-long, and thanks for not telling on me—when I lied about being old enough for France, I mean. Take care. I'll write the minute we get there. Write back, sometimes, won't you?'

'I'll write, lass.'

He stood at his door, watching the bobbing light of her candlelamp grow smaller in the twilight, then slammed it shut with a cold, seething anger. It was either that or tears—and men couldn't weep. Not even old men...

Alice and Julia spent the first night in a hostel in Bloomsbury with a dozen other nurses, all bound for France. Their room had eight beds in it and precious little else. From one of them came a muffled sniffing.

Alice wanted to weep, too, but for what she didn't know. She ought to feel happy. Julia was happy, had hardly been able to wait to get into the motor taxi that was to take them to Holdenby Halt.

From the steps, her ladyship had waved them goodbye, head high, a smile on her lips. She'd done the same, Alice all at once thought, to Robert and Giles—now her daughter was leaving, too.

Miss Clitherow had been there, and Cook and Tilda and Jinny Dobb. Tilda had waved frantically; Cook had plucked at the corners of her apron, ready to weep. Miss Clitherow had smiled; only Jin had stood still and silent.

Catchpole had waited by the the gate lodges with wheelbarrow and hoe, pretending to be working there, removing his pipe from his mouth, raising his straw panama as they passed.

They had almost missed Reuben, standing at the fence with his dogs, at the place where the single-track railway ran alongside Brattocks Wood for a few score yards.

'Reuben!' Julia had cried, pulling down the compartment window, waving her hand wildly as the train had slipped out of his sight. 'Did you see him, Alice? How kind of him to be there!'

'Aye,' Alice had sniffed, her voice unsteady. 'Remember when we came back from London that first time? I was happy; you were sad at leaving the doctor. Remember that Tom stood there an' all?' The tears she had kept in a hard lump in her throat had all at once welled up and ran down her cheeks. 'Oh, miss...' she had choked.

'Alice—don't cry. Please, *please*, don't cry or I'll think it's all my fault for taking you to France with me. What is it?'

'It's nothing.' Alice had taken a folded handkerchief from her pocket. 'And you aren't taking me to France. I *want* to go. It was just—just...' She'd mopped her tears, then taken a deep breath, smiling shakily. '...just that I'm leaving home, I suppose.'

And, if she'd admit it, it was also partly because of what Jin Dobb had said that moonlit night she'd told her fortune, and the fact that Jin hadn't smiled when

264

they left. Sober-faced, she'd been; as if she'd remembered—as if she had known something...

The sniffing from the far corner of the room stopped. It wasn't any use crying, Alice sighed, though she'd indulged her own tears that morning. Now she lay in an unfamiliar bed in unfamiliar darkness and thought of Tom. Tomorrow they would leave for France; before another day had run, they would have arrived. Monday the third of July would be the start of her new life. Two days journeying nearer to Tom; two days nearer the end of a war that could not, must not, last into another winter.

They had crossed a millpond Channel in a troopship filled with soldiers. Most wore new uniforms; others—a few—had the sad eyes of men returning from leave.

They sailed in convoy with three merchantmen, all supply ships, carrying ammunition and horses, whilst three small warships fussed around them

'Destroyer escort and two frigates,' said someone who knew about such things.

Laying off, riding at anchor, another trooper waited for a berth. Its upper deck was thick with soldiers, crowding the rails for a first sight of home. They all wore full kit and broad smiles. The destroyer whooped three times in greeting. The homecoming soldiers cheered and waved. The sky was bright and cloudless; the Channel glistened blue-green. Reluctantly, almost, the turbines beneath their feet began to turn and throb; hawsers were released, a last link with England. Ahead, as they nosed slowly out to sea, lay France. Astern, Dover's cliffs shone creamily and ever smaller in the sun.

'Look at Ruth Love,' Julia whispered. 'She seems upset, almost...'

'Yes.' Alice had noticed. 'Happen a bit of sea-sickness.'

'On a calm day like this?' Oh, no. It was something deeper, more secret. Julia knew it. 'I'm glad she's with us, though.'

Above them, seagulls cried; the bows lifted and fell gently. Beneath their feet they had felt the steady throbbing of engines. There was no going back now.

French railway stations, Alice noted, and French trains, were little different from those she had left behind her. Calais terminus could be York, or King's Cross even, had it not been for the strange language.

They carried their cases to the luggage van, then found a compartment with four empty seats. Sister shepherded them inside, determined to keep them together. In a brown paper carrier bag were sandwiches, apples, and two bottles of water for the journey. Sister did not trust foreign water; was wary of anything foreign she could not scrub down, disinfect or sterilise.

When the train left the platform, she lapsed into silence, her face wearing a thank-God-we're-almost-there expression. Ruth Love's face was pale and taut. Perhaps she, too, had not slept.

'You may take off your hats and coats,' Sister murmured as the train gathered speed, hooting, just as English trains hooted, at a river-bridge ahead.

Alice pulled her finger round the inside of her high, starched collar. Not even after six months could she abide the tightness at her neck.

The sun beat down. It would be a hot, uncomfortable journey. Her stockings made her legs itch. She smiled across at Julia, then turned to look out on her first real glimpse of France.

Sister looked around the compartment, ascertained the other occupants were French and therefore would probably not understand English, then said, 'Our destination is Celverte. As far as I know, it's a small place between Abbeville and Amiens.'

They would leave the train at Abbeville, she told them, where transport would be waiting. They would be able to unpack and settle in—get a good night's sleep. Tomorrow they could expect to be on duty.

Ruth Love leaned towards Sister, lowering her voice to a whisper.

'Will we be far from the Front?'

Sister held up ten fingers—twice. *'Miles.'* She never bothered with kilometres. 'Is anyone hungry?'

She passed round sandwiches wrapped in greaseproof paper; took out two tin mugs. The sandwiches were spread with margarine and potted fishpaste.

The French family took out sausages, crusty white bread and wine. The woman sliced the sausages, speared a piece on the end of her knife, and saluted the English women.

'Bonne chance!' she smiled.

The heat in the compartment became overpowering; Sister lowered the window. Julia rubbed her hot, itching legs.

Alice eased her collar, gazing out, squinting into the sun. Outside was a France exactly as she had thought it would be. Now they sped through villages of small, brightly painted houses, their shutters closed against the afternoon sun. In each garden, vines showing bunches of small, unripe grapes clung in orderly fashion to wires. In every garden, too, grew clumps of arum lilies, white and waxy, their

268

leaves glossily dark green. They reminded Alice of Mr Catchpole and Rowangarth and Tom.

Tom. She knew from her familiarity with Julia's wall map they would be nearer to him than to the doctor, though she had not remarked on it because doubtless Julia had realised it too.

Celverte. She wanted more than anything to arrive there; to unpack her case, take off her dull green cotton frock and shoes and stockings and walk barefoot on a floor of cold linoleum. Then hopefully, she could wash. She felt such discomfort that even one tap dripping cold water would be welcome, whilst a real bath would be complete bliss.

Celverte? If it were only twenty miles from the Front, then surely it was close to Tom who was billeted near Albert? If he hadn't been moved on, that was.

She revised her thoughts. Before even taking off her shoes and stockings she would write to Tom; send him her address. It would be like posting a letter in England; he would have it in no time.

More vines, more lilies; cows being driven to be milked. Was it always this hot in France? She leaned back her head and closed her eyes. When she opened them, Ruth was shaking her arm, saying, 'Abbeville. Alice...'

269

Celverte was indeed a village, but so humming with war that Alice was taken aback. Transports and ambulances of all kinds were everywhere, crowding the narrow streets outside the railway station, while high above them a chateau stood beautiful in the sun, its windows sparkling.

'That big house on the hill—that's the hospital?' Sister asked, checking her cases.

'One of them,' offered the driver sent to meet them, 'but my orders say you're to go to the school.' The chateau, he said, was more of an emergency place—a clearing-station—and a right shambles it was, so he'd heard. More wounded there than they could cope with; lying all over the place—even in the courtyard, outside.

'Wounded?' Sister snapped, instantly alert. 'From where?'

'From the fighting—where else? Listen...'

They stood, breath indrawn, until in a quiet moment they heard a noise like distant thunder, continually rumbling.

'Hear it? That's *their* guns. And they tried to tell us it'd be a walk-over. Such a barrage of shells we were going to put up that there'd be no Germans living, they said, by the time our gunners had finished with them. Walk in, then, the infantry could. Just walk in through the gaps the sappers had made, take the Jerry trenches, then press on to the Belgian border.

'The war'd be over before we knew it, they kept telling us. We'd all of us be back home for Christmas. That's what they told the lads,' the driver said bitterly, 'and the poor sods believed it. But how can you run a war from a desk in London? Why don't they come over here; have a look at what it's really like?'

His face was fiercely indignant; he spat his disgust on to the dust-dry cobbles. 'You're going to be needed here. Get in—I'll take you...'

'One moment!' Sister took the man's arm, holding it tightly. 'You're saying that more fighting has broken out? We've been travelling for two days, you see—no newspapers.'

'That's right. Been building up to it for months. Never seen so much stuff: guns, mortars, flame-throwers, the lot. One big push, they said. One barrage from the artillery like no one had ever known before, then over the top, my handsomes! Brussels and blighty in time for Christmas!'

'And it wasn't like that?' Tight-lipped, she let go of his arm.

'It flaming wasn't! Our lads went in all right—only the Germans weren't lying dead in their lines like they should have been. Their trenches were empty. The crafty sods had a second line, further back. They must've been laughing like drains, seeing our gunners getting it wrong—everything falling short.

'They waited till our lads were standing there like they were looking for the war, then those machine-gunners just let them have it. Slaughter. Hundreds—*thousands*—of them. The lucky ones are up there.' He pointed to the big house on the hill.

'Get in, Nurses,' Sister said, tight-lipped. 'I think they're going to be glad to see us...'

Their quarters looked gaunt from outside. Above the door of the building *Institut des Filles* was chiselled in the stonework. A girls' school, taken over by the authorities and now a home for nurses. Inside, they were greeted warmly.

'Hullo. I'm the housekeeper.'

Not unlike Miss Clitherow in her dress and bearing, Alice thought, though her smile was wider and brighter.

'You'll be thinking it is unusual to have a housekeeper in quarters like this—but they told me I was too old for nursing, so I came here to look after things. Unpaid, but I hope not unsung. I try to make things a little more comfortable for you all.'

Sister nodded her approval, then excused herself to go in search of the matron; all others followed the housekeeper. Hot and dirty, they lugged cases up the wide, uncovered stairs.

'You'll be in this dormitory. Once, when this was a convent school, it had twelve beds; now, we have improved it a little.'

She swished aside a curtain. 'Each cubicle is curtained to give privacy when required, and you must remember to darken your window at night. We are very near the Front. To show a light after dark is not allowed.

'Outside is a little chapel, for all denominations. Chaplains visit each week. Times are on the noticeboard. Now—each of you take a bed, except—' she studied the list in her hand '—Staff Nurse Love.'

'That's me.' Ruth Love stepped forward.

'Here you are.' She opened the door to a small, partitioned-off room at the top of the dormitory. 'This was once occupied by a nun—I hope you'll be comfortable in it. It's less austere than it once was...'

'Thank you. I hadn't expected—' Clearly she was surprised. 'Just one thing: are you allowed to tell us where the fighting is?'

'I don't see why not. It began three days ago, and as far as I can tell, it's about twenty-five miles away—in the area of the River Somme.'

The Somme. Albert. Alice closed her eyes, pulling in her breath. Tom was there. She slid back the heavy green curtain that separated her bed from Julia's.

'You heard? Tom's in it now.'

'Yes, and I'm sorry, Alice. But you *are* near him. Just think—he could even be billeted just around the corner!'

'He might...' Alice was not comforted, even though Julia had been through the same when there'd been fighting at Verdun.

'Cheer up. The first thing we must do is let our men know where we are. What's our address?'

'Care of Voluntary Aid Detachment, General Hospital Sixteen, BEF Two,' Alice recited flatly. 'They told us when we got here...'

'Thanks. I forgot.' Julia opened her writing case, carefully printing the address at the top of a sheet of pale blue notepaper. Then she wrote,

We have arrived and I love you, love you, love you. Letter follows. J.

'We mustn't seal them down. The Censor has to read them first,' Alice frowned.

'Who cares? Censors are human, aren't they?'

Alice unscrewed the top of her ink bottle, dipping in her pen. Tom might get this letter, she thought, in a couple of days. If he were still near Albert, that was. If he hadn't been among the thousands the machine-gunners had—were *supposed* to have...

'Hurry up.' Julia broke into her thoughts. 'I'll take them downstairs. We leave them in the basket in the hall. Then we'll unpack and get our bearings. Supper's in an hour. It'll be all right, just you see. We're hungry and tired. Once we've cleaned ourselves up and had something to eat, things are going to seem a whole lot better.'

'I know. And this is streets ahead of York Military.' At the end of the long, narrow room was a cubicled bath and, beside it, curtained off, two washbasins. 'There might even be hot water.'

'And the housekeeper seems very nice...'

'I suppose we'll be at the big house tomorrow.' Alice looked up from her unpacking as Julia returned.

'We might be. But the chateau is only a clearing-station. Seems there's another hospital, just across the field, at the back. Wooden huts, but newly built. We might be there. By the way,' she dropped her voice to a whisper, 'when I passed the end cubicle, Ruth was sitting on her bed. Just sitting, staring. I said hullo to her, but she seemed not to hear. She looks sort of strained, somehow. Do you think she's sorry she came?'

'Don't know.' Alice laid her Bible on

the chest beside her bed, the buttercup she was pressing for Tom inside it. 'Maybe we should ask her, though really it isn't any of our business.'

'No, it isn't. Not really...'

They spun round, gasping. Staff Nurse stood there and they knew she had heard.

'Look—we didn't mean...'

'Only concerned. We do care for you,' Julia whispered.

'I know. And I suppose I'd better tell you and then, if sometimes I seem a little—well, *distant*—you'll understand. And if I didn't hear you just now, Julia, perhaps I was listening to the plane going over...'

'A plane? You've been bombed?' Julia offered. 'Oh, sit down, won't you?'

'Not bombed.' Ruth sat on the bed, hands clasped tightly. 'It's James, you see. Have either of you lost anyone?'

Alice shook her head. Julia whispered, 'My brother—last year...'

'James was in the Flying Corps—an observer in a spotter plane. I was out here. I'd done my year, was going back to England. James had been promised leave too. Flyers seemed to get it more easily—they needed it...'

'And James was—?' Julia prompted, gently.

'He was shot down, two weeks before.'

'How *awful,*' Alice choked.

'More awful than you know. It's bad enough, being told about it, but I had to find out the hard way.

'I was on duty; the ward was bordering on chaos. They'd sent us some stretcher cases from the dressing-station—all of them in a mess. Then someone said they'd brought in a flyer; there'd been two, they said, only one of them was in the mortuary.

'I went to have a look. A nurse was just pulling the sheet over his face. I asked her if he was dead and she said, "Just this minute. I'll find a couple of orderlies. He was horribly burned..."

'I pulled back the sheet: God knows why, because all the while there was this voice inside me saying, "It isn't. It won't be..." That flyer could have been anybody. His face and hands were awful—unrecognisable. But I knew. They'd taken off some of his uniform, you see, and I could see the strawberry mark on his left arm.

'Then I looked at his identity disc—that hadn't burned, either. J.M Love. God! I'd not been ten feet away while my husband was dying. Some other nurse had been with him.

'I started to scream. I just stood there, screaming. Then someone slapped me: two of them took me by the arm and ran me outside. Imagine? A staff nurse behaving like that? But I wasn't a nurse at that moment. I was a wife, a widow. Such rage in me...'

'Don't!' Julia choked. 'Not while it hurts so badly.'

'Oh, it hurts. It won't ever go away. They sent me back to Blighty to pull myself together—to Denniston House. Both men were buried with indecent haste, but I found his grave before I left. Just a marker on it.'

'You shouldn't have come back, Staff,' Alice said, fighting tears. 'Every time you see an aeroplane—hear one—it's going to bring it all back.'

'No, Hawthorn. It's got to be faced. There won't ever be any peace for me if I don't. Sister knew. She understood. Said I should give it a try—one day at a time.'

'Will it help to tell us how?' Julia asked, gently.

'Oh, the usual. One of theirs—shot them up whilst they were taking off. Bill—James's pilot—was killed instantly. Pity James wasn't. He was hours dying, and what's so awful is that I could have been with him.'

'We didn't know you'd been married,' Julia said. 'No ring, you see.'

'I took it off. When you are wearing a ring they ask you where your man is—patients, especially.'

'Put it back,' Julia whispered. 'Keep faith?'

'I will, MacMalcolm. Just as soon as I can bear to—to admit I'm a widow and that I'll never see my Jamie again.' She rose to her feet. 'Well, best finish my unpacking—I've got four drawers and a wardrobe. Very posh!

'And thank you for listening. This is the first time I've really talked about it—actually said out loud that he's dead. Well, best be off...'

'Staff!' Alice cried, making to follow her.

'No! Leave her!' Julia hissed, grasping Alice's arm. 'What she told us took a lot of doing. Let her pull herself together.'

'This is a *terrible* war.'

'I know, Alice. But we'll feel a whole lot better about everything in the morning. And when we wake up, there'll be another night to cross off my calendar. I cross them off, you know. Nights, not days...' Nights spent wanting Andrew. 'And we are so very lucky; we're so much nearer to them, now, that there's a fair chance we might be able to see them, even if only for a short while.'

An hour would do.

13

Tom Dwerryhouse blinked his eyes rapidly, then relaxed. It hadn't been a movement on the skyline; just a trick of the moonlight. He leaned his rifle carefully beside him, then took a drink from the water-bottle at his side, sliding his eyes left and right.

He was hungry and the biscuit in his pocket was hard. He broke off a piece, tonguing it into his cheek to soften it. All was quiet, still, from Geordie's end. Were they all asleep across No Man's Land? On a night as bright as this, dare they be?

Geordie Marshall hated Germans. They had killed his sister in the bombardment of Hartlepool eighteen months ago, and his anger went deep. Now he found comfort in killing; the dummies on the firing range, even, became objects of his hatred. Tom had seen the look in his eyes; the way his finger caressed the trigger, almost with love. Geordie had not joined the army for his mother's sake, or even for the sake of England. He had become a soldier to avenge the death of a girl called Dorothy. He was at the far end of the village—if village you could call it—now. For so long,

Tom had looked across No Man's Land to the distant cluster of ten cottages and a church, standing deserted: the army had moved out those who lived there months ago. Now, since the shelling started, it had become a ruin, the little houses no more than empty walls that in the moonlight looked like great, hollow teeth.

Geordie was in the end cottage; the one with its stone staircase still intact. He'd be at the little landing window, passing his tongue round his lips, squinting into the distance like a green-eyed night cat.

Tom crouched in the shattered belfry of the church. He felt safe behind the thick stone wall; had taken up his watch at a slit-like window high enough to support his rifle, narrow enough to give him protection. Tonight neither he nor the man in the end cottage were sniping. Tonight they kept watch over stretcher-bearers who had slipped out into the wastes between to bring back wounded. No betraying rifle-cracks; only a shot in the air to warn them they had been seen; a shot to alert our artillery—start up a protective barrage from guns already ranged and primed.

Tom prayed the silence would continue. He wanted those fools of men to get out safely, if only because he himself had survived the first awful days of the fighting.

They would be all right, they'd been told before it all began; told so often they had come to believe it.

There'll be nothing moving when our gunners have finished. You'll just go in—take prisoners. Fritz will be glad to surrender—if you can find one of them alive, that is.

Into battle. After almost five months of waiting and time-wasting, it would be good to go in. Then on to Brussels: because that was where they expected to be by Christmas. He'd been put out when they'd called him for special duties—duties Tom called sniping. A sniper waited alone, motionless and hidden, for the slightest movement from the trenches opposite; to keep the enemy always on his guard, make sure no one looked over the top of the sandbags, much less tried to advance. You waited for the *second* glimpse of a grey, steel helmet. You didn't fire first time. The first sighting could be a helmet on the end of a bayonet—a toe in the water, a try-out. Second time you shot the bastard and, if you were Geordie Marshall, you smiled as you did it.

Now, Tom was put out no longer; was grateful, almost, that his special skill had separated him from the slaughter of that first, foolish advance. No Man's Land was

282

no longer a spread of bonny, flower-filled meadows. Tonight it was exactly as he knew it should be: a churn of shell-holes; torn, jagged trees that only seven days ago had flourished green. And only seven days ago there had been cottages in No Man's Land, and a church.

Tonight, they had waited for the brief darkness that came before moonrise—Geordie and himself and a dozen men with stretchers. Conchies, all twelve; men who merited white feathers in civvie street yet were the bravest of the brave. On their arms and steel helmets they wore a red cross, their badge of courage. He'd been proud to go in with them.

Two chaplains were out there, too; one British and a priest to give last rites to the dying and absolution to the dead. Brave men who also refused to carry a gun.

The moon slipped behind a cloud; Tom chewed on the biscuit. There would be hot tea when they got back to the rear trenches—rum in it, if they were lucky. Surprising how cold a July night could be—or was it fear that chilled him through?

Nathan Sutton, Tom thought, could well be out there, or in some other No Man's Land, every bit as dangerous. Happen that applied to Sir Giles, an' all, not so far down the line.

What would her ladyship think if she knew? God in heaven, but this was a wicked war.

A stone hit the wall at his side. He clicked back the bolt of his rifle, pointing it downward.

'*Tom?*' It was Geordie. 'We're on our way. They reckon they can get back while the moon's hidden. I've got two walking wounded here—can you take one?'

Tom felt the ledge beside him, making sure he had left no signs of his being there, then lowered himself to the ground, stretching his cramped limbs.

'Been out there long?' he asked the soldier. Tom could hardly see him, but he felt the warm damp of his uniform, smelled the blood.

'Only since afternoon. I hoped they'd come and get me. My arm and leg...'

'You're all right now.' Tom wrapped the man's waist round with his arm. 'Hang on to my neck...'

The wounded man clung like a dead weight. Their progress was slow. 'Easy, mate...' Just as long as the darkness lasted, they could make it. 'Lucky devil. Got yourself a Blighty wound there.'

'Yes—lucky...'

Doctors were waiting for them, and orderlies. The stretcher-bearers handed over their burdens and were given tea.

Geordie carried two mugs. He felt disappointed—cheated almost. He hadn't fired a shot. A wasted night; not one killing.

'They say we can stand down now.' He offered a cigarette and Tom shook his head. Geordie always offered one, always forgot Tom didn't smoke. 'It's me for my bed. G'night, then...'

He slouched off to his billet. Geordie wasn't a smart soldier; didn't snap to attention and salute correctly when addressed by an officer. Geordie's eyes often held contempt for the fancy uniforms of his superiors: dumb insolence, it was called, yet the Tynesider got away with it. He was the best shot in the battalion—better even than the gamekeeper—and he knew it. He'd taken more Germans than most.

'So long,' Tom murmured, hands wrapped round the hot tin mug. At times like this, he tried to stand quietly and apart, emptying himself of the horror of it, and the fear; willing himself back to sanity.

And sanity was a place called Brattocks Wood; a lass called Alice. To think of her was the only way to relax the tension from his limbs. She was on her way here—might even have arrived. What had he been about to let her do it? It was three weeks since her birthday. Twenty now, yet still too young to be here; too young to marry.

He sent his thoughts to her, wherever she was. Only weeks ago they'd been sure it would soon be over. The Germans were cracking and the offensive on the Somme would finish them once and for all. Yet now they knew—that lot in London, an' all—that the enemy was as strong as ever and no one was going anywhere at Christmas.

He wanted, all at once, to weep his frustration at a world gone mad. Instead, he spat with contempt on the ground at his feet. Tears wouldn't bring back the dead, heal wounds, or help blinded eyes to see again.

He looked up at the sky. A soldier could be forgiven for thinking that, at times such as this, God was on *their* side. He drained his mug, hitched his rifle on his shoulder, and made for his billet.

There had been no mail for days. He hoped tonight that there might be a letter from Alice, and that someone might have put it beside his bed space.

When he got back, he was amazed to find there were three: two from England, and one that bore the red stamp and scribbled initials of the Censor.

He opened it with the blade of his pocket knife; he always opened her letters carefully. Partly because he was tidy-minded, but really because he wanted to savour the moment when he dipped his fingers into the envelope and pulled out a sheet of paper she had touched, written on, most likely laid to her lips.

The spray of buttercups fell to the floor. Gently he picked it up, slipping it back into the envelope. He read the address at the top of the page and a shock of pleasure tingled through him.

BEF Two. The Somme area! She was somewhere near; might be so near that—

He shook such thoughts from his head. The area of the River Somme was large and wide; she could be well out of his finding.

My darling Tom,

I am here, safe and well. Write to me soon? Take care. I love you.

Alice.

'Oh, my lovely lass...'

The single candle guttered; the wick sank into a pool of wax, the flame died. Tom pushed the letters into his pocket to read tomorrow in the daylight. Alice, near Albert? To see her, touch her. To hold her, kiss her...

He unlaced his boots, unwound his puttees, then lay down in the darkness, the straw in his palliasse crackling beneath him.

287

He smiled. All at once, God had changed sides.

A few days after their arrival, Julia and Alice were on duty at the chateau. Make yourselves useful, they were told. VAD nurses weren't properly trained; there were things they weren't allowed to do, said the time-served nurse of the Army Reserve, scathingly. Yet now, when ambulances brought in the injured in long, slow-moving convoys, and the walking wounded limped up the hill in an endless straggle, every nurse was needed.

Alice cut open a mud-caked, blood-stained trouser leg, carefully easing back the rough khaki cloth, laying on a dressing, offering a cigarette.

Don't let them bring Tom in; don't let me see him like Ruth did...

The sun beat down. Already her apron was soiled: whoever had thought up this uniform—all bits and pieces to button, take off, scrub and starch—hadn't know what they were about!

'Hawthorn!' She responded quickly to Sister's summons. 'Get this man's jacket off...'

This was like the frosty February morning at Denniston, only now there were forty times forty wounded and would be, every day, until the fighting eased.

This morning she had awakened before six—out of habit, she supposed—and, wrapping her night shawl around her, had walked without sound to the washbasins at the end of the room. Neither was in use; weary nurses slept until the last minute possible and, anyway, half the beds were empty, those to whom they belonged counting away the minutes to the end of their night duty.

Breakfast, in the early morning cool, had been good. The porridge had been free of lumps, milk to pour on it plentiful; there had even been a bowl of sugar on the table.

Last night, before she slept, she had written again to Tom, telling him she would be working at the chateau, hoping it would help him locate her, though probably every chateau in Picardy was now a hospital.

A stretcher was carried past her. The man who lay on it had been given morphia, his purple cross a passport to the top of the queue.

'That man,' Sister pointed to a soldier she had satisfied herself was not in need of surgery, 'can have soup. See to it, Hawthorn.'

The man smiled his thanks, then lowered himself to the ground, leaning his back against an ornamental urn; glad, in spite of his pain, to be out of the fighting. Soon, he would sleep in a bed; might even learn he'd got himself a ticket to Blighty.

'Can you manage it all right?' Alice placed the mug of soup on the ground beside him.

He told her he could. He looked almost happy, she thought as she washed her hands in the bucket of disinfectant, shaking them dry, thinking that tonight, when she wrote to Tom again, she would tell him that before long she would be working at the new hospital, just as soon as a ward was ready for their use. Such information would help, for where was there a place with a chateau *and* a newly built hospital? Somehow, bit by bit, he would work out where she was.

'Nurse Hawthorn.'

'Coming, Staff!' A plane droned low overhead; a British one, with red, white and blue roundels. *Their* planes had black crosses on them.

'You want me, Staff?'

'Yes.' Ruth Love took her eyes from the sky. 'Find Sister, will you—ask her if she can spare a minute.'

The soldier at whose side she knelt was feverish, mumbling in delirium. His shoulders and back were covered in bright red pinpoints and the spreadings of a rosy rash.

Alice frowned. She had long ago learned to recognise flea bites, but this was something more. 'Is it...?' Some called it trench fever.

'Typhus, I think. Go find her, will you? And *don't run!*'

Alice had not enjoyed the injections she had been given, but now, Staff's message delivered, she had reason to be glad of the headache, high temperature, and swollen arm she had suffered.

'Want a hand?' She hurried to Julia's side.

'Please. Hold that dressing, will you?'

Julia's hands were so sure, Alice thought as she watched her wind and secure the head bandage. Everything she did oozed confidence. It was, Alice supposed, because of her upbringing. Miss Julia's sort were like that.

'Want to know something?' Julia lit a cigarette then passed it, smiling, to the soldier. 'Rumour has it there'll be a break soon. Soup and bread in the kitchen, about noon. Know where the kitchens are?'

'Yes. This is awful, Julia. All these wounded, I mean.'

They lay around the courtyard, most of them not sufficiently ill even to warrant being carried inside, yet all of them seriously wounded.

'I know. Sister thinks the same. She

was muttering about being glad when she got her own ward so she'd know what she was about.' Six huts—wards—at the new hospital were still unfinished. 'I think they're only waiting for the paint to dry and the linoleum to be laid. Wonder if there'll be letters tonight?'

Since their arrival, there had been nothing. They had come away, disappointed, each morning from the letter-board.

'Not if they're in the fighting,' Alice shrugged. 'And look out!'

Sister approached; and caught them gossiping.

'You two!' Sister Carbrooke was smiling. 'Cut along to the kitchens and get something to eat. You've got fifteen minutes...And for heaven's sake, clean yourselves up and put on fresh aprons! By the way, my ward is finished. Tomorrow we'll be busy moving in!'

She walked away, still smiling. Like a cat who'd been at the cream, Julia thought or, more exactly, like a sister who'd been given a ward...

'Come on,' she grinned. 'Food!'

All at once, they felt inexplicably happier.

That night, there were letters.

'Four!' Alice gasped, sorting through

hers for sight of Tom's handwriting; frowning at the postmarks. 'One from Tom's mam, one from Mrs Shaw—and *two* from Tom!'

'And I,' smiled Julia serenely, 'have got one from Giles, one from Mother and three from Andrew!'

'Let's read them over supper,' Alice laughed, wondering which she would open first.

'Best we scrub up before we do anything. Did you know they sent a man into isolation?'

'Yes—typhus. Ruth Love found it.'

'That's fleas for you!' Julia took her spongebag from its hook. 'We'd better have a good look at ourselves, I think.' High on the heady delight of five letters, she let out a shout of laughter. 'I don't know why, but suddenly I got a picture of Aunt Clemmy! What *would* she say if she thought her niece had fleas!'

Alice neither knew nor cared. Tom had written, and the awfulness of the dressing-station was behind them. Even with Sister hovering like a hawk, a ward would be nothing short of heaven. She even looked forward to the smell of carbolic.

Julia pulled back the green curtain that separated their cubicles, then lay on her bed, newly bathed and almost content.

'There are days, Alice, you never forget...'

'Mm,' Alice smiled.

'And isn't it amazing—Andrew, I mean. I wondered how on earth I was to let him know where I was. I used Tom's trick about seeing Nathan's younger brother, though I wasn't at all sure if he'd remember what his younger brother is called. Just imagine it all being so simple...' He had added it to the bottom of his letter, almost casually.

By the way, darling—don't forget that because of my exalted position in the Medical Corps, I can keep tabs on you. So see that you behave yourself!

'It was his way of telling me he knows where General Hospital Sixteen is! What news from Mrs Shaw?'

'They all seem in the best of spirits. The Pendenys cook swopped her a pound of sugar for a quarter of tea!'

'Wonder how the Place comes to have sugar to spare?' Julia grinned.

'I bet Mrs Clementina had sacks and sacks of it put by when she thought there'd be a war.' Mrs Clementina was like that. 'Anyway, Cook made two sponge cakes with it, so everybody was happy.'

'And Tom?'

'He loves me. How is her ladyship?'

'Mother's fine. Remember McIver—the blind soldier at Denniston? We'll both be pleased to know, she says, that he's got back his sight in one eye. Wonder how the old convalescent ward is doing? We've come a long way since then, haven't we?'

They had, Alice agreed. 'When your contract is up, will you stay out here, Julia?'

'I think so—as long as Andrew is in France. We'll be due leave, then. I wonder if we can spend it here.'

'Might be a bit risky, going to Reims,' Alice cautioned. 'We don't know what it's like there. It could be as badly knocked about as Albert. You might even have to get permission to go there.'

'I realise that. All the same, it's worth thinking about.'

A sudden evening breeze moved the window curtains, bringing with it the scent of blossom. 'Isn't it lovely and cool—and listen!'

Alice raised her head. 'Can't hear anything.'

'Exactly! That's just it—they've stopped!'

'No guns.' Suddenly, after firing so constant it had become a part of the background, the guns of neither side could be heard. 'Do you think they've stopped fighting?'

'I don't know, but oh, will you listen to that lovely silence...'

As she said, there were days you would never forget.

There were days, Clementina Sutton frowned, when she had had enough, especially of Elliot who was in trouble again—though for the very last time, did he but know it!

This journey to London was totally unnecessary. She had not planned another visit to the house in Cheyne Walk until the decorators were finished and all the carpets laid. Now she must scurry down there to sort out his most recent misdemeanour, before his father heard of it!

Sometimes, she shuddered, she feared for her eldest son. His schooling had been of the most expensive; his grand tour the most prolonged. Before this irritating war began, she lamented, gazing out at telegraph poles that slid past the window, there had been young girls aplenty, all of them more than eager to exchange maidenhood for motherhood. But now they were getting ideas that could lead to nothing but the undermining of our very society! Married women going out to work was bad enough, but unmarried ladies walking out unchaperoned with skirts above their ankles took some getting used to!

And now—and she wouldn't have believed this had she not seen it with her own eyes—young ladies smoking *in public,* and attending tea dances without an escort; partnering young men to whom they hadn't been introduced!

It was on this subject she intended to speak to Elliot most earnestly. Young women on the loose in London could lead to nothing but trouble; and as for young, lonely wives with husbands at the Front—well, it didn't bear thinking about.

It was the fault of the war, of course. Men taken from their homes, and hastily married women left alone to pick up the pieces of their strange new lives as best they could, created an explosive situation from which nothing but trouble could come—*had* come.

She had always thought, Clementina reflected, that she had managed the matter of Elliot's army service rather well; had secured him a posting to the War Office where, had he been in possession of one iota of the sense he'd been born with, he could have sat out the war and returned to his family unscathed. What was more, she had worked extremely hard to convince her immediate social circle that her eldest son was employed on a project so secret that he simply couldn't be spared for active service in France.

She sighed deeply. Elliot's secret project, it seemed, was the seducing of a young wife whose husband was fighting in France! Aunt Sutton had written in high indignation to tell her so; said the whole of London was talking about it, and that it was only a matter of time before the cuckolded husband received an unsigned letter and up the balloon would go!

Spiteful old maid! Clementina couldn't think why Edward liked her so. Mad as a hatter, of course.

Yet, for all that, Clementina could cheerfully clatter her son's ears for his stupidity, though to stop his allowance would bring him to repentance far more quickly! And that was not all! There was the matter of an unpaid mess bill and a gambling debt to a fellow officer not honoured. Oh, Mary Anne Pendennis, you have much to answer for!

The train began to slow at the approaches to Grantham, and she hoped no one would invade the privacy of the empty compartment she occupied. People these days thought nothing of engaging one in conversation, and it simply did not do—even if they *had* purchased a first-class ticket.

Beatrice, the woman's name was. The daughter of a baronet, married to the second son of a peer, she should have known better than to engage in an affair with an unmarried man, no matter how attractive she found him. She'd set her cap at Elliot, of course. Good looks, of a good family and money—or so he gave the impression—to burn. *Her* money, Clementina thought savagely.

Why couldn't Elliot have been more like his younger brother; been blessed with his sunny nature, his fairness of looks? Why had her firstborn been a direct throwback to the Cornish washerwoman, and why, in spite of all the heartache he caused her, did she love him so much?

Was it because he and she were so alike; would never be totally accepted by the society into which her father's money had bought her? Was Elliot tilting at windmills, just to show he didn't care? And who were they, anyway, those blue-blooded aristocrats whose lineage went back to the Plantagenets and who hadn't a sixpenny-piece to scratch their backsides with?

She understood Elliot's rebellious ways —she really did—and most times she would have been prepared to deal kindly with him. But he was due for a reckoning-up, a jerking in of the reins; after which he usually behaved himself for a six-month at least.

If only her Elliot were married: women would leave him alone then...

Clementina hoped her bed would be made up and aired when she arrived. She kept no servants at the London house, only an elderly woman who, grateful for a roof over her head and a fire to sit beside, kept watch over the property in her absence for three shillings and sixpence a week and a daily pint of milk. And a hamperful of cast-offs sent down by carrier, Clementina added. The caretaker did well out of that hamper, she shouldn't wonder, selling off most of it to better-off friends and making a nice little sum with which to buy the gin Clementina supposed she drank. Drink was the downfall of the working classes. It had made them what they were and would ever remain. Mary Anne Pendennis had signed the pledge the moment she'd been able to print her name, and never a drop of liquor had passed her lips; that at least Clementina gave her credit for.

She knew Elliot was in the house. The minute she opened the door the stink of his Turkish cigarettes met her. Why couldn't he smoke cigars? At least they smelled of good breeding. Turkish tobacco made Clementina think of brothels, though for the life of her she couldn't think why.

'*Elliot!*' She gave him the full force of her displeasure. He'd be lolling in the study—the only habitable room in the house—and if he thought he was getting away with this latest carry-on, she hoped the tone of her summons would warn him otherwise.

'Mama, dear! How lovely to see you.'

Oh, but he was handsome in his uniform. She wavered just a little, then snapped, 'And what kind of mess have you got yourself into this time?'

'Mess, Mama? Let me take your coat?'

'*Mess!* With the Beatrice woman. Your Aunt Sutton knows about it, and half of London too. Have you got her into trouble?'

It was the worst, most frequent nightmare of all. Elliot, in Court, cited as co-respondent, and a greasy little man reading intimate details from a tattered notebook. And always in those nightmares, Helen sat beside the divorce judge, smiling sweetly, eating sugared rose petals.

'Trouble?' Elliot's deep brown eyes opened wide, their expression one of hurt. 'I don't know what you mean.'

'Trouble, son. Let me explain. It comes of taking liberties with another man's wife. Is she pregnant?'

'Beatrice is a lady, Mama!'

'Is she, now? So damned ladylike that the minute her husband's back is turned she's in your bed!'

301

'Please!' He had been about to remark upon her crudeness, but thought better of it lest she flew into a rage and threw him out without so much as a penny-piece. 'You've got it wrong, Mama.'

'All right, then! You were in *her* bed.'

Unspeaking, Elliot sized up the situation. His mother's face was chalk-white, her eyes small slits of anger. When she was really angry, the only solution was to throw himself upon her mercy—grovel, if he had to. Because if he didn't settle his mess bill at once he'd be in trouble enough; to renege on a gambling debt was even worse.

Thus far, he'd been able to keep out of the way of Authority at the War Office; had managed to look busy at all times—even to walking the corridors, frowning studiously, with a large brown envelope inscribed OHMS SECRET beneath his arm.

Trouble—even a whiff of it—and Authority could well seek to discover who this officer was and what he did with his time. He could be off to France so fast his feet wouldn't touch the ground!

'I thought you were an officer and a gentleman, Elliot,' Clementina pressed. 'And gentlemen don't play cards with money they haven't got!'

'I'm sorry. I got carried away. I promise I won't let it happen again.'

'*Promise?* Your promises aren't worth the breath you make them with! Now it's me, your mother, you're dealing with; *me,* who'll get you out of trouble, same as always. So stop your play-acting and tell me how much it is you want this time?'

'My mess bill is fifty pounds; I owe Billy Smythe two hundred...'

'Now say that again,' she challenged.

'We-e-ll—it's thirty-nine pounds fifteen shillings to the mess steward, and a hundred and fifty to Smythe. And neither will take a cheque. I've already tried.'

'And the woman?'

'I think just a few pounds to Molly will ensure that on any date anyone cares to mention, I was here, all night, *alone.*'

'And who the hell is Molly?'

'The scrubbing-woman you keep in the basement, Mama.'

'The caretaker, don't you mean?'

'Caretaker, then. Though why you don't have staff here, I don't know. That woman's an embarrassment sometimes, answering the door.'

'That woman comes cheap! And when staff is needed here I bring them down from Pendenys, you know that.' It was more economical to bring down a cook and two or three maids third class by railway than to keep servants here, eating

303

their heads off, their followers having the run of the place the moment she returned to Pendenys Place. 'I'll arrange for you to have a couple of hundred, though as to the caretaker, you'll have to bribe her out of your own pocket if it comes to the worst. *That* kind of trouble you get yourself out of from now on. When you find yourself a suitable wife—or let me find one for you, Elliot—then you'll realise I can be more than generous. But I will *not* pay for your whores, and that is my last word! And you might as well tell me the worst. How far has this scandal gone? Is your Aunt Sutton right? *Are* people talking?'

'Not any longer. I've finished with Beatrice—told her so a while back. I don't think she'll make trouble, but if she does, it's my word against hers.'

'Were you indiscreet, Elliot? Did anyone see you in public?'

'Not that I know of. Don't know why Aunt says people are talking—we mostly came here...'

'You did *that!* In *my* bed!'

'Of course not, Mama dear. I wouldn't be so foolish. Sufficient to say that I saw to it Molly kept her mouth shut.'

'Dear, sweet heaven—where will it all end? When are you going to learn sense? You'll drive me to my grave, and that's a fact? Why can't you see how lucky you are, safe in London for the duration? Why must you take such delight in rocking the boat?'

'I don't know,' he whispered contritely, because she was right. He'd gone too far with Beatrice, and if her husband were to hear about it and kick up a fuss, he'd be in the trenches without so much as a by-your-leave.

'Please, son, try to behave yourself. Try to keep out of trouble—be more like Nathan...'

'I will. I promise. I truly do.'

'Good,' she said wearily. 'And now, since there's nothing to eat in the house, I suppose we'd better telephone for a taxi and see if we can find somewhere with food to serve.'

'Better than that—I'll drive you! My motor is round the back. I keep it here, didn't you know?' Poor Mama. She really looked tired. Showing her age, these days. Not a patch on Aunt Helen when it came to looks. 'Now off you go and put on something nice and I'll take you to the best little restaurant in London.'

'That will be nice,' she smiled briefly, knowing who would be picking up the bill. 'Very nice indeed...'

And oh, *why* did she feel like bursting into tears?

14

Their new ward had smelled of paint, unseasoned timber, and never-before-used cotton bed-covers. Within two hours of moving in, it smelled crisply of carbolic.

'Almost like Denniston House,' Alice sniffed.

'Only tonight, when we go off duty, we'll walk the field path back to quarters instead of pedalling home.'

Home to Rowangarth; to that far-away, creaking old house with the remembered smell of beeswax polish and precious old furniture and the roses that climbed its summer walls.

'They'll be busy getting in the hay,' Alice sighed, though who was left there to scythe it she couldn't for the life of her think.

'Forty-four,' Julia murmured, not to be tempted into nostalgia. 'Everything comes in forty-fours...'

Beds, bed-mackintoshes, feeding cups; forty-four trays, bowls, cups, saucers, plates, spoons; and every one to be accounted for before their reliefs took over at duty's end.

'The patients will be moving in to-morrow.' Alice still thrilled to the title of 'nurse', though she and Julia would never be proper nurses like Sister and Ruth Love. They should not even, yet, dress a wound, though no one seemed to complain when there were too many wounded and too few to nurse them.

'I would like everything to be counted, cleaned and in place by the time we go on duty,' said Sister, unable to disguise her satisfaction. 'Tomorrow, all the beds will be filled and we'll begin a week of day duties.' And after that, she told them, a week of night work, though when and how they would get a rest-day she would better know when she had consulted with her opposite number—a sister she had yet to meet. 'It will be good, though, to get into a routine again.'

The near chaos at the chateau had appalled her orderly mind. From now on, with her own ward, things, she thought, grimly satisfied, would be vastly different. Now it was no longer Hut Twenty-four, but Sister Carbrooke's ward.

'And since everything seems in good order, I think that when you, MacMalcolm, and you, Hawthorn, have cleaned the windows, you can take what remains of the afternoon off. I'm sure you have things to catch up on in quarters.'

Hawthorn, she supposed, would spend her hour cleaning and pressing her uniform; MacMalcolm would spend it writing to her husband and Love would—

Sister frowned, unsure. Staff Nurse Love's eyes were still troubled, as if returning to France had awakened memories instead of laying them to rest.

'You, Staff Nurse, will check the contents of the poisons cupboard with me, if you please.'

It would be a long time—if ever—before Ruth Love accepted the death of her husband. She would have to be watched most carefully, Sister decided; for her own good, as well as that of the patients.

Such a horrible war, and the end of it nowhere in sight! How had it been allowed to happen? It made her glad she had been born a woman. Men were so *utterly* stupid!

Sister Carbrooke's ward was not to become a haven of well-ordered tranquillity. Before many hours had run, they were all to realise it was to be little more than an extension of the chateau dressing-station; a staging-post, Sister snorted, between the trenches and a hospital ship to England. Since the Somme fighting began, ten thousand wounded had been disembarked at Southampton alone, a nursing colleague had written, and heaven only knew how many more at other ports. Those who came to Hut Twenty-four had first to be divested of mud-caked uniforms and made as comfortable as possible. Thereafter, medical officers called briefly to assess the order of priority in which they were shipped to England. It made a mockery, Sister mourned, of the profession of nursing. It was, said Julia and Alice, Denniston House stableyard all over again, without the bitter cold.

Ruth Love said little, scanning each khaki uniform for the wings of a flyer; feeling guilt-ridden relief when her fears proved unfounded and she was not to be reminded of another death in another ward in another life, it seemed.

Night duties followed day duties. The distant guns began their barrage again. Hopes of a rest-day faded; it became almost unpatriotic even to think of one. In the midst of such killing, merely to be alive was something to be wondered at.

That night, they trod the well-worn path from huts to quarters without speaking. It was Julia who broke the weary silence.

'Penny for them?'

'I was thinking about home—about buttercups and Brattocks Wood and—' Alice stopped, her voice trembling.

'And Tom,' Julia whispered. 'With me, it's usually Holdenby Pike I think of when things get bad; the feeling that everything up there is clean and untouched and away from the taint of war. And Andrew with me, of course...'

'It's far worse for the men,' Alice shrugged.

'I know. It's the only thing that helps me to carry on.' That, and the chance that, around the next corner, she might see him...

'It would seem,' said Helen Sutton, 'that Julia is well and happy, though how she manages to be so amazes me.'

The Government had been unable to keep back the news of the slaughter around the River Somme. The country was stunned by it. There had even been talk about the shortage of Post Office telegraph boys, so many telegrams of death and wounding were there to deliver.

It would be better now, though. It *must* be better. Lord Kitchener had been replaced as War Minister by Mr Lloyd-George, that forthright Celt who cared little for the conventions of polite society. He thundered instead for the rights of the men at the Front, and mocked the stupidity of some in high command who thought that wars were still fought by gentlemen in pretty uniforms and white gloves.

'Well, my dear Helen, between the new man at the War Office and your precious tanks in action at last, we might soon see an end to the wretched business in France,' Judge Mounteagle said. He had called to collect a small bag of Sutton Premier tea. 'Six of these tanks at the Front, so the papers say. Let's hope they frighten the trousers off the Kaiser!'

Not that they would, he reasoned, but Helen, for some peculiar reason, set great store by their development—stupid, new-fangled machines that they were. Clumsy, too. Still, if they gave the dear lady comfort with all her children at war—and one of them never to return from it—then who was he to tell her they were a flash in the pan and would never catch on! And things had come to a terrible pass when a man had reason to be grateful he was old. Calling all men to the Colours from nineteen to fifty-five now!

'Most grateful for this tea, m'dear,' he smiled. 'Not been able to buy so much as a spoonful lately.'

'We are lucky.' Helen believed in sharing her luck. 'So far, all our tea-chests have reached us safely.' And lucky, too, that by this morning's early delivery there had been letters from Julia, Giles and Nathan. She was proud of her family, but how desperately she wanted them home! 'And do you know, I have a feeling inside me—call it woman's intuition, if you wish—that before next year is all that old, we shall see an end to the war. I truly believe it.'

'Do you realise, Alice, that in just three hours it will be 1917?'

'It's been a funny old twelve-month,' Alice acknowledged.

'A bad one,' Julia shrugged. 'All right, so the fighting seems all but over around the Somme, but it has started up again at Verdun.'

Verdun, where Andrew was stationed, and Tom, too, for all Alice could tell. All she was sure of was that his regiment had left Albert—*I won't be seeing Mr Nathan's brother for a while* had been Tom's first intimation. Then there had been almost two worrying weeks without hearing from him, after which came a letter bearing the mark of a different Censor. *I'm still with Geordie, though our billet is little better than a cowshed, now...*

'That's it,' Alice said flatly when the relief of hearing from him had subsided. 'I'm sure of it. Tom *has* been moved.'

'Any idea where?' Julia looked at the watch on her wrist, impatient for the New Year, new hope.

'Ypres or Verdun,' Alice sighed, 'and

both of them further away.' She had rounded many corners hoping to see him, but Tom had never been there, even though he'd been so near to Celverte. Now there seemed less chance than ever that they would meet, especially since single men were never given leave—nor married ones, she sighed, glancing across the small kitchen to where Julia was making tea for last rounds.

Last rounds? Not tonight. Hardly any of the patients would sleep, for wasn't the New Year just hours away, and weren't all of them Blighty-bound just as soon as maybe? And by the time their wounds were healed and their blue uniforms exchanged for khaki ones once more, the war would be over!

'They aren't going to settle down,' Ruth said. 'Not until after midnight, anyway. Might as well accept it. Take the mugs round, Julia, and warn them that any New Year rowdiness will be punished by ice-cold bedpans at dawn—only don't let Sister hear you!'

Ruth Love was improving. Some of the tenseness had left her—she had even shown them a photograph of a young nurse and a handsome flyer, taken on their wedding day. Then the shutters had gone down again; she had spoken his name just once since then.

'Today is—would have been—Jamie's birthday,' she said briefly.

Not a lot, Julia thought, but a beginning. Sufficient that she had told them; been prepared to share her grief. Time was a great healer, said people who knew no better. Time would never heal her own wounds should Andrew be killed, Julia thought fiercely. Nothing would.

'Hey!' Alice snapped her fingers. 'You were miles away! Tell me?'

'Forget it!' Julia's voice was sharp. 'This war *is* going to be over soon, isn't it?'

'It is,' Alice said firmly. 'Didn't we agree not half an hour ago that it would be? So how about us having a drink before we see to the ward? There won't be a lot of time afterwards. I'll take a cup to Sister.'

The ward—Hut Twenty-four—had been decorated for Christmas with flags and trails of greenery, gathered from the lanes outside Celverte. It had been the best Christmas some of the wounded had known for three years. Now they were the lucky ones, awaiting a berth on a hospital ship and Blighty; bloody lovely Blighty! Their pain was as nothing. They were alive, would remain alive until summer at least, when it would all be over! Soon they would cheer in another year, and who amongst them cared if the dragon lady called Sister Carbolic frowned!

Sister Carbrooke said yes, of course she would take the flyer. She always tried to keep one bed empty for extreme emergencies.

Prognosis nil? she frowned at the telephone. Very well. He would die in a haze of morphine and receive just the same care as—

'Nurse Love—there's a patient arriving. Top bed,' she said tersely. 'Will you special him, please?'

The top bed was the only one to have curtains around it; curtains to hide the ceremonial of dying from the rest of the ward who, but for a whim of Fate's choosing finger, could each have lain there.

'Yes, Sister.' Ruth Love pulled back the bed-cover and lit the bedside lamp, drawing the curtains quietly. She was no stranger to death. After the night Jamie died, nothing could pierce the shield she had drawn around her emotions.

The stretcher-bearers carried him in. On his forehead was the purple mark of his suffering; on the lapel pinned to his collar were the details of his condition and drugs injected. His name was Hans-Rudolf Kliene, his rank *Leutnant*.

'No! Sister, I will not...' she choked. 'I will *not* nurse him!' Her eyes were fear-filled, her face paper-white. The young

315

man who lay dying was her enemy—and a flyer! He could even be the one who, not so very long ago, had swooped in low over Jamie's aerodrome and—

'Will *not?*' Sister's voice was low with anger. 'Please step outside the ward, Staff Nurse. And close the door behind you. *Quietly...*'

Any other woman would have recognised the threat in that voice; any woman other than Ruth Love who was being ordered to live again her own husband's death.

'Sister—I beg you. It isn't fair—it isn't right to ask it...'

'What is right or fair in war, Nurse? What was right or fair about *her* death?' She pointed to the photograph of a nurse called Edith Cavell that hung in the corridor. 'You and I are bound by the ethics of our profession to nurse the sick and the wounded, no matter who they be. We tend them regardless of creed or colour because they need our skills. The boy in there is dying and in his rare moments of lucidity he will know it. He needs the comfort of a handclasp. The young fear death. Help him?'

'Nurse MacMalcolm—can't she special him?' Her voice shook with emotion. 'Please, Sister...?'

'Nurse MacMalcolm can and would, but I am asking you, Ruth. You may refuse and I shall try to understand. But if you do, you will have betrayed not only your profession, but your husband too. It is your choice. Yes or no—quickly! A man is dying!'

'I'm sorry.' Ruth Love lifted her chin. 'Forgive me? I'll go to him...'

Hans-Rudolf Kliene had white-blond hair and, had his eyelids not been closed, she knew his eyes, too, would have been the same brilliant blue as Jamie's. He lay, moaning softly, wanting to die yet fearing it, resenting it.

Ruth moved the chair nearer and sat down. He was so young. Jamie had been young, hadn't wanted to go to war. University first, then a house in the country and the life of a veterinary surgeon—only there hadn't been time.

'Mutter...' The eyelids flickered, and were still again.

Only a boy. He wanted his mother. Tears scalded her eyes and she dashed them angrily away. She was a nurse; she could not weep. God! It was all so unfair! She bent closer, her lips close to his ear.

'Ja, Hans?' she said gently.

Taking his hand she held it tightly, then whispering her lips over his cheek she laid them to his closed eyelids. His lips moved in a small smile; his hand relaxed inside hers. She sat quietly for a moment, the hand inside hers warm and fragile and afraid. Her fingers searched his wrist for a pulse beat. His dying had been gentle in the end.

'*Jamie!*' Her cry was harsh with pain. She laid the limp hand to her cheek. She had screamed out her anger at the death of her husband, then locked her grief inside her, so terrible had it been to bear. Now, at the dying of his enemy, this boy so like Jamie, she allowed herself the tears she had been unwilling and unable to shed; that had lain so long in her heart in an ache of bitterness.

'It's all right, Nurse.' Sister reached out, gathering her close, holding her tightly. 'Let it come. Weep for him, for them both...'

A long time afterwards, when the joy of a New Year had subsided and Hut Twenty-four was quiet again, Ruth Love stripped the top bed, folded the blankets and drew back the curtains.

She was calm, her eyes dry of tears now. Sister, who missed nothing, saw with sad satisfaction that she was once again wearing her wedding ring.

There was a covering of snow at Holdenby, that New Year's Eve, changing Rowangarth into a picture-postcard house, disguising its shabby comfort with a sparkle of white.

Cook always kept the New Year watch. You had to say goodbye to the twelve-month gone, to be thankful for its blessings, vow to learn from its mistakes. Tonight, as she always did, her ladyship would wait with the sherry decanter and a sup of whisky in an old crystal glass and a man—it was to be Reuben again tonight—would knock loudly on the front door at the first stroke of midnight from the church clock.

'Come in, and welcome.' Agnes Clitherow answered the knocking before the clock had finished its striking.

'I'm come to bring in the New Year,' Reuben said formally, wiping his boots carefully, 'and to wish health and content to all. And the Almighty's blessing on absent ones,' he added, glad the speechifying was over.

'Thank you most warmly, Reuben.' Helen offered her hand. She never called him Pickering, which would have been too demeaning, nor *Mr* Pickering, which wouldn't have suited his position, but Reuben—which was friendly between her and him; special, too.

'Thank you kindly, milady.' Reuben accepted the glass, offering a piece of coal, a salt cellar full to the brim and a crust of bread in return. Then he downed the whisky at a gulp, savouring the bite of it and the warmth, tucking the cigar the housekeeper gave him into his pocket.

'Bid you goodnight, then...' he never outstayed his welcome. On the doorstep he replaced his best tweed hat, brought his forefinger respectfully to its brim, then walked briskly down the steps.

'A Happy New Year, Miss Clitherow.' Helen smiled.

'Thank you—and to you, milady.' She bobbed a curtsey. She always curtseyed at certain times of the year, just to keep things straight. 'Are we to go below stairs? I know Cook would appreciate it.'

'Of course.' Nothing must change. Once, in the good days, there had been a party for servants; now they were almost all gone to war and a party would have seemed out of place, even had there been food. 'We must have a glass of sherry.' New Years at Rowangarth were always made welcome.

'May we come in,' Helen peeped round the kitchen door, 'and share your fire?'

'You may, milady, and welcome,' Cook beamed, rising—as did Tilda and Jinny—to her feet.

Agnes Clitherow poured sherry, passing it round. Helen settled herself comfortably in one of the rockers and all sat down again.

'Do you suppose,' Helen pondered, 'that Mr Lloyd-George will make a difference to things; now that he's Prime Minister?'

She shouldn't talk about the war, she knew, but everyone did, if only to comfort each other.

'Oh yes, indeed, milady.' Agnes Clitherow nodded, sipping daintily from her glass.

'And it's a known fact,' beamed Mrs Shaw, 'them Germans is hungrier than we are. They had a poor harvest an' all, this summer.'

'Bread ninepence a loaf.' Jinny Dobb gazed mournfully into her glass. 'How's a soldier's wife with bairns to feed to afford that kind of money, milady?'

'They're hungrier in Germany,' Cook insisted. 'Be thankful for small mercies, Jin. We have tea here, and potatoes; and there's always rabbits. Mr Pickering sees that every household has its fair share!' The sherry was going to her head. It always did, but she didn't care. 'Though it's got to be said it's time for official rationing—fair shares of food at fair prices!'

'I think Mr Lloyd-George will see to that,' murmured Agnes Clitherow. The old guard had done nothing for the war; perhaps the hot-blooded Welshman with the gift of words would do better.

'I worry about Russia,' Helen frowned.

'The Czarina—so foolishly influenced. Her poor son, though—she has so much to worry her...'

'That Rasputin,' said Jin, 'is a nasty, evil old man.' Jin could recognise evil; could smell it almost. 'Needs locking up in prison,'—or wherever it was they put mad, meddlesome monks. 'You can't blame the Russian peasants for getting fed up about it.'

'No. But it couldn't happen here.' The housekeeper shot a warning glance across the room. The British working man knew his place. Always would. That was why Britain was great.

'Happen not.' Jin drained her glass and gazed meaningfully at the decanter. The housekeeper replaced the stopper firmly.

'I think,' said Tilda, 'we should drink to our soldiers and nurses, milady, and that next year they'll all be back home.'

Tilda disliked the war. Not for her the high wages of factory work. She hid from it happily at Rowangarth, in spite of the extra tasks thrust upon her.

'Most happily.' Helen raised her glass. 'To my son and daughter and Hawthorn and the doctor. And to my nephews and Will and Davie and Dwerryhouse. May God keep them safely—and grant us all a Happy New Year.'

They all said Amen to that. There had

been one taken already from Rowangarth; they wanted no more. And as for the Almighty taking a hand in things, Jin Dobb thought darkly, it was in the tea-leaves that Mr Lloyd-George, now that he was Prime Minister instead of that Mr Asquith, would make a great difference to the war.

But it was in the stars, she was forced to admit, the war hadn't anywhere near run its course. There were deaths and woundings aplenty yet to come. And terrible rumblings from a far-away country.

Nowhere near over, this war wasn't. Jin *knew*...

15

1917

Spring came suddenly to Rowangarth. All at once, the sharpness left the air, the weeping willows on the edge of the wild garden grew green, and the avenue of linden trees began to burst bud.

In Brattocks Wood, celandines glowed like small yellow stars, and violets peeped from beneath their leaves. In and out of the tallest trees in the wood, rooks carried twigs, repairing nests. The worst of winter was over, Reuben noted with satisfaction. Now, the third spring of the war was here, bringing with it a gentleness to compensate for the misery of a cold, hungry winter. It made him hopeful that this year would see an end to the fighting; that Himself-up-there had finally decided who would win this war. Us, Reuben thought, without a doubt!

Helen Sutton stood at her wide-open bedroom window. On a day such as this, anyone could be forgiven for feeling happy. Half-way into March; skies a pale, clear blue and the air so heavy with the scent of green things growing that just to breathe it in made her dizzy. It would be better, too, at the Front; no mud-filled trenches or soldiers keeping watch with frozen fingers.

This morning there was such joy in her heart she knew beyond doubt that all those she loved were safe. This was not a telegram day. Soon, Miss Clitherow would bring her morning tea—Helen never ate breakfast now; her personal contribution to the war effort—and she would be wearing the expression that meant she was bringing letters from France, Helen was sure of it.

She shrugged into her wrap, quickly pinned up her hair, smiling at Helen-in-the-mirror, listening to the measured tread along the passage, waiting for the creak of the floorboard half-way along it.

'Come in, please,' she called. 'Good morning, Miss Clitherow!'

'Milady.' The housekeeper nodded her head. 'There are no letters—well, not from France and—' She hesitated, offering the folded newspaper. 'I think you should see this—well, sooner than later...'

She busied herself pouring tea, eyes downcast. Helen read the headlines. They were half an inch high and screamed: CZAR NICHOLAS ABDICATES.

'Oh, dear heaven!' She shook open the paper, ignoring the offered teacup. 'Please don't go, Miss Clitherow.' News such as this she did not wish to read alone. 'You've seen it?'

'Not read it, milady, but Cook has. She could hardly tell it, she was so upset...'

'Then it would seem the Czar of Russia has given up his throne—or been dismissed from it. So *awful*...'

The King's cousin, forced into ignominy! There had been rumours, of course; undercurrents of discontent in Moscow and St Petersburg, with the Mensheviks and the Bolsheviks at each other's throats for the support of the peasants. *Peasant.* A word long gone in these islands. Here, a peasant was a part of history.

'It couldn't happen here, Miss Clitherow?' Helen's hands shook so much that the paper made little crackling noises.

'Absolutely not, milady. Here, we are a democracy,' said the housekeeper with conviction. 'Now, drink your tea, then I'll have Tilda run your bath. The newspapers always make things sound ten times worse.'

'But what of the Russian troops holding the Eastern front? The Czar was their commander-in-chief.' Who would command them now?

'They'll have it all worked out, be sure of that,' Agnes Clitherow soothed. 'We won't be losing an ally. It's the fault, though, of that monk Rasputin,' she offered in a rare show of opinion. 'Men in holy orders shouldn't meddle in matters of state! He asked to be killed.

'And had you thought, milady, that the Czar has many loyal supporters? The Russian aristocracy will back him, and the Cossacks to a man would die for him. Don't worry. He'll soon be Czar again.'

'Yes. Yes, of course.' Helen picked up her cup, but the tea in it had gone cold and tasted bitter on her tongue. Strange, she pondered, gazing out of the window, that the sun continued to shine and the birds to sing.

But the sun cared nothing for wars or Czars, she shivered, and oh, how lucky those birds who could not read.

'I've said it all along,' muttered Jinny Dobb, 'and there's none present as can contradict me; that Czar of Russia should have put his foot down over his wife and that Rasputin, the mucky old devil. Spiritual adviser, indeed...'

'What do you mean?' Cook demanded, sliding her eyes in the direction of Tilda whose ears she considered too innocent for Jin's implications.

'She means,' offered Tilda blithely, 'that he's had carnal knowledge—'

'*Tilda!* You're talking about a Czarina —an Empress!' Cook's cheeks flamed red. 'And where did you hear such a word? *Carnal,* indeed! You don't even know what it means!'

'I heard it plenty when they murdered that Rasputin at New Year. Served him right, folk said. Shouldn't interfere in politics, some said; others said he shouldn't have interfered with the—'

'*That will do!*'

'The lass is right,' defended Jin. 'Was only what folk were saying at the time. And now they'll be thinking it's all going to blow over in Russia; that we'll send troops to help put the Czar back in power. But why should we? Why should one drop of British blood be spilled, just to save a man who treats his subjects like they was dirt? An' I'll tell you something else, Cook. There's worse to come from that quarter of the globe. Jin knows...'

'I said that would do, and I meant *do!*' Cook banged the flat of her hand on the table-top. An Emperor having to abdicate was bad enough, without Jin Dobb's prophecies to make it worse. Trouble was, when Jin went into one of her utterances, she was rarely wrong.

'All right,' Jin grumbled. 'I'll shut me mouth. Pity you don't want to hear the good news...'

'Good news!' Tilda gasped. 'Is the war going to end?'

'Nay, lass. Not this twelve-month. We shall lose an ally, too: they'll be little help to us now, them Russian soldiers. But we'll gain another friend, and before so very much longer, an' all. One so powerful as will make that Kaiser wish he'd never started the dratted war!'

'Who, then?' Cook asked reluctantly.

But Jinny Dobb, having had the last word, kept her mouth tightly closed on the subject. 'I'll see to the vegetables and peel the potatoes,' she said stubbornly, and not all Tilda's soft-soaping nor Cook's cajoling could draw forth another word.

Julia hurried to Matron's room, a summons

which had her worried. Usually, a reprimand from the matron of General Hospital Sixteen was first passed to a sister who passed it to a staff nurse to deliver. Interviews with Matron were so rare—unless you were a sister, of course—that a nurse so summoned shook with trepidation.

'What have you done?' Alice demanded

'Nothing.' Julia swallowed hard. 'Nothing, truly.'

'Said, then? There's got to be *something...*'

Each skirted round what she really thought—that it was news of such seriousness that only Matron could give it.

'I shall never get through the night,' Julia choked. 'I shall worry and worry...'

'Have you asked Sister?'

'Of course I have! All I could get out of her was that Matron said that when MacMalcolm came off night duty she would like to see her—see *me!*'

'There you are, then! If it were anything —well, *awful*—she'd be bound to tell you at once. So stop your worrying.'

Julia said she would, but it was a white and shaking nurse who tapped timidly on the door marked 'J Campbell, Matron'.

'Yes? Who is it then?'

'It's MacMalcolm, Matron. You wish to see me?' Her voice sounded hoarse; she cleared her throat noisily.

'Ah, yes. Sit down, please.'

Julia remained standing. to be invited to sit in Matron's presence meant only bad news to follow. And even had she wanted to, her feet refused to move one step towards the chair.

'To get to the point, Nurse, I have a message from your husband.'

'From?' Not *about!* She sat down heavily, grasping the chair seat.

'From Major MacMalcolm. And I have to say at once that I strongly disapprove of army telephone lines being taken up for personal messages,' she said in a rounded Scottish accent. 'However, on this occasion...' She paused to smile—to *smile*—which gave Julia time enough to gasp, 'Major? He's a captain, though...'

'Then he's been promoted, girl! On this occasion, and because we are all of us of the same professional calling, I agreed to tell you that he'll be in Paris on army business on Friday next—the 6th. Can you meet him, he asks, at the Gare du Nord between one and two p.m—in the vicinity of the main entrance? He could not be more specific, timewise, than that.'

'Meet him! Oh please, Matron *please,* let me go?' Julia was on her feet again, her heart thumping, her cheeks flushing hotly. 'Friday I'll be sleeping, anyway, and

330

I haven't had a rest-day for six weeks. We haven't seen each other since we—'

'Aye. Since you were married, he told me.'

'More than two years ago.'

'This meeting will only be in passing, as it were. You'll not be getting any time off, Nurse...'

'I can go? You'll give me permission to travel, ma'am?'

'On this occasion—yes. But do *not* make a habit of it. I can't have my nurses gallivanting off when they should be sleeping after night duty. Be that as it may, there will be an ambulance convoy leaving on that morning for Calais. You may have a ride as far as Amiens with them; from there you can catch a train to Paris. At seven a.m, that will be...'

'But I don't come off duty until eight!'

'I am well aware of that, Nurse. However, Sister Carbrooke agreed that you can leave the ward at six-thirty.'

'She *knew?* She knew all along and she never said—never breathed a word!' Tears of utter happiness filled Julia's eyes and she dashed them impatiently away. 'Thank you, ma'am, so very much. And is that all? Can I go now, if you please...?'

'Away with you! And don't shout it all over the place or they'll all be wanting permission to meet their men in Paris!'

came the dour parting shot.

Friday April 6th Spring in Paris. The loveliest time of the whole year. A time for lovers!

Julia picked up her skirts and ran; down the field path, past the farm buildings, up the wooden stairs.

'Alice! Where on earth—' She swished back the green dividing curtains. 'Oh, thank goodness...'

'It's all right then!' Alice saw the shining eyes, the flushed cheeks. 'Now sit yourself down. I won't have you spoil it in the telling—because it's good news, isn't it?'

'*Good?*' Julia collapsed on her bed. 'Andrew! In Paris on Friday! He managed to get Matron on the telephone! Round about midday at the railway station I'm meeting him. I can't believe it!'

'Matron said *yes?*'

'Mm. Oh, she tut-tutted a bit about using army telephones and all that, and at first I thought it was some awful April Fool's joke, but—'

'Oh, *hush*, will you! Just take a deep breath and start at the beginning,' Alice beamed. 'I want every word of it, right from start to finish.'

So, just a little more calmly, Julia told it, punctuating each sentence with little happy laughs.

'And all I know for certain is that he'll

332

be in Paris on army business, that we'll be able to have a few hours together and, oh! I forgot—he's a major now! Major MacMalcolm. Sounds good, doesn't it?'

'Sounds *very* good.'

'And listen to this! Carbolic must have known all along what it was all about! She must've, because she told Matron I could go off duty early. Yet not by a wink or a nod did she let on!'

'Sister's an old poker-face.'

'Yes, and I love her!'

'Letter for you, Alice.' Ruth Love had collected the morning mail. 'Nothing for you, Julia—but you can't expect letters *and* telephone messages,' she grinned.

'You knew! You and Sister both!' Julia gasped. 'And neither of you said a word!'

'Indeed not,' Staff Nurse smiled primly, 'and why should we? It's only the bad news that travels fast. Good news gets even better for the keeping. I'm so glad for you, Julia.' She turned quickly and left, and they heard the gentle closing of her cubicle door.

'Poor Ruth,' Julia sighed. 'I have no right to be so happy, have I? Oh, Lordy—I've just thought. Nothing will go wrong this time, will it? Andrew won't have to cancel?'

'Not this time,' Alice said firmly. 'Now we're going to get some breakfast then we're both going to sleep. And no tossing and turning!'

'I'll try not.'

What a lovely, *lovely* morning this was. Julia raised her eyes to the bright April sky.

Thank you, God. Thank you with all my heart for this happiness...

Paris had never been so beautiful, nor would ever be again—the entrance to the Gare du Nord station, and the tables outside it, that was.

Ten minutes to one o'clock. The local train had crawled, but here she was, with minutes in hand to savour their meeting, to wonder what she would say, what Andrew would say.

If she turned a little to the right from where she waited she could see a clock. She fixed the minute hand with her eyes and began to count. It took her to seventy before it jerked forward. She slowed down her count and began again.

Five minutes to go. She became impatient with counting, and turned her attention to the motor taxis and cabs drawing up at the entrance. It was them she should be watching. And what was Andrew doing in Paris? Was the Medical Corps moving him on to another theatre of war; to India, even? India would be safer, but did they have VAD nurses there and how was she to get to him? Please—not India?

A flower-seller nearby tied up bunches of violets; a poilu strolled past, his girl on his arm; a one-legged man on crutches rattled his tin at her, begging with his eyes for money. Smiling, she gave him a coin.

One o'clock. Very soon, Andrew would come. Any minute now they would wipe out thirty-one months—almost a thousand nights—of being apart. Soon she would see him, touch him, kiss him...

At half-past one she was wondering, panic-stricken, if she had heard Matron aright; if their interview was only in her imagination. Had she got not only the time wrong but the place and day too? Perhaps she had dreamed the whole thing; an illusion born of her desperate need of him.

There were other entrances; two, perhaps three. Should she try them? Could she find them? Would Andrew do the same? Would they spend the entire afternoon shuttling from entrance to entrance, missing each other by seconds?

She should wait here! If she had got it wrong then Andrew would find her. In desperation she turned to the clock as if God Himself pushed round the minute hand. Between one and two, Matron had said. Oh, *please* don't let her have got it wrong.

She pulled her eyes from the clock, searching the station approaches, the cabs outside it, the flower-seller.

Darling, as you love me, come now! Don't let it all come to nothing, again.

Another cab drew up. She hardly dared look. It was the eleventh she had counted. She smoothed down her coat, straightened her cap again, then looked up.

He was there, crossing the street towards her. *He had come!* Andrew: thinner, taller, more good to look at than ever she could remember from her dreamings.

She whispered his name but no sound came. *Over here, my darling! I'm here!*

He sidestepped a porter's trolley, then turned to see her. For just a second he stopped, as if the sight of her was beyond his believing. Then he smiled, quickening his pace.

'Andrew!' She ran to him, arms outstretched, and they were holding each other close. Cheek on cheek. Not speaking nor kissing. Clinging, desperately reluctant to let go; as if each were afraid that, if they did, the other would vanish like a mirage.

'My darling love.' He was the first to find words. 'It *is* you.'

She pulled herself a little way from him. Her eyes filled with tears and his image blurred.

'Sweetheart!' He tilted her chin and his mouth found hers, and it was their first kiss at Aunt Sutton's house all over again only a million times more lovely.

'I'm sorry,' she whispered as tenderly he dried her eyes, her cheeks. 'I wasn't weeping—just happy...'

'Tell me?' he said softly.

'I love you, love you,' she whispered. 'I can't believe any of this.'

'It's happening.' He kissed her again. 'Let me look at you. You're so beautiful —even in that ridiculous hat.'

'I'm in uniform. This is my walking-out hat.' She pulled it off.

'That's better. You haven't had your hair cut?'

'No. I just pin it up tightly.'

'Never have it cut...'

'I won't, I promise. And we're wasting time. It's half a minute since you kissed me...'

'I think,' he said eventually, 'you are even more beautiful. Sometimes, when things were bad, I'd blot it all out and see only your face...'

'Darling—don't?' She began to weep again, then impatiently pulled her hand across her eyes. 'And we *are* wasting time.

I want you to make love to me. Where can we go?'

'Sweetheart, sssh...' He took her face in his hands. 'Not this time. The Reims train leaves in just over an hour and I must be on it. There isn't time, even, to find a room...'

'Andrew, *no!*'

'That idiot at HQ—he went on and on. I wanted to yell at him that my wife was waiting!'

'I want you,' she said, stubbornly.

'Darling, listen. There is so much to tell you, let's sit down.' He nodded towards the pavement tables. 'Please?'

'Sorry, Andrew. Just a few days ago I'd have given all I had in the world just to see you walk past the bottom of the lane, yet now I'm complaining. Forgive me?'

He took her arm, finding an empty table. 'Now will you listen to me, woman?' He reached across the table-top, taking her hands in his. 'First—I am now Major MacMalcolm!'

'Matron told me. I should have said congratulations, darling. I'm proud of you, but they won't move you because of it?'

'They will—they *are.* That's why I came to Paris. Oh, I'll still be in France, but going to a hospital which is soon to open, so I've just been told. There are too many wounded being shipped to blighty who ought to be treated here...'

'I know, darling,' she murmured, pouring coffee.

'Of course you do. Well, I shall get surgical experience now, and at a place called Cotterets. It's well behind the lines. No more forward dressing-stations. I've had almost three years of them; it's someone else's turn now.'

'You'll be safer at a base hospital, won't you?'

'Much safer. I can hardly believe my luck. But the best thing about the move is that, if we all work together—each do extra duties for the other—there shouldn't be anything to stop any of us getting time off. Not leave, of course, but it's going to mean that sometimes I shall be able to get away. How will that suit you, wife?'

'It sounds too good to be true,' she murmured, 'especially since I've been bargaining with God for only an *hour*.'

'Two nights, it should be. We'll have to decide which place will suit us best to meet—can't waste time travelling. And I'll go on the leave rota, too, which might eventually give me seven days. We could take a long leave in Paris, then—make it a second honeymoon...'

'So we'll be together—*really* together—soon?'

'With a bit of deviousness and a spot of luck—yes.'

'Don't! And keep your voice down. The Fates might hear you! But it doesn't matter where we meet, darling. As long as there's a bed—a big, soft, sinful bed—and oh, my goodness! I've only got uniform with me! I'll write home and ask mother to have some clothes sent out.'

'The blue dress with the white lace collar—that's a must.'

'My wedding dress...'

'Aye. The one you were wearing when I asked you to marry me. And be sure she sends a nightgown—the one with the little blue ribbons on it.'

'But *why?*' she teased. 'Whenever I wear it you take it off at once!'

'I know. Pity to crease it,' he grinned, 'and you'll never know the delight it gives me, unfastening the ties at the shoulder!'

'Don't talk like that, Andrew. It makes it even worse. I wanted so much for us to be together. I'm a selfish creature but I have such need of you. And here we are, sitting either side of a table, when all I want to do is hold you and touch you and kiss you...'

'We'll be together soon. I promise we will.' He dipped into his pocket, leaving coins on the table. 'And I've got an idea. We'll go into the station and—hey!

Over there! What's the commotion!' A boy was selling newspapers, and around him men and women snapped them up eagerly. 'Hurry, darling. Let's see what it's about!'

It seemed important; good news, too. Everyone smiling, chattering excitedly in a language he hardly understood.

'Here—your French is better than mine...' He passed her the newspaper. 'Something about the USA, isn't it?'

'Oh, my goodness! They're in the war! The United States has come in—on our side! America declared war at one o'clock. Then they seized eighty-seven German ships in American ports! And Cuba and Panama have declared war on Germany too! I never thought they'd come in with us—after all, it isn't their war. But what a difference it's going to make!'

'Amen to that. But Germany *has* been asking for it—stirring up trouble for the United States in Mexico; breaking off diplomatic relations. And sinking American ships, which were neutral, after all.'

'You could hardly call them neutral, Andrew, when they were bringing food and supplies to British ports.' Her cheeks throbbed; she could hardly believe what she had read.

'I never thought it would happen. Americans of German and Irish origin were so much against them coming into the war. Do you realise what this will mean, Julia?'

'I realise we've lost the Russians and gained the United States—that's *got* to be important,' she frowned.

'Yes, but *think,*' he urged. 'We are weary of the fighting. Three years of it! We've drained ourselves! This will be like a shot in the arm! The Americans are strong and so full of confidence...'

'Yes, and I'm glad—relieved. It takes a bit of getting used to, though.'

Why, all at once, was she thinking about Kentucky and Amelia and all the women the length and breadth of that country? Did they want their men to fight? Were American women allowed a say in it?

'Sweetheart! I promise you it's going to shorten this war by *years.*'

'Yes—but will they actually send troops over here, Andrew? Will they fight in the trenches?'

'It's almost certain they will. I'll bet the German High Command is feeling pretty sick at this moment! And look around you—the French are pretty pleased about it!'

The streets around had all at once filled with people; talking, gesturing, shaking hands, hugging. And all of them smiling, laughing.

'I'm pleased too. I truly am. I'm so relieved I could cry. But, darling, I want us to have children—sons—yet I couldn't bear to have them and love them then see them taken from me to fight some senseless war. Do you realise almost all the world is at war now?'

'Sweetheart, there *won't* be another war. This one will be so terrible to look back on that no one will let it happen again. And it's my bet they'll give the vote to women, once it's all over—if only for what women have done for the war effort. So you'll be able to rise in your monstrous regiments and say, "No more wars!"'

'But do you realise, wife, that we're just about the only two people not jumping for joy?'

He wrapped her in his arms, swinging her off her feet, kissing her soundly.

The flower-seller called, *'Bonne chance, mes enfants!'* as they passed, and Andrew stopped to buy a bunch of violets. 'For you, my darling Julia,' he whispered, 'to remember this day...'

'I love you,' she whispered, breathing in the sweet, soft perfume. 'Did you know—Tom gave Alice buttercups—she has some pressed in her Bible. They are her special flower now, and these shall be mine. April violets. I shall keep some of these in my own Bible, and when I want you so much I can't bear it, I shall look at them and remember lovers' meetings.'

'Lovers' meetings *to come*,' he said softly. 'We are so lucky. The worst of our war is over, I know it. Now, let's find the Reims platform and I shall take you in my arms and hold you and kiss you for the rest of the time we have left. A long goodbye, and I don't care who sees us!'

'Not goodbye,' she murmured, her lips close to his cheek. 'We'll say *au revoir*—so long. And it doesn't matter at all who sees us. The French love lovers. They won't care. And, darling—I'll remember this lovely afternoon for the rest of my life.'

'Away with your bother,' he laughed. For the first time since their parting, Andrew MacMalcolm's cautious heart beat with happiness and hope. 'Just be writing to Rowangarth for that nightdress!'

16

June blazed brilliantly. The trenches dried of their mud and the walls, beginning to crumble, were repaired in the lull in the fighting. For lull there seemed to be. Those at the hospital realised it. Nothing official;

just the sure knowledge that beds were being filled less quickly.

Alice and Julia walked the field path that connected the hut-wards to the school and convent. Their eyes pricked for want of sleep, even though the night duty had been one of comparative calm. No soldier had called out in a fearsome nightmare; most had slept peacefully. Without the often-present tension, they had carried out morning routine: temperatures, bedpans, washing bowls, tea. Bed-mackintoshes, creased into discomfort in the night, had been smoothed, beds made, the floor mopped. The ward was in perfect order for the day staff who had arrived at five minutes to eight with the breakfast trolley rattling behind them.

'You've forgotten, haven't you?' Julia demanded as they passed the empty farm building once occupied by the convent cows. 'After all the bother it caused you, you've forgotten the date!'

'I haven't,' Alice laughed. 'At three o'clock this morning, I remembered it was the twentieth of June!'

'Nineteen-seventeen. It's the *year* that's important. Twenty-one! You are your own woman now. Congratulations!'

They linked hands and did a little jig, then hugged Alice close.

'I'm so glad for you. Now you can marry

Tom at the drop of a hat! No more asking permission.'

'Mm. Just to think about it makes me feel giddy. I wonder if there'll be a letter from him. I haven't heard for days.'

'Yes you have, though you didn't know it. There was one for you two days ago. I was going to bring it up to you and then I saw he'd written *Not to be opened until 20 June* on the back of the envelope. So I put it in my locker in case you were tempted.

'I left it on your bed last night—other letters, too. Come on! Let's run!'

'They clattered up the stairs two at a time, then pulled back the cubicle curtains.

'There you are! You didn't think we'd forgotten, did you?'

'Just look!' Tom's letter was there; one from Julia, too. And envelopes from Reuben, Tilda and Tom's mam.

'This is for you from me with dearest love.' Julia held out a small blue box with a jeweller's name in gold letters on the lid. 'I tried to find something to bring with me when we left England—something special. But there was nothing in the shops. So I hope you don't mind these being secondhand, sort of. I thought they'd match your engagement ring. They were Grandmother Whitecliffe's...'

Alice opened the box. Pearl ear-drops lay

on a tiny cushion of black velvet, glowing creamily.

'Julia! You shouldn't have, but I'm glad you did. They are *beautiful!*'

'Wear them on your wedding day.'

Tears filled Alice's eyes. 'I'm so happy...'

'Me, too.' Ever since that April afternoon in Paris. 'Are we too happy, Alice?'

'No. Jinny Dobb always said folk get what they deserve.'

She stopped abruptly. Not today Jin's prophecies! Alice Hawthorn wasn't walking into any wood: not three times; not even once! She had found her straight, stout stave long ago, and now she was old enough to marry him of her own free will.

'Thank you,' she said simply, shyly kissing Julia's cheek. 'And can you give me a couple of minutes? Save me a chair at breakfast? I'll follow you down. Just want to read Tom's letter...'

'And have a little weep?'

'Just a little one. And we aren't too happy, Julia. It's just that now it seems our turn has come round. Off you go now!'

They were *not* too happy, she repeated inside her, and the Fates *wouldn't* get jealous. She laid Tom's letter to her cheek.

'I love you, Tom Dwerryhouse,' she whispered. 'Wherever you are, my love, take care...'

July came, and with it a starting again of the fighting, which they soon learned from passing drivers was further away, in the region of Ypres.

Tom was at Ypres; he and Geordie Marshall, still together. That morning, before she went on duty, Alice opened the door of the tiny chapel the nuns once used and, kneeling at the altar, she begged God and the Virgin whose face gazed down benignly, to take care of her man.

'And let this war end soon. Please God, let there be a finish to all this senseless killing.'

The war had taken the sweetest years of her youth, yet she would count them as nothing if only Tom could come home safely.

'And *all* our soldiers and sailors and flying men, please? Keep them safe?'

She knew she was asking for a miracle, but still she prayed, because miracles *did* happen.

That same month, Julia and Alice sewed the narrow scarlet bands to their sleeves—a band a VAD nurse was entitled to wear for every year of service. They had signed a new contract, too, for another year's duty in France.

'We're entitled to leave, you know,'

Alice snapped off the cotton, gazing proudly at her right sleeve. 'And to a travel warrant, too.'

'I know, but I shan't go home. There's a rest home for nurses at Etaples. Think I might go there instead and sleep for a week. See if I can find a hairdresser, too, and get my hair sorted out. It's grown too long to manage.'

She ached for England; for sight of Rowangarth and all those she loved; longed, too, to be away from the awfulness of the war. But she couldn't go on leave when any day she might hear that Andrew had got time off from duty.

'On that first day at Denniston House,' that first, carbolicky day, 'I never thought I'd stick it for a year. I'm proud of this, you know.' Alice squinted this way and that at the red band, making sure it was straight. 'I feel like an old hand, now.'

'It wasn't Denniston for me—oh, bother! We don't have to sew these things on everything, do we?'

'Only on our frocks. Here—give it to me—I'll sew it on for you.'

'Bless you.' Julia lay back on her bed, hands behind head. 'Not Denniston House. It was the York hospital that nearly finished me. We were about half-way through Ward 3F and I seriously thought about packing my bags...'

'Your poor hands—I remember.'

'Not just my hands, Alice. It was my dignity more than anything. Being ordered about as if we were the lowest of the low.'

'We were. Completely useless, as nurses...'

'We aren't now, though. We've got a stripe up. Does our red band mean we're lance-corporals?'

'No, it doesn't,' Alice giggled. 'It shows we've got some service in, though.'

'Hmm.' For a while Julia contemplated the ceiling. 'I got a letter from Aunt Sutton this morning and I realise the matter might still be taboo, but I think I should read you some of it.' She pulled open her locker drawer, taking out an envelope. 'Listen to this.

"In case you should hear a garbled version of the latest air-raid on London, this is to let you know I am all right; continuing to do my bit for the FANY whilst still managing to live at home. But for those arrogant sods to come in broad daylight to drop their bombs made me furious at the cheek of it. Suppose it was their way of cocking a snook at all the American troops who have arrived here.

"The raid made quite a mess. Dead horses in the streets—poor dumb creatures —and motors blown sky-high. Rows of houses gone. Hundreds injured and killed. Poor London.

"Figgis was very upset, poor old girl. Had to give her a drop of brandy, but all's well now and they won't try it again, be sure of that."

'Now here comes the bit I thought you should hear.' Julia paused, then said, 'It's Elliot. He's on his way here.

"They have caught up with Elliot at last; even Clemmy wasn't able to do anything about it this time. Scandal, of course. He was his own undoing. Playing around with the wife of an officer serving in the trenches. Stood to reason the husband would hear of it, sooner or later.

"Simply not done, but Elliot will never be the stuff a gentleman is made of, in spite of Clemmy's money. I warned her; told her people were talking. Yesterday she was on the telephone to me, blubbering like an idiot. Not worried about me and Figgis and if we were all right after the raid; not even worried if her London house was still standing. All she could say was that Elliot had arrived at Pendenys with all his kit—on ten days' embarkation leave!

"I tell you, I could have burst my stays laughing at her performance. Mind, I'm sorry any young man has to go to war and, however awful Elliot is, his mother loves him, let's face it. But I am firmly of the opinion that it will do that young man the power of good to get some of the mud of the trenches on his fancy boots!"

'Well?' Julia looked up. 'Thought at least you'd be glad to hear that his womanising has caught up with him at last, even if it does mean he'll be coming here. I'm not a bit sorry he'll have to do his share of the fighting. Why should Elliot sit it out at the War Office?'

'I don't care one way or the other about the War Office.' Alice's needle jabbed fiercely. 'That was up to him and his conscience. I hope I don't meet up with him, that's all.'

'Alice! You *won't!* Out of all the soldiers in France we're going to run into *him?* When we are both aching and praying for just a glimpse of our own men? The Fates wouldn't be *that* cruel! And even if he were wounded—which heaven forbid,' she added hastily, 'he wouldn't come to us. We don't nurse officers here.'

She laughed, which caused Alice to demand, frowning, what was so very funny about any of it.

'None of it, really. But I just thought that if Cousin Elliot was in one of my beds, I'd take the greatest pleasure in waking him up in the middle of the night and plonking him on an ice-cold bedpan! And I'd so enjoy giving him an injection. *Bang!* in his backside! He'd hit the roof!'

'You know we aren't allowed to give injections,' Alice said crossly.

'I know—but what a thought!'

'I'd rather *not* think about it. And I don't want to talk about it, either. You don't know how much I hate that man—still. He tried to treat me like a street woman!' Even now, she was reluctant to speak his name. 'I wish Morgan had bitten his face, spoiled his good looks. I wish Tom had knocked his teeth out!'

'Alice, lovey! If I'd known—well, I thought you were over it. I'm sorry. I truly am.'

She gathered Alice into her arms, hugging her tightly, laying her cheek on her hair.

'We'll never see him, I know it. It's against all the laws of average. And if it's any comfort to you, Alice, I hate him too. He was a nasty little boy and he's grown into a nasty man. Cheer up, or I'll be sorry I told you.'

'It's all right. I've grown up a bit since the Brattocks Wood affair.' Nursing had taught her a lot—given her a greater respect for herself, too. 'Sorry, Julia. I shouldn't have taken on so. Forget the man. And in case you hadn't noticed, it's suppertime.'

They hurried to the rest-room in search of bedtime bread and jam and mugs of cocoa, each proudly wearing the red mark of a time-served nurse on her sleeve. Tom would be proud of her too.

Her fingers found the locket at her throat and the pearl ring that hung with it. The wedding ring, too, that once belonged to a mother she had never known; the ring Tom would one day place on her finger.

Tom, I need to see you, touch you. Take care, my love.

Ellen's farmer husband cut Rowangarth's hay in return for half the crop, which suited Helen nicely, since they had never replaced the carriage horses the army had commandeered. The mare and her foal had long since been sold, and only the pony remained. The hay crop was no longer of such importance.

Helen breathed in deeply. There wasn't a scent quite like it in all the world. Hay, lying in the fields, almost dry enough to stack, with the scent of high summer on it; the sure promise of winter fodder. Wars began and ended, but haymaking, planting and harvesting went on as it had always done; always would. The seasons did not acknowledge war; the thrush in

354

the far linden tree singing in the early evening cool didn't, either. And the rooks, sensible old creatures, cawed lazily home to roost after a day's scavenging, not knowing about France or that Robert would never come home again.

Or did they know? Some said they did. She shrugged, turning to look at what had once been her lawns. Last year, potatoes; cabbages and turnips growing there this year. Food. It was more important, now, than pretty green grass. Almost everyone felt hunger. Rowangarth managed better than most, though what they had she shared. Tea from India; rabbits, hares and game-birds from the estate; turnips and cabbages from what had been her lawns.

She thought of France. British troops there were better fed, people said. If that were true, then she minded little that here they were sometimes hard put to it to find the next meal. But never again, she vowed, would she take for granted sugar in her tea or butter or good red meat. Or bread. Some days, they had to make do with only one slice. Why, she fretted, did the Government not order rationing—*real*, honest rationing, so that everyone had fair shares and food was not all bought by the rich. Because food was mostly for those who could pay for it. Rumour had it that there was no shortage of butter at Pendenys Place, but that was between Clemmy and her conscience. Poor Clemmy. Elliot gone to the Front now...

Helen straightened her shoulders. There were some good things to think about. American troops had brought hope to British soldiers in France, and the King had at last changed his name. Politic, really, especially after what had happened to the Czar, poor foolish man. And you couldn't in all honesty have an English King with so German a name; not Saxe-Coburg-Gotha. Windsor sounded far more British as a surname, although, Helen sighed, she would have better liked it had His Majesty adopted the surname Plantagenet. So romantic, those long-ago medieval kings.

She shivered and pulled her shawl round her. The dew was falling heavily and her feet felt the cold through her flimsy shoes. It was almost dark. Best go inside; sit out another lonely evening with only the creaks and small bumps of an old house settling to rest for company. She had never been so alone, felt so desolate.

A bat swooped above her head and she flinched, then hurried up the garden steps for the safety of her home. Dear, old dependable Rowangarth. Come what may, at least she would always have her house...

Tilda waited, arms folded, for the kettle to boil, gazing at the photograph over the fireplace. David, Prince of Wales, beloved of all women for his boyish good looks, adored to distraction by Matilda Tewk. David Windsor, she supposed he was now, though the name Saxe-whatever-it-was had sounded grander. But, like Cook said, you couldn't have a German name now, in England. Even German shopkeepers who had lived in England for ages and taken British nationality before ever the war started, had had their windows smashed and their doors daubed with paint. And anyone who had a dachshund for a pet had to keep them indoors now, for fear of them being kicked on the streets. Even German dogs bore the brunt of British hatred for all things Germanic.

Yes, she conceded, sighing; better in view of what had happened in Russia that the royal family should become a little less foreign-sounding.

'Will you hurry up with that cocoa, Tilda!' Cook snapped. 'There's some of us as wants to go to our beds!'

'Just coming up to the boil, Mrs Shaw.' You didn't back-answer Cook when she had one of her moods on her, and Cook had been in a mood all day. Jin's fault, of course. Jinny Dobb would never learn sense.

'If I have to cook another rabbit or pluck another pheasant, I'll go off my head,' Cook had grumbled. 'Everybody knows that rabbits is vermin.' And out-of-season pheasants were scraggy and didn't even taste anything like a bird taken proper in the shooting season.

'Food is food, Mrs Shaw!' Jin had retorted, 'and vermin or not, a rabbit tastes very nice when the butcher hasn't had sight of red meat for nigh on a week. There's some in towns as would give a lot to get their hands on a few of your vermins!'

To which there had been no answer, really, except for Mrs Shaw to retire on her dignity and keep a tight-mouthed silence for the remainder of the day.

It was awkward, though, when you were piggy-in-the-middle, Tilda sighed, longing for days past when there had been food aplenty, cream on Sundays and six house staff to fetch and carry.

'Ready now, Mrs Shaw,' she murmured soothingly, having received a rakish smile of understanding from her beloved. 'I've made it nice and milky for you. Now sit you down and enjoy it. You've had a busy day.'

To which unsolicited sympathy, Cook's eyes filled with tears and she set her chair rocking furiously.

'Thanks, Tilda lass. Oh, if only you knew how weary I am of this war.'

'I do know. We're all sick and tired of it.'

They were. Just to think of another winter, with not enough coal and houses freezing cold; grey skies and queuing hours for a bit of margarine, a pound or two of flour, and most folk dreading a knock on the door and one of those telegrams.

'Just you drink it up and get yourself off to bed. I'll see to the fire and lock the doors. We'll all feel better in the morning.'

In the morning there might even be something good to read in the newspapers!

'Would you ever have believed it?' demanded Reuben of Percy Catchpole, laying a rabbit on his kitchen table.

'Thank you kindly and believed what?'

The gardener, himself a widower like Reuben, hung the stiff, furry creature on a nail in his pantry, selected a large onion and two carrots to give in exchange, then offered his tobacco pouch.

Reuben accepted a fill for his pipe from it, then settled himself for a chat. 'Why, that Mata Hari woman, though that isn't her real name. Spying for the Jerries and her born in Holland. I thought the Dutch were supposed to be on our side. It only goes to show, Percy, that there's nowt so queer as folk.'

'They're putting her on trial, aren't they? Talk is if they find her guilty, our lot'll shoot her.'

'They can't shoot a woman.'

'Can't they? Them Germans shot Nurse Cavell and all she did was to help some of our soldiers escape.'

'All the same,' Reuben puffed thoughtfully on his pipe, 'it's a terrible thing, even for a German, to shoot a woman. Our lads wouldn't like doing it—if they find that Mata Hari woman guilty, that is.'

'Our lot is soft; too gentlemanly for their own good. They'll let her off!' Catchpole spat derisively into the fire. 'What else did the newspapers have to say today—that was worth reading, I mean?'

'Nowt,' said Reuben flatly. 'But it's the Government; won't let them print the half of what happens.'

'It's a poor carry-on,' sighed the elderly gardener gloomily. 'If things get any worse, there'll be trouble here, like in Russia. Mark my words if there isn't!'

'Nay!' said Reuben, shocked to the tips of his toes at the thought. Such a thing couldn't happen here, could it? Our soldiers were loyal to King and country. 'Wonder how young Alice is getting on.' Hastily he changed so dangerous a subject. 'Tom Dwerryhouse, too.' Aye, and Sir Giles and Mr Nathan an' all. With things not going so well for us at Ypres, it was a rum do and no mistake. There were times, Reuben sighed, when he was thankful to be old!

Private Tom Dwerryhouse felt a brief, rare peace, but then he always felt that way at stand-down when men from the rear trenches came to relieve them. Two, sometimes three days and nights on duty, rifles at the ready, one foot on the firing step, head down, listening, waiting. Or perhaps, with Geordie, nerves raw, creeping under cover of darkness into No Man's Land, following the dim tape to lead them through a minefield to a high, forward position to snipe: to justify his doubtful title of marksman, earn the few extra shillings that came with it.

Geordie was never so pleased as when ordered out. By now he thought himself indestructible, possessed of a cunning that would see him safely to the end of the war. Of no concern was it to the Tynesider that the war was going better for the enemy in spite of the arrival of the fresh, well-armed, well-dressed American troops.

Our side always won, in the end, and the German was yet to be born who could see off Geordie Marshall.

'I'll kill those bliddy fleas,' he said viciously. 'C'mon, Tom lad. Let's get out of these stinking togs...'

It was one of the things about war he hated most, Tom acknowledged, unstrapping his ammunition belt, throwing down his cap. It was not the blind obedience to those above him, nor being deprived of a man's right to live his life as he pleased, wed the lass he loved, go to his bed alive and wake up alive. It wasn't even the killing and maiming around him. It was, in truth, the complete loss of his dignity; the foul stink of his body after three days in the forward trenches. Never taking off his clothes, his boots, even. And peeing where he stood. The trenches reeked in summer like middens. It was worse, almost, than winter's mud and slime.

They had been billeted for a time in stables. Now, as the fighting intensified, the army had moved out the farmer and his family, who left, possessions piled on two carts, driving their livestock in front of them, cursing the Boche volubly. It would have been a sad sight were it not for the empty farmhouse, taken possession of at once by grateful soldiers, each man's sleeping space guarded jealously. Their new billet was dry, clean and free of vermin, so that to enter it without delousing themselves, no matter how desperate for sleep, was considered a sin: bodies and uniforms must first be cleaned. There was a well in the farmyard; better still in this blazing July day, a shallow river across the empty pasture.

It was beside this clear, slow-moving river that Tom's platoon had stripped naked, examining underclothes for lice, turning uniforms outside-in, running a candleflame up and down the seams to kill the fat, incubating eggs. They did it with a ritual satisfaction, then plunged naked into the river, soap secured on a string, to wash heads and bodies, splashing like bairns let loose from a sweltering schoolroom.

Then clean, straw-filled palliasses and blessed oblivion, to sleep the clock round, sleep away one of their precious safe days to be awakened only by the ache of hunger in empty bellies.

Three days on stand-to; two days on stand-down; the pattern of a soldier's life with only sometimes the satisfaction of a properly cooked meal over a field-kitchen fire. And letters. News of Alice, of Mam and his sisters and brothers. Strange intrusions from a life almost forgotten and which would never come again, because this war would go on until there wasn't a man left on either side to carry on fighting it.

All at once Tom felt kinship with those in strange, far-away Russia, who had deposed their Czar. It made sense. Those men fought for their motherland, they were told, just as he was fighting for King and country. Only his King hadn't even heard of Tom Dwerryhouse, and his country seemed no longer to care. Only Mam and Alice cared. Alice, walking the daft dog, calling his name. Only there had never been a place called Brattocks Wood, and Rowangarth was all in his imagining.

He held his soap tightly, pulling in his breath, plunging beneath the water, only surfacing when his lungs seemed near to bursting. Then he shook his head and opened his eyes and Geordie was standing beside him, hair sleeked back.

'Come on, bonny lad. Sit yourself on the grass and dry out while I have a fag.' He offered the packet he had hidden on the riverbank.

'No, thanks, mate.' Tom lay down, eyes closed, hands behind his head. 'Shake me if I nod off...'

His brief, rebellious anger was over. Soon he would return to the billet to blessed, beautiful sleep. And the near certainty of a letter from Alice.

The fourth winter of the war was almost upon them. At home, Britain looked on it with despairing dread. Those who had money spent it on food; those without it tried to blank out their minds to yet another twelve months of war, reminding themselves that they, at least, existed in comparative safety and that soon the Government would bring in a fair-shares-for-all rationing of food. Mr Lloyd-George was a man of the people; he surely must understand.

Leave from the trenches began again for married men. The Flying Corps, no longer a flash in the pan, had been changed in title to the Royal Air Force. Aeroplanes, like tanks, had proved themselves; become a force to be reckoned with.

That winter the armed forces opened their ranks to women volunteers.

'They'll give us the vote after this,' some said. Other women cared only about keeping their children fed and clothed and the day their man would come home. And never, ever, would they let him go to fight another war in another country in strange-sounding places most women couldn't even pronounce! This war must be the one to end all wars, they vowed, or there would be fighting here at home as they fought in Russia now.

Those Russian soldiers knew what they

were about, said the man in the street grimly; were leaving the trenches to join the revolutionaries in Petrograd—and let the French and British get on with it! Rather those men should fight for the piece of land Lenin promised them and an end to serfdom. And, as the soldiers returned to their motherland, so the ruling classes left their townhouses, their country estates sewing jewels into their clothing, taking gold and silver and only things of value they could carry with them; seeking refuge in any country that would take them in. A tiara bought a passage from Lisbon to New York. Their land was useless now.

Some aristocrats stayed behind to join the fight against Bolshevism; to seek out their Czar from wherever he had been imprisoned, get him and his family to safety. Some not of Russian birth rallied to the romanticism of their cause. British battalions were ordered to Russia to fight with them, which angered most people, since King George had done nothing to help his cousin in his peril.

Yet why should he? some reasoned. The foolish Czar and the arrogant Czarina had begged on bended knees for all their troubles, said most, and anyway, the house of Romanov was already doomed by the strange blood disease brought into the family by the Czarina. A woman passed it to her sons. Sons could bleed to death just from a scratch.

There was only one small and doubtful satisfaction in that sad October. Mata Hari, convicted of spying, her appeals against the death sentence refused, faced an Allied firing squad, bringing with it a strange justice.

At least now the unlawful killing of Nurse Cavell had been avenged.

Winter came to Celverte, not with snow, like in England, but a final falling of leaves and frosted morning grass. Alice pulled her night-cape around her and hurried after Julia, who had run ahead to collect the letters she was sure would be there.

'One for me from Andrew and one from Nathan—and one for you, from Tom,' she smiled.

They spread their letters on the table-top, hugging both hands round mugs of hot tea. Soon they would fill bed-warmers, snuggle beneath the sheets, sleep off the fatigue of a busy night. But these minutes between were a precious unwinding. Time to drink the tea they had been longing for all night; to read letters, eat a slice of bread and jam they didn't really want.

'Andrew is well,' Julia announced.

'Tom, too...'

'There's a leave rota at the hospital now.

This time he says he'll be lucky. Sometime after Christmas, he thinks.' They would give the Christmas leave to men with families, Julia supposed.

'Tom says his platoon found an abandoned cart piled high with wood. They had fires in the farmhouse and washed and dried their clothes.' The letter had been written four days ago. Tom would be back in the forward trenches now.

'Listen to this, Alice! Nathan met Giles last week. He was at a dressing-station, and who should walk past him but my big brother! I'm glad he's all right. Nathan wrote especially to tell me. He's a dear, good man. And, oh my goodness. Nathan met—' She stopped, her cheeks flushing.

'Met who?' Alice demanded, knowing she had no need to ask.

'Met Elliot. Nathan said he'd been to Calais with a convoy of wounded—chaplains sometimes do, you know—and there on the quayside was Elliot! And would you believe it—Master Elliot has been posted to Paris! To Combined HQ. God! How does that blighter manage it—keeping out of the trenches, I mean? He must have friends in high places!'

'He's got a rich mother who hasn't a shred of conscience,' Alice snapped.

'Yes—well, never mind. Nathan says he has a good idea where I am and hopes, soon, to be seeing me. Which means, I suppose, that he's expecting a posting to these parts.'

'I'll go and get the warmers.' Alice rose to her feet, tucking Tom's letter in her apron pocket. 'There's plenty of hot water in the geyser. I'll fill them...'

Damn Elliot Sutton and his luck, though she'd rather he were in Paris; rather he were still in England, truth known. Anywhere but Celverte.

She filled a jug with boiling water, unscrewed the stoppers then, with a steady hand, filled the earthenware bed-warmers.

She was pleased at the steadiness of her hand; glad that Elliot Sutton's name could no longer upset her.

'*Bed!*' she said crisply to Julia.

17

1918

The war that was supposed to have been over in months, began its fourth year. That first Sunday of January was declared a national day of prayer, when women, children and elderly men—for now there were no young men left at home—prayed for an end to the madness.

At home, women with too little food and warmth waited in dread for the telegram that would devastate their lives. The entire country took on a greyness: grey skies, a grey future. It seemed to many women that all hope was gone; many children were too young to remember peace and plenty; had never known childhood.

Air-raids on London increased. In Berlin, the High Command was jubilant. They were winning the war in spite of the intervention of mighty America!

At the Western Front, the tommies and poilus hung on with fatalistic desperation. They had endured it for three years; had become immune to feeling, almost. Now it was less trouble to accept it without resentment, for surely death waited just around the next corner.

Some soldiers began to have strange thoughts. The dead had come back to Mons, hadn't they? Angels had protected them in that first winter of the war, and now, when they so desperately needed help, their comrades, long since dead and buried, returned from the darkness to fight beside them.

Some soldiers said they had seen and talked to men they knew to be dead; others said those ghosts walked in clean boots that made no sound in the squelching mud, nor left a footprint behind them.

At Celverte, nurses worked until they were desperately weary, only to be summoned from sleep by the call of a bugle as an air-raid threatened or a convoy of choking, gasping soldiers was brought in, spitting away lungs poisoned with mustard gas. They died protesting, arms flailing as they fought to breathe.

French civilians, scenting danger, began to leave homes too near the fighting. The Boche was about to start his breakthrough, and poison gas could be carried on the wind. Better homeless than dead.

Then, from out of the greyness, a light shone. Only a penny-candle light, but how it glowed golden with hope. On the sixth of February, women were given the vote. Not the young ones; not those who would be foolish enough to waste it by encouraging women into Parliament, but those who had reached the age of thirty and would have the sense to be guided by the opinions of their menfolk.

Then—and of equal importance to women—official food rationing came at last, passed by an Act of Parliament. Fair shares for all now; no more queuing in the wet and cold. Official food cards, to be distributed at once, would guarantee rations on demand.

'Well now,' Mrs Shaw beamed. 'There's

four of us lives in and one who lives out, so we can't count on Jin's card. But according to the paper,' and this morning Cook was prepared to believe that for once the newspapers had got it right, 'we shall have two pounds of sugar, half a pound of margarine, a pound of bacon and red meat enough for two good meals. And half a pound of *butter!*

'Mind, that's between the four of us, but her ladyship has got used to tea without sugar, she says, and she'll let me have her half-pound for baking.'

'And bread is to be rationed an' all, don't forget,' Tilda offered.

Four pounds of bread a week for a woman and child. Two fair-sized loaves, that was—*each*—which was more like it, thought Cook, who had already decided to convert their bread ration into flour and bake her own loaves.

'Sense at last,' she exulted. 'And now we've got the vote, it's up to us to get some women into Parliament.'

A woman would have understood what it was like to be hungry; to stand hours for a loaf and a few scraps of mutton, aye, and with crying bairns clinging to her skirts an' all! Women would have seen to it that food rationing had come sooner.

She sighed contentment and bade Tilda put on the kettle for a sup of tea. Now she might even be able to make cherry scones again—if she could lay hands on a few cherries. February was almost over, spring and warmer days just around the corner; and though nobody was going to get fat on their food cards, at least the poor and the old would have food they could afford.

Happen soon, she thought, crossing her fingers tightly, we might even win this dratted war!

Julia lit a cigarette. Once, she would never have thought to smoke, but she always carried a packet in her pocket to offer to wounded soldiers. 'You wouldn't have a fag on you, Nurse?' She had heard it so often. Now she used them—*needed* them—herself. Many nurses smoked. Cigarettes soothed and comforted and often took the place of the meal they were too busy to eat.

'Want one?' she asked of Alice.

'No thanks. And that's your third since we came off duty.'

'Yes, but I'm worried. Not so long ago, Andrew was hopeful of getting a few days' leave, yet there hasn't been a mention of it in his last two letters. It's ten months since Paris. Something's wrong, I know it.'

'He's busy. You don't have to tell *us* that, now do you?'

'I suppose not. And I'm a spoiled brat

for wanting to see him. I should be glad he's alive and not at a clearing-station at the Front. But I've tried counting my blessings and in the end it all boils down to the same thing. I miss him. I want him!'

'I know, love. I've got a man of my own, remember? I'm beginning to forget what he looks like, it's so long since I saw him. Let's go down to the rest-room. Ruth said some new records have arrived for the gramophone. Why don't we find ourselves a cup of tea, then listen to some music?'

'Oh, don't be so patient with me! Just say what's on your mind and tell me I'm a self-centred little beast and give me a good thump!'

'All right! Nurse MacMalcolm is a self-centred little beast and she's too big for me to thump, or I'd do it! Now are you coming downstairs?'

'Yes—and I'm sorry, Alice. If I can't have Andrew, a cup of tea and a spot of jazz is just about the next best thing. You got a letter, didn't you—how is Tom?'

'Fine, I think. It was only a hasty note, though. Said he'd been sent back to the billet and told to get into his best uniform. Going on a special duty. Said he'd write later. I don't know whether to be pleased or worried about it.'

'Special duty,' Julia frowned, throwing her cape around her shoulders against the cold of the early March evening. 'Don't suppose it'll be anything dangerous or he'd not need his good clothes. Probably being sent to some inter-regimental shooting contest or something. Or maybe a special guard duty. They do sometimes pick men out at random.'

'Shooting contest? When there's fighting all along the front line from Ypres to Verdun! They wouldn't be so daft!'

'Want to bet? That lot at HQ don't know the first thing about what it's really like. Or perhaps there's some big-wig from London paying a visit. I wouldn't worry if I were you. Anything that gets him out of the front line is good.'

'You're right. I tell you this, though. When I get Tom Dwerryhouse safe home from the army—'

'And married!'

'—and married, I'll not let him out of my sight for a minute!'

Special duties? Perhaps they were going to give him a stripe. She wondered if Geordie would be going with him.

'You're going to Epernay,' the platoon sergeant had said when Tom arrived smartly dressed and breathless at Company HQ. 'Are your boots blacked, lad? Best bib and tucker? There's a motor waiting; you'll pick up another two lads on the way. Got to be there before dark, so get a move on!'

It was all he knew. The sergeant couldn't tell him any more. Dropping a hastily written letter into the post—Alice would worry if the duties turned out to be so special he wasn't able to write—he threw his knapsack into the back of the waiting motor, laid his rifle carefully beside it, then heaved himself inside. Little more than two hours ago he'd been in the firing line; now he was dressed up like a dog's dinner and heading for a jaunt to Epernay where, if his memory still served him, there would be a lot of brass-hats since Brigade Headquarters was stationed there.

He took off his cap and unbuttoned his tunic. What it was all about he had no idea—but then, his was not to reason why...

The three marksmen—Tom and two they had collected on the way—arrived at Epernay a little before sundown.

'You're part of the special party are you?' asked the guardroom corporal glumly. 'Best go to the quartermaster's and draw your palliasse and straw. Then go over to the cookhouse and get yourselves something to eat. That's all I know, 'cept that you're to see the RSM at nine. There's your chitties. Enjoy yourselves.'

He slammed three requisitions on the

desk-top, then went back to his figuring.

'I'll tell you summat,' remarked one of Tom's new companions, a red-haired soldier with a Leeds accent, 'this is a rum do and no mistake. They tell you nowt around here. What are we supposed to be up to, then?'

Tom neither knew nor cared. He hadn't eaten since morning and the thought of a hot meal drove all else from his mind.

'Happen the RSM knows about it. They'll tell us,' he grinned, 'when they want us to know.'

The regimental sergeant-major did not know, or if he did he kept the knowledge to himself.

Their numbers had risen, now, to a round dozen; all of them privates, all wearing the badge of a marksman.

'You will all get to your beds,' they were told. 'Number Three hut behind sick-bay is empty. Kip down in there. And no sloping off into the town, mind. Epernay is strictly out of bounds.

'Get your heads down, the lot of you. You'll be given a shake at half-past four, after which you will shave and see to it your boots are well-polished. You'll get a hot drink, then you'll be here at five. *Five a.m,* that is! You'll report to RSM Poole.'

'What are we supposed to be doing, sir?'

asked one of the twelve.

'You'll know, all in good time,' came the trite reply. 'Now get yourselves off; and no playing cards into the small hours—do I make myself clear?'

They murmured yes sir, he did, and stood smartly to attention as he rose and left the room.

'It's a queer carry-on,' repeated the red-haired soldier.

'Happen it is,' Tom grinned, 'but I'm not complaining.'

The meat stew was good; the tea that followed it hot and sweet. He had spent two wakeful nights forward of the line with Geordie, now all he wanted to do was sleep. 'Let's find that hut,' he said.

At exactly five in the morning, when the sky to the east lit slowly with pale streaks of gold, they presented themselves at the guardroom asking for RSM Poole. From a billycan they had drunk hot, sweet tea; breakfast, they were told, would be later. A corporal eyed them cagily, counted them, then ordered them into two ranks. A door opened. The RSM walked out. All twelve sloped arms in salute.

'Carry on, Corporal. Issue each man with one round.'

The corporal ordered, 'Stand at ease', then dipped into his pocket, handing out twelve small, slim bullets. His eyes were downcast as if, Tom thought, he had no wish to look at them. Then he gave the order to shoulder arms, and 'Squaaad, quick march!'

They were brought to a halt at a field a few hundred yards away. They were not the first to arrive. Two horses were tethered by the field gate, an ambulance and a small truck were parked farther down the lane.

'What the 'eck's going on?' the Leeds man demanded.

'No talking in the ranks!' the corporal hissed.

Tom slid his eyes left and right. A chaplain spoke to one of the officers standing a few yards away, then hurried off. The corporal saluted the regimental sergeant-major.

'All present and correct, *sah!*' He stamped his feet, then stood stiffly to attention.

'At ease.' Even the RSM seemed not to want to look at them. 'You'll want to know why you are here. Special duties, you were told, and when you go back to your regiments you'll not speak of this to anyone on pain of severe reprimand!

'You are all marksmen, for which you draw extra pay, I would remind you, and you have been selected for your skill.'

He drew a deep breath, lifted his chin, clasped his hands behind his back and walked the length of their ranks, lips pursed. Then he swung to face them.

'You are here as a firing party. You are required to carry out the execution of a man condemned by his own actions to death by shooting.' He spoke quickly, quietly. 'No man present has the right to refuse to take part,' he added, his eyes narrowing to warning slits.

There was a terrible, stunned silence. No one moved. One of the twelve drew a shuddering breath, then let it out slowly.

'Did you hear me? Do you understand?' the RSM rapped.

His mouth had gone dry. He hadn't wanted this. No man in his right mind wanted it. And why were they all looking at him like that?

He cleared his throat, opened his mouth, shut it again, trap-like. Then he motioned to the corporal to take over, walking quickly to where the officers stood, glad to be away from stares of hatred.

Like automatons the twelve loaded their rifles.

'I don't like this any more than you do,' hissed the corporal.

'Then why the hell are you doing it?' The Leeds man was the first to find words.

'For the same reason as you lot. I can't refuse!'

'Who says we can't?' asked one in the rounded accents of a west country man.

Tom stood still and unspeaking. To his left more had joined the officers and the chaplain; to his right was a wood, the trees in it leafless, still. Ahead, the sky was brightening into morning. Soon, the light would be good enough for them to—to—Almighty God! To shoot a man!

His mouth began to fill with spittle. Sniping, shooting at an enemy at long range was what he was trained for and a part of war. In return, an enemy sniper was entitled to shoot him, were he daft enough to let him. But to shoot a man in cold blood, enemy or not; to take aim and fire at a defenceless man was asking too much of any soldier!

He glanced at the man on his left. At his shoulder he wore the badge of the Durham Light Infantry. He had thick black hair and a thick black moustache. His face was chalk-white; he stared ahead, unblinking.

'You will carry out your orders briskly and without comment.'

It was the corporal again; the bloody corporal!

'When commanded, the first rank of six will kneel, rifle to the ground to his right. The prisoner will be brought in, blindfolded. A white envelope will be pinned to the left of his tunic. You will aim for the envelope. Those in the rank behind will fire first.'

To the left. His heart. Tom swallowed noisily, realising he stood in the rear rank of six; he would be one of the first to fire.

They couldn't do this! This wasn't war. This was cold-blooded, deliberate killing.

'When the prisoner is brought in, you will observe that to one side of him will be a medical officer. Don't shoot the MO.'

Funny? That's supposed to be funny? White-hot anger thrashed inside Tom.

'After the first command to fire, the medical officer will quickly ascertain if the prisoner has been despatched. If he is dead, the MO will walk away. If, in his opinion, the prisoner is still alive, he will raise his hand and the front rank will rise smartly, take aim, and await the order to fire—which will be quickly given.'

'And what if we *all* miss? What if he's still alive, even then?' It was asked with contempt by the black-haired man.

'Don't get any ideas! If that happens, then an officer who will be standing close by, will take his pistol and...' He left the sentence in mid-air.

Tom gritted his teeth. The corporal had done this before, he knew it. He recited the paraphernalia of death exactly as, when a boy, Tom had recited his multiplication tables each morning at school. *I hope you catch the pox, you nasty little sod, and die slow of it...*

'And should that become necessary, you will all be deemed to have disobeyed an order given by a senior officer and you know what'll happen, then...'

Tom knew. They all knew. *No man shall disobey an order; shall fall asleep at his post; shall cast away his arms.* The penalty for all three was death; death by firing squad like the poor wretch they would bring in just as soon as the light was good enough.

He looked at his right, wondering if the leaf buds were swelling in Brattocks Wood. Alice used to go there. Once, in another life, she walked the daft dog there, then ran to meet him. *Alice, lass, I'm sorry.* Sorry? He'd never tell her about this day; never admit to anyone they had turned him into an animal.

...you will not speak of this to anyone on pain of severe reprimand. Speak of it? He'd be ashamed of this until the day he died.

The regimental sergeant-major returned. With him was one of the two officers. A bit of a lad, dressed up to the nines. His face was pale, his hands tightly clenched in brown leather gloves.

The senior of the officers walked across

the field to where a lone tree stood. At his side hung a pistol.

The field gate opened. It was the medical officer. He walked to the opposite side of the tree, stopping a few feet away from it. He did not look up; not even to glance at the captain with the pistol.

Tom's hands were numb with cold and he blew on his right one. He had started to shake. It started at his knees and went right up to his diaphragm. The shaking stopped there and turned to a spasmodic retching. He clenched his teeth, then held his breath to stop the jerking inside him.

A small motor bumped into the field, then drew up beside the tree. Two sergeants jumped out, helping down a man who was already blindfolded. He stumbled and fell and they helped him to his feet. The van drove away, stopping beside two stretcher-bearers. Tom pulled his eyes to the front again. He had to look at the prisoner, beg his forgiveness and—*No!*

They were tying the man to the tree. He was not wearing field grey uniform; was not a German or an Austrian. The man they were going to shoot was a British soldier. Nor was he a man! He was a boy! Even the bloodstained bandage around his head and the black cloth that bound his eyes could not disguise his youth.

'*God in heaven!*' whispered the black-haired soldier. 'What did he do?'

'Cowardice,' the corporal mumbled. 'They give them a shot of morphine, though,' he added, as if in mitigation. 'Or a cup of rum...'

The boy lifted his head, turning it from side to side as if to find one last small slit of daylight.

'Squaaaaad...'

It was the young officer; the RSM was standing behind him.

Tom jerked his gaze to the boy. His lips were moving. He was trying to pray, to follow the intoning of the chaplain.

'*Aim...*'

Aim. Not at that white envelope. There was a quicker way. Deliberately, carefully, Tom squinted down his gun sight. *Sorry, lad...*

Six shots rang out, almost at once. The medical officer ran quickly to the sagging body, searching at his neck for a pulse. Then he rose to his feet and walked to where the stretcher-bearers waited.

The kneeling rank rose slowly, dizzily, leaving their rifles where they lay. The stretcher-bearers ran quickly, supporting the lifeless body as the captain with the pistol slashed the ropes. Then gently they lifted the boy on to the stretcher; lifted him with compassion as if he were a small, helpless child.

They walked quickly to the ambulance, slid the stretcher inside it, then pulled across the back flaps. The twelve men stood like statues, watching the ambulance manoeuvre through the field gate.

Tom ran his tongue round his lips. It was finished. Minutes, it had taken. He was glad the stretcher-bearers had been gentle. Conchies, they were, who had shown pity. Like Sir Giles. One of them could have been Giles Sutton.

The man from Leeds broke ranks, running to the hedge to fall vomiting to his knees; the black-haired man hissed, *'Bastards. Bloody bastards...'*

'He was only a lad,' one said. 'A bit of a lad. They'd no right...We shouldn't have...'

Anger took Tom; shook him. Blind with rage he strode to the young officer who had taken off his cap and was mopping his forehead with a white handkerchief.

'Sir!' he rapped. He lifted his rifle into the air, then flung it with all the contempt of his pent-up hatred at his feet. 'With respect, sir, I will *not* do that again!'

He lifted his head high, gazing defiantly into the eyes of his superior.

...shall not cast away his arms... But it had been all he could think of to do.

386

'Pick up your rifle, Private,' the young officer said quietly.

'Go on, lad. Pick it up,' said the regimental sergeant-major. 'Don't be a bigger fool than you need...'

Alice. Alice who loved him, waiting in Brattocks...

He bent and picked it up. He'd made his protest, now he was drained of feeling. He turned and ran towards the wood. He wanted to be sick, too; wanted never to have to look into the eyes of the other eleven again.

'That man there! Return to the ranks!'

Tom's foot hit a sod of grass and he stumbled and fell. He lay there, his burning face in the cold, wet grass. He had plumbed the depths; he despised himself, despised the army and the King and country in whose names he had been ordered to war.

Get up! The voice echoed above his head. *Get up, you fool. Go back...*

It's all over now, said the soft voice of reason inside him. *Think of Alice. Think of yourself. You've survived, this far. What's done is done...*

He pulled himself to his knees, reaching for his cap. His rifle lay where it had fallen, several feet away, and he walked unsteadily to the bole of a tree to pick it up.

The familiar, screeching whine made him stop. Instinctively he threw himself flat, hands over his head, breath indrawn.

The shell exploded in the field. A barrage! They were being shelled! The Germans—they couldn't be *that* near? Another explosion and another; more and more. A shattering continuous roar.

The earth shook beneath him. He cringed closer to the tree, holding his nose, blowing into it to ease the pain inside his ears as the roaring increased.

'There'd be no one left alive; nothing left standing. He hadn't a hope in hell! He turned his face as a shell slammed into the transport that had brought them here, then closed his eyes, wincing as it exploded into flames.

He pressed himself closer to the ground and began to pray. A scream, louder than the first, filled the air around him and he felt the thud as the shell struck.

There was a roaring in his ears. The earth beneath him moved, flew high in a million pieces.

The breath left his body; a pain pierced his head. He cried out as a red mist blotted out his sight. Then the blessed blackness took him...

'Will you listen to this!' Julia exulted, waving Andrew's letter. 'Good news at last, he says.' Quickly she scanned the single sheet, then passed it over. 'You read it, Alice. Tell me I'm not dreaming!'

'The lovey-dovey bits too?'

'There aren't any,' Julia said impatiently. 'Go on, read it. He's got five days—well, four, plus his sleeping day. He'll be duty-surgeon that week and,' she did a rapid calculation, 'and we'll be on nights, too. The twenty-second, that is...'

'So you'll be able to travel on your sleeping day as well. Julia, love, I'm so pleased for you. Go and see Ruth right away, then she can put in a good word for you with Sister, though they'll have to give you leave. They can't refuse a married woman.'

'Even though we're so busy we none of us know which way to turn?'

'We'll all double-up for you—and what makes you think you're so important, *Norrrse,* that you can't be done without for a few nights?' Alice giggled, doing an excellent imitation of Matron.

'Oh, I do love you,' Julia sighed. 'I love the whole world—except the Kaiser's lot. You don't think it'll go wrong again?' she whispered, suddenly serious.

'It will *not.* Andrew has got leave—dates, everything—and they won't refuse it to his wife. We'll have to get out your civilian things and press your dresses. You'd better try the blue on and see if you think the hem needs taking up. They're wearing them a lot shorter now.'

'I will. It'll be like old times again. Me meeting Andrew in the park in that dress. Remember?'

'Mm. And you getting married in it...'

'And being disappointed in it, too...'

'He'll come, this time. That blue frock has been waiting here to be worn for ages. And I'll press your wedding nightgown too. You must take that with you.'

'I must.' Julia's cheeks pinked, thinking how little she would wear it. 'And it'll be your turn next. Who's to know that Tom's special duties won't land him here, right on your doorstep. Goodness! I've just thought—you could get married! Would it be legal, here in France?'

'I don't know.' It was Alice's turn to blush bright red. 'If an English vicar read the service and there were witnesses, I don't see why not...'

'On a ship at sea, the captain can marry you—well, that's what I heard.'

'Don't! Please don't! We're tempting Fate. I'd settle for just seeing him, knowing he was all right. All I want is for this war to be over and Tom safe. We didn't know how lucky we were, did we?'

'It seems so long ago, that night in Hyde Park.' Julia's eyes misted over.

'It *is* long ago. Just before my birthday, you both met; nearly *five* years gone!'

'And now I'm going to see him again in—' She drew a ring around the date on her wall calendar. 'Friday the twenty-second of March. I'll be seeing him in sixteen days!'

'Where?' Alice asked, ever practical.

'He didn't say. Once we thought Paris was too far, but now, with the extra day, we could make it there. And Paris in early spring would be wonderful.'

Come to think of it, Paris in freezing mid-winter would have been equally marvellous.

'*Anywhere* will be wonderful. Now mind you tell Ruth about it. And don't be fobbed off. A wife is entitled to leave with her husband, remember.'

'Mmm.' Julia's sigh was long and blissful.

'What news from Rowangarth?' Alice ventured. 'Her ladyship's letter—you haven't read it.'

'Nor have I!' Laughing, Julia slit open the envelope then. 'Oh, my goodness! News, you asked. Aunt Clemmy is a grandmama!'

'She's *what*? Mr Albert?' It *had* to be Albert.

'The very same! Out of the blue, it seems. They kept it a secret because—well, everybody thought Amelia was past child-bearing—anything could have gone wrong.'

'Seems it didn't...'

'I think Amelia always secretly hoped —but she has a fine, healthy son, it would seem. Mother says she's green with envy: she does so want a boy for Rowangarth. Aunt Clemmy, it seems, isn't at all sure if she wants to be a grandmother yet.'

'Well, there's nothing she can do about it. She *is.*'

'Yes, officially this time,' Julia giggled wickedly. 'Bet she'll be nagging her Elliot to get married now. Well, there's one thing certain: when some brave woman takes him on, there'll be no shortage of pregnancies, Elliot being what he is.'

'Don't spoil good news by talking about *that* one,' Alice admonished. 'I'm pleased for Albert Sutton and I'll bet his father is pleased, an' all.'

'He is. It was Uncle Edward told Mother about it. Went over to Rowangarth in high good humour, especially to give her the news. But I think Mother wishes it could have been her. When the war is over, Giles really will have to get himself married. I don't know why some girl hasn't snapped him up. He's very good-looking. If he doesn't get on with it, people are going to think he's a pansy.'

'Oh, for shame. He's never that! Nor

Nathan Sutton, either. I suppose,' Alice defenced, 'they're both slow starters and the pair of them will surprise us all one day. My word, but they say good news always happens in threes and you've had two lots already. Wonder what the third will be?'

'It'll be for you. I've had good news enough for one day. You are due a letter from Tom—there'll be one soon.'

'Yes, and maybe he'll be able to tell me what his special duties were. Mind, if I don't hear for a while I won't worry overmuch. When things are special, sort of, maybe he won't be allowed to write.'

'I agree absolutely. There'll be nothing at all to have worried about, just you see. Our luck is in at the moment.'

'And not before time!' Why, even now, Tom might be so near to Celverte that—

Alice shut off such thoughts firmly. All she wanted was for him to be safe. She could wait.

Take care of yourself, my lovely lad...

Elliot Sutton regarded his newly shaved face, his glossy, brilliantine-sleeked hair with satisfaction.

'You've got to admit,' he whispered to his smirking reflection, 'that you were born with the luck of the devil.'

Posted to France. It had struck fear into

his guts, and all because of Beatrice and the meddling old biddies—Aunt Sutton had been one of them—who had stirred things up till her husband was bound to hear of it.

He'd been called a cad and a womaniser; his immediate superior at the War Office had read him a solemn warning about not honouring gambling debts, let alone his mess bill. His stock had been pretty low when he had arrived at the Place on embarkation leave, his mother alternating between screaming, floor-pacing anger and drooping depression. She had called him all the nasty things he'd ever heard, and a few he hadn't, then relented, spending a lot of time on the telephone, eyes narrowed, mouth tight as a sprung trap. And she had done it!

Got him a posting to Combined Allied Headquarters in Paris, and though he had been relegated to the meanest, smallest office in the darkest, dreariest room in the whole building, his spirits were on the up again.

Good old Mama! She had a way of getting anything she set her heart on. She could bully and bluster and put the fear of God into anyone who stood in her way. Mama, with one of her moods on her, could put the fear of God into God Himself!

She wasn't a bad old stick, all things considered. A little on the earthy side, sometimes, but who cared about that when her pockets were bottomless?

So now, he thought, when he could wangle a spot of absent-without-leave, he might just look up Nathan, because even from the smallest, darkest office in CAHQ, Paris, he could find at once exactly where, at the Front, any regiment was quartered. Nathan, newly posted to another division, was somewhere in the region of the Somme, it seemed. Giles, too, wasn't all that much further away. It might be rather fun to look him up too; to have Giles salute him and call him Sir! Private Giles Sutton having to stand to attention and tip his cap to his cousin Elliot would help make up for the demeaning position Giles had placed him in when he'd had to make the most grovelling of apologies over the sewing-maid affair.

It would be possible to get near to the front line. Some messages were still delivered by hand, in spite of wireless telegraphy. If it meant seeing Giles, he didn't mind being a messenger boy. And going near enough to the trenches would, he considered, give him place-names to drop when later it was all over and men talked in their clubs about the war.

'Ah, yes—the Somme. I was there in

'18. Bad job, that,' he would say, refusing modestly to be drawn further.

He sighed long and deeply and with great satisfaction. Nathan and Giles could wait. At this moment Paris called, and Paris could knock spots off London and Leeds when it came to finding a good time.

He reached for his greatcoat, arranged his cap at a rakish angle, and gave a satisfied smile to the handsome young officer in the mirror.

Be damned if Elliot Sutton didn't always land on his feet!

18

Days that were so deliciously slow-moving for Julia, became increasingly worrying for Alice. Each morning, as Julia crossed off another day on the calendar, Alice came to dread the arrival of the mail and the letter that did not come.

Two weeks without hearing from Tom; almost three since the date of his hastily pencilled note. Just to think of special duties, whatever they might be, made her shake inside, all the while insisting that no news *must* be good news.

In her less bleak moments, she would tell herself it would all come right; that this was the very day on which a platoon of West Yorkshires would come marching down Celverte's main street and Tom with them.

Daydreaming, for all that. Better she should take solace from Julia's joy and her often repeated, 'Your turn next, Alice!' with always the final comforting thought that, since the Kaiser's armies had started a massive attack on all fronts, the army post office seemed the first affected by it, because, in all honesty, no nurse in quarters seemed to be getting her usual quota of letters.

On the Wednesday before Julia was to leave for Paris—for Paris it would be—all hospital units in the area of the Somme front were put on emergency alert. This meant, amongst other irritating restrictions, that no nurse could leave the vicinity of the hospital without permission, even to walk down the lane into Celverte.

'It's serious,' Ruth Love frowned. 'Gas. They can send it inside shells now.' No longer was an adverse wind their friend. 'And I've heard—though for pity's sake don't tell Julia—that the Germans have made a breakthrough somewhere in the Verdun area.'

'Andrew isn't in the front line now.'

Alice spoke with genuine relief, whilst wishing with all her anxious heart she could be as certain of Tom's whereabouts.

'Only two days to go.' Julia began to pack her case. They were working night duties and, though Julia was exhausted at the end of each one, sleep was impossible. She lay, alternately thinking of lovers' meetings and the telegram which would begin, 'Sorry, darling, but—'

I'll never forgive You, God, if You do it to me again. She sent her thoughts high and wide, then relented at once. Poor God, who was blamed for everything these days and thanked for very little. *I'm sorry. It's just that I love him so much. I'm grateful You've kept him safe for all this time. It's just that I couldn't bear it if anything went wrong.*

The next day she folded the blue-ribboned nightdress and laid it in her case. It was an act of defiance, a tilting at Fate. That morning, when they came off duty, she placed the final cross on the calendar.

'There, now. Tomorrow, I'll be on my way to Paris. Oh, Alice, nothing will go wrong...?'

'*Nothing* is going to go wrong. You will come off duty and get yourself to the station. And had you thought, it's almost certain that Andrew is on his way

398

to Paris already. He's got one day extra, remember?'

'Mm. He said he'd spend it finding somewhere for us to stay and getting his uniform sponged and pressed—and a decent haircut. I think he'll have had my letter telling him when I'll be arriving. I hope so...'

'Stop your worrying! So he hasn't got the letter? All he's got to do is to ask the times of the trains arriving from Amiens and meet each one. He isn't stupid! Tomorrow you'll see him. You *will,* so for goodness' sake let's find something to eat then get ourselves into bed. I'm so tired, I could weep.'

Alice did not look at the criss-crossed letterboard as they passed it on the way to breakfast. There would be no letter from Tom.

Just one letter, God—a card, even?

'Sorry, nothing for you. Nothing for me either. The mail has gone all to pot,' Julia comforted.

Let Andrew be there tomorrow, God. Let him be on the Paris train this very minute.

'I know. I think things are getting bad, Julia. We are still on emergency alert.' She would be glad to see Julia on her way, if only because of a crawling inside her that refused to go away; a feeling of something being very wrong. It was so strong, it made her afraid.

She clucked irritably. She was getting as bad as daft Jin Dobb. It would be all right! Tomorrow, Julia would catch the early train and there would be a letter from Tom. There *would!*

'Breakfast,' she said firmly. 'Then bed.' Only, like Julia, she wouldn't sleep.

That night, the noise of shellfire was so loud, so near, they were afraid.

'Is it our guns or theirs?' Alice whispered as she did the rounds of the beds with Julia, plumping up pillows, enveloping blanket corners.

'Ours, of course! Got to be!' Julia stopped, frowning, as Ruth Love answered Sister's unspoken summons. 'Did you see that? Ruth almost ran!' No one ran, except in an emergency.

'It's gas,' said Ruth, when they were out of earshot of the beds. 'The shelling we can hear is *theirs*. They're getting nearer. Sister just said there's a big push on. She wants us to fill palliasses: we might have to take in a lot of wounded, bed them down on the floor...'

'We'll manage,' Julia whispered. 'I only hope they don't send us gas cases.' There was so little they could do for the victims of mustard gas—save watch them slowly die.

'Best get on with it. I've got the stable

key. The straw is in there; we can fill them, then leave them ready in case they're needed.'

The stable was dry, the straw clean. Long before daylight they had filled a dozen palliasses.

'We did well,' said Ruth, relieved that so far there had been no call to use them. When their morning relief arrived a little before eight, the ward was calm, though the sound of gunfire could still be heard.

'This is it, then! You've got half an hour to bathe and change and get to the station. Just think, Julia. In a few more hours you'll be with him!'

'*Hours...*' Julia's eyes took on a far-away look. The time had come, and still no telegram had arrived; no letter. Andrew would be in Paris, waiting for her. She wanted to cry; she wanted to laugh. She hugged Alice tightly.

'I know I keep saying it, but your turn will come. And I'll give your love to Andrew. I'll be back on Tuesday—late. You'll have had a letter from Tom by then and there'll be so much to talk about...'

'I'm happy for you—you know that?' Alice laid her cheek to Julia's.

'Mm. 'Bye...

'MacMalcolm! You're still here!' Ruth Love pulled back the cubicle curtains impatiently. 'I thought you'd have gone!'

'What is it?' Something wrong, Alice knew it. Ruth's cheeks were bright red, her eyes wide.

'It's stand-to! Didn't you hear the bugle? Day staff to remain on duty in the ward—night staff to go to the chateau!'

'But I'm asleep on my feet!' Alice protested.

'So are we all. But I'm to tell you both to go there at once.'

'*Both?*' Julia's face drained slowly of colour. 'Ruth, I'm going to Paris.'

'Matron said I was to stop you. Heavy casualties. They need all the help they can get.'

'Please?' Julia's voice was little more than a whisper. 'Andrew is waiting for me. Didn't you tell Sister?'

'I did, but you know how it is with her...'

'Don't ask me, Ruth! I beg you, don't ask me!'

'I'm asking you nothing. I'm telling you what Sister said, that's all.'

'So you might have missed her...?' Alice breathed.

'Exactly!' Ruth picked up the suitcase, thrusting it at Julia. 'So *go!* All right—I was too late—you'd gone. But go to him! *Go,* you little fool...'

'Down the back stairs!' Alice hissed.

'Out the back way, past the stables. Run, Julia! *Run!*'

'But—'

'Will you *go*,' Ruth urged. 'Just get out of here! I'll tell her I missed you!'

'I'm sorry.' Still Julia hesitated, eyes trouble. 'The wounded, I mean. I—'

'*Out!*' Ruth yelled.

They stood, breath indrawn, as Julia's footfalls echoed along the narrow staircase passage.

'She's gone. I was too late. When I got there she'd already left, Hawthorn!'

'Yes.' Alice let go her indrawn breath. 'Gone by five minutes. Wait for me, Ruth?' She threw on her night-cape. She ached for bed; to take off her shoes, her stiff collar. 'Things are bad at the Front?'

'Heavy casualties. Come with me to tell Sister I missed Julia, then I'll walk up to the chateau with you.'

'Thanks for what you did. It was good of you.'

'No, it wasn't! If Sister ever finds out we'll all be in trouble, so watch what you say!' Ruth snapped. 'And she had to go, Alice. I'd never have forgiven myself if she hadn't.'

'I don't know what you mean...'

'No? When it might be the last chance they'll ever have of being together?'

'Don't, Ruth! You're wrong!' Alice's

mouth had gone dry; her words came out roughly. 'Say you didn't mean it?'

'I mean that the war isn't going well for us—surely you'd realised that?'

'Yes, I suppose I had.' She'd thought it for a long time, only she hadn't dared to say it. 'But Andrew is going to be all right!'

Tears pricked Alice's eyes; tears of despair and fatigue.

Tom. Where are you?

Julia leaned back, eyes closed. She was on her way now. The train was an express; no stopping between Amiens and Paris. It would be all right! She pushed all thoughts of guilt from her mind. She was leaving when they needed her, but Andrew came first. She had been so obsessed with want of him she would have gone, even without Ruth's help.

Dear Ruth. Dear, lovely Alice. But they wouldn't regret helping her. Afterwards, when she was back at Celverte, she would work extra hard, do anything asked of her. She would do extra duties, be more kind to Alice on mornings when there were no letters for her. Only let Andrew be waiting at the station and she would never again ask anything of God.

Andrew stood at the barrier, checking his

watch with the station clock. The previous train from Amiens had arrived on time, but Julia had not been on it. The one due was already late, but what was a few minutes when it was almost a year since their last kiss?

A ticket collector arrived to take up his position; the train was coming. *Please, my darling, be on this one...*

A signal down the line dropped with a thump; he heard the train before he saw it. Then it came into the station, slowly, importantly; hissing and clanking, its brakes squealing, coming to a stop with a final hiss of steam.

There was a long, drawn-out second, then windows dropped, hands reached out for handles. All along the train, doors swung open.

His eyes searched the bobbing heads for her ridiculous cap. She was almost at the barrier before he saw her.

'*Darling!*' He reached for her hand, taking her case, pushing through the waiting crowd.

Then he gathered her in his arms, searching for her mouth, knowing again the exquisite delight of the scent of her soap, the sweet, clean smell of her hair. She felt fragile in his arms.

'You've lost weight, and I love you,' he said eventually.

She looked at him through eyes bright with tears, trying to speak, shaking her head impatiently because the words wouldn't come. She reached up, cupping his face in her hands, mouthing, 'I love you, too.'

'Darling, darling Julia.' He held her to him, resting his cheek on her cap. 'You are here. I can't believe it. I wanted you so much I was afraid something would go wrong.'

'It nearly did.' She took in a calming gulp of air. 'We were on stand-to. Alice and I had just come off night duty. Sister sent Ruth to tell us we were to go to the chateau—it's a dressing-station. I wanted to scream and shout and say I wouldn't, but I just stood there, not believing it.

'Then Ruth told me to go; said she'd tell Sister I'd already left. I ought to feel guilty. I do, I suppose, but I promised in my mind I'd make up for it—and I will!'

'I don't feel guilty being here. I have a wife I love to distraction, and I've been kept from her for more than three years—allowing for the odd hour. I did more than two years in a front-line dressing-station: I think we deserve these few days.'

'They say we get what we deserve,' she laughed shakily, feeling a little less guilty about her flight from quarters. 'And,

Andrew—have you found us somewhere to stay?'

'I have indeed!'

'What is it like? It isn't madly expensive is it?'

'Like? It's a room, I suppose. Haven't taken a lot of notice. But it has a splendid bed. Big and soft—I slept in it last night. Bliss.'

'Then take me there this instant. Is it far?'

'Only a few streets away.' He picked up her case, then drew her arm through his, smiling down at her. 'I love you, Julia MacMalcolm—did I tell you?'

The *patronne* at the *pension* was middle-aged and plump, though her smile, when she allowed one, transformed her face completely.

'Ah, monsieur, you are back!' She felt a stab of guilt. 'I am going,' the young soldier had said, 'to meet my wife,' and she had thought, may God forgive her, that he was going to find a woman. Not that she could blame him, with the war going so badly. A fighting man, when he had leave, deserved all the comforts he could find.

But the *fille* beside him *was* his wife —there was no disputing it; a woman in love, and that love showing in her smile, her eyes, the way her hand clung to his.

407

And may Our Lady bless them both and grant them a splendid time together!

'The bed was to your liking last night?' she asked solicitously.

'It was absolutely *magnifique,*' Andrew beamed.

'*Le déjeuner*—it is still being served if Monsieur wishes a table?' She returned his smile, handing over the key.

'Thank you but no!' He picked up the case, walked purposefully past the dining-room door and up the stairs. It would not surprise her, thought the *patronne*—and she wasn't often wrong when it came to matters of *amour*—if they stayed upstairs for a very long time!

They proved her suppositions well-founded when they came downstairs, hand in hand, just as the dining-room doors were being opened for the evening meal: he, handsome in his uniform; she looking exquisite in blue. And, *Dieu!* How the colour suited her. It made her positively glow!

'*Bon appétit,*' she beamed as they passed the desk. 'The bed? Did Madame also find it to her liking?'

'Oh, very much to my liking,' Julia laughed, eyes shining with mischief. 'Very, *very* much...'

They spent three days which, were the

Fates to decide they should be their last together, would compensate for a lifetime of aloneness, Julia thought. The sun shone especially brightly, the flowering trees were at their most beautiful, and the river, when they walked beside it, winked sunshine back at their happiness.

They laughed, drank coffee at pavement tables, walked hand in hand down narrow, unexpected streets, visited the church of the Sacred Heart, leaving a candle for their happiness at the feet of the Virgin.

They made love passionately and often. No one other than themselves existed. Paris was theirs and theirs alone; their happiness wiped out the years apart.

'Will you always love me like this?' Julia asked softly, her hand in his.

'For ever, my darling—if you'll promise never to stop loving *me*.'

'Always, I promise. I can't bear to think we have only one day and one night left.'

'Don't be sad. We shall be so happy, my Julia! It's at times like this when I love you so much I can hardly bear it, that I send my heartfelt thanks to the fat policeman who was the cause of our meeting.'

'And to Alice, who pushed him!' She reached up, clasping her arms around his neck, searching, eyes closed, for his lips not caring at all that they stood in view of every passer-by.

'Let's go back to our room,' she whispered, throatily. *'Please?'*

It had been unbelievably easy. It had not even, Elliot Sutton exulted, been necessary to await the call to deliver a message. When no one had entered his small room at Combined Allied Headquarters for two days, when the telephone on the wall had not demanded his attention either, he'd thought, and rightly, that no one knew he was here. That far emboldened, he had taken a large, thick envelope, tied it round with tape, then sealed it all over with blobs of red wax. It could not have looked more secret, more important. Then he wrote: BY SPECIAL MESSENGER, FOR SIGHT ONLY OF GO/C 52ND DIVISION, hoping that such a division existed, placed the envelope in his case, and took a train to Amiens. From there it would be easy to find Celverte, where Julia nursed, and the clearing-station twenty miles away to which Cousin Giles had lately been sent. He was wasting his time, Elliot considered, as he settled himself on the train, being one of a number, when he would have made so excellent a spy. The ease with which he'd obtained the whereabouts of his cousins had amazed him. Small wonder the Allies appeared to be losing the war.

He adjusted the cushion at his neck, then lit a cigarette, considering what his defence would be in the event of his absence being discovered. Having decided the odds against it were in his favour, he turned his attention to more mundane matters.

He must first look up Nathan at Brigade Headquarters at some obscure castle five miles out of Amiens on the Abbeville road. Nathan, always eager to help, would find him a billet for the night, were a bed not available in more salubrious surroundings. After which it would be easy, because of the identification he carried, to obtain transport and a driver and go where the whim took him. Perhaps he would meet none of his family, he shrugged, but no matter. A jaunt near enough to the fighting would relieve the boredom of his existence at CAHQ, though had it not been for Beatrice's stupidity and the wagging tongues of London matrons, his posting would not have been necessary.

Yet Paris was the place to be, though Parisian women were notoriously expensive as well as expecting to be wined and dined at expensive restaurants. Perhaps the brothel women would be easier and cheaper out in the countryside, he mused.

He hoped so. His allowance was spent and until April he was living on his army pay.

But something would turn up. It always did. In his case, he could never be sure if it was heaven taking care of the righteous or the devil looking after his own. A bit of both, maybe.

He smiled, stubbed out his cigarette, and closed his eyes.

'Nathan, dear fellow! How good to see you!' Elliot clasped his brother to him. 'My, but you took the devil of a time to find!'

'I can't believe this!' Nathan Sutton's pleasure was genuine and evident. 'What on earth brings you here?'

'Oh—you know. Least said..' Elliot tapped his nose with his forefinger in a say-no-more gesture. 'Something to deliver to someone in high places. Took a chance on finding you.'

'And I'm glad you did. How long can you stay?'

'Must be away by morning,' Elliot smiled, still smugly satisfied at the ease with which he had located his brother.

'Then I'm sorry—I'm going up to the line. Almost certain I won't get back before tomorrow afternoon. The troops you see: many like to receive the Sacrament before they—well—go over the top into action, and I am duty chaplain.'

'Bother!' Elliot's smile was easy. 'But I suppose the Lord's work must come first. Never mind. Surely we can have a little time together. When do you leave?'

'In half an hour. My, but it's splendid seeing you. You look so well,' Nathan laughed. 'I'm sorry not having more time, but I'm new here and so far I don't seem able to have sorted out any free time for myself. I plan to look Julia up soon, though. I'm pretty sure she's only four miles from here. A little place called Celverte. There's an enormous chateau—a hospital, now—perched on a hill. It's probably there that she works.

'Still, I can at least introduce you to the adjutant. You'll be welcome to eat here; use my bed tonight, if you'd like. I'll get back as soon as I can, but—'

'Your work takes priority,' Elliot finished smoothly.

'It must, but come with me to the mess. At least we can have a drink together before I leave. And did you know that Giles isn't all that far away? I haven't managed to meet him yet, but I've already written, and I hope it won't be too long before we can fix something up.'

'David and Jonathan—that's what the two of you are. Inseparable,' Elliot teased.

'I might just look him up too. Got a pass that'll take me past most guardrooms, you know.'

'I wish you would. Stretcher-bearers don't have it very easy, and it's time you patched up your differences. I know he'd be glad to see you—if he isn't on duty, that is. So many of his kind spend long stints at the Front, I'm afraid.

'But let me show you to my room. It is small, yet I have a bed, which is more than the poor beggars at the Front have. I'll introduce you around; I know you'll be welcome.'

They made him very welcome. Elliot said his farewells to his brother, then took advantage of the invitation to dine. The arrangement suited him well. Free bed and board was most opportune at this time, and an evening spent in the mess might be altogether more entertaining than spending it with his earnest, saintly brother. Or, he considered, if the evening promised to be stuffy, with no card-games in the offing, he could always look up Cousin Julia. She just might offer him a welcome; tell him where exactly he could find Giles. There were many possibilities open to him; his visit to the Front—or as near as dammit—might prove most entertaining. He would make up his mind when he had eaten.

He smiled into the small mirror, tweaked his tie straight, then went in search of a meal.

It was something of a shame, Elliot was to think afterwards, that his early welcome so quickly ran thin. It could have been blamed, of course, on the fact that he ate too little and drank too much and quickly became the worse for it. Half a bottle of good red wine and several brandies had taken charge of his tongue. In no time at all, the commanding officer was obliged to ask the adjutant to deliver a message to the padre's brother, reminding him he was a guest, and please to conduct himself accordingly. To which gently whispered words of advice, Elliot had flushed deeply, pushed back his chair noisily, and left the table.

It was simply not done. He knew it, but was powerless to curb his impetuosity. He knew better than to leave before the senior officer present, but Elliot in his cups cared not one jot for tradition or rank or age. He'd be away from here first thing in the morning; to hell with the lot of them!

But first a walk in the evening air to clear his head, then be damned if he wouldn't find himself transport and look up Nurse Julia! Even her thinly veiled disapproval would be better than having

415

to make his apologies, then creep away to his brother's bed. Pulling on his cap, making sure his hip-flask was full, he set off in search of his cousin.

The duty officer in charge of motor transport was young, inexperienced, and easily impressed by Elliot's air of command and the imposing pass that gave him entry into the Paris headquarters.

'Celverte, sir? No—not all that far away. We have a convoy leaving for St Omer: I could arrange to have you dropped off as near as possible, perhaps?'

Elliot thanked him charmingly. He was always charming when things went his way, and in less than half an hour he was travelling in the direction of Celverte.

The driver, beside whom Elliot sat, knew the place well. Very small, but with a large chateau. They would reach the crossroads very soon. From there, it would only be a short walk into the village.

The chateau was easy to find. It stood high and arrogant, dominating the village, a splendid target for a German gunner with a good eye—if they got any nearer, Elliot thought. In the courtyard he waylaid a nurse, asking for Julia MacMalcolm, but she shook her head impatiently.

'No one of that name here,' she snapped, 'though we get them from time to time from Sixteen-General, when we are busy—which we are,' she added.

'Then can you tell me—'

'Over there—through Celverte.' The nurse pointed in the direction of the woods. 'Ask for the convent or the school; the nurses will be there if they're off duty. Huts, the hospital's made up of. You can't miss them.'

'Is it far? Will it take me long?' Elliot demanded, having had exercise enough for one day.

'Depends how quickly you can walk,' she shrugged, turning abruptly, hurrying away.

She had no time to waste on dandily dressed officers with brilliantly polished boots, when another convoy of wounded was expected within the hour. A cup of hot, sweet tea was more to her liking! And he had smelled of drink. Maybe the walk to Sixteen-General would sober him up a bit!

Tuesday. Soon, Julia would be back. Not that she wished it, but Alice had missed her more than she had ever thought possible.

She was tired. Julia's extra hands had been missed, especially since Sister had been unable to find a relief for her.

She walked the field path back to quarters, hoping there might be a letter from Tom. It was three weeks now, and she was getting more and more worried. But Julia should be here by ten tonight; Julia would tell her things would be all right, urge her not to worry.

She stopped briefly at the letterboard, then went at once to the dining-room, pleased at last that in the morning her friend would be beside her at breakfast, still talking about Paris and Andrew and so starry-eyed she'd be not one bit of use on the ward for the whole of the day. Alice took her place at the table beside Ruth Love.

'She'll be back soon, won't she? Do you suppose we'll get any sense out of her?' Ruth grinned.

'I was thinking much the same thing myself.' The soup was hot and thick. Alice had not realised how hungry she was. 'Any news?' she murmured.

'From the Front, you mean? No, though if things had got worse, surely we'd have been warned—to evacuate, I mean.' It would be far from easy, were the German divisions to get nearer, to carry the wounded to safety. 'But cheer up. There's a bit of good news—for you, at least. I put a letter on your bed. Did you find it?'

'I haven't been upstairs yet.' Alice jumped to her feet, hunger forgotten. 'I'll go and get it!'

'There's no hurry!' Ruth called, too late. Poor love. She thought it was from Tom and she was going to be disappointed. The letter had borne an English stamp.

Breathless from running, Alice flung aside the green curtain, then gazed with disappointment at the envelope on her bed.

Not from Tom. Not from anyone she knew. She turned it over and read the name of Tom's sister on the back.

But of course! His family had had news of him! Eagerly she tore open the envelope.

It was a long time before the words stopped swimming in front of her eyes, the floor tilting beneath her feet. She stood in time suspended, trying to sort them into some kind of order, make sense out of them.

...and Mam is so beside herself that I am writing to let you know that Tom—

'No! *No!*'

Tom was *not* dead; had *not* been killed in action! At Epernay? There was no such place!

...died at Epernay on Tuesday 5 March. I am sorry to be the one to have to give you such terrible news. I hope in time you will bring yourself to forgive me. I share your grief. I loved Tom, too...

'*Julia!*' For God's sake, where was Julia!

Her cry was raw with terror. She crumpled the letter in her hands, flinging it on the bed. Julia would know what to do; would tell her it was all a mistake. She should be back by now. Why wasn't she here? *'Julia...'*

She began to run, blindly, wildly; away from that letter and the cruelty of a world that had caused it to be written. Tom wasn't dead! He *wasn't!*

Her heel caught a hole in the path and she hurtled to the ground, the palms of her hands and her knees taking the brunt of her fall. She stayed there, hugging herself as pain tore through her. Then she pulled herself unsteadily to her feet and looked into the face of Elliot Sutton. Only it wasn't Elliot Sutton and the letter hadn't happened! It was all part of a nightmare and she wanted to awaken from it.

'Tom!'

A hand grasped her wrist and held it tightly. She closed her eyes, shutting out a world gone mad.

'Well, if it isn't the little sewing-maid!'

'No! Don't touch me! Tom! Help me, Tom...'

'There's no Tom here, my girl,' he laughed. 'And no damn dog, either!'

His words were slurred; his breath smelled of drink. She kicked out wildly, but he held on to her wrist, laughing at her efforts to be free.

Her struggling excited him. He felt a stirring in his loins. Dammit, but she'd be cheaper and cleaner than a whore!

He pulled her towards the building, kicking open the door. In the dimness he could see the straw-filled palliasses. Be blowed if it wasn't all laid on for him; all there for his comfort!

He flung her down, then straddled her, ripping open the bodice of her dress, tearing at it wildly. His mouth covered hers and she bit viciously at his lips then, digging her heels into the soft, shifting straw of the palliasse, she put her weight on them, heaving up her back in an effort to throw him off.

He tore at her skirt. She screamed, *'No. Help me! Someone please help me!'*

His mouth found hers again. His moustache was rough and hurt her lips. She ceased to struggle. It was no use. There would be no awakening from this nightmare.

He thrust into her; viciously, cruelly, laughing triumphantly, throatily, trailing his mouth over her neck, searching for her breasts.

She wanted him to kill her. She wanted to be dead, like Tom. The face above her began to swim as dizziness took her. She closed her eyes and surrendered to the darkness that shifted and slipped before her eyes, blotting out her sight.

Tom. Wait for me...

She stirred, opening her eyes. She was alone in the cowshed. It hadn't happened. Elliot Sutton's cruel thrusting had been a part of the nightmare, too.

She rose slowly to her feet, her body throbbing with pain. She put her hands to her breasts, pulling her bodice over them.

'Julia!' She began to run. Please, Julia *must* be there!

She clattered up the stairs, flinging open the dormitory door. Julia had not come. It was Ruth Love who stood at her bedside, the crumpled letter in her hand.

'Alice, I came to look for you. What is it? What have you done to yourself?'

'The letter—you read it?'

'Yes—I'm sorry, but I—'

'It says he's dead, doesn't it? He's dead, isn't he?'

Sobs shook her body. She paced the cubicle like an animal caged.

'Ssssh, now.' Tenderly Ruth took her, cradling her, clucking softly. 'Alice, I *do* understand.'

'Why Tom, Ruth...?'

'Why my Jamie? Why any of them?'

'I wish he'd killed me. I wish I were dead, Ruth.' She lifted her eyes skywards.

'Do you hear me, God! You should have let him kill me!'

'*Kill* you? Alice—what has happened?'

It was Julia. She was back! Moaning softly, Alice went into her arms. Over her shoulder, Ruth held up the letter.

Tom, she mouthed. *Killed.*

'Dear God, *no,*' Julia gasped. 'Alice, what did you do?'

She cupped the tear-ravaged face in gentle hands, mopping it with her handkerchief.

'Do? It's all right, Julia. My face is all right. He didn't hit me, this time...'

'He?' Julia stared with disbelief at the torn frock, the marks on her neck, her shoulders. '*This* time? *He* did this? Elliot Sutton did it?'

'I ran out. In the stable, it was. I went dizzy, then everything went black. I thought I was dying. I wanted to die!'

'Alice—tell me? Did he? This time, *did* he?'

Mutely, Alice nodded.

'She's been—*raped?* I'm going to find Sister!' Ruth gasped.

'No! Please, Ruth—don't! Not yet. Let's try to get things straight first. She's been through this before, you see. Same man...'

'Then we *must* tell Sister. He can't be allowed to get away with it!'

'No, Ruth,' Alice whispered. 'Just leave

423

me alone—please?'

Ruth's eyes met Julia's, questioningly. Julia nodded.

'Very well. I'll be in my room, though, if you want me.'

'Thanks,' Julia whispered as the staff nurse left, pulling the curtains together behind her.

'Now, let's have those clothes off,' Julia said softly, 'and get you into the bath.'

'Yes.' She wanted to wash herself; get rid of the touch and smell and memory of him—scrub her body clean. 'Don't tell, Julia? Don't tell anyone?'

'No, love. I won't tell.'

'And Ruth won't?'

'We'll ask her not to.'

'It was awful, Julia. He hurt me.'

'Ssssh.' Julia undressed her friend as if she were a helpless child; wincing to see the bruises showing already on her body. 'But there shouldn't be any damage done. They say it can't happen—not first time...'

'But it wasn't the first time—Tom and me, just the once—you know we did. Oh, God!' The sobs began afresh. 'Julia, I want Tom!'

'Hush now. Tom's going to be all right.'

'Maggie wrote that he's been killed...'

'Well he *hasn't*! It's all a mistake. Tom's

all right. I know it. He'll have been taken prisoner. Let's run that bath...?'

Gently, she slipped Alice's arms into the sleeves of her dressing-gown; tenderly, she guided her down the long room to where the bath stood curtained.

God! Listen to me! I swear on the love I hold for Andrew that Elliot Sutton will answer for this! I swear it!

19

Julia watched over Alice like a hen with an only chick, trying never to leave her too long alone to brood, insisting that Tom had not been killed. Nor was her optimism merely for Alice. She truly believed he was alive; that soon there would be a letter from him.

'I won't even let myself *think* things won't come right for you,' she insisted, again and again. 'Something inside me says it. Don't stop hoping, please?'

Yet Alice had lost hope; lost all faith. There could be no God when that awful thing had been allowed to happen; when she was reeling from the shock of Maggie's letter. That night, she would never forget. Each year she would remember the anniversary of the dying of her happiness.

Then Sister gave them the grave news.

'You are to pack your cases,' she said, sadly. 'Put everything in them you are least likely to need, then push them beneath your beds. It seems we must all be ready to evacuate the hospital at short notice, and since the wounded will take priority over all else, it is up to each nurse to prepare herself as best she can.'

'But how are we to leave—even if the Germans come?' Ruth had whispered. 'Most of our wounded now are gas cases—in no fit state to be moved. How can we leave them?'

'There I cannot help you. It will be up to each nurse to search her conscience, then decide whether to stay or to leave. As perhaps you already know, nurses from a forward dressing-station arrived here last night. They were completely without possessions. German troops overran their post, taking our wounded soldiers prisoners, allowing the nurses to go free. Two wanted to stay, but they were made to leave.

'Let us hope the enemy will not reach Celverte. I think we should carry on as best we can, and leave the rest in God's hands. Sometimes, I have found, He does know best.' She cleared her throat noisily, then tilting her chin defiantly she whispered, 'Before we go on duty, shall we say a prayer?'

Stunned, they bowed their heads.

'May God, in the troubled days that lie ahead,' Sister whispered, 'grant to us all at this hospital the serenity to accept the things we cannot change, the courage to change the things we can, and the wisdom to know the difference.

'There now, ladies,' she smiled, almost with relief. 'It is out of our hands now. Shall we collect the breakfasts for the ward, then relieve the night staff?'

'She's one love of an old dragon,' Julia said shakily as she and Alice pushed the breakfast trolley to Hut Twenty-four. 'She and Aunt Sutton would get on like a house on fire. And cheer up, Alice! No one has had a letter in ages. Everything has just gone haywire. I've only had a couple from Andrew since our leave—and that was almost three weeks ago. He writes every day—you know he does—so somewhere in the pipeline are nearly twenty missing letters. Tom is alive, I know it. Do you think I'd be so cruel as to say it if I didn't believe it? Word of a Sutton, I wouldn't.'

'No, you wouldn't. But there's something else.' Alice took a deep, shuddering breath. 'I'm pregnant.'

'*What!*' The trolley stopped with a

clattering of cups and plates. 'You can't be!'

'I can. I'm a week overdue.'

'Nonsense!' Shock hit Julia hard in the pit of her stomach. 'It's all the worry: the letter from Maggie; Elliot doing what he did; all the talk of the Germans advancing.

'It isn't. I'm always regular, no matter what. And when you smoke, it makes me feel sick, and it never did before. I've fallen—I know I have. What am I going to do?' Her voice was thick with tears. 'Where can I go? There's Reuben, but how can I go back to Rowangarth? Folks are going to say that I asked for what I got. The men always stick together, and the women are no better. Where am I to go with my shame?'

'You are going nowhere, that I promise you! Rowangarth is your home, and we'll take care of you if you really are having a baby. And Elliot Sutton isn't going to get away with it!'

'Julia—it'll be my word against his. And what was he doing in Celverte? Who saw him? What proof do I have?' She sighed, despairingly. 'Tom's dead and I wish I were. Perhaps I'll die, having it. Women do...'

'Stop it!' Julia's voice was rough with anger. 'Just stop it, will you? You are *not* alone! What we'll do, I don't know, but we're going to think calmly about it. And I'll ask Ruth if there's anything you can take—anything safe, that is—to help bring you on. Ruth's a proper trained nurse. If there's anything at all, she'll know about it.'

'There's nothing to know, Julia. And even if there is, Ruth wouldn't tell us about it. It's against all she's ever been taught as a nurse. She can't help me. Nobody can. And I don't want you to tell Ruth just yet.'

'All right. But I'll help you, I promise. And as for Elliot.' Her eyes narrowed into vicious slits. 'May God help him if you really are pregnant. I'll make him wish he'd never been born.'

'Leave it for now, Julia? And Sister's glaring. Come on—or we'll be in trouble.'

Trouble? She was already in more trouble than she knew what to do with.

Tom—please don't be dead.

It was not long after they had finished duty, after they had eaten a supper they neither wanted nor could taste, that the bugle sounded. Its strident notes sent alarm slicing through those who heard it, for a bugle-alert meant either an air-raid threatened or that off-duty nurses were on stand-to.

'It isn't a raid,' said Ruth, 'but Sister

says we can expect a convoy of wounded. They can't cope with them at the chateau, so somehow we've got to fit them in here.'

It was almost with relief they put on clean aprons and fastened on caps, hurrying to what had once been the school yard to wait for the ambulances.

'Where are they from?' Ruth asked of Sister Carbrooke.

'North of Albert, I believe. So far, I think our lines are holding, but with so many wounded, who can tell?'

'How many can we take?'

'I'm not sure. But we can find room for five in Hut Twenty-four. There's the emergency bed and we can put four on the floor. Thank heaven for the palliasses. Can you tell Night Sister where they are?'

There were twelve ambulances. The stretchers were laid in rows on the ground; those of the wounded who could walk were tended at once by nurses; those seriously hurt waited examination by a doctor.

Beside each medical officer walked a nurse with trays of syringes and dressings; another wrote down the names and numbers of the wounded.

Some tried to smile in spite of their pain. They were out of the fighting; little else mattered.

Others lay pale and still, eyes closed.

Some would die before morning, their wounds such that it was kinder to let them slip away from their pain in a haze of morphine.

'This man is bleeding badly—can he be found a bed?' a doctor asked.

'There's always a bed kept empty in Hut Twenty-four,' Sister said at once. 'He can have that. How bad is he?'

'I can't say. He's lost a lot of blood. He might make it, though.'

The wounded soldier wore the red cross of a stretcher-bearer on his arm. His face was paper-white, his yellow hair wet with sweat.

'Nurse Hawthorn!' Sister held up a hand. 'Take down this patient's name and number, then show the orderlies the way to our ward. Tell Night Sister he's to have the empty bed—MO's orders.'

Alice dropped to her knees, searching beneath the rough shirt for the discs that hung there. Then she pulled in her breath sharply.

'Sister—can I stay with him? They're going to need all the help they can get tonight in Hut Twenty-four.'

'Why, when you've just done a full duty? You look fit to drop where you stand. *Why*, Hawthorn?'

'Because he's bad, I know it.' Alice dropped her voice to a whisper. 'And if he's going to—to die, he should have someone he knows beside him. I know him well, only don't let Julia hear about it suddenly. Tell her gently? He's her brother, you see.' And Giles Sutton could die, if not from his wounds, then from loss of blood. 'Let me stay with him, Sister?'

The night nurses in Hut Twenty-four laid Giles Sutton on the emergency bed, then pulled the curtains round it. Alice stood at Duty Sister's desk, coughing to gain her attention.

'What is it?'

'Sister Carbrooke said—if it's all right with you, that is—that I could stay and special that patient.' She nodded in the direction of the curtained bed.

'Why?'

'Because you are busy enough and the MO agrees. I'd like to stay. I know him, you see.'

'Your young man, is he? Going to have a fit of hysterics, are you?'

'He isn't my young man, and I'll be all right, Sister. He's Sir Giles Sutton—I used to work for his mother. Best, when he comes round, he should see a face he knows.'

'Think you can manage?' Sister demanded brusquely.

'Yes. He's had an injection. When he

needs another, someone else will have to give it to him. Apart from that, I'll be all right.'

'Very well.' She seemed the sensible sort, Night Sister decided. 'Go to him. I'll be in as soon as I've had a word with the MO about him. Bad, is he?'

'They think it was a land-mine.'

'I see.' Land-mines were the very devil. A dirty way of fighting. 'All right. Away with you...'

The white-haired sister covered her face with her hands. She had been a nurse more years than she cared to remember, but never had she seen such wanton wasting of good young lives. Once, she had been a midwife. Now every waking day she wondered how many of the boy children she helped to be born were already dead. She rose to her feet as the medical officer came into the ward.

'Good evening, sir,' she said softly, all traces of her despair gone.

'How is he?' Night Sister came to stand beside Alice's chair.

'No change, though he's been stirring as if he's going to come out of it. And I think the dressing has stopped the bleeding. Sister, do you think—' Alice stopped, embarrassed.

'Go on, Nurse. I haven't got all night!'

'Well—when first I was nursing, we had a patient just like this. Another land-mine. He lived though. Nurse Love was in charge of that ward and she'd whisper in his ear. I think she thought it might help him hang on a big longer. I'm not meaning to be forward, Sister,' she dropped her eyes to the floor, 'but can I try?'

'Whisper about *what?*' the elderly nurse frowned.

'I could tell him that it's me, Hawthorn, and I could talk about Morgan—that's his dog. I used to take it out for him. And I'd talk about Rowangarth, where he lived. Familiar words might help.'

'They might. It won't hurt to try.' Sister's voice was gentler. Anything that might help save just one young life was worth a try. She turned and left abruptly, swishing the curtains behind her.

Alice reached for Giles's hand, her fingers automatically searching for a pulse. There was the slightest movement in his fingers, as if he knew.

'Sir Giles?' She laid her hand over his. 'When are you going to finish those old books? Morgan needs a run.'

There was a flickering of his eyelids, the slightest moving of his lips as if he had heard her and was trying to speak:

'I'll take Morgan out for you. To Brattocks...'

Brattocks. She shouldn't have said that word. She would never see Brattocks again. How could she go back there?

'You're going home, Sir Giles, to Rowangarth. Her ladyship is waiting at the top of the steps. Can you see her?'

Sister parted the curtains, scanning the chart that hung at the foot of the bed. 'No change?'

Alice shook her head, rising to her feet. 'I think he can hear me, though. Just small signs. I'll carry on talking to him.'

'It's probably that he's in need of another injection,' Sister murmured, tight-lipped. 'I'll give him it now. Then I'll stay with him for a while. I've been talking to Sister Carbrooke; we've agreed MacMalcolm should be told. All the wounded have been seen to, found beds. She'll be going off duty soon. Will you tell her, Nurse? Are you up to it?'

'I don't know. I'll try, though. Best it comes from someone close. What am I to tell her, Sister?'

'That he's very ill; that he's being special-nursed. Will she make a fuss, do you think?'

Alice shook her head. 'Her husband is a doctor; she'll be all right.'

'Then will you ask her if she wants me to send for the padre?'

'He's *that* bad?' Alice sucked in her breath sharply.

'I'm afraid so.'

'I'd better hurry.' Alice was cold with shock. 'Can she see him? Can she come back with me?'

'Nurse! You have worked one duty, and half the night too. You'll be expected here as usual in the morning. A few hours' sleep would do you more good.'

'No. I'll stay with him.'

She found Julia in the yard of the school, hugging her cape around her, ready to leave.

'Alice! I haven't seen you for ages—are you all right?'

'Yes—but come inside, will you? There's something Night Sister said I was to tell you.'

'What is it?' Julia's face drained of colour.

'Tonight they brought a soldier in.' Alice turned to close the door behind them, give herself a moment in which to think. 'I've been with him. They took him to our ward—the top bed. He's not so good...'

'Who is he?' Julia demanded through clenched teeth.

'Sister says you can come and see him. He's just had another injection, so he's not in pain.'

436

'Alice—*who?*'

'It's Giles—and wait!' She grasped Julia's arm as she made for the door. 'Sister thinks he's in need of a priest. Will I ask her to send for one?'

'Yes. Yes, of course!' Julia was running, stumbling in the darkness. Then she paused, holding out her hand, taking Alice's in her own. 'I'm sorry you had to tell me. Be with me when I see him?'

'I'm staying with him.'

'But I should do it. I should be with him!'

'You're too close. Sister wouldn't allow it. Just be with him for a while. You'll be near him all day when we go on duty—he's in our ward, don't forget.'

They entered the familiar ward, nodding to the staff nurse, opening the green curtains. Night Sister sat beside the bed, and she rose to her feet as they went in.

'You are his sister?' she asked, tersely.

'Yes. Thank you for letting me know.' Julia bent to touch the white cheek with her lips, saying his name softly.

'Giles, it's Julia.' She turned to Sister, her eyes begging. 'Can I stay for a little while? Alice says you want to send for a priest. I agree. Can I stay until he comes?'

'I don't know if one will get here in time. And I have already sent...'

'Thank you,' Julia said gravely. 'And can I stay?'

Sister pursed her lips, then shrugged. 'For a while, perhaps.' She would be all right. Her sort knew how to keep a hold on their feelings.

She left, shaking her head. She hoped a padre would be available. It could well be too late, if he didn't come soon.

One long, sad hour later, the army chaplain came. Julia lifted her head wearily, then flung herself into his arms.

'Nathan! Oh, my dear...'

Sister followed close behind, eyebrows questioning.

'They're cousins,' Alice offered. 'The padre and Sir Giles grew up like brothers.'

Sister nodded, accepting the explanation. Nathan moved to the head of the bed, his face taut with pain. 'The Sacrament,' he murmured. 'I'd thought he would be...'

Sister shook her head.

White-faced, Nathan knelt at the bedside. Julia and Alice sank to their knees. They heard the swishing of the curtains as Sister left, then Nathan softly intoned prayers for those about to die.

'Giles,' he whispered, taking his cousin's hand, holding it to his cheek. 'Why did it have to be you?'

'Can you stay?' Julia whispered. 'Just for a little while?'

Nathan lifted his hand, giving Absolution, signing his forehead with the Cross.

'My dear, dear friend,' he whispered. 'I wish I could have done more...'

'You must go?' Julia whispered.

'I'm sorry—yes. But I'll be back as soon as I can. Are you all right, Julia?'

'Yes. But will you pray for us, and for Mother especially?'

'I will.' He kissed her cheek then, nodding his thanks to Night Sister, he left.

When Julia returned, Alice was seated beside the bed once more, Giles's hand in hers.

'I've been talking to him,' she smiled. 'Just softly, about Rowangarth and Morgan —things he knows about. Ruth did it at Denniston, remember? That boy had just the same injuries. We didn't lose him, did we?'

'And you want another miracle?'

'Yes, I do,' Alice said stubbornly, leaning closer.

'Here's that Morgan again, Sir Giles. He's been down to the kitchen, soft-soaping Cook for scraps. We're going to Brattocks, him and me. It's Hawthorn, come to take him to Brattocks...'

'It isn't any use.' Julia bit hard into

her lip. 'He can't feel pain. We must be grateful for that.'

'Go, Julia. You're upset. I'll stay.' Stay all night, if she had to.

'No. We'll stay together.' She sat down, opposite. 'Dear Giles, who never harmed a soul. Why him, Alice? Is it only the good who die young?'

Her mouth was set traplike and Alice knew she was thinking about Elliot Sutton. And hating him for being alive.

In the morning, when the night nurses left and Sister Carbrooke and Ruth came to take over, Giles Sutton still held on to life. Sister read his chart, frowning.

'One of you must take some rest. You, Hawthorn—go back to quarters. Get some breakfast and a few hours' sleep. I'll send MacMalcolm to wake you at noon. You're neither of you any use to him half asleep. That's an order. I'll give him another injection, then change his dressings. Staff will keep an eye on him.' And on MacMalcolm, too, who looked pale and strained, the smudges beneath her eyes dark against her cheeks.

'I want to stay,' Julia whispered. 'He's my brother. And anyway, Nathan is coming back. I want to see Nathan.'

'The chaplain,' Alice whispered. 'Nathan —their cousin.'

She drew her cape around her shoulders. Her eyes felt dry and full of grit and there was a dull ache inside her. Hungry, she supposed. Tea—that was what she wanted. Hot, sweet tea—and to sleep the clock round.

'Talk to him, remember,' she said, softly.

In the early afternoon, Alice returned to take her place at Giles's bedside, whilst Julia, too tired to protest, touched her brother's cheek gently and allowed Ruth Love to push her towards the door.

Not long afterwards, the duty medical officer stood at the bedside as Sister changed Giles's dressings.

'The bleeding has stopped.' He bent to examine the gaping wound. 'It seems clean. No indication of—?'

'No gangrene,' she said firmly, anticipating the question.

'Then perhaps, Sister, no more morphine, would you say?'

'I agree, sir.' She could not disguise the triumph in her voice.

'I'll leave you a prescription when I've done my rounds. I didn't think, you know—'

'No.' No one had thought it. MacMalcolm's brother, by the law of averages, was lucky to have seen another day. Only get him through this one, and the next, and they could begin to hope.

Alice wiped Giles's forehead with a cool cloth, then moistened his dry lips, listening to the medical officer's murmurings as he stopped beside each bed in the ward.

'Sister says you are to go, Alice.' Ruth parted the curtains. 'We can manage until the night nurses come on. And as soon as Julia wakes up, tell her that her brother is being taken off morphine. He's being put on a different pain-killer now; one not nearly so drastic. So if she's able to take it in, tell her that's good news, will you?'

'There's hope?'

'It's early days yet...'

'Then I'll tell her it's early days yet, but there *is* hope.'

Alice leaned over the bed. 'It's Hawthorn. I'm going now, Sir Giles.' Then her eyes flew wide. 'Look!'

His lips were moving. He was trying to speak.

Ruth took the feeding cup, easing the spout between his lips. Carefully she tilted it; weakly he sucked on it, then swallowed the cool water slowly. Then his eyes opened and he looked around him in bewilderment.

'Hawthorn?' he whispered.

'It's Hawthorn,' she smiled, eyes wet with sudden, happy tears. 'I've been in Brattocks Wood with Morgan!'

'Julia!' Asleep or not, this news was too important to keep. 'Listen! Giles is—'

'What is it?' Julia sat upright, eyes blinking, still half asleep. *'Giles?'* She made to get out of bed, but Alice pushed her back.

'Good news! He's to have no more morphine. He's on a milder pain-killer now!'

'But that's good. It *is!*'

'Yes, an' Ruth said especially to tell you. Said it's early days yet, but—'

'But there's a chance? He's going to be all right!' Julia covered her face with her hands and wept.

'Hush, now. Stop that noise!' Alice lifted the sheet corner, mopping Julia's eyes. 'Get yourself dressed and go over. He might have drifted off again, but he took a drink of water, and he spoke.'

'He was lucid? What did he say?'

'Clear as a bell, it was. He saw me and said my name,' Alice choked.

The agony of her own troubles faded a little and she smiled tremulously. Giles Sutton was going to get well. He *was!*

Back to night duties again, and so far, the Somme line had held. Giles, too weak yet to be sent to England, improved a little each day. Nathan was a constant visitor;

443

Sister, though she tried not to show it, became fond of the softly spoken young man who had been wounded in No Man's Land, trying to bring help to those unable to help themselves.

'They spoil me outrageously,' he smiled to Nathan. 'Julia, of course, cannot nurse me, but Hawthorn is a dear creature, and they both pop in for a talk when Sister's back is turned. They tell me I shall soon be leaving for England, though I shall miss being here.'

'I have written to Aunt Helen, Giles; told her to try not to worry. Heaven only knows how long it will take to get to her, but at least she'll know at first hand that you are getting well and that we are all together here. I long to see Holdenby.' Nathan's eyes spanned the miles to the little railway station and the hills behind it.

'I shall be discharged, they tell me.' Giles fidgeted with his bed-cover. 'I haven't told this to anyone yet; the MO only sprang it on me yesterday, but I'm a poor creature, it seems. I've been a fool, Nathan. Mother was right. I should have found myself a wife.'

'But you can't fall in love to order, old chum! When you get back home, a hero, they'll be falling over themselves to flirt with you.'

'No! Mother knew, you know. After Robert was killed she would talk about grandchildren. But what she really wanted was a boy, for Rowangarth. Now it's too late, though it seems I'm going to make it. I'll always be a bit of a weakling; never one hundred per cent...'

'Nor will a lot of men.'

'I know. I've got a lot to be thankful for. At least I have my lungs and my eyesight. But, Nathan, the MO was as certain as he can be that I'll never father a child. It's going to break Mother's heart.'

'It won't, Giles. She'll be so relieved to have you out of the army she won't care. I'll bet Julia agrees with what I say, too. I'm sorry though; desperately sorry.'

'Thanks. Julia doesn't know, by the way. I'll tell her, of course, but she isn't going to like the title leaving Rowangarth. You know how she feels about that? She won't want it to pass to Elliot when I've snuffed it. She can't abide him. I mentioned his name only yesterday and she bit my head off.'

'Elliot isn't everybody's cup of tea,' Nathan grinned, 'but one day he'll mend his ways. Perhaps the love of a good woman, as they say, might well be the making of him.'

'Elliot isn't interested in *good* women,' Giles murmured, his eyes mischievous.

'But I shall tell Julia, next time she pops her head through the curtains. And I'm thankful to be out of the war, Nathan. I did my best—now I can't wait to be home again. How are things going, by the way? I suppose the fighting is as bad as ever?'

'It is. And the Germans are by no means finished. One good push, just one breakthrough and—' He shrugged eloquently. 'The war could go either way, you realise that, don't you?'

'I do, yet sometimes I think I wouldn't care who won it, if only the killing would stop.'

'We'll win,' Nathan said quietly, sadly. 'But what a price we'll have paid.'

Alice was eating breakfast when someone called, 'Hawthorn! Young man to see you!'

'*Me?*' She jumped to her feet, heart thumping. 'Where?'

'At the front door. A soldier. Off you go, then!'

'Oh, God, *Tom!*' She began to run. It was him. It *was!* Julia had been right all along!

She ran down the hall, flinging wide the door. 'Tom?'

The soldier turned. His hair was fair, his eyes bright blue; at his shoulder he wore the insignia of the West Yorkshire Regiment.

'Nurse Alice Hawthorn?' he said. 'I'm Geordie Marshall. Tom was my mate...'

Despair took her, held her. She wanted to smile, to hold out her hand, ask for news of Tom. Instead, she stood there, unspeaking, wanting to fall to her knees and beat the floor with her fists. For just a few seconds, it had been Tom. She wished Geordie hadn't come because she knew what he would tell her.

'I haven't got long,' he said, gently. 'We're on our way to Ypres. The lads are covering for me, but I can't stay. Tom had got it worked out where you were, and I took a chance on it—finding you, giving you some of this things.'

'It's true, then? Tom is really—' She couldn't say the word.

'He was sent on special duties. That's all I know for sure. But I did hear he was in a motor transport that got hit by a shell. At Epernay, it was. All the blokes in it—gone. But he wouldn't have known any pain. Not like some...'

'It's good of you to come.' She held out her hand. 'He wrote about you in his letters.'

'Aye. I miss him. We were a good team. When they came to collect his things, I got in there quick. I've brought you his Testament. He usually had it in his top pocket—we all do. Daft, I suppose.

They're supposed to stop a bullet. But even if he'd remembered to take it with him, it wouldn't have helped him a lot.

'I've brought the letters you wrote him. Been carrying them around with me for ages. They meant a lot to him.'

He handed them to her awkwardly and she smiled and thanked him, reaching up to kiss his cheek.

'I'll have to be off,' he murmured.

'Yes. Thank you, Geordie. God keep you...'

She watched him walk away, then break into a run. She laid the Testament to her cheek and something fluttered to the ground at her feet.

She bent to pick up a spray of buttercups. It was as if he were saying goodbye to her.

Tom, my love, what's to become of me...?

20

'So you see, Sis, that's the way it is.' Julia sat at her brother's bedside, his hand in hers. 'I dilly-dallied, left it too late. There'll be no sons, now, for Rowangarth. But at least Mother will have grandchildren to fuss over—yours and Andrew's.'

'But are you sure?' The enormity of his words hit her like a slap. 'Doctors can be wrong. How could he make such a snap diagnosis? I shall write to Andrew—he'll know of the best specialist in London.'

Write to Andrew? Much good would it do her. No one got letters these days. You just had to write them and post them and hope.

'I think the MO is right, but it seems I shall live. There are millions who'll never be so lucky.'

Julia drew in her breath sharply. Had Giles not survived that awful first night, his title would already have passed to Pendenys, to Uncle Edward. She didn't mind that; Uncle Edward was a Garth Sutton. But for it to go one day to Elliot made her cold with fury. This war, dammit, would have handed to Aunt Clemmy on a plate what her father's money had failed to do: obtain a knighthood for the Pendenys Suttons.

'Yes, lucky,' she hastened, suddenly ashamed. And was a title really so important? When Giles had pulled through, did it matter?

Yes, it did! It damn well did! She'd rather it went to the first tinker who knocked on the door than to Elliot. Elliot Sutton was evil; a changeling. If only some land-mine had taken *his* manhood...

'You are right, old love.' She lifted his hand to her cheek. 'Just to survive this war is a small miracle but oh, it's so ironic. You will never father a child; Alice is carrying a baby she doesn't want. It's a strange old world, isn't it?'

'*Alice?* Our Hawthorn? But that's awful —Dwerryhouse being killed, I mean. What will she do now?'

'God knows.' Despair trembled on Julia's words. 'And it isn't Tom's child. She'd have wanted it if it had been. It's Elliot's,' she finished bitterly.

'You mean—*again?*' Giles's cheeks flushed crimson.

'Again. Only this time Reuben wasn't there, or Morgan or Dwerryhouse. Alice was out of her mind with grief that night; didn't know what to do. I hadn't got back from Paris, and she'd just had a letter telling her that Tom had been killed. There was no one to turn to. She ran blindly, she said—literally bumped into Elliot Sutton. And he'd been drinking. Life can be rotten, can't it? He'll deny it, of course; swear he was never near Celverte!'

'Poor little Hawthorn. I feel so disgusted, so angry.'

'Don't we all? Ruth Love wanted him found, but Alice begged her not to. It was bad enough that time in Brattocks;

all Rowangarth knowing about it. I think she didn't want to face it again. But she'll have to, now, because she's as sure as she can be that the worst has happened. And only Ruth and I know about it, so don't say anything, will you?'

'You know I won't. But it makes me feel so useless having to lie here, too shot-up to do anything about it,' he said, bitterly. 'How can we help her?'

'I don't know. She's worried sick. Losing Tom has been bad enough and now this. She has no parents to go to—Rowangarth is all she's got. But I'm going to ask Aunt Sutton to have her. No one need know then. I know Aunt will take her in. She doesn't like Elliot either.'

Eyes closed, Giles lay back on his pillows, wanting more than anything to thrash his cousin half to death.

'Giles! I haven't upset you? I'm sorry! I shouldn't have told you, but it just slipped out. I don't know what to do for the best. I'm so fond of her, you see...'

'It's all right, Sis. I am upset, but not in the way you think. I'm glad you've told me and I want to help. Best I talk to Nathan about it—she wouldn't mind Nathan knowing? When do you think he'll be here again?'

'Tomorrow morning. He's holding early Communion in the chapel. I intend going, when I come off duty. Shall I ask him to look in on you?' And whatever God was about, she thought despairingly, at least He had sent Nathan to them.

'Would you? And don't worry. We'll help Hawthorn. Nathan will know what to do. Off you go now. That's Sister calling for you!'

'Sure you're all right?' Hurriedly, Julia rose to her feet.

'I'm fine. Just let me think...'

'I talked to Julia after Communion,' Nathan said, sitting down at Giles's bedside. 'She asked me to look in on you. Desperately urgent, she said.'

'That's my awful sister for you, but I do want to talk to you. Can you spare me a little time? It's advice I want.'

'Be only too glad, you know that.'

'And you'll hear me out? You won't tell me I'm half out of my mind?'

'Army chaplains have to be good listeners. I won't interrupt.'

'I've been awake half the night thinking about it, and I know I'm right. But it's all up to you, really. Tell me, Nathan; can you marry people?'

'*Marry*—yes, of course...'

'Here in France?'

'I suppose so: if there were witnesses, I don't see why not. I don't know about the reading of the banns, though, but out here, on wartime emergency footing, sort of, I don't know they'd be all that necessary. But why do you ask—though I know you're going to tell me.'

And Giles told him, holding nothing back, about Tom's death and Alice and Elliot and Alice having to bear the shame of it alone—she innocent, too.

'Elliot is a Sutton—your brother, Nathan. Alice carries a Sutton child and we are in part responsible for what has happened,' Giles finished.

'Responsible—yes. And God forgive my brother and his ways. I'm deeply ashamed.' Nathan shook his head, wearily. 'And Hawthorn: one sorrow on top of another. What can I do to help her? Find a good home for the child when it's born, perhaps?'

'No. I've already found that. You might though, on my behalf, give your brother the hiding of his life. I would, and gladly, if I weren't so weak still. But if your calling prevents such a thing, then at least help by marrying us—Hawthorn and me.'

'Marrying...?'

'That's what I said.'

'But, Giles, had you thought? Has the girl thought? She might be unhappy as your wife, as lady of a house where once she had been a—an employee. And there is no snobbery in my reasoning,' he added, hastily. 'I'm only thinking of her.'

'So am I, and her shame as a mother unmarried. And I'm thinking of my mother, too. I can't father a child, Nathan, yet Hawthorn has a babe in need of a father. And Rowangarth has need of a son, or—'

'Or Elliot will one day inherit?'

'Yes. Not only the title, but Rowangarth too. A knighthood is Aunt Clemmy's dearest wish for him; he would like it, too, yet it's the one thing she has never been able to get him. I'm sorry to be so blunt, but you know it's true.'

'It's a thought that pleases me.' Nathan's smile bore out his words. 'Mind, the child could be a girl...'

'It's slightly better odds it will be a boy. I've heard that more boys are being born now than girls. Nature's way of compensating for this war. Can you marry us, Nathan?'

'I'd have to go into the legalities of it, but I see no reason why not. An English service said by an English priest and with witnesses...'

'Bless you, Nathan! I'll talk it over with Julia. She'll agree with me, I know it. I can take it there's probably nothing to stand in the way of it then—except Hawthorn. She knows nothing of this.'

'Then you'd do well to consider she might want nothing of it. She's a straight, sensible girl, what I know of her. She might thank you kindly, and refuse!'

'She might, but I hope not. I want her to say yes. It would make so many people happy: the child would grow up without the stigma of illegitimacy; marriage would protect Hawthorn and ease my own conscience. And, best of all I think, Mother might have her boy for Rowangarth.'

'Or a granddaughter, don't forget?'

'I won't; but at least I'll have tried. Do you think the deceit is justified? As a priest, do you?'

'As a priest, no. As Elliot's brother, *yes!* But talk to Julia first. Heaven only knows she's a bossy, self-opinionated love of a girl, but in this she'll talk sense!'

She would, Giles thought. If it were entirely left to his sister, she would most likely push him to the chapel in a bathchair *tomorrow!* Julia would back him, but what of Hawthorn?

'Had you thought, you idiot,' Julia demanded of her brother, 'that it's perfect in every way but for two things. Not only must Alice agree, but the dates must too! A baby, from start to finish, takes about nine months; yours would be born in *seven*—from the date of your marriage, that is.

'When were you wounded? The middle of April, wasn't it? And you are going to marry Alice after you'd received wounds that made you—well, you know—and have a seven-month baby into the bargain; because that's what everyone would have to believe it was!'

'Doc James would help with the dates...'

'Yes. I think he would but, even so, you'd have to tell people you were married in March—or earlier. Would you be prepared to do that, for Mother's sake, because she must never know it isn't your child?'

'I'd do it. And since I can't give Elliot a hiding for what he's done, I think what I propose is the next best thing. Mind, Elliot must never know either.'

'He might put two and two together, Giles. He's a devious swine.'

'What? Say publicly that Alice's child isn't mine because on the twenty-sixth of March *he* raped her. Because that's when it was. Nathan told me. Elliot *was* here. He slept in Nathan's bed that night—made a fool of himself in the mess, too. It all adds up. That's why this time Elliot can do nothing about it!'

'There's still Alice, remember?'

'You mean she wouldn't fit in? And why not?'

'I'm not saying that at all. I care for Alice a lot. I once said if I could have had a sister, I'd have chosen her. I'd be happy for her to be my sister-in-law.

'But there's Tom. She'll never love you, Giles; not like she loved him. No man will ever take his place. It would have to be a loveless marriage; oh—not *loveless!* She cares for you; she always has. But you know what I mean?'

'Only too well. And I accepted that when I was told I was unlikely ever to father a child...'

'Oh, dammit! That was an awful thing for me to say! I'm a fool! Forgive me, Giles?' Tears glittered in her eyes.

'It's all right, Sis. But you do see why I'm so desperate to have Hawthorn's child for my own, for Rowangarth? And I care for her too. I always have.'

'Then are you going to ask her, or shall I sound her out? And remember, she might want to wait the war out to see if Tom comes back.'

'I accept that, and I'd like more than anything for him to be alive—a prisoner. But I don't think he is.'

'Then I'll talk to her; see if I think there's a chance she'll say yes?'

'I'd be grateful. It could be made to work, I'm sure it could.'

'All right. I'll do a bit of fishing, but

457

you do your own proposing, don't forget. I practically proposed to Andrew; I'm not going to make a habit of it!'

'You are an extremely nice lady, Mrs MacMalcolm—did you know that?' he said softly, a smile softening his pale gaunt face.

It was good, Julia thought, to see him smile. She hoped with all her heart that Alice would say yes.

As they left the ward that morning, cold with fatigue, Julia said, 'I had quite a long chat with Giles last night, when Sister was out of the ward.'

'Mm. It's good—if there's anything good about being wounded, I mean—that he ended up with us. Even Sister and Ruth know Rowangarth and her ladyship from her hospital-visiting at Denniston.'

'Yes—and Aunt Clemmy, too! But he was lucky, though he's such a dear person that he deserves to be in our ward. You like him, don't you?'

'You know I do—always did. He's a lovely gentleman.'

'So would you marry him?'

'*Julia!*' Alice stopped in her tracks. 'That's a cruel thing to say. It's Tom I love, only—' She hid her face in her hands, taking deep, gulping breaths, fighting the sobs that writhed in her throat. '—only he's never coming back. He'd have stood by me, though. Tom would have married me.'

'If they hadn't hanged him first for beating Elliot to death. Giles said he would've thrashed Elliot if he could.'

'You told him, Julia? How *could* you?'

'Giles is going to have to know. Everyone is. Sooner or later, it's going to show. And Giles is on your side, Alice. But let's get into breakfast. We'll find ourselves a quiet spot and talk about it. I was serious, you see, when I asked if you'd marry him...'

'No!' Alice shook her head violently.

'I see. Giles not good enough for you? You don't want me for a sister?'

'Don't talk so daft,' Alice flung. 'Tom isn't coming back. Geordie Marshall confirmed it, as good as. I'll have to learn to live with what happened. And don't think I wouldn't want to marry some decent man who'd accept the child and not hold it over me that I was no better than I ought to be...'

'No better? God, Alice, you were *raped!* But just think. Giles wants a son for Rowangarth; you need a father for your child—'

'Not for my child, Julia. It isn't *my child*. It's something lying inside me like a great *sin!*'

'Oh, love, I'm sorry.' Julia grasped her friend's hand, squeezing it tightly.

'Let's get something to eat. And hear me out—please?'

'No, Julia. Sir Giles is a gentleman born. I'm a servant. There's nothing more to be said.'

'Isn't there? Oh, but there *is*, and you'll listen, Alice! Now—do we talk?'

That night, when Sister was taking her usual ten-minute tea-break with Night Sister in Hut Twenty-three, Julia whispered, '*Now*, Alice! He's not asleep. I just looked in. Talk to him?'

For the first time, Alice felt embarrassment as she pulled aside the cubicle curtains, then slowly, carefully, pulled them together again.

'Sir Giles?' she breathed.

'Mm?'

'Are you in any pain?' she demanded, taking his wrist, checking his pulse.

'Not too bad. Anxious, though...'

As if to put off the question she knew he would ask, Alice ordered, 'Open, please,' then placed a thermometer in his mouth.

'It won't do, Hawthorn.' Giles removed the impediment. 'Julia says you've had a good long chat...'

'Yes.' Her eyes were fixed steadily on the chart she held.

'And?'

'I've given it some thought—no! I've

thought about little else since breakfast —and perhaps, if we mind our p's and q's, some good might come of it. Only how I'm going to go home to Rowangarth afterwards, I don't know.'

'You agree, then?' he said softly.

'Yes, I thank you. Mind—I'm not doing it lightly, and there'll be a lot to be sorted out one way or another, but I think it's up to us both to make the best of a bad job, though the way my luck is running it won't be the boy you want, but twin girls!'

'Oh, dear—we sound so awkward, don't we? And never once the most important word. Do you suppose we could start again, at the beginning? Hawthorn, will you marry me?'

'Yes, sir, thank you. I will—with reservations, that is.'

'Reservations accepted—and you won't have to worry about *that*,' he said, so softly she could hardly hear him. 'And do you think we might be a little less formal? Could you bring yourself to call me Giles, do you think?'

'I'll try. It'll come after a while, I shouldn't wonder. I felt awkward with Julia at first, but now—well—it isn't any bother. Now, are you going to let me take your temperature or is Sister going to come back and find us chatting together as if I've got all the time in the world, which

461

I haven't! Open your mouth, please—and Sir Giles, I do thank you.'

It was, Giles Sutton thought as he lay awake into the small hours of the morning, the most peculiar proposal—and acceptance—or marriage ever. Poor Hawthorn. She had been so embarrassed, yet there had been relief in her eyes and gratitude, though it was he who should be grateful. And he *must* learn to call her Alice. Alice Sutton. Lady Alice—oh, hell! Had she grasped the full significance of it, he wondered. Would a title sit heavily on those thin shoulders?

Poor little Alice. He'd do his best for her and no one—absolutely no one—would be allowed to treat her with anything less than her position deserved.

And Mother—what of her? Should he write to her now, or should he wait? Soon he would be fit enough to make the journey back to an English hospital. No private soldier was allowed his own nurse to accompany him, even if she were his wife. Alice would have to return to Rowangarth alone; by the time she did, his mother would have had time to get over the shock of their marriage. For shock it would be.

There were so many ifs; so very many buts. Here, wide-eyed and with nothing

462

else to do but think, he was only too well aware of them. Would Alice, when she'd had time to think about them too, call the wedding off? And where, he thought in sudden cold panic, were they to find a shop with wedding rings to sell?

He closed his eyes, pretending to sleep, as the curtains at the foot of his bed parted. Then a voice said softly, 'I know you are awake. I'll bring you in a drink if you'd like. And don't worry. We'll manage, somehow...'

Alice. Practical as ever. And dammit, they *would* manage!

One week later and with Sister Carbrooke —who'd had to be told or how else were they to get Giles to the chapel?—and Ruth Love as witnesses, Nathan Sutton joined together till death did them part, his cousin Giles and Alice Hawthorn.

'You're all right?' Julia had whispered as they washed and dressed. 'Even though this isn't how you'd hoped it would be?'

Alice looked pale and tired, a condition which couldn't be entirely blamed on a night duty more hectic than usual.

'I'm fine.' She took a long look into the wall mirror, unfastening the chain at her neck as she did so, taking from it the wedding ring with which her own mother had been married. 'Will you give this to

463

Giles—unless there's going to be a best man, that is?'

'No. Just you and him and me, and Nathan marrying you and dear old Carbolic and Ruth to sign the certificate afterwards—make it all legal and above board. You *are* happy about it, Alice?' she demanded. 'And you needn't worry; no one here will know about it, and we can trust Sister. She was just a bit annoyed that we hadn't told her about—well, what happened that night.'

'I know. I only hope it's going to be all right at Rowangarth.'

'When mother goes to visit Giles in hospital and hears what he has to tell her, she'll be giddy with happiness.'

'Even though it might be a girl? Even though she might find out it's Elliot Sutton's? It might be black dark, like him.'

'But you've got dark hair too, Alice. A son often favours his mother. And she won't ever find out it isn't Giles's child, even if we have to lie through our teeth for the rest of our lives. You aren't having second thoughts?'

'No.' Alice shook her head. 'It's just that—'

'That it should have been Tom? I understand. But we've agreed to make the best of a bad job, so shall we pick up Ruth and Sister? It's almost time.'

'Yes. And thanks, Julia. And no one will find out?'

'They won't—not here, anyway. Everyone thinks it's a special Communion —thanks for Giles's recovery. A family Communion, sort of. And, Alice—I'm glad I'm getting a sister. When this war is over, we'll visit each other and talk about our children, and—'

'We will, Julia.'

And Tom, my lovely lad, forgive me? And try to understand?

'So!' said Sister. 'Your husband is on his way home! Before so very much longer he'll be a civilian, with the medal he deserves if there's any sense left in the British army. But why you aren't going too, I don't know. In your condition it would have been easy to get your release. We might even have been able to get you on the same hospital ship.'

'I want to stay, Sister, if it's all right with you. In just a few weeks I'll have done another year and my contract will come up for renewal. I'll just not sign on again. It'll be a lot simpler to do it that way. And if I don't have to apply for release on grounds of pregnancy—well, the less who know, the better. Besides, I'm not showing yet. I can work a little longer, surely? And you need

465

every pair of hands you can get.'

She wanted to stay; she wanted to leave. She didn't want to part from Julia; she dreaded returning to Rowangarth. Lady Alice, indeed! It was enough to make Jin Dobb's cat laugh! Putting off the moment, she was.

'Work? You'll have to remember to be very careful when you are lifting—if at all. I shall see that MacMalcolm keeps an eye on you.'

'She's at it already, Sister. Don't do this! Stop doing that! It's a wonder the entire hospital hasn't found out. You'll never tell, will you?'

'You know I won't. Sir Giles deserves a son—a child, and a child born in wedlock belongs to the marriage. He's a fine young man. He'll never be fully fit, you understand, but he should do well enough. It's you I worry about.'

'I'll be all right, Sister. I'll manage. And one way or another, it won't be all that long before Julia's home.' In a rare burst of insubordination she reached up to kiss Sister's cheek. 'Can I go now? They're busy on the ward.'

'Yes, indeed! Be off with you!'

Sister Carbrooke dabbed her eyes and blew her nose loudly. *Damn* this war! And damn the fools who let it start and the idiots who didn't seem to be doing half enough to help our soldiers win it!

And thank goodness young Hawthorn —*Sutton*—would be on her way home to England soon. A pregnant nurse in all this mayhem was something she could well do without!

Alice stood at the ship's rail, hugging her coat around her, determined to stand there, in spite of the cold wind from the sea, until the coast of France could no longer be seen. She worried about Julia; about Andrew too. She worried about the hospital at Celverte and all the patients and nurses there.

The Germans were advancing—there was no denying it. Balanced now as the fighting was, one stroke of good or bad luck could give victory to either side. And Julia was there, separated from Andrew and hardly a letter from him recently.

We've been together so long, Julia. Ever since that night in Hyde Park we've been close. We are sisters now.

Yet she didn't know how her ladyship had taken it; didn't know how Giles was doing because there had been no letters for anyone from anywhere. She hoped Giles was getting better quickly. It was summer now; the days were warm and long. He'd be able to spend time sitting quietly in the sun; help him forget the nightmare he'd been through. He might even have gone home now to Rowangarth, and Morgan licking him and fussing and slobbering all over him.

The ship's engines began to throb. The gap between the ship and the quayside widened.

Goodbye, France. Take care, all of you. I wish I could have stayed there, right up until the end...

She gripped the rail tightly. France was little more than a grey blur now: somewhere beyond that long, flat streak of coastline a war was being fought to the bitter end, and young men were being killed every second of every minute.

Goodbye, Tom, my lovely lad. I'm going home to Rowangarth. I shall see Reuben again and that daft dog and I'll take him walks like I used to, in Brattocks. But you won't be there. You'll never whistle me and I'll never again run to you.

There would be buttercups now, at Rowangarth. The pastures would be yellow over with them.

I don't know where you are, Tom, where they have laid you. But one day I'll find you, stand beside you. And when I come, my darling, I'll bring you buttercups, so you'll know I have been...

21

Alice sat in the waiting-room at Holdenby Halt, cases and bags at her feet. She had given the stationmaster a sixpenny-piece, asking that he telephone Rowangarth, tell them she was here.

She was tired. The slow, late-night crossing had been without incident, but the turmoil inside her had prevented sleep. she was in need of food, too, to stop the rumblings inside her and the empty ache that went with them.

She thought back to the long, lonely train journey north, and England so heartbreakingly dear, slipping past the window.

At York, the Holdenby train stood at a side platform, letting out puffs of smoke, little hisses of steam, ready to leave. A few more miles more and she would be home—but to what? Perhaps it would be better if she sat here for ever and people became so used to her being there that they treated her as part of the furniture, and dusted and polished her every day.

The door opened. The stationmaster lifted his top hat.

'I did the telephoning. They're coming to fetch you, miss.'

He was looking at her strangely, doubtless thinking her face was familiar, yet not knowing who this Nurse Sutton was. A porter loaded her luggage on to a trolley. He was too old to be working, but there were no young men left now.

'I'm to tell you Sir Giles is on his way, miss. Is there owt you need?'

'No, thank you.' She smiled because he, too, gazed at her questioningly. She would have to get used to such looks.

Her fingers twisted on her lap, making her aware of her wedding ring. Married, yet not married; wanting Tom still. She was glad Giles was coming to meet her; it could only mean he was getting stronger.

She had no way of knowing. Seven weeks married and only two letters: one hurriedly written on arriving in England; the other giving the address of the London hospital to which he'd been sent. It told her that the situation on the Western Front had not improved—for the Allies, that was. Shifting positions, small advances and counter-attacks did nothing to help the army deliver letters. And letters were so precious; so necessary to those over there.

She closed her eyes, thinking of Julia and Ruth and Sister, hoping they hadn't been overrun, that the Allied lines were holding. Celverte was so near, now, to the fighting. She should be glad to be away from it, but she wasn't. Hut Twenty-four, with all its dangers, was better by far than what might await her here.

From the minute she'd left Celverte she had felt lonely and alone. She wanted, *needed*, to be back there.

'Alice!' Giles stood in the doorway, a walking-stick in either hand. 'No crutches, you see!' He swayed awkwardly towards her, then kissed her cheek.

'You shouldn't have come,' she said, all at once shy.

'I wanted to. When the station telephoned, I rang Pendenys. Aunt Clemmy is in London so I knew Uncle Edward would offer a car. I persuaded Mother to wait at home—told her I could manage all right. I've got to talk to you first, you see.'

The porter pushed the trolley ahead of them. Alice took one of Giles's sticks. 'Put your arm round my shoulder, it's better that way. Take it slowly,' she murmured, still the nurse.

Pendenys had sent their biggest, shiniest car. The driver opened the door, helped Giles in, then covered his knees with a rug.

'They treat me like a wounded hero,' he murmured, reaching to close the glass panel between the front and back seats. 'I came because I've got to tell you,' he said softly as, slowly, majestically, they left the station yard.

'It's her ladyship, isn't it?' Alice choked. 'She's upset.'

'She is *not*. She's as pleased as can be. Only Mother knows, and Aunt Sutton. Mother's longing to tell everyone, but I asked her not to—not yet. I told her all about it; said the baby was the result of one brief loving.'

'*Loving,* Giles?'

'Yes. You and me, I said. Just the once, before I was—injured...'

'But why? She'll think I'm—*common.*'

'No! Exactly the opposite! She said it was as if it had been meant to be. I told her, you see, that I met you the night you'd heard Tom had been killed. that *I* met you, Alice—not Elliot. I told her I held you, comforted you and—well, it happened...'

'But you shouldn't have. I don't know what to think.' She shook her head, bewildered.

'Then don't think—not anything. Especially don't think about Elliot. You and I—*we* got the child. Can you accept that, Alice? You were upset, needing comfort; I forgot myself and—'

'We're deceiving her. It isn't right.'

'It *is*. And we knew we'd have to tell

some lies. But she doesn't care that I lost my head. She even said it would be a special child because love children are always particularly beautiful. She refuses to be anything but glad about it. She's happy—truly. Some good has come of it, after all.

'She came to visit me in hospital in London—stayed with Aunt Sutton whilst she was there. I'm afraid Aunt Sutton knows; Mother just had to tell her. Aunt is delighted, but sworn to secrecy—about the baby, that is.

'Did you get any of my letters, by the way? I'm officially a civilian now. And in case you hear it from someone else, I've been recommended for the Military Medal.'

'Giles! I'm so pleased! Yours was a special kind of bravery—and don't try to say it wasn't. I was there, remember? And I didn't get your letters; only two telling me you'd made it back.'

'Letters still not getting through? Things must still be bad.'

'They are. People here at home don't realise how bad. Things are being kept back. The papers aren't allowed to print the half of it. But I won't say anything to her ladyship. Julia's still out there, and Andrew, remember.'

'Well, she's got you and me to fuss over

now. And her precious grandchild. But you agree with me—telling her that it was the result of a slip, kind of? It's better than the way it really was. I want her to think the baby is mine. It's what Nathan would call a permissible untruth.'

'I'll admit it's better than what Julia suggested—trying to tell people we were married before we really were so it wouldn't have to be a seven-month baby.'

'My sister is a great one for her spot of drama. The way I told it sounds far more believable.'

'With you taking the blame for what Elliot Sutton did.'

'And taking his child for my own, don't forget. So no more talk about him. Let's try to make this a happy day, Alice?'

'All right. You don't think he heard any of what we said?' She nodded towards the driver who was steering the car through the lodge gates.

'No. We whispered, and anyway, I think he's a bit hard of hearing. Probably why Aunt Clemmy engaged him in the first place. Chin up? Look! There's Mother waiting at the door. I knew she would be!'

'You are a good man, Giles Sutton. I'm grateful to you, and I'll try my best—I promise.'

She stared ahead, chin high. And it

would have been all right—it really
would—if a dog hadn't dashed out to
join them; a big, daft lovable spaniel.

Does this creature belong to you...?

'Alice, my dear, don't cry! Please don't
cry.'

Her ladyship, hugging her, kissing her,
and the familiar sweet smell of her special
soap so easy to recall.

'I'm sorry.' Alice dabbed her eyes, took
a deep, calming breath. 'Only it's so long
since I went away—so good to be back.'

'And it is so good to have you home.
Come inside, child. You look exhausted.'

Over his mother's shoulder, Giles smiled.
It was going to be all right, Alice insisted
silently. Only Brattocks Wood to face now,
and Reuben. Reuben wouldn't ask any
questions, point any fingers, and the rooks
kept secrets. There'd only be the ghost of
a lost love to face...

Miss Clitherow stood in the hall at the
foot of the staircase, hands clasped in front
of her, a half-smile on her lips.

Nothing had changed.

Alice was sent at once to bed. She had
been travelling for twenty-four hours, and
with very little food, it would seem,
Helen Sutton told the housekeeper. First
something light to eat, then sleep.

'You must not overtire yourself,' Helen

smiled, offering daintily cut sandwiches and a glass of cool milk. 'In your condition,' she settled herself on the bed, 'you must have peace and quiet. No visitors at all until tomorrow.'

'My *condition,* milady—' Alice whispered. 'What must you think of me—of us?' She dropped her eyes to fingers nervously plucking at the bed-cover. 'I want to say I'm very sorry...'

'Sorry, my dear good girl? Sorry you are giving me what I have wanted for so long! It didn't help at all when Clemmy told me Albert had a son; now, soon, I shall announce my own grandchild!'

'But the way of its getting—don't think too badly of it?'

'The way of my grandchild's getting is nobody's business but yours and Giles's. The fact that he chose to tell me was only to explain Dwerryhouse's death—and I was so sad to hear about it. But I do understand—and I thank God that He didn't create any of us entirely perfect, or where would the baby have been now? There wouldn't have been one, Alice. Giles would never have had a son—or daughter,' she added hastily. 'Just remember that I adored Giles's father; that I know how easily the act of love can happen.

'Julia, too, I am glad to say, knows just such a happiness.' Her eyes took on a remembering sadness, then she said, 'How is Julia? How was she when you left her?'

'She was fine, milady. She'd finished her second year, just as I had. I wanted her not to sign another contract. I begged her to come home with me, but she would have none of it. Andrew is out there and she wants to be as near to him as she can. They had a lovely three days together, in Paris. She looked so happy when she got back.'

But only for a while, milady. When she got back I was there, beside myself, weeping, half out of my mind.

'Julia made a good choice, you know. Andrew will be a splendid husband—when finally this war allows him to be. Some say the fighting is going badly for us, that we aren't being the told the truth about what it is really like in France. Are they right, Alice?'

'That I can't say.' Not for anything would she add to her ladyship's worries. 'I only know about my part of the war. We were always busy at the hospital. It was like another little world, all wrapped in cotton wool and bandaged round to keep everything else out. You learned to live from duty to duty, and always the wounded must come first, no matter what.

'So I can't tell you how things really are—except that at one time letters came quite quickly and regular, like. Lately though, hardly any mail was getting through.'

'I'd noticed that myself...'

'But it'll be all right,' Alice hastened. 'Since the doctor got to be a major he was sent to a hospital much further away from the fighting. Julia's ever so thankful he's away from the front line now. And nurses would be moved out at once if they were threatened. Don't you worry none. They'll both of them be home soon, milady.'

'I do so hope they are. Thank you for those words of comfort, Alice. It's going to be such a joy, having you and Giles to fuss over and spoil. I've been so lonely. And, my dear, do you think you could remember not to call me milady? It is you who must be called that. *You* are Lady Sutton now.'

'Aye. It bothers me.'

'Then you mustn't let it. And will you remember that I am your mother now?'

'Oh, I couldn't!' Not calling her ladyship 'Mother'. 'Oh, my word no!'

'Then perhaps you could make a start with "Mother-in-law"? I suppose, really that's what I am. And in time you might try "Mother", or even "dearest", which is what Giles mostly calls me. Will you, Alice?'

'I'll try.' It had been strange, at first, using Julia's name—or calling her MacMalcolm.

Faraway days at the York hospital: that huge, empty dirty ward, and Julia's poor chapped hands. Then Denniston House and France and being able to sew two years' service on uniform sleeves. Five years of being friends, being together—until two days ago, that was.

'I don't want you to go, Alice. What will I do without you?' Julia had whispered.

They had held each other tightly as if it were the last time each would see and hold and touch the other; as if there was to be no more laughter together or whispered secrets or shared tears.

'Come home with me, Julia? Two years out here is more than enough.'

'No! Oh, I long to see Rowangarth. Sometimes I ache for its sanity and safeness. But Andrew is here and I must be near him. Just think—the door at the top of the ward might open and in he could walk, demanding to know where his wife was. She couldn't be in England, could she?'

'No. I'll give your love to Rowangarth, though.'

The honeysuckle and foxgloves would be

flowering when she got back; buttercups, too. Tom had picked buttercups. Tom was there now, in Brattocks. She had only to take Morgan's lead, cross the wild garden, climb the stile. Then Tom would whistle and she would run to him...

'Alice?' Gently Helen touched the hand lying so child-like on the bed-cover. 'Bless the girl—she's asleep already.'

She bent to kiss the pale cheek. Alice had thickened at her waist, her breasts were fuller; signs of the child she carried—Giles's child. But her hands, her arms, her once-bonny face, were all painfully thin.

It was the fault of the war. Its horror even reached out to touch young girls who by rights should have been home with their mothers with nothing more to worry them than which hair ribbons to wear that morning.

'Welcome home.' Helen tiptoed across the room. 'Don't worry now, Alice. I shall take care of you—and the baby.' She raised her eyes to the sky. 'And thank you, God, with all my heart. Thank you for this day...'

'I am extremely put out, Edward.' Clementina Sutton paced the floor, heels tapping. 'I ordered the car to meet me. You knew I needed the Rolls-Royce at York at five.'

'Yes, but it was out; I'd offered it to

480

Giles, so I sent you another. He had to go to Holdenby. And I really don't see why you can't change trains at York—it's only a cockstride to the Place from Holdenby station.'

'I dislike the local train; you know I do. It is slow and dirty and often there are no decent seats on it.'

'That is because there is so little demand, locally, for first-class travel. But why are you so agitated, my dear? I asked you not to go to London. There is always the risk of an air-raid and you always come back upset these days.'

'Then don't blame me! Blame this awful war that parts a mother from her sons and causes shortages and restrictions and—'

'I think our soldiers in the trenches would be happy to take on your shortages and restrictions, Clemmy.' Her husband's retort was touched with reproof. 'And why did you hare off to London without so much as a word when there was really no need?'

'There was *every* need! I heard from Molly that things are happening next door.'

'Molly?'

'Of course *Molly!* You know of her! The basement woman at Cheyne Walk, the one who caretakes! She wrote to me.'

'You said next door was empty,' Edward

reasoned gently. 'Has someone broken in—done damage?'

'No, but I was right! As soon as I got there—'

Signs not of occupation, exactly; curtains at the windows, though. Heavy curtains. And a tall strange man with a thick beard appearing from the basement area, marching glowering around the house, disappearing again. Not so much a caretaker like herself, Molly had confided in awed tones; more of a *keeper*. Most likely they'd got someone locked up in the attic like in that novel. And not English. Molly had heard the bearded one shouting at a stray dog, chasing it away, slamming the gates shut. Swearing, he'd seemed to be, though she hadn't understood one word of it. But not French, she was sure of that. She'd have recognised swearing if it had been in French.

'I always knew it, Edward, from the minute next door moved out when the air-raids began! Refugees! "There'll be refugees in that house next door, mark my words if there isn't!" I said, and I was right!'

'But don't you feel some small compassion for them, Clemmy? To have had to leave their homes; not knowing whether they are still standing, probably leaving most of what they had behind them.'

'Why should I? Did I start the war, Edward? *Did* I? Oh, no, it was *them* started it. Molly said those people next door aren't like us; aren't even Europeans, if you ask me! But there'll be no more trouble. I've seen to that!'

'I wasn't aware there had been any,' Edward frowned.

'No, and there won't be now. I've had a carpenter in. He has built an eight-foot fence all round the back. That should keep them out!'

'And your daylight too. But are you sure the refugees want to invade the back garden?'

'Those peculiar people will invade anything, if the mood takes them. It's why this war started; why it has lasted almost four years. *Four* years it'll be, come August, and the end of it nowhere in sight! I swear my nerves are in shreds! And why did Giles need the car? Are they so down-at-heel at the Garth that they can't buy a motor?'

'You know how Helen feels about motors, though I fear she's going to have to acknowledge their existence soon. They are here to stay. When the war is over, they'll be much in demand.' Change the subject. Refugees upset Clemmy; especially refugees living next door. 'It wouldn't surprise me if they don't turn out a small motor most people can afford—just as Mr Ford does, over in America.'

'A *people's* car?' Clementina's eyebrows rose. Every Tom, Dick and Harry on the roads, honking and tooting? Trippers all over the place? Oh, but she hoped not! 'And what did Giles need with our motor when he's still supposed to be an invalid?'

'Giles *is* an invalid and will always be so. He's been given a medal because of it. And he needed the car to meet his wife at Holdenby. She was returning from France, where she was a nurse.'

'Ha! And that's another thing! Why was I the last to hear of it? Why wasn't I told? Had to get it secondhand from Aunt Sutton last night that Giles had married a nurse! Don't gawp, Edward. Kept it quiet, didn't they? How long have you known?'

'Since Giles was discharged from hospital, about a week ago.'

'And it didn't occur to you to tell me?'

'You were in London.'

'So didn't you think to pick up the telephone?'

'No. I imagined—quite rightly, it seems —that you would hear of it from Aunt Sutton.'

'Hm. Well...I shall call on Helen in the morning! What else do you know about it? You'll have been to Rowangarth, I take it?'

'I have. Helen told me Giles is discharged on medical grounds; a civilian now. Oh, and there was a letter from Nathan this morning. I read it, then left it on your desk.'

'How long did it take to get here?'

'About three weeks. At the time of writing he was well. He said he'd met Elliot, though they hadn't had much time together. But read it for yourself.'

Edward reached for his jacket. A walk was indicated, for when Clemmy read Nathan's letter—read that Giles's wife was the pretty little sewing-maid from Rowangarth and that Nathan himself had married them in the chapel of a convent in France, they would hear her dismay as far away as Creesby! He hadn't been married to Clemmy all these years not to know that. And be blowed if he wasn't going to go over to the Garth tomorrow with her and wish the youngsters well; congratulate Giles on his medal.

Strange, though, that Helen hadn't thought to mention the wedding until recently, Edward frowned, or even put an announcement in the papers. But likely Giles hadn't been able to tell her, being wounded so soon afterwards; and anyway, it seemed to have been a quiet affair. Rather nice to think Nathan had married Giles and his lady—Alice, wasn't she called?

485

Clemmy wouldn't like it, mind; had called the poor girl all manner of names after the Brattocks Wood affair, even though Elliot had been entirely to blame for it and deserved all he'd got. But that was forgotten now, and rightly so, he thought gratefully.

Quietly he crossed the huge, echoing hall and slipped out of a side door. Poor Clemmy. Got herself into such tizzies; mostly over nothing, too.

He breathed deeply on the soft evening air until his lungs were full to bursting, then made for the hills. A walk to the top of Holdenby Pike was exactly what he needed.

Alice awoke, threw on a shawl, then tiptoed to the attic room that once had been her own. Closing the door quietly, she switched on the light, blinking in its sudden glare.

She ran a forefinger, Sister Carbrooke fashion, along the dressing-table top. Everything was clean, exactly as it had been more than two years ago. Her trunk stood beneath the slope of the ceiling still: slippers, hand-knitted by Tilda, lay beneath the bedside chair. She pushed her bare feet into them and their warm softness gave her comfort.

What now to wear? Her uniform had

accommodated her swelling figure; the white apron, tied less tightly at her waist, disguised her swelling breasts. She had been a slip of a thing when she and Julia left for France; thinner than she'd ever been with all the running about there had been at Denniston House.

Now her best grey costume wouldn't go near her, she frowned, taking it from the wardrobe. She had always thought to wear it to her wedding, but there would be no wedding, now—not to Tom. She would never see him again and she didn't know why she was allowing herself even to think of him when such foolish indulgences sent white-hot pains slicing through her. And it were best she should remember she was married to Giles now, and be thankful for it, though she'd never be his wife; not really a wife.

She returned the costume to its hook, then quietly opened a drawer, lifting out the black cardigan her ladyship had given her at the end of her mourning for Sir John. It had been a little on the large side, but far too good to refuse. Now, unbuttoned, it would disguise her thickening figure, and it wouldn't take her long to ease out the waistband of one of her skirts, move the buttons on her best blouse.

Carefully she crept down the back stairs, walking softly to the sewing-room, closing the door with hardly a click. Someone had been using the sewing-machine. It was threaded with black cotton; a pair of sharp-pointed scissors lay beside it.

She began to snip at the waistband resisting the urge to stand at the window, look down at the bothy. But no one lived there, now. Davie and Will and Tom had all gone and the garden apprentices and improvers. How many would return, and would Jin go back there to care for them when they did?

Tom wasn't coming back. She hugged herself tightly, fighting back tears. She was Lady Sutton now, and she would have to learn to act as Lady Helen acted and not allow herself to burst into tears like some foolish housemaid.

But she *was* a housemaid; under-housemaid, before she'd taken over the sewing. Glad of the scrubbing and cleaning an' all; to be away from Aunt Bella and learn to laugh and have second helpings and fall in love.

Leave me, Tom? Leave me be? I'll always love you. It isn't possible for me to love again. I'll be a good wife to Giles; he'll need nursing for the rest of his days. But never think, Tom, that I shall forget you, or that every leaf on every tree in Brattocks won't whisper your name to me, nor every buttercup that ever grows won't remind me of what I lost.

488

She sniffed, pulling the sleeve of her nightdress across her eyes; taking a shuddering gulp of air, pulling it down into her stomach. Then she glanced up sharply.

'Tilda!'

'Ooooh! I heard someone—I never thought...' She dropped her eyes to her shoes, embarrassed.

'Tilda, it's good to see you! So long, isn't it? Two years...'

'Yes, milady.' Tilda bobbed a curtsey, eyes still lowered.

'Tilda—*no!* Don't do that! I'm home again!'

'Home. Aye, but to upstairs. We've got to watch ourselves. Miss Clitherow said so. You're a milady now.'

'But not here? Not in the sewing-room, Tilda? I suppose it's going to take some getting used to—me being married.'

'Married to the *gentry.*'

'Tom was—Tom died...'

'Aye, so he did. Him and millions of others.' She said it with condescension as if, partly, to excuse Alice's haste in finding herself another man to love.

'Tilda, *please?* Oh, I know things will have to be different, but you and me were friends. In the sewing-room, can't we be Tilda and Alice? It's going to be lonely here, for me...'

'You've got Sir Giles, milady. And might

I be excused? There's the fire to see to for breakfast. And to save time, will I bring yours to your room? The hens are laying well, now; it's boiled eggs this morning.'

'Thank you. I won't have an egg. Just a little bread and marmalade. I'll be giving my food card to Miss Clitherow. They gave me one when I left France. I'm not a nurse any longer. I get civilian rations now.'

Her words hung on the air, a silent appeal for understanding, but they were wasted on the housemaid.

'Will you take it in the morning-room or your bedroom, milady?'

'Neither, thank you. I'll have my breakfast here, in the sewing-room, Tilda.'

She smiled, trying to do it as Lady Helen would have done, and the effort hurt her lips. Teeth clenched tightly, she returned to her sewing.

After breakfast, and when she had made sure Giles was comfortable, she would take Morgan and walk the long way through Brattocks; visit Reuben. Reuben would understand that it was Alice come to see him and not milady. She would have to learn to walk again in Brattocks, lean on the rearing-field gate, aye, and even look at the buttercups she knew would be growing golden in the pasture this very day; learn to do it all again. Without Tom.

She felt a sudden upsurge of nausea and hoped that Tilda wouldn't be long in coming. Dry bread, Ruth had told her, or a plain biscuit, often helped relieve morning sickness.

Where are you, Ruth? And you, Julia?

She glanced at the mantel-clock, still ticking away as if the years between had never happened.

Day duty, that's what. Just getting dressed, they would be, then off to breakfast and to collect the trolley for Hut Twenty-four.

Who would be sleeping in her bed, now; sharing the curtained bed-space with Julia, folding her uniform into the drawers that Alice Hawthorn had once used?

I miss you, Julia. I wish the letters came more quickly. I need to hear from you. And it isn't any of Alice Hawthorn's business who sleeps in her bed in the schoolhouse because Alice Hawthorn is gone. She ceased to live and breathe one night in March. The twenty-sixth of March, if you want to be exact. A little after half-past eight. On a straw-filled palliasse in the shed where the nuns once kept their milk cows. That was when Alice Hawthorn ceased to be—she and Tom Dwerryhouse both.

So get on with letting that skirt out, Milady Sutton, or the whole of the Riding is going

*to know you are pregnant with a bairn you
don't want...*

'Come in,' she said sharply, in answer
to Tilda's knock.

Alice cast a practised eye on the thermometer, let go of Giles's wrist.

'You'll do,' she smiled, 'though you
shouldn't have met me yesterday. It was
more tiring than you thought, wasn't it?'

'Yes, Nurse,' Giles smiled. 'I'll admit
it, but every day I'm a little better; I
know it.'

'I'm bound to agree there's a lot more
to recommend you than the pour soul they
brought into Hut Twenty-four that night,'
Alice sighed. 'And there's still the best
of the summer ahead of you. Peace and
quiet and sunshine are great healers. By
Christmas, when Julia and Andrew might
be home—'

'And the baby born—'

'Aye. By then, you'll be stronger in every
way. Your just being here is a miracle.'

'I know it, Alice. I remember so much
about it. That awful explosion that made
me feel as if I were blind and deaf and
dumb for a moment. Then lying there
wondering if I were dead.'

'Don't, Giles. It's over—a bad dream.'

'It won't ever be over. And I want to
tell you about it because that miracle very

nearly didn't happen. I remember lying there, wanting to die, wanting to live. Then someone came for me.'

'Like you so often crawled out into No Man's Land to bring some other soldier to safety, Giles.'

'I felt a jab. I knew what they were giving me, Alice, that I would soon feel a kind of peace; floating above my body, not caring. The darkness came then and I seemed to slip in and out of it. A part of me wanted to let go—to die; the other part of me couldn't because there was a voice in my head. It wouldn't go away. I tried not to listen to it, but it kept calling me back to Rowangarth; all the time insisting that Rowangarth needed me.

'It was your voice I heard, and I know it was your hand, holding mine so tightly that I couldn't float away. It *was* you, wasn't it? It was you wouldn't let me die that night?'

'We were all willing you to live, not only me. I just sat with you, talked to you, that's all. Julia would have, but Sister said she wasn't to. Nathan came that night—did you know that? He prayed for you and blessed you.'

'So many good friends...' Then he smiled, his eyes bright with mischief. 'Do you think I might sit in the conservatory? It's such a lovely morning and, that way,

I can hide behind the plants when Aunt Clemmy comes. And you don't have to be there,' he hastened, seeing the look of alarm that widened her eyes. 'Mother wants all the glory this morning—if you'll agree to her telling people about the baby now? She wants to. Can she, Alice?'

'Aye. It's all right. Folk'll have to know sooner or later. She can tell them it'll be a Christmas baby.'

'And will it?'

'I'm not sure, but Christmas will suffice for now. And I'd like to go to Keeper's—see Reuben. He'll know I'm back. Wouldn't be right if I didn't.'

'Good idea. Take Morgan with you. He'll take care of you. Mother will understand—and, Alice...' He grasped her hand, holding it tightly. 'Thank you for making Mother so happy. We won't regret what we did, I promise you.'

'What *we* did? We got married, that was all.'

'I know. But thanks all the same.'

'It's me should thank you. I hate him, you know. I'll hate him as long as I live. You said yesterday you were taking Elliot's child. Well, you aren't. I give it to you gladly, for I don't want it.'

'Alice! Please, *no?* You'll love it when it's born!'

'I won't. I try not to look at my body,

Giles. It's getting ugly and it'll get uglier. It's a nightmare I've got inside me, not a child—so you'll understand how grateful I am to you and her ladyship. And if you could bear with me, try not to let my bitterness spoil things for you? You want this child; if it wasn't for that, I couldn't go on living.'

'Poor little Alice. Off you go and see Reuben—tell him about it. Reuben will understand.'

'I shall tell him the truth, Giles. He'll say nothing; he'll keep it a secret. But Julia knows and Ruth Love knows and Nathan, too. It's only right I should tell Reuben. For my sake, he'll never tell.'

'I know he won't, and I agree he should know. So come on, Nurse Sutton. Give me a hand to the conservatory, then be off with you, into that lovely sunshine. Reuben makes a mashing of tea round about this time, if I'm not mistaken.'

'You are a kind man.' Fleetingly she laid her lips to his cheek. 'And I hope it's a boy. About time you had a little of your own goodness back.' She smiled fleetingly, picking up his walking-sticks. 'Let's disappear before Mrs Clementina arrives...'

Reuben's kettle was indeed on the hob, and when Morgan burst into his kitchen, did a wild circuit, then skittered out again, he knew it would be Alice he would see, walking up his path. He held wide his arms, his pale eyes dimming with tears.

'Lass!' He held her to him, his unshaven cheek rough on hers. 'Eh, lovey, but I've missed you. Come on in and tell me if it's right that the nurse young Giles wedded in France was our little Alice. I couldn't believe it when I heard.'

'It's true. I did write, telling you, three weeks ago, but the letters haven't been getting through. Perhaps it'll arrive soon.'

'It's all right. I'm only teasing. I'm that glad to see you I'd forgive you anything.'

He took the teapot from the mantel, setting it to warm.

'Then will you forgive me for having a baby, Reuben, because I am.' Best say it quickly.

'A babbie,' Reuben gasped. 'Giles's, or Tom's?'

'Bless you for not saying "Are you sure?"' Alice laughed shakily. 'And it belongs to neither. It was the night I heard about Tom—that he'd been killed. There was no one I could tell about it: Julia was in Paris with Andrew. I just ran and ran, crying all the time. Then I met up with Elliot Sutton.

'I thought he was a part of the nightmare, but he wasn't.

'I had to tell you, Reuben. Only me and Giles know about it, and Julia, and Nathan Sutton who married us. Giles won't ever have a child—his injuries, you see—that's why he married me. And you're not to say a word to anyone about that either. Her ladyship thinks the child is Giles's, and that's the way it'll always have to be. You'll never tell?'

'Eh, lass.' Reuben shook his head sadly, sitting down heavily. 'I swear that if that arrogant young swine was to walk through that door, I'd take a gun to him!'

'No you wouldn't. Elliot Sutton was so drunk the night it happened that I doubt he even knew it was me he—he—'

'Aye, lovey. Aye. Best we try to forget about it. Some good came of it. Her ladyship'll get her grandchild, after all. Let's hope you give her a lad. It would make up for losing one son to the war and the other being sent back only half a man.'

'But say you won't *tell?*' Alice insisted.

'You know I won't! When's it due, then?'

'Round about Christmas.'

'Well now. Christmas is a nice time to have a babbie born. And what you told me is forgotten already. Only I'll not forget

497

about Elliot Sutton. I'll bide my time, lass, but I'll do him a mischief if ever I can.'

'Forget him—and can I stay with you for a while? Her ladyship has been bursting to tell folk about her grandchild, and this morning she's going to. She'll be telling that Mrs Clementina and I can just imagine the sneer on that woman's face when she finds out it's me that's having it.'

'And you as is Lady Sutton now. That'll not please her, either. Does it please you, lass?'

'No, Reuben. I'd rather have lived here at Keeper's with Tom, but I've got to count my blessings. Giles wanted a son; I have one that I didn't want to conceive. It seemed the right thing to do—for us to marry. If Tom hadn't been killed I'd have told him, hoped he'd have stood by me.'

'He would have, lass. But then—' Reuben rubbed his chin reflectively. 'If Tom hadn't been killed you'd not have run out all upset and straight into Elliot Sutton's path. It's a queer carry-on, and no mistake. Treating you all right, are they?'

'Aye. Her ladyship is so pleased. This morning she kept giving little smiles and I knew she was thinking about the baby and that Mrs Sutton from Pendenys was coming and how she couldn't wait to tell her.

'But Miss Clitherow is polite—too polite—and when I wanted to talk to Tilda Tewk she went all uppity on me and reminded me of my position. I haven't see Mrs Shaw yet, nor Jin Dobb. I hope they'll take it a bit better. If they knew the truth of it, they'd be on my side.'

'But you can't tell them the truth, Alice, so you'd best stop fretting about it. And *I'm* pleased for you, no matter who fathered that babbie. And, like you say, happen Elliot Sutton doesn't remember it happened.'

'And he'll never know, will he, Reuben?'

'Not from me he won't, so let's have that tea. And Lady Sutton or not, you'll sup out of the same mug as Alice did!'

'You're an old love, Reuben,' she choked, blinking away a tear. 'I hoped you'd understand—and about Tom, too.'

'Aye, well, it's a funny old world we're living in.' Reuben blew his nose noisily. 'And I'm here, don't forget, if things get a bit too much for you. If you want to unburden, I'll listen. And I'll never ask you anything you don't think fit to tell. So don't fret none, eh lass?'

'Thank you, Reuben,' she said softly.

She had never loved him more.

22

July, and the enemy armies almost at Reims, driving further on to a place on the map called Epernay. And all along the front line, heavy attacks at Vimy and Ypres and the Somme and nearer to Celverte than they had ever been.

Was Julia still there, Alice fretted, laying aside the newspaper. Had General Hospital Sixteen been evacuated or had it been overrun?

There had been one letter only, written a month ago. Fighting lines could change overnight, Alice knew. The letter, though Lady Helen had opened it with relief, did not guarantee Julia's safety, nor that of the wounded in her care.

The Germans did not kill babies nor rape nuns—that was a nonsense put out by men in small back rooms to whip up hatred for the enemy—but a screaming shell was no respecter of persons. One only could wipe out the ward on which Julia worked.

Why didn't you come home with me, Julia? Why must you stay there so stubbornly Sutton when you have done all and more than is required of you?

But would Alice Hawthorn have even considered returning to England? Would she have given up, given in, left Tom in the trenches when well she could have stayed—to meet him, perhaps, at the turning of a corner?

But she was no longer that girl, and Alice Sutton was pregnant, and pregnant women were of no use on the Western Front. And it wasn't a pregnancy, it was a punishment, and when her labour began, every pain would be inflicted by Elliot Sutton, and the child would nurse at her breasts with *his* mouth. It would live and thrive because of who had fathered it, but maybe she would die at the birthing? She sometimes hoped she would.

She jumped, clucking, to her feet. There was so little to do, save eat as many of the right things as were available to a woman in her condition, take gentle exercise, keep her mind peaceful and her thoughts beautiful, Doctor James had stressed, so her child might be perfectly born.

Julia! I want to come back to Celverte! I want this nightmare never to have happened. I want to be Alice Hawthorn again and Tom still alive!

Damn this war and damn the German who wiped out Tom's life as if it were of no consequence! And she was sick and tired of being a sewing-maid with a title that insisted she was a lady!

They would be having tea-break downstairs—she would go and share their pot, sit at the table as she had always done! They couldn't refuse her; wasn't she Lady Sutton now? If she insisted, surely they would allow her back?

She heard Cook's sobbing before ever she pushed open the kitchen door; heard the agitated rocking of the fireside chair.

'Mrs Shaw—what's wrong?'

'This whole world is wrong. It's gone mad; *mad*, I say,' came the muffled cries from the depths of her apron.

'Tell me?' Alice laid an arm around the quivering shoulders.

'You haven't read the papers, then? Surely you've seen it?'

'I know the Germans are advancing, but they can be thrown back just as easily,' she comforted.

'But what about that poor King of Russia, eh? How could they do it? And his bairns an' all...'

Alice picked up the newspaper from where it had been flung. It was a special edition; four pages only, printed later than the one she had just read.

RUSSIAN ROYAL FAMILY MURDERED, blazed the headlines. *At a house in Ekaterinburg, Nicholas II, Czar of all the Russias, his Consort and children were put to death by a Bolshevik firing squad on or about Tuesday 16 July...*

'It can't be true, Mrs Shaw,' Alice whispered. 'They couldn't kill their Czar. The papers have got it wrong again.'

'They've done it, all right, and him crowned and anointed. And what harm did that sick little lad of his ever do to anybody, aye, and them Grand Duchesses, too?' Cook was a Royalist through and through, extending her respect to the Czar even though his soldiers hadn't done all that well for us in the fighting and taken themselves off when we'd needed them most. 'If it can happen there it can happen here. If we don't win something, soon, there'll be revolution on our streets an' all, and the gentry stood up against a wall and shot! They had a revolution in France—now Russia. Who's to say it won't—'

'Of course it won't happen here. This is England, Mrs Shaw. It could *not* happen to us. Come on, now—dry your eyes. I'll put the kettle on and we'll all have a cup and a chat, just like it used to be. I haven't seen hide nor hair of you since I came home. Let's pretend, shall we, that this war never happened and that Bess and Mary will be coming down for a —'

'But it *has* happened.' All at once, Cook was on her feet, taking the kettle from

Alice's hand. 'Bess and Mary are gone and you can't turn back the clock. It isn't right you should come down here, supping tea with servants!'

Breathing deeply, defiantly, she dabbed at her eyes with her apron corner.

'But it's *me*, Alice!'

'No. You went away Alice and you've come back her ladyship. I'd like it if you'd go or Miss Clitherow'll find you here and it'll be me and Tilda and Jin what gets the sharp edge of her tongue!'

'No!' Alice wanted to cry that they wouldn't; that Miss Clitherow could not say her nay if she wanted to drink tea in her own kitchen!

But it wasn't her kitchen. It was Lady Helen's and ever would be, and you didn't make a silk purse from a sow's ear, though try telling that to the straight-laced Agnes Clitherow who was the worst snob in the riding. And upstairs and below-stairs didn't mix. Giles Sutton wouldn't have looked at her twice had he been choosing a wife as he should have; wouldn't even have considered her, but for the bairn he so desperately needed.

Yet she *was* Lady Sutton, and though Doctor James and Mrs Effie had been kindness itself, and Mr Lane and Mrs Letty—aye, and Lady Tessa an' all—they'd only done it from genteel politeness, and

504

because she carried her ladyship's precious grandchild.

And how was she to rear that child when it was born—she who knew nothing of the ways of the gentry? Would she be allowed to take over its upbringing? Wouldn't it be best, once it was all over, if she were to go; vanish as if Alice Hawthorn had never been; leave them their child and find some place to start afresh, alone?

'I'm sorry.' She backed towards the door. 'I wouldn't want to get any of you into trouble. I didn't think, Mrs Shaw. I won't come down here again; please forgive me.'

'Nay—oh, that's not what I mean!' Cook's face flushed red. 'You are mistress of this house, now—or could be if you wanted to. And by right, an' all.' The plump, elderly woman looked down at her anxiously twisting fingers. 'But what I'm trying to say is that you aren't one of us any longer. You are Sir Giles's wife, and we've all got to remember it. And that's an order from Miss Clitherow.'

'What have I ever done to Miss Clitherow to deserve this?' Alice choked.

'Nothing, I suppose—and everything.' Cook lifted her head, gazing into Alice's eyes. 'I'd appreciate it if you'd bear in mind what I've just said. With respect, that is, and remembering the fondness I've

505

always had for you. I'm mistress in this kitchen, but your place is upstairs now. It has to be said...'

Alice turned and, closing the door quietly behind her, walked slowly up the wooden stairs. Cook was right. She didn't belong below stairs now, any more than the saying of the wedding service and the ring she wore meant that all at once she was as good as her betters.

Best she should run away—but where to? Who in all of this world wanted her?

She crossed the hall, sped down the stone steps outside the sturdy front door, and made for Keeper's Cottage. Reuben knew; he would understand. She could pour out her unhappiness to him; weep until there were no tears left in her.

Then he would take a clean handkerchief from the top, left-hand drawer, mop her eyes, and send her back to where she now belonged.

I want to die when this bairn is born, God, and You'd be doing me a service if You'd let me!

And for shame, Alice Hawthorn! For shame to think such dreadful things when there are young men fighting with their last breath to stay alive. At this very minute, there were at least two score of them, in Hut Twenty-four and oh, Julia, how I wish I could turn back the clock...

The tide of the war began to turn. High summer had seen an Allied counter-offensive on the Western Front, though the newspapers were not allowed to print the entire truth for fear of raising hopes too high. Then, to Cook's great joy, it began to be cautiously admitted that the enemy had not only been halted but pushed back, in places. She read and reread the newspapers now, sure as ever she could be that by Christmas it would all be over. The lads would be home and there'd be all the flour and sugar and butter that any cook could ever want and she would roast the biggest piece of sirloin that dratted oven could accommodate!

'I think,' said Helen, 'that our little baby might well be born into a world at peace, Alice. And we must never let such a terrible thing happen again. We have the vote now. We must use it!'

'*You* have the vote, Mother-in-law,' Alice shifted uncomfortably in her chair. 'And please don't set your hopes too high on a boy? It must just as easy be a girl.'

'Does it matter? It will be *my* grandchild. Clemmy doesn't know how lucky she is, yet she rarely talks about that little boy in Kentucky.'

'Sebastian,' Alice murmured. 'An un-usual name.'

'Yes. He's starting to talk. In Albert's last letter he said the little one calls himself Bas. Do you know, Albert's marriage was one of convenience—no one tried to deny it. There were hurtful remarks, too, from some quarters. Yet now he seems so very happy. I think he will bring his wife and son to England when the war ends. Clemmy hasn't met her daughter-in-law and—'

The conservatory door opened and a red-cheeked Tilda offered a salver with a flourish nothing short of triumphant.

'Milady! Did you ever see so many letters? Eight, and nearly all from France. Miss Clitherow says it's a good sign.'

'Two for you, Alice, and oh! six for me. Thank you, Tilda.'

Helen rewarded her housemaid with a brilliant smile, sending her back to the kitchen on a cloud of contentment, she being the one to have brought such good news.

'Mine are from Julia.' Alice tilted the envelopes, the better to see the postmark. 'Written some time ago, but to get so many at once—it's got to mean that things are getting better over there.'

'Mine are from Nathan, Andrew and Julia—and one from India, from Cecilia. Such a feast. Let's read them, then exchange news?'

'Would you mind if I shared mine with Giles?' Alice worried about him. What little she knew about nursing confirmed that his return to full health would never be. For the rest of his life, Giles would have good days and bad days; might never walk again without the help of sticks.

It was because of this, and because of his goodness, that she was able to show her affection in small ways: by never leaving him alone for too long; by anticipating his periods of silence that indicated pain he was reluctant to admit to; by talking about the child she carried, though it pained her to do it.

'I shall claim a father's right and choose the name if we have a son.'

Already the child she carried was his own—Rowangarth's—yet to her it was still a child of rape, conceived on the day she had learned of Tom's death.

'I have letters,' she smiled, 'from Julia. And Mother-in-law has six.' She settled herself at his side. This was one of his good days; he should be outside, she frowned. Already it was August; the warm days, soon, would grow less.

'And I have two. Tilda brought them to me. One from Julia and one from Nathan. He asks after your health, by the way.'

'He's a kind man. I think if he were here, he'd want you outside in the sunshine.

They're cutting the wheat. Why don't I take you there?'

Every grain of corn was precious; the harvest had never before been so important.

'No. You mustn't push my chair now.'

'But from here to the field isn't far, though if you really want to go, I can ask Reuben to give a hand.'

'Do you think he might, Alice? I'd like to go out.'

'Then you shall!'

Reuben was not at Keeper's; Morgan sniffed him out at the far end of the wood, looking up into the tallest trees.

'Now then, Alice lass.' His smile was one of pleasure. 'Summat I can do for you?'

'Yes, there is.' She could be herself in Reuben's company, and she smiled happily. 'I want you to help me push Giles to the ten-acre field. He'd like to watch the harvesting, but won't let me take him there.'

'Nor must you.' He bent to fondle the spaniel's ears. What time shall it be?'

'About two, if you can spare a couple of hours.'

'Time is what I've got plenty of, these days. No rearing, no growers to see to; no shoots like there used to be. Just showing myself from time to time to warn the poachers off—though there's little in the way of game-birds to take now. That old war has a lot to answer for.'

'That it has, Reuben—I should know. But tell me—what do you find so interesting about those trees?'

'Trees? Why do you ask?' His reply was too sharp. 'A keeper has to have his eyes everywhere, you should know that.'

'Then tell me—where are the rooks? Because that's why you haven't had your eyes off those elms all the time I've been here.' She said it lightly, yet all the time knowing she should have known better than to ask. 'I haven't heard them, come to think of it, these few nights past...' She liked the rooks in Brattocks Wood; they were a part of Rowangarth, with their lazy, sunset cawing as they settled to roost. They were her friends, keepers of her secrets, and if they ever left... 'And do you believe what folks say, Reuben—that if those birds ever leave Brattocks sorrow will strike the Suttons?'

'Who's been telling you nonsense like that? Jin Dobb, was it, the daft old biddy?'

'No one told me; I think I've known it all along. And they aren't there, Reuben. They've gone.'

'Happen not at this moment. They'll be out, foraging. They'll be back.'

'They *must* come back. They can't go, Reuben...'

'Lass! Stop your fretting. It's nowt but a nonsense. Rooks are canny birds; have better instincts than humans. And those elms are old; rooks know when a tree might blow down. Like as not they're just flying round, looking for a safer place to nest,' he comforted.

'The elms aren't old. Sir John had them planted, the same year as him and her ladyship were wed. You told me so. They're good for fifty years yet. And the rooks *have* gone...'

'Will you give over nattering? All that talk is superstition. They'll be back, I tell you. Now, about this afternoon. I'll be up at the house after dinner and we'll take Sir Giles round the back way—no steps, round the back. I reckon we might go by way of the garden. Percy'd like to see him; might appreciate a visit. Us'll have a rare afternoon, Alice, if you think the master's up to it.'

'He's grand today, though other times I know he's in pain. What do you think to him, Reuben?'

'He's no worse'n he was when he comed home. Better, in fact. He looked right badly the day they brought him back to Rowangarth. And he's a better colour now,' he added for good measure. Reuben

512

set great store by colour. A body was either a good colour or a bad colour; healthy or ill. As simple as that.

'We'll make it a good afternoon, Reuben —not let him tire himself?'

'Us will, lass.' An outing would do Alice good an' all; her looking that pinched and tired sometimes, and dark rings under her eyes that had never been there before. 'Come on, then.' He offered his arm. 'Let's walk back nice and gentle and forget those rooks, the daft old things.'

She smiled up into his eyes. 'I've forgotten them already. I'm not superstitious.'

But she *hadn't*—and she *was*...

By early September, when the harvest stubble had been ploughed in and a nip in the air warned of autumn, it became certain the war was going in favour of the Allies. French, American and British troops pushed the enemy out of France, then began the slow liberation of Belgium.

By the end of the month, Bulgaria sued for peace and, soon after, came reluctant offers of co-operation from the German High Command. Austria surrendered, and Turkey; it was becoming almost too much to bear.

Cook could not so much as open a newspaper, and Tilda was obliged to read the news to a Cook terrified it would all come to nothing; that the Germans would produce some fearful weapon even more deadly than Big Bertha and the awful business would begin all over again.

In November, the Kaiser abdicated his throne and fled his country. The Allies had won the war. Nothing, now, could stop them! Weeks—*days,* even—and it would all be over. No more killing; no more sacrificing young lives to the god of Teutonic arrogance. Lovers would love again; fathers see children for the first time. No more trenches, lice, the stench of death.

At daybreak on the eleventh of November 1918, all fighting ceased. At eleven o'clock, an armistice was signed. *It was over!* Telephone lines sang the news all over Britain; church bells rang out, motor horns blared, women banged tin trays with wooden spoons; many a pan on many a hob boiled dry from neglect.

'Helen!' It was Edward, telephoning. 'We are opening champagne! Come over?'

'Can't! We are opening it too! Oh, Edward, I can't stop weeping, it's so wonderful!'

In towns and cities, work came to a standstill, and men and women from shops and factories and offices spilled out on to the streets, dancing, hugging, laughing, singing. At noon, Big Ben chimed out for the first time in years and the King and Queen stood on the balcony at Buckingham Palace, Queen Mary waving a Union Jack, would you believe!

'I've taken the liberty, milady...' Miss Clitherow emerged from the cellar carrying a bottle of champagne.

'Miss Clitherow! *One* bottle? For shame!' Helen laughed. The housekeeper disappeared to return, flushed and triumphant, with two more.

'Tilda—be a dear, good girl and find Reuben and Catchpole, will you? We must all celebrate!'

Crystal glasses unused since Julia's wedding, were quickly polished; corks popped, champagne fizzed and spilled.

'Alice, darling—it's *over!*' Helen hugged her son's wife, kissing her soundly. 'I knew we'd have a peacetime baby; I *knew* it!'

Over. Alice took her place at Giles's side. Helen held up her hand.

'Please—everyone...Shall we first thank God it is all over and remember those who are still away from us and,' her voice fell to a whisper, 'those who will never come home.'

Giles reached for Alice's hand, holding it tightly. 'Over,' he said softly. 'No more killing...'

'And Julia and Andrew home for

Christmas,' Alice murmured. She would like to have Julia beside her when her time came. Julia would understand.

'Let's try to be happy today, Alice. You and I—we know how it was over there—but let's try not to think too deeply about *anything*...'

He raised his glass to Agnes Clitherow, who smiled back broadly, tilting her glass with her little finger genteelly raised, whilst on the bottom step of the great staircase from which Sutton ancestors gazed down, Jinny Dobb lapped contentedly at her glass, not at all sure she could ever quite take to champagne, but appreciating the feeling it gave to her. It was why she had been obliged to sit down, truth known.

Cook drained her glass and thought happily about pounds and pounds of butter, sugar by the sackful, dinner parties every week. Tilda shared her dreams with David, who had been in the fighting—well, *near* it—even though he needn't have bothered.

Percy Catchpole regarded his daft little glass balefully, wishing it were a pint tankard and full of ale; Reuben gazed over to Brattocks to the almshouse he'd waited four long years to move into, hoping that Jin Dobb would shift herself sharpish and be off back to the bothy, where she rightly belonged. He looked over to where Alice stood, giving her a smile and a nod to let her know that he, too, was remembering.

'I can't stop weeping,' Helen laughed, taking a fresh handkerchief, dabbing happily at her eyes. 'And Julia will be home and Andrew and oh, Miss Clitherow, pour yourself another glass, *do!*'

It was a good day; a day four years too long in coming. There would be no work done today at Rowangarth; no rhyme or reason in anything anyone did, but who cared? It was over! *It was over!*

That night, when Giles slept, Alice walked in slippered feet to the sewing-room. Every light in every window made Rowangarth a blaze of light, but the bothy, locked and silent, stood dark and apart.

...those who will never come home. Her hand reached for the locket at her throat.

It's over, Tom. When we thought we'd lost, almost, the war turned round on itself and we won! I want you to know there won't ever be a day I don't think of you and send you my love and want you till it hurts.

I'm all right now. Giles will look after me and the child, when it is born. And one day I shall find you, Tom. And I'll bring you buttercups, like I promised...

Alice was the first to see Julia. She was

517

crossing the cow pasture, hands in pockets, head down, as if she had walked from Holdenby.

Frowning, she reached for her shawl, then ran quickly down the back stairs. How like her! How exactly like Julia to arrive, not in the carriage or the station cab or even in one of Pendenys's cars. No! She must savour the moment; leave her luggage at the station, then walk the last miles home in the crisp cold of an early December afternoon.

'Julia! My dear, you're back!' Alice ran, arms wide, then stopped in her tracks. 'Julia—what is it? What's wrong? And what on earth made you want to walk? You're blue with cold!'

Julia's eyes sought those of her friend. They were dull; dark with pain. 'Cold? Yes, it *is* cold,' she murmured as if the thought had only just occurred to her.

'Julia.' Alice's voice was low with concern. 'Tell me what's wrong? You look awful. Have you been ill? Have you caught this 'flu that's about? Hurry, let's get you to bed; then we'll call Doctor James.'

'Alice—listen, please? I haven't told anyone. I was waiting to tell *you...*'

'Tell me?' Alice tried to speak but no sound came; just the moving of her lips.

'Tell me what, Julia?'

'Andrew. Dead...'

'No! Oh God, *no!*'

Julia nodded, her face a mask, then the words tumbled out in a rush of pain.

'Ruth Love first told us. It was over! The whole ward went mad. I'd never felt so happy. Then, just before we went off duty, someone brought me a telegram. On the sixth of November, it had happened—and I'd thought he was safe...'

'He isn't dead! He can't be! Come home?' Alice held out her hand. It would be all right, once they were home.

'Home? Dear God—how am I to tell Mother? How am I to face people? This pain inside me—it won't go away...'

'Come home?' Alice pulled Julia's arm into her own. 'We'll go in by the back door. There's a fire in the winter parlour. Mother-in-law is out. There'll be nobody but us—only please, Julia, don't look at me like that?' It was as if she were dead with only the fierce pain that blazed in her eyes to show she lived and breathed.

And please let it not be true, God? Let there have been some foolish, careless mistake? Not Andrew? Not Julia's love taken, too?

'On the sixth, the telegram said. He was up at the front line. He shouldn't have been there. I went to his hospital.

I wouldn't believe it—had to find out for myself. Just walked out of the ward. I didn't care...'

'And?' Alice opened the back door, closing it quietly.

'He would have been all right, Alice. Four years he'd kept alive, and then a toothache got him. A bad tooth it was, not a bullet!' Her voice rose to a wail of torment as if her agony, once released, must have its terrible way.

'Sssssh.' Alice closed the parlour door, turning the key. She wanted no one here; no one but her and Julia. 'A bad tooth?'

'They told me at the hospital. One of the young doctors at a dressing-station at the Front had a raging toothache. Driving him mad. One of the stretcher-bearers brought back the message: could someone at the hospital give him something to take back with him to ease the poor man's pain, he said; something to put in the tooth to numb it. And Andrew said he could do better than that.

'He wasn't on duty, so he went back with the ambulance, said he'd take out the tooth, then put a dressing in it. Only he didn't. He never got there. The ambulance drove into a minefield—one of our own minefields, left behind in the advance, and unmarked. Four of them killed. Two stretcher-bearers, the driver and Andrew.

My husband died because someone had an aching tooth...'

'There now, there, there...' Alice gathered the shaking body to her. 'Let it come, love? Alice understands...'

Tears ran silently down her cheeks as her friend, her sister, cried out her grief in great, tearing sobs.

'They gave me his things at the hospital—his instruments and clothes—and transport back to Celverte. I told Sister I was going home. I was so full of rage, of disgust. Ruth wanted me to cry, but I couldn't. Sister went to see Matron. They knew I'd be no more use to them, so they sent me home on sick leave...'

'But where have you been till now?' Alice brushed away her tears with an impatient hand.

'I went to Little Britain. D'you know, I thought I'd find him there, but there was only Sparrow. I slept in our bed. All London seemed happy and I hated them for it.

'Then I made myself open one of his cases. I suppose I needed to find something there—some sort of goodbye to convince me it really was true. Then I knew it was. There was his uniform in that case—the one he'd been wearing when it happened. They hadn't the decency to keep it from me. The front of his jacket and his shirt and vest—all blood-soaked and ripped. That mine must have torn his heart out. So what do I do now, Alice? Shall I go to Brattocks—tell it to the rooks? Do they bring dead lovers back?'

'The rooks have left, Julia...'

'Gone? Left Rowangarth? So it's sorrow to the Suttons, then. Which one of us is next?' She closed her eyes, shaking her head. 'Alice, I'm sorry! I shouldn't have said that—not to you, the way you are.' She looked at the swollen body as if seeing it clearly for the first time. 'Please, love, I'm sorry. And you *do* know. You've been through all this. How do you bear it? Is it going to get any better for me?'

'I don't know, Julia. I only know I shall never forgive those who allowed that war to happen. Let them that want a war fight it themselves, I say. They've taken your brother and your man—my Tom, too—and sent Giles home a poor wreck. Jin Dobb knows how to ill-wish, some say. I wish with all my heart I could do it.'

'Bear with me, Alice? When it gets too much to bear, be kind?'

'I shall be here, always. And your mother—she knows how it is, too.'

'Yes—but oh, Alice, less than a week and Andrew would have made it home.

And there'll be no children now, for me.'

'Then you shall share this one—show me how it should be reared. I don't know the ways of the gentry, Julia—I need you, too.' She dropped awkwardly to her knees, unlacing Julia's shoes, placing them in the hearth. 'Your stockings are soaking an' all. Take them off. Your feet are like blocks of ice.' She took off her shawl, wrapping it round them. 'I'll build up the fire—stay by it, warm yourself. That's the pony and trap—your mother is back. Best leave it to me, to tell her...'

She turned the key in the lock, then closed the door behind her, doing it slowly to put off the moment. Her heart ached dully—not with grief, but with blind, passionate hatred for those who had caused the war, fuelled it uncaringly with young lives.

Perhaps you didn't have to learn how to ill-wish. Maybe it was there inside you all along and all you had to do was hate.

She did not know. All she was certain of was that Helen was smiling and waving, calling out to her to walk carefully on the stableyard cobbles—and that she, Alice, must tell her that Andrew wasn't coming home.

23

'I'm glad to have met you.' Alice stood at the open front door, saying goodbye to the midwife. 'It was thoughtful of Doctor James to send you.'

'I think it was two birds with one stone, Lady Sutton. The doctor is run off his feet with 'flu—an epidemic now—and he wanted me to look in on you. I shall be with him when your time comes, assisting...'

'This influenza—is it really bad?' Alice frowned.

'I'm afraid so. As if we hadn't had enough with the war—now people have more to worry about. A lot have no resistance to it—been undernourished for years, you see. But you are not to worry.' She believed in keeping mothers-to-be serene. 'Take a little gentle exercise when the weather allows, and keep away from anyone sniffing or sneezing, and you'll do nicely.'

Against all her instincts, Alice thought about Elliot Sutton, wondering how soon he would return to Pendenys Place.

Not yet, she hoped. She wouldn't want

to think of him so near when her labour began. People said you forgot your labour when you held your child, but she wouldn't want to hold it; it would be like touching *him*. She shivered, visibly.

'You aren't worrying, Lady Sutton?' The nurse was quick to notice the worried frown. 'Believe me, if birthing was that awful, this world would be full of only children. I shall tell Doctor James you are a healthy young lady and that all is well. And don't fret. I am just a telephone call away,' she beamed.

Alice closed the door, walking carefully across the hall, avoiding rugs that might slide beneath her feet, having care for small objects underfoot she was not able to see now. She was so big, so ugly.

'That was the midwife, coming to check up on me.' She opened the library door, smiling at Giles who lifted his head from the book on his knee. 'Doctor James is busy with 'flu visits; I was warned to keep away from sniffles and sneezes.'

'And the baby?'

'Fine. She seemed well pleased. Doctor James puts great trust in her.'

'I'll be glad when it is over.'

'So shall I.' She threw back her head, forcing a laugh. 'Do you know—I swear I haven't seen my feet for over a week.'

'Poor little Hawthorn.' He took her hand

and held it to his cheek. 'I'm grateful to you.'

'And me to you, so let's hear no more of your thanks. But I do so miss Julia. I wish she hadn't gone back to London. She says she wants to end the lease on Andrew's lodgings, but she doesn't really. She just wants to be near him. If she had given it a little time, waited until spring, I could have gone, too—helped her through it.

'I was there the night she met Andrew, you know. It would be better if I could be with her when finally she says goodbye to him: one day she must let him go.'

'I think she'll never get over it, Alice.'

'Maybe not—but at least the pain gets less bad. In time, she'll be able to call him back without hurting inside.'

'You know how it is, don't you?'

'I know. Life can be very unfair. And you deserved better than this, Giles, but I'll try, always, to do what I can to help you.'

'We'll have to lean on each other.'

'We'll do that. And I'll build up the fire, then perhaps we could have tea together.' She felt such pity for him, such gratitude, that she cupped his face in her hands, gentling his forehead with her lips.

'That was to say thank you,' she whispered, pink-cheeked. 'For everything.'

The first Christmas of peace was quiet at Rowangarth; subdued, almost. Food rationing had not miraculously disappeared with the signing of the armistice, nor shortages ended. Julia became a shadow, a wraith of the loved and loving woman she had been, taking long walks to the top of the Pike, returning exhausted, eyes dark with pain and red-rimmed from weeping.

'I didn't give up the lease on Little Britain,' she confided on her return from London. 'I meant to, but I couldn't. It would have been like a betrayal. Sparrow will take care of the place still, and I shall use it whenever I go to London.'

'You'd do far better to stay at Aunt Sutton's,' Alice urged. 'Think of the expense of keeping the lodgings going—and empty, most times.'

'The army gives me a widow's allowance,' she said, tight-lipped. 'Let that pay for it. And did you know that Figgis has left Aunt Sutton; gone to her sister in Bristol. She's too old to work now. Aunt misses her, but she plans to spend as much time as she can in France, now it's possible for her to travel there again.

'She can't wait to get back to her Camargue, see how her friends there fared during the war. She plans to go for New Year. Did I ever tell you she's left her house to me?'

'No. It's kind of her, though. One day you'll be able to have a home of your own if the mood takes you; later, when things get easier for you, that is.'

'Things won't get easier, and I don't want a home if Andrew isn't in it with me,' she shrugged, her voice flat with indifference.

'Julia, I do know what it's like. Let me share it with you?' If only she would rage and weep and slam doors like the Julia of old would have done, it might be the first step along the road to acceptance. But she was like a woman in a dream; a half-alive creature with wide, troubled eyes in a face pinched with pain. And all the time getting thinner, more pale. 'And please don't go back to London just yet? The baby—it could happen any day now. I want you, *need* you, with me.'

'I'll be here—but there'll be Doc James and the nurse. You'll be all right.'

'But, Julia, it's you I shall need, *really* need. And there's something else—' she hesitated.

'Mm?'

'Listen, please!' She was away with her dreams again. In Paris, was it, or Hyde Park, with Andrew? 'Giles didn't sleep, last night. And his temperature is up.'

'How do you know? Did you take it?'

'No, but it's up. His forehead was

burning. Take a look—see what you think, will you?'

Julia removed the thermometer from her brother's mouth, read it quickly, then passed it to Alice, reaching for his wrist.

'It's up—just a little,' she murmured. 'Feel a bit off, do you?'

Up a *little?* Alice read and read again the thin line that showed an unacceptable high. Her eyes met Julia's. *I told you so.*

'Any chest pains—tightness?' Julia was the nurse again, her cool hand on his forehead.

'No—*yes!* Oh, I don't know! It's just that I've had a bad night...'

'You should have rung your bell: I'd have heard you,' Alice scolded.

'You need your rest.'

'It wouldn't have mattered. I'm not sleeping too well, these nights. And Julia would have come...'

'Of course I would. And if you aren't improved by tonight, I'll have Doc James call. So let's make you comfortable. I think we might start with a wash down, and dry sheets.'

Alice rang the bedside bell, grateful that something had taken Julia's interest; worried that Giles should be the cause of it.

'Julia, you *can't!*' Giles whispered. 'My

sister, I mean, undressing me...'

'Idiot! I've given more bed-baths, rubbed more male buttocks than you'll ever imagine. And done far worse!'

There was the glimmer of a smile in her eyes, in her voice. It was like a snatch of sunshine on a grey day, and Alice latched on to it gratefully.

'We were the terrors of Hut Twenty-four, weren't we, Julia? Brave men trembled at our approach.'

'No. That was Sister Carbrooke.'

The moment soon passed; the sudden smile was gone when out of earshot Julia whispered, 'I'm going to phone Richard James at once. Giles says he's cold, yet he's wringing with sweat. Where is Mother?'

'Gone to Denniston; but she must be told as soon as she comes back. I think Giles has caught 'flu. He's got all the symptoms.'

'But how could he? He hasn't been out of the house since before Christmas.'

'It's 'flu,' Alice insisted. 'The doctor should see him, straight away.'

Richard was out, Effie James told Julia flatly. 'He was up half the night, now he's trying to catch up on house calls. If he rings in, I'll get him to you at once, but it could be ages before he's back. This influenza is serious, Julia; you don't think it's that, with Giles?'

'I don't know what to think, but Alice is certain it is. Can you treat it as urgent, Effie? I'm worried. His temperature is too high.'

'The doctor's on his way,' Julia said brightly, closing the door behind her. 'I'll just clear up in here. Aspirin and plenty of water to drink,' she said lightly to Alice, who had pulled a chair to the bedside. 'I'll see what I can find in Andrew's bag.'

On his way? He could be hours, Julia frowned, collecting sheets and towels, carrying out the water bowl. And Alice was right. Giles, somehow, had caught 'flu, and Effie James said people were dying of it. What, she demanded silently, bitterly, had Rowangarth done to deserve such punishment? Robert, Andrew—Alice, even. And now Giles, bright-eyed with fever, and God only knew when Richard James would get here.

Andrew, where are you? Andrew would have known what to do, made it all come right. And may hell damn toothache into eternity!

'It's influenza.' Richard James told Helen, who had waited downstairs. 'I'm sorry to have been so long coming, but half the Riding is down with it. Five deaths, too—a

531

vicious strain; either that, or people are so frail after four years of war they have nothing to fight it with...'

'What more can we do?' There was fear in Helen's voice.

'Nothing that hasn't already been done. All the fluids he can take... There'll be a crisis, though with two nurses in the house, Giles is luckier than most. I don't know which way to turn. And my own nurse is laid up too.'

'The midwife? But she was here recently. Is it she who brought the germ into the house?'

'No, Helen, it is not. She, poor soul, fell on the ice yesterday. Her arm is broken, and a badly bruised nurse with an arm in a sling isn't a lot of use to me, I'm afraid. And I'm sorry to be the bringer of such bad news, but—'

'I'm sure Giles will be fine.' Helen tilted her chin. 'When will crisis time come, do you think?' The crisis, people called it, when a fever reached its height; when a strong person survived it and a sickly one did not.

'I should say in about twenty-four hours. This influenza isn't like other diseases. There is no known medicine to fight it with. It's all a question of waiting and hoping—and praying, Helen my dear. I'd send Effie to you, but I need her at the surgery. I'm sorry, but—'

'I understand. You have all your other patients to think about.' And with most of the young doctors still not released from army service, Richard must surely be hard put to it to cope with the sudden epidemic. 'Thank you for coming. We'll take every care, between us.'

'And keep an eye on Alice. By rights she shouldn't be in that sickroom.'

'No! Of course not!' Helen took the stairs in a panic. How thoughtless of her to let Alice near Giles. Her labour could start any day, any hour; the midwife with a broken arm and Richard not knowing which way to turn!

'Alice, I think you should go to your room—have a rest,' Helen said, closing the door behind her. 'I will sit with Giles—you mustn't overtire yourself.' *And oh, my dear, you must not catch influenza. Not now when your time is so near.*

'It's all right, Mother-in-law. I was a nurse, don't forget? Often we worked so hard we didn't take off our shoes for days at a time.'

'But you were not carrying a child then.'

'I shall stay with him,' Alice insisted. 'Julia is resting; she will take the night duty. We must try to get his temperature down; cool drinks, cold cloths—anything

533

to fight the fever. And pray for him, dearest? He hasn't got his strength back yet, after his wounds. Prayers do get answered, I know it.'

'Alice! I'm not being a fuss-pot. Richard James said you shouldn't be in here.'

'I'm sure the doctor means well, but he must not order me out of my husband's room,' Alice said softly, returning to take her place at the bedside. 'I'm sorry to disobey him—and you, too, mother-in-law—but I will stay, until Julia takes over. And I need cold water and more cloths. And drinking-water, too. Will you ask they be brought up, please?'

'Alice—I *beg* you...'

Unspeaking, Alice shook her head and, taking Giles's hand in her own, laid it to her cheek. And wasn't it too late? She and Julia had been in the sickroom for most of the day. No use, now, to start worrying...

Julia built up the fire, pulled back the curtains, staring out into the night.

'Poor Giles.'

She looked down at her brother's flushed face. His eyes were closed, but he wasn't sleeping. How could he, when his breathing was so laboured, his temperature so high?

Richard James had called again, white-faced with fatigue, had shaken his head at the questioning in Julia's eyes, then turned to leave.

'Perhaps I had better look in on Alice, if she is awake?' he murmured. 'Just to make sure all is well.'

'Mother checked up on her half an hour ago. Her light was out; she seemed to be sleeping...'

'I shall be out on calls half the night, but I will ring Effie every time I'm near a telephone. I will come at once if I am needed here.'

'Look, I know it couldn't happen at a worse time—the midwife laid up too,' Julia said softly, 'but if anything starts, Mother will sit with Giles and I'll take care of Alice. We'll manage till you can get here. We've been together a long time, she and I. She trusts me.'

'Yes—well...' He picked up his hat and gloves, wrapped his muffler round his neck. 'Best be off. I'll call again in the morning—if not before,' he added, his thoughts with the woman upstairs whose time was so near.

He sighed loudly. It was going to be a long, weary night.

Alice awoke suddenly to the certain knowledge that her labour had started. She reached for the light-pull over her bed, blinking her eyes, focusing them on the lock. Three in the morning; an ungodly hour, when a night nurse's body screamed for sleep.

She shivered, reaching for her night shawl, pulling on her slippers. No need to fuss yet, though she'd better tell Julia.

She walked quietly along the passage towards the welcome strip of light that shone beneath Giles's door.

'Are you awake?' she said softly, pushing it open.

'Hullo, love,' Julia smiled. 'Can't sleep...?'

'I woke up. I think it's started.'

'Pains? Are they bad? How often?' Julia was instantly alert.

'Not bad at all, honestly. More like niggles. I'm all right. Knew you'd be awake—just wanted to be near someone, that's all.'

'You're sure?'

'Absolutely certain. And now that I've told you, it'll probably stop. How is Giles?' Alice laid her hand on his forehead, pulling it sharply away. 'He—he's burning...'

'He's delirious, too—rambling about the war. I phoned Doc James. Effie, poor love, sounded worn out. Said he was out on a call but should be back soon. When he comes, we'll tell him it's started, shall we—just to be on the safe side?'

'If you want to. But it's nothing I can't cope with yet. Like I said—'

'Forgive me, milady, but is anything the matter?' The housekeeper stood in the open doorway, her hair down her back, a shawl clutched around her. 'I heard footsteps outside my door.'

'I'm sorry, it was me. Did I wake you?'

'No, milady, I couldn't sleep. Been tossing half the night. How is Sir Giles?'

'Poorly, I'm afraid,' Julia said softly. 'I've sent for Doctor James.'

'Then I shall dress, and put up my hair. I'll let him in when he comes. And I think I'll stir up the kitchen fire—set a kettle to boil.'

'Would you, Miss Clitherow? I'd appreciate a cup of tea,' Julia smiled.

'Then I'll make a large pot and we can all have one. Won't be long, Miss Julia, milady...' She was gone, quickly, silently.

'Good old Clitherow. She can be a pain sometimes,' Julia smiled, 'but she's all right underneath.'

'Wish she wouldn't call me milady.'

'Sorry, Alice, you're stuck with it, I'm afraid. But are you sure you are all right—*really* all right?'

'Fine. And it might turn out to be nothing that a good hot cup of tea won't take care of.'

It might, but it wouldn't; not when she was six days past her time...

Richard James laid aside his stethoscope, then confirmed Julia's fears. The crisis time of Giles's illness had begun. Within the span of twenty-four hours, they would know the worst—or the best.

'It is so awful,' Julia fretted. 'Such advances in the war; the best brains of the country finding better and more deadly ways to kill, but no one thinks to look for something to help fight a fever.'

'One day they will, be sure of it,' the doctor shrugged. 'So many advances, even since my student days...'

'One day—but not tonight. Nothing to help Giles,' Julia accepted bitterly. 'And I think Alice's pains have started.'

'Oh, dear.' It was all he could think of to say.

'Not pains,' Alice insisted, 'but there's —well—*something*...'

'Then you must go back to bed at once!'

'I will, later.' When the waters broke, she would. She knew about such things. Didn't she once help Sister deliver the baby of a refugee? A small, roadside miracle, it had seemed. A noisy one, but quite wonderful. And the look on the face of the father when—

No remembering! This is *now*, Alice Sutton. Soon your own child will come bawling into the world, but there'll be no joy of it...

By late afternoon, Alice's pains could no longer be brushed aside. Helen Sutton had taken her place at her son's bedside; Julia mopped Alice's face and Miss Clitherow and Tilda hovered within earshot of either room.

In the corner, made up with dainty sheets and blankets, stood the cot used by all Helen's children. Alice tried not to look at it. A prettily draped cot should have been a comfort, a joy; a promise that soon she would hold her child to her.

But she didn't want to hold it, to love it. She wanted Tom's child and Tom pacing the floor downstairs. She had imagined it so often in her dreamings. Their first bairn; born in springtime and a whole world of happiness theirs just for the taking. She had been so sure.

'I think I'm going to be sick, Julia.'

'*Sick?*' Without panic, Julia reached for a basin.

'No. Maybe not. But I feel—*peculiar.*'

'How—*peculiar?*'

'I don't know. My head hurts and I'm so hot. Can you take the blankets off?'

Julia lifted the sheet, bellying it out to make a rush of air. 'That better?' There had been no blankets on the bed. And

Alice was right: she was too hot, and she shouldn't be. 'Won't be a minute,' she said softly, reaching for the bell-push. 'I won't leave you...'

She opened the door and stood there, waiting. Her ring was answered at once.

'Miss Julia?' Tilda stood there, wide-eyed and breathless from running.

'Ask Miss Clitherow to telephone Doctor James at once,' she said softly, urgently. 'Tell her I don't care what he's doing—he must come, *now*. Tell him it's Lady Alice. She's in labour, and I think she's got 'flu!'

'Ooooh, miss...' Tilda clattered down the stairs, heart bumping. Sir Giles was badly—maybe couldn't last the night out—and now Alice.

'Miss Clitherow, ma'am!' she yelled.

Alice's child was born in a scream of pain. Her body hurt, her head ached blindingly and there was a tightness in her chest that prevented her, almost, from drawing breath.

There had been a moment, minutes ago, when she had wanted to give in to the pain; to close her eyes and slip high and away, over Brattocks and up and up towards a sun that shone brilliantly.

'Push, will you! One more push, Alice...'

Julia, urging her, holding her hands

540

so tightly she couldn't get free, fly to Tom.

'Alice—*try.* One more push...'

And then there was peace. This was dying, a release from pain. Yet why was she on fire, her whole body burning? Was it hell she was going to? Had they judged her already, and must she pay, now, for her sin?

'Alice, love, it's all right!' She heard a mewling, a baby crying. 'You have a fine son! It's all over. We have a boy!' Julia laughing, crying.

Go away, Julia. Go, and take my sin with you. I want to go to Tom

She tried to breathe deeply, but the pain inside her was too great. She let go a little gasp, then darkness came. Sweet, gentle darkness.

'I'll see to her now.' Richard James threw off his coat and began washing his hands. 'Sorry.'

He tied, then cut the cord that bound mother and child; then, swaddling the baby in a towel, cleaning out the little mouth, he whispered, 'Take him to Giles. Don't go in. Tell him he has a son. Let him hear him!'

Eyes bright with tears, Julia sped to her brother's room, flinging open the door.

'Giles! Can you hear me?' she called.

'It's over?' Helen sprang to her feet. 'She's all right?'

'I mustn't come in, but tell Giles? Tell him he has a fine son—and Sutton fair! The image of Uncle Edward!'

Briefly, Helen closed her eyes against tears of relief and joy, grasping her son's hand.

'Giles, can you hear me? You have a son—a fine son to get well for!'

His eyes opened, his hand stirred in that of his mother. His lips moved in the gentlest of smiles.

'A son!' Helen exulted.

Julia stood at the window of Alice's bedroom, her heart beating with pain, watching the slow, black procession that carried her brother away from her.

Poor, broken Giles; too weak from his wounds, still, to fight back.

She was glad she must remain here, take care of Alice and the baby; Alice who tossed and muttered in delirium, and the little one, so hungry, so sick.

No milk had come to Alice's breasts; the fault of the influenza. Giles was dead; Rowangarth's son must live at all costs.

Yet he could not feed. They had searched, but no wet nurse could be found; no woman with breast milk to spare for a baby who vomited back the cow's milk they gave him. He sucked at the bottle hungrily, but it was all no use.

The last coach of the funeral procession was lost to her sight as it rounded the bend in the drive.

'Goodbye, Giles,' she whispered. 'You were too good a soul for this world, but your son will live, I swear it. And I'll watch over him and love him always, I promise you.'

Rowangarth was deserted, save for herself and Jinny Dobb. Jin watched over the baby in the warmth of the kitchen; she, Julia, sat with Alice until her mother returned. Outside the skies were grey, the January wind bitter from the east.

Andrew, I need you. Our lovely world has gone mad. We are being punished for I know not what. The rooks have deserted us and Alice is sick. The baby can't feed. He's losing weight and crying with hunger. What am I to do, my darling? Help us, please?

Jin Dobb could stand it no longer. She had offered to mind the bairn because she detested funerals and especially the burying of a young man on a day so bleak as this. But the bairn had cried solid for half an hour and not even her little finger in his mouth to suck on had silenced him for long.

The mite was not just hungry; he was

slowly starving. First Sir Giles and now his bairn; a little scrap with a title already to hang on him, but no name. Alice must choose the name, Miss Julia had insisted, yet Alice wasn't capable of thought at the moment. Fighting that 'flu, and her weak from a long labour because the doctor hadn't been able to get there in time to be of much help.

But that was men the whole world over, she thought bitterly, pacing the floor yet again, patting the little back, stiff with anger. Never there when you needed them. And no use giving the bairn more water. It only gave him gripes. It was sustenance he needed; something his little belly could keep a hold of and not throw back. Cow's milk for a new-born babbie, indeed! They hadn't the sense they were born with. For two pins she'd go upstairs and tell Miss Julia now!

Wrapping the baby tightly, she mounted the stairs with determination, knocking on the sickroom door.

'I'm come to tell you, ma'am, that this bairn is fading slow and I can't stand by and see it!'

'I know, Jin; I know! And don't bring him in here. We've enough on our plate already.'

'Then if I might suggest—' and if someone didn't do something soon, the lass would keel over and go the same way as Alice on the bed over there—'that it isn't milk from a cow this babbie needs.'

'Then tell me,' Julia flung, her face red with anger and frustration. 'Just tell me and if I have to go to the ends of the earth to get it, I will!'

'Nay. No need to put yourself out. Soon as they gets back from the churchyard I can get it from my sister for you. He'll keep it down, or I'm a Dutchman!'

'Keep *what* down?'

'Goat's milk, that's what. And proved times over. My sister never could feed a babbie—not with breast milk—so she brung hers up with the help of a nanny goat; though much good it did her, them lying dead in a foreign country and begging your pardon, Miss Julia, for reminding you of such sorrow.'

'Tell me,' Julia urged, 'can you bring some milk and how will I give it to him?'

'Well, you make it weak at first, it being so rich. One measure of milk and two measures of good fresh water—and sugar for energy, of course. That's what my sister did and fine young men they growed into and never a suck of mother's milk did they ever have!'

'Then you'll get me some? You think it's worth a try?'

'The state this babbie's in, anything's worth a try. He'll either keep it down or he'll throw it back. We'll soon know.'

She stuck her finger into his mouth and he sucked on it eagerly. Then he turned his head in anger, crying out again.

'We'll try it, Jin. And bear with me? Give him some more water—keep him quiet. I'll take him from you once Mother is back.'

She would try anything. Rowangarth's child must not die. She loved him already; loved the way his fingers clung and his cheeks went into tiny hollows as he sucked down his bottle milk. And she loved him because he was Sutton fair; so like her uncle and not a trace of the blackness of the man who had fathered him. Mary Anne Pendennis's darkness had skipped a generation, and Alice had borne a child that was a true Sutton.

Now Elliot would never know about his son; never suspect. He would see his child grow into manhood and envy Rowangarth their fine young heir. Because he *would* grow into manhood: somehow she would find sustenance for him, even if she had to hawk the streets in desperation for some woman with breast milk to spare. She would beg for it on her knees.

But they would try Jin's way first. The little one could only vomit it back. She closed the door on the crying child, returning to the bed, taking Alice's hands in her own.

'Don't go! Not you too. Giles has gone and our baby is sick—I can't go on, Alice, if you don't get well. You are all I have left now. Please, *please* don't leave me?'

The frail hand in hers stirred; there was a moving of the head on the pillow. Alice's eyes opened, blinking, looking questioningly about her.

'*Alice!* Alice, it's Julia!'

'Drink?' Her lips formed the word, but no sound came.

'Yes! Oh, yes!' Julia reached for the feeding-cup, holding it to the dry, cracked lips. Alice sucked weakly at first, then greedily. Then she smiled.

'I'm not leaving,' she whispered.

'You're going to be all right, Alice! You *are.*'

'Feel dreadful. How long...?'

'You've been ill—very ill. For four days. But the baby—well, we managed between us, didn't we; though Doc James got here in the end.'

Alice turned her head on the pillow. Somewhere, in her dark, giddy floatings, she knew there was a baby, a boy, safely born; but she had tried to run from it; not to touch it, touch Elliot.

'Did I—did I *say* anything?'

'No. No names, though you yelled

something awful at times. I'll bring the baby to you as soon as Doc James says it's safe, but there's something I've got to tell you first.' There was no easy way to say it so she whispered, 'Giles. He was too weak. It beat him in the end...'

'Did he know?' Alice closed her eyes, her mouth set tightly against the sudden choke of tears in her throat.

'He knew. I stood in the doorway so he could hear his son crying. He smiled, Alice.'

'Yes.' She didn't want to open her eyes again. She wanted to rest here and not have to see the baby.

'They took Giles to the church at two. It'll be over now.'

'Poor, dear man,' Alice murmured. 'I wanted to die, too. I didn't want to hang on. I wanted to be with Tom.'

'I know, love; I know. Do you think I haven't thought things like that too? But there's a child to bring up now. I love him already, Alice. You'll love him as well.'

'I don't want to see him. Don't bring him in here?'

'Ssh. You're weak and hungry. When they all get back, I'll ask Cook to make you some pobs. Pobs will slip down nicely, won't it? And Mother will be so glad you are on the mend.'

Alice closed her eyes. It was no use. So

Julia loved the child—let her, then. She, Alice, wanted nothing of it; not Elliot Sutton's child. Even to touch it would be impossible.

'I want to go to sleep,' she whispered.

When the mourners had left Rowangarth, Helen Sutton let down her guard. The war was over, ah yes, but today it had claimed another life. Both her sons taken and the son-in-law who had been so unbelievably like John. Now Alice lay ill: she, who had braved the dangers of nursing in France, lay in delirium, struck down by the epidemic sent to torment more these already tormented islands.

Black again. No sooner out of mourning than back into it; and the child whose coming had raised her flagging spirits now daily becoming more sickly.

She must get out of this house of widows, she thought desperately; walk the anger and bewilderment out of her whilst the daylight lasted.

She stood at the top of the steps, Morgan beside her, determined to follow where he led—anywhere, save to the sickroom where Alice lay so ill and from where she could hear the crying of a hungry child.

The spaniel, who had been neglected of late, made for the wild garden stile with the joy of a captive released. He had

had little petting or spoiling, and been dismissed from the kitchen each time he poked his nose round the door. Yet there was one place left and he made for it, nose down, yelping with joy.

'If it isn't that daft dog Morgan.' Reuben stroked the head of the creature who sat on his doorstep, eyes beseeching. 'And her ladyship. Taking him out, are you? I'd be careful in the wood, milady. It's muddy underfoot.'

'I think rather that he's taking me, Reuben.' Helen sighed deeply. 'Though truth known I need to be out of the house. I can't even bring myself to go and see how Alice is...'

'Don't take on, milady. Things aren't all bad.'

'No? Alice is so ill and the baby sickening still? He can't feed. So robust a child born, yet now he can't keep milk down.'

'Oh, dear. Your ladyship is in a worse state than Russia,' Reuben chuckled. 'And since I'm in my best suit still, it might be fitting if I walked with you through the wood. It's slape underfoot; don't want you to fall over.'

He took a crust from his pocket, offering it to the spaniel who swallowed it greedily. By rights he shouldn't be talking to her ladyship in so familiar a fashion, but it was clear she was in need of comfort. A body could take only so much, and she was at the far end of her tether, poor sad woman. He crooked his arm gallantly, tipping his hat, bowing his head in deference.

'If you would please take my arm, milady, there's something I want you to see. You'll mind what folks have always said about the rooks over the years?'

'That if ever they should leave Rowangarth, then sorrow would follow? I know. Sir John believed it too, Reuben. And they left, suddenly—and what has happened since? More sorrow, when we might have expected some happiness. Giles taken, Alice so ill and the child—' She stopped, shaking her head, fighting back tears. Then she slipped her hand through the crook of Reuben's arm. 'What is it, then, that I must see?'

'Come with me. And don't you worry none.'

'How can you say that, today of all days? And Alice and the baby getting no better...'

'Milady—I was upset, too. Couldn't get the worry of it out of my mind, till this morning. See now, up there.' He pointed to the elms, the tallest trees in the wood. 'Look and listen.'

Above the topmost branches, birds

wheeled and dived. Black birds, cawing loudly, slipping in and out of the leafless branches.

'I heard them yesterday, milady, but I couldn't see them; thought I was dreaming. Then this morning I looked again and there they were—just a pair of them, but nesting; carrying twigs like they do to repair old nests. So count, milady. How many do you see now?'

'Several. At least six.'

'Three pairs, maybe more. Them old rooks is back. There'll be no more sorrow now. I reckon the bad luck has run its course. Nothing lasts, milady—good luck nor bad—but Rowangarth has had more'n it's share of bad luck. Things are going to pick up now.'

'I shouldn't believe this, Reuben.' She smiled up at him, eyes bright. 'It's superstitious nonsense and we shouldn't take any notice of it.'

'No more we should, milady,' he chuckled. 'But I'm right glad to see them back—and mending them nests as if they intend staying.'

'And so am I, Reuben. Oh, so am I!'

Jin Dobb said she couldn't wait for teatime. Got things to do more important than bread and jam; an errand for Miss Julia.

She'd be back in about half an hour, she called over her shoulder, breathless to be gone.

She returned with a milk can which she deposited on the cold slab in the pantry, then made for the housekeeper's sitting-room.

'Will you tell Mrs MacMalcolm that Jin has got what she wanted for the babbie, and if she'll come below stairs with a feeding bottle, I'll be glad to oblige.'

'I'm to say *what?*' The thin eyebrows rose.

'Just say *goat's milk,*' Jin snapped, impatient to be about the business in hand. 'She'll know what I'm on about!'

She had the mixture prepared in a well-scalded jug when Julia appeared in the kitchen, a red-faced child cradled in her arm, a feeding bottle in her hand.

'You're sure?' she asked anxiously.

'Sure as I can be. Us'll soon know, Miss Julia,' she sighed, filling the bottle.

The baby stopped crying, pulled the offered teat into his mouth, and began to suck hungrily. Then he closed his eyes, taking the feed more gently, making little smacking noises with his lips, stopping, sometimes, to rest.

The bottle emptied with a squeaking of air; Julia removed the teat from the puckered, milky mouth.

'There now, miss. Pat his back—gentle like. See what comes up.' Only wind, Jin hoped, but they'd soon know.

Julia rubbed the little back with gentle, circular movements; the tiny head lolled against her arm. Ten perfect toes, touched by the fire glow, spread themselves fanlike in its warmth. His eyes opened briefly, his mouth contorted.

'Ah, bless the little love—he's smiling at us,' Cook sighed.

'Smiling be blowed,' said Jin derisively. ' 'Em can't do that for weeks. That's wind he's trying, to get up. Rub careful, Miss Julia.'

Wind—*flatulence*—it was indeed. It came in two resounding burps, to the delight of those who watched.

'There now,' Jin smiled proudly. 'If he'd been going to throw that feed back, it'd have been then. He'll keep it down now. Just see if he doesn't!'

'You think so?' Julia whispered. Her eyes were bright, her cheeks flushed from the heat of the kitchen fire. A smile tilted her lips and she looked, for just a moment, Tilda thought, like the Miss Julia of old.

'I think,' Jin said, 'that the little fellow is going to do all right on that old nanny's milk. Oh my word, yes!'

'He's nodding off,' Cook whispered, rising from the chair by the fire. 'Would you like to sit there, miss, and rock him?'

'No thank you,' Julia smiled. 'You shall get him to sleep for me. I need a cup of tea. Shall you set the kettle to boil, Tilda, and will the rations run to a slice of bread and jam? I don't think I've eaten for days.'

'Spare it and gladly.' Cook nestled the baby to her. 'It's just like when you was a little lass, come down to my kitchen for jam sandwiches.'

'Then can I eat it here with you—a celebration, sort of? Alice is much improved, you see. Her fever is gone. Mother is back from her walk, sitting with her now and looking so relieved.'

'Then thanks be,' Cook sighed. 'I was getting to think there was a curse on this house.'

'Not any longer,' Julia smiled; not when the rooks had come back to Brattocks Wood. 'I think some good things will happen to us now.'

Not that she really believed such nonsense; she never had—even as a child—but if it made her mother happy, then who was she to scoff? Or to question the wisdom of those old black birds?

24

1919

'You will *have* to go out,' said Julia flatly. 'Today is so lovely.'

It was a rare February afternoon, with a silver-blue sky trailed with fat white clouds, and everything touched to life by a pale gold sun.

'I'd rather not. You go. Take the child.'

'Listen! You had a bad confinement and 'flu—of course you feel frail. But that was weeks ago! We could tuck the babe up warm in the perambulator—you could push. And that's another thing. His birth must be registered. All right! I know things were upside down here when he was born, but I want him named.'

'Giles said he would name a son; I was to choose for a girl...'

'Alice—why are you so listless, so uninterested?' Julia flung, impatiently. 'You aren't trying. It's as if you don't want to get well. You call your son *the child*...' Julia was worried. Things had to be brought into the open.'

'He *isn't* my son,' Alice countered

556

defiantly. 'He's Rowangarth's. He belonged to the Suttons the minute Giles married me.' It had been a silent bargain she'd made with the Madonna in that little chapel—and with Tom.

'Please, can't we try to make the best of things? We both lost the man we loved...'

'I was fond of Giles, an' all!'

'I know you were. But we understand each other; we are sisters now. There is a little boy to be brought up and you are his mother!'

'*You* are that, Julia!' she flung in a rare blaze of anger. 'I thought I'd died, I really did. After all the pain there was a lovely floating feeling and a long, warm passage to walk down—all echoes, it was. I wanted to get to the end of it. Tom was waiting for me; I know he was.'

'Well, I didn't let you die—neither you nor your child!' Julia flamed; the Julia of old. 'And do you think I didn't want to die? Do you imagine your love for Tom was any greater than mine for Andrew? You sit there in a dream. Once, just *once*, you've held the baby, and you gave him back to me so quickly it was as if you didn't want to touch him!'

'I was afraid I would drop him, he wriggled so.' Alice walked to the window, staring out. It seemed, she thought dully, that the world was coming alive out there; waking after a four-year nightmare.

She looked across to the wild garden. There would be hazel catkins, fluffily gold, and pussy-willows, round and soft like palest moleskin. And beyond, in Brattocks Wood, would be the scent of the earth awakening and buds swelling and wild snowdrops beneath the trees.

Yet no matter how often she walked there or stood beneath the tallest elms, Tom would never come; would never whistle her; stand there, arms wide.

They had been lovers; why hadn't that one coupling made a child? Why had it happened on a straw-stuffed palliasse in a cowshed?

Evil, evil *evil!* She could not love a child of so cruel a getting. Julia adored him; had taken him to herself. He had been born when she yearned for someone to love, ached for Andrew's child in her arms.

'You are more his mother than I shall ever be,' she said softly, sadly. 'The child must be reared by one of his own kind—not by a sewing-maid. You and he are bonded. I give him to you as I gave him to Giles.

'And you are right. You must register his birth. I would like him to be called Andrew Robert Giles—can you bear it, him being Andrew? Call him Drew, if it hurts...'

'It doesn't hurt. I am pleased and proud.

And Drew shall be his pet-name until he is shortened and breeched—till he's a real little boy. Sir Andrew Sutton...' She gathered Alice to her. 'Come out into this lovely afternoon, please try? You have been so long away from us. I want you back, Alice Hawthorn. I want us to be as we were.'

'We can't be. Those days are gone. But we'll have to make the best of a bad job, I'll grant you that.'

'Then come out? I'll go and get Drew—tuck him in all snug.'

'No! A walk round the garden, if you'll give me your arm—but just you and me?'

'Very well. Put on some thick shoes and a coat and muffler...'

Julia watched her go, acknowledging the wisdom of her words. Things would never, could never be the same again. They could neither of them turn back the clock, return to yesterday. But the pale sun of February promised that spring was just around the corner and, please God, a new, brave beginning.

'Andrew,' she smiled softly. 'Andrew Sutton...'

The first of March: days were lengthening and daffodils grew in thick drifts in the wild garden. Most of the married soldiers were back home now, and the single ones impatient to follow. King and country had no use for armies now. They cost money to feed and house; the sooner they were demobilised, the better.

Will Stubbs returned to the stables, horses still his first love; and if her ladyship would trust him with the buying of a decent pair for the carriage, he'd said, he'd be glad to oblige. Horses came cheaply now, the army no longer needing them.

Motors were the rage now, he stressed. He had learned to drive during his last months in the army, and knew enough about internal combustion engines to look after any motor in his care, he'd hinted.

He had smiled at Alice, glad to see her again, advancing with hand outstretched until he remembered.

'Mornin', milady,' he said instead, hand at his side.

'Will! So good to see you safe and sound!' She had offered her own hand, smiling gently, hoping he wouldn't ask about Tom.

Jinny Dobb left Rowangarth kitchen at about the same time. The bothy was to be opened again and needed a good bottoming, she declared, bucket and scrubber at the ready. It would be good to care for the garden boys again; move out of the almshouse and let Reuben move in.

'Mother isn't going to replace Reuben

when he retires, and he agrees,' Julia confided. 'He'd like to be out of Keeper's as soon as he can. He feels he'd be better replaced by a woodman: there'll be no more shoots here; not until Drew is old enough. Reuben says we can worry about stocking up with game when the time comes.'

'And the woodman—he'll have Keeper's?' Alice murmured.

'Mm. He can keep an eye on the wild game and see to the trees and hedges at the same time.'

Alice was glad about that. She hadn't wanted a new, young keeper living in a house she should have shared with Tom.

'I think the child should learn to shoot—handle a gun properly—though Giles wouldn't have wanted it,' Alice shrugged. 'But there's time enough for that...'

Alice was slowly regaining her health, taking walks with Morgan, most times to Reuben's cottage. She felt at home there; had no need to watch what she said or the way in which she said it; could be Alice Hawthorn from the minute she stepped over his threshold.

Her first real test had been the child's christening. Never had she been so thankful that Rowangarth was in mourning. Because of it, the ceremony had been simple, with no celebration afterwards.

Julia, as godmother, carried the child to the font, announcing his names proudly; Nathan, at Pendenys on leave, stood at her side, a godfather. Alice felt safe with the two of them there, who knew her secret and would keep it always.

Andrew Robert Giles Sutton cried lustily at his christening, which pleased his grandmother to dwell upon as she held him tightly to her on the carriage ride home.

'I like a child to cry at the font,' she smiled fondly. 'It cries the devil out of them, you know.'

Edward and Clementina Sutton called briefly to drink the health of the child; Clementina reluctantly acknowledged her nephew's wife, asking archly after *Lady* Alice's health.

'I am much improved, I thank you, ma'am,' Alice replied softly, exactly as Lady Helen would have done. And such magnanimity she could afford in her relief that Elliot Sutton had not been there.

'Awaiting his demobilisation; having a gay old time in Paris, I shouldn't wonder,' Clementina said fondly as she took her leave, telling Helen what a beautiful grandson she had and how lucky she was to have him so close.

'I have only photographs of my Sebastian,' she sighed, even though she wasn't remotely interested in her youngest son's boy. She wanted Elliot married; needed him to give her the grandson to whom Pendenys Place would one day pass.

'I think, Alice, she would like to see Elliot married,' Helen murmured as the motor bore them back to Pendenys. 'Elliot should have a son.'

'My thoughts, exactly, Mother-in-law.'

And she, Alice, had that Sutton-fair son. And she hoped, when Elliot Sutton married, that he fathered a dozen bairns —and never a boy amongst them!

'Where,' demanded Helen, closing the door behind her, 'is my grandson? Julia surely hasn't made off with him again? She is becoming quite bossy about him. You must put your foot down, Alice!'

'She and Nathan are wheeling him round the garden; they have a lot to talk about. They haven't met, remember, since Giles and I were married.'

'Nor have they. Nathan is such a dear soul. He'll be missing Giles, too.'

'He will. And don't scold Julia for the way she feels about the child, Mother-in-law. He was born when she needed someone to love; he gave her something to live for. She laughs, now. We must be grateful for that.'

'She and Nathan,' Helen frowned. 'You don't think—one day, perhaps...'

563

'One day, maybe, but not yet. Not for a long time. After Andrew, any other man would be second-best. You of all women know that.'

'I do.' Then frowning, she said hesitantly, 'Alice, I know there is a strangeness between you and little Drew: it often happens, Richard assures me. You suffered shock and the trauma of war; you had a far from easy delivery, then succumbed to influenza. It would not be unnatural in the circumstances, he says, for a mother to seem to reject her child for a while. Nature, he says, sorts it all out in the end.'

'Yes, thank you for understanding. Things will come right, I'm sure of it. At the moment, Julia's need of him is greater than mine; she thinks of him as Andrew's son; and it doesn't matter to a young baby,' Alice hastened, 'who loves him and feeds him and cuddles him. Leave him with Julia for the time being?'

'You have a wise head on those young shoulders.' Helen kissed her daughter-in-law tenderly. 'And I am lucky to have you. We shall stay here together, the three of us, and comfort each other.'

'And rear a spoiled little boy between us if we aren't careful,' Alice warned.

'May heaven forbid!' Helen laughed with delight. 'One Elliot in the Sutton clan is enough, surely!'

'More than enough.' Alice matched her mood to the moment of laughter, though her heart was sad because of the sin that would never be far from her innermost conscience.

Much more than enough, and may you never need to know the truth, dearest lady, of your grandson's getting...

Mary Strong returned to Rowangarth a week after the christening. Having received three proposals, she had weighed up the pros and cons of marriage, and turned all her suitors down to return to her position as parlourmaid to her ladyship as she had left it: a spinster.

The factory in which she worked for most of the war years had closed with amazing speed once the need for shells ended, and she had returned to her parents' home to take a well-earned rest and allow the pink and white of her complexion to return.

Bess, chaperoned by an elderly aunt, had already moved in with her young man above the shop in which he sold tobacco, newspapers and periodicals and, when the sugar situation again allowed it, boiled sweets, chocolates and toffees. Bess Thompson had done very well for herself, she not minding the squint in his right eye that had kept him out of the army, and him not caring that she looked as yellow as a Chinaman. It was all most upsetting, thought Tilda, who hadn't had one offer in any shape or form.

'I shall be moving out afore so very much longer,' Reuben told Alice. 'Lady Day, the new man should've started, but he'll not be coming till the first of April. Seems a decent young chap, the woodsman. Got a wife and bairn—came with good references. That housekeeper woman showed them to me; asked my advice.'

'I shall miss you not being at Keeper's, though you won't be far away, in the almshouse.'

'I'll be glad to go. I've made a start, sorting things. I had it in mind to get myself out a few days before—give the man's wife time to get the place to her liking. You wouldn't care to give me a hand—pack things into boxes...?'

'I'll have some tea-chests sent over and a few old newspapers, if you like. And you know I'll come.' Tomorrow would be best; just one year since Tom was killed, since Elliot Sutton thrust into her with as little feeling as a dog taking a bitch on the street.

She covered her face with her hands, shutting out the memory, angered she could allow such crudeness into her head.

'What is it, lass? Tell old Reuben?'

'It's just that—' She took a shuddering

566

breath, tilting her chin as her ladyship would have done. 'Just that tomorrow is the day I heard that Tom was killed. A year, it'll be. And—'

'And the day you happened on young Sutton,' he finished. 'Well, just you arrange to have tomorrow at Keeper's. Miss Julia will have the bairn, won't she?'

'She has him all the time, Reuben. Won't even consider a nursemaid. He's hers, as far as I'm concerned. She loves him like her own—like I shall never be able to, God forgive me. But it's best, that way. He'll get his bringing up from one of his own kind. I'll come to Keeper's tomorrow—and gladly.'

'Aye. Then if you feel like a little weep, or having a talk about it, I'll be near. So shall us have a sup of tea? Have you got the time?'

She had time. She had all the time in the world.

'I would like, Miss Clitherow, to borrow a bucket and scrubber,' Alice said to the housekeeper who had come to see what her ladyship was doing in the broom pantry.

'*A bucket and scrubber?*' Her words were a question that demanded an answer.

'Reuben moves out of Keeper's soon. There may be floors that need a scrub.'

'But, milady—*you* cannot! Tilda must do it!'

'Miss Clitherow, *I* wish to help Cousin Reuben, and I will be taking a bucket, floorcloth, scrubber and—'with unnecessary force she sliced a piece of soap from the end of a long yellow block—'*and* a piece of primrose soap!'

She threw them one by one into the bucket with a clatter, then marched up the wooden stairs. She crossed the great hall, shaking with dismay at her outburst, and opened the door of the bedroom beneath the eaves. There she took out her cotton housedress, a pinafore and a scrubbing apron, and drat Miss Clitherow and her snobbish eyebrows! And be blowed if Alice Sutton couldn't still scrub a floor with the best in the Riding!

Her anger had gone by the time she reached Reuben's cottage; anger that in truth had helped rid her of the feeling of doom that wrapped her round the moment she opened her eyes that morning; would help her, if she scrubbed hard enough, to forget the awfulness of today, this first anniversary of her sorrow.

'Are you there, Reuben?' Strangely, the door was locked and she peered through the window, relieved to hear footsteps crossing the kitchen flags.

'You forgot to unbolt the door,' she said

accusingly, taking off her coat, hanging it on the clothes peg. 'I'm dressed for scrubbing, if there's any to be done. Did the tea-chests come?'

'Aye. Will Stubbs left them last night, but lass—' He grasped her arm, eyes troubled. 'There's something I must tell you afore anything else. Sit you down. Kettle's about boiling—a sup of tea first, eh?'

'Yes, please. But what—'

Her eyes lit on the kitchen table. Milk and sugar had been laid there, and three mugs.

'You're expecting someone?' She held her hands to the fire.

'Not expecting, exactly.' His back was towards her; she was unable to read the expression on his face, but there was no mistaking the agitation in his voice.

'What is it, Reuben? Is someone coming?'

'No. Someone's comed. And best you sit down.' He laid his hands on her shoulders, pushing her into the chair. Then he walked to the staircase door, opening it, holding it wide, saying not a word.

A man was sitting on the stairs. Alice jumped to her feet, taking a step towards him, not seeing the bucket she had left there, knocking it over with a clatter. The noise of it filled the room sharply, the echoes hanging there strangely menacing.

The man rose to his feet, walking carefully down the three remaining stairs, and stepped into the light.

He was tall; his eyes were blue—so blue you had to notice them—and his short-cut hair was Viking-fair.

She blinked her eyes, the better to see him; the floor tilted beneath her. She cried out for Reuben and felt his hands hard on her elbows.

There was a churning inside her, a shaking she could not control. Her lips moved, but only the whispering of his name came from them.

Tom? Tom Dwerryhouse...

'Sit down, lass.'

Reuben's voice, echoing above her head; Reuben, guiding her to a chair, helping her into it.

Her hands gripped the wooden arms until her knuckles showed white. It was Tom! It *was!*

She rose, swaying, watching as he closed the staircase door. Then she stumbled towards him. 'Tom, Tom, bonny lad! Say something so I'll know it's you?' She held wide her arms, laughing, weeping.

Unspeaking, he looked at her as if she were someone he knew but whose name he had forgotten, taking a step away from her, placing the table between them. Then slowly he brought his finger to his forelock;

did it unsmiling, his face a blank.

'Bid you good day, milady,' he said.

'There's no call for that, lad,' Reuben said sharply. 'I told you how it was, told you she wed, now...'

'And what else, Reuben?' Her eyes were wide with fear. This was a nightmare. The man she loved—had never stopped loving—could not have hurt her more had he slapped her. 'What else did you tell him?'

'Nowt, 'cept you had a babbie and that Sir Giles has been dead these three months. What else is there to tell?'

'You must be proud of your son, Lady Sutton,' Tom offered. His words were clipped acid-tipped.

'Reuben,' Alice choked. 'Can you leave us?'

'I'd intended doing that—let you talk things over. But I'm not so sure now that I will, or you'll be fratching and fighting and I won't have that! I warned you, Tom. You knew the way it was before ever she got here.'

'I want you to go—please, Reuben?' she whispered. 'And there'll be no cross words.'

Unspeaking, Reuben fixed his gaze on the younger man.

'There won't be,' Tom said quietly. 'Give us an hour, will you?'

'Slip the bolt when I'm gone.' Reuben reached for his shotgun. 'If anybody knocks, don't answer.'

'If you say not,' Alice whispered, 'though why?' She picked up the teapot with hands that shook. Her mouth had gone dry; her voice sounded peculiar when she tried to speak. 'Why the bolt, Tom? And where have you been till now?'

'I'll tell you, if you'll tell me why you got yourself wed and pregnant within weeks of my being killed—leastways that's how it seemed, the way Reuben told it.'

'Geordie Marshall came to see me—he was passing through Celverte. He told he he'd heard there were twelve of you in a transport, blown up by a shell. Best I didn't hope, he said.'

'And does it give you a grand feeling, being Lady Sutton?' His mouth was set traplike, as if every word he spoke came out only with the greatest effort.

'No, it doesn't. And I need a cup of tea—you, too?'

'Please.'

He was standing too close; his nearness set her heart beating. Every woman's instinct told her to fling her arms around him as once she had done, searching for his mouth, eyes closed, lips parted. She wanted to say, 'I love you.'

'What else did Reuben tell you?' she

said instead, pouring milk into the mugs, her hand shaking so much it slopped on to the table-top.

'He said you'd been wed to Giles Sutton in France and that you'd had a boy.'

'And that Giles died the night it was born? Did he tell you I'm a widow?'

'He did, though much good it did me to hear it. That bairn has bound you to Rowangarth: you're one of them now.'

'I'm Alice,' she whispered. 'I never forgot you; used to talk to you with my heart. I thought you'd been killed, Tom. Maggie and Geordie said so.'

She passed him a mug, pulling out a chair, sitting at the table. He moved a step to sit down opposite.

'Are you going to tell me? Were you taken prisoner? It's a year today since I knew. It's why I'm here. I wanted Reuben to help me through it.'

'He told me that an' all, yet none of it rings true. What are you keeping back?'

'Say my name, Tom? Say *Alice*. Or is it so awful to you that you can't bear to hear it?'

Her face was paper-white, her eyes wide with pain, and he hated himself for hurting her because all through that year it had only been thoughts of her that had kept him going; thinking how it would be when they met.

'Your tongue's got sharp, milady.'

'Happen. And as for ringing true—I'll admit if I sat where you are sitting now, I'd not be satisfied with half a story. But it concerns other people; people I couldn't hurt. There are things I can never tell you.'

'Not if I tell you where I was?'

'Not even...' Her eyes begged understanding. 'I'm asking you, though. Where were you, Tom? Tell me?'

'I went home, to see Mam. Only Mam died in January of the 'flu.'

'I'm sorry.' She truly was. 'And before that?'

'Before I got back to Blighty, you mean?' Silently Alice nodded.

'I was on a farm, about fifteen miles from the Front. I spent the last year of the war there. Safe. I wasn't killed like they said; I wasn't taken prisoner. I was a deserter. I still am.' There. He'd said it!

'*Deserter...?* No, Tom! Not you!'

'*Me!* And don't think it was cowardice. Going out into No Man's Land sniping —that was a part of the war—getting Jerry before he got me. But taking cold aim; snuffing out a bit of a lad accused of cowardice was a different matter. Taking life like that was murder, and I had to do it—all of us had to—or we'd every one of us been shot. They could shoot you for

574

disobeying an order, did you know that? Once, a platoon down the line from us refused to take any more of it; said they wouldn't go over the top to be gunned down. They stood their ground when the order was given, so an officer picked out two of them; shot them as an example to the others. One of *our* officers did that.' He stopped, shaking his head. 'I wasn't a coward, though.'

'Tom—I'd never think you had been. I was there, don't forget. I saw men with terrible injuries. I cut filthy stinking uniforms off wounded men. I had to clean men of lice and fleas; stand by and watch them die of mustard gas. And not just spitting up their lungs—their faces burned by it, and their eyes. Don't tell *me* about that war! If you deserted I can understand why. But it was those special duties, wasn't it?'

'Aye.' He looked down at his hands, ashamed still. 'You'll never know how special! Do you really want to know?' he flung, bitterly. 'I was one of a firing party. They made an executioner of me!'

'Tell me, Tom.' She reached over the table, but he pulled his hands away.

'It was at Epernay. One morning, early on. He was one of our own—a lad too young even to have been in the fighting.'

And so he told her; haltingly at first,

then the words came out as if he'd waited for nothing more than to cleanse his soul. Tom had a sin too.

'That's how it was,' he finished. 'Like stepping into hell. I tell you, the only men there with any compassion were the stretcher-bearers—conscientious objectors —white-feather men. They lifted him gently, like he was a new-born bairn.'

'Giles was a stretcher-bearer, Tom. I wonder if Andrew was ever called to an—an *execution...*'

'I hope not. He was a decent man. But there'd have been no need for the doctor that morning at Epernay. They told us to aim for the white envelope on his tunic. I aimed straight between his eyes. I suppose if there's to be any salve for my conscience, it's that. I did it clean, and quick. I couldn't trust the other five, you see. They were shaking, useless, when they found what those special duties mean. If they'd missed...' Still he refused to meet her eyes. 'Do you despise me for what I did?'

'No. I went to France a girl, wanting to be near her young man. I came home a woman who'd seen things, experienced things, no one should have to endure.'

'And *I* came home a murderer. Can you wonder I deserted?'

She shook her head, then whispered,

576

'What then? Where did you go?'

'There was a terrible silence when it was over—none of us could believe what we'd done. Then I went wild. I knew what I intended doing could get me shot like the lad they'd just carried away, but there was such rage in me.

'I walked over to the officer who'd given the order to fire, and I flung my rifle at him. Everybody there was in a bad way, and I got away with it. I just walked away from them all, into the wood: I remember thinking it was like Brattocks. And then the shelling started—Jerry, giving us all he'd got. I thought I'd copped one, thought I was dead. The last thing I saw was the transport I should have been in—a direct hit. Eleven of them, just wiped out. They must've thought I was in there too...'

'Go on,' she urged.

'I woke up. It must have been afternoon. It had been just another bonny place before the shelling started, but the tree they'd tied that lad to was blown out of the earth, and the wood was like something out of No Man's Land. Trees splintered, the earth churned and pitted. And not a sound.

'I was like a man in a dream. I picked my rifle up—it was caked with mud—and I started walking. I thought that before long I'd meet up with some of our lot, but I didn't. It was getting dark when I realised

I'd been walking away from the front line, not back to it.'

'I'm glad, Tom, that you walked into that wood. You'd really have been killed, if you hadn't. That protest you made saved your life,' Alice comforted. 'Perhaps God saw that act of pity, and remembered it...'

She ached to touch him, hold him to her, tell him everything would be all right. But the man who had come back was a stranger.

'There was a farm,' he said. 'It was so peaceful I wondered if I really was dead. I had a drink of water from a well, then I went into the barn and slept. And I knew that when I woke up, I wasn't going back to the front line. No more fighting. I swore on that dead lad's life I'd never fire another shot.'

Alice shook her head, not able to speak, dashing away her tears impatiently.

'Don't weep, lass. That war wasn't worth anybody's tears.'

'No, it wasn't. But where did you hide, Tom?'

'I went no further. I awoke and this little lass was standing there—not a bit frightened.

'Hullo. Have you come to help Papa?' she asked me, and I told her I had.

'Seems her father was sick and the

578

farm work wasn't getting done. He'd been kicked by a horse—hurt bad. She spoke English, that little lass—Chantal, her name was.

'She took me into the farmhouse. Her mother looked at me old-fashioned, then started gabbling in French.

'Maman says if we take you in we'll have big trouble,' the lass said. But she made me understand that if I pretended to be shell-shocked and not able to speak so folk wouldn't know I was English and a deserter, I was welcome to stay if I would work.

'They needed me, you see—they didn't have a lot of choice. Chantal told me I must be their cousin who'd been wounded—badly shell-shocked—and couldn't speak or hear. The farmer agreed to it; I began to think I'd be all right. All I had to do was keep my mouth shut and act daft. And it wasn't hard. Anyone who came would jabber away in French to me. I didn't have to act gormless—I couldn't understand a word of it.'

'And no one ever suspected?'

'No. People felt pity for me, I think—a poor poilu shocked out of his mind. And it was an out-of-the-way place; they didn't have many visitors. I hid my uniform and my rifle and wore old clothes they gave me. Henri, the farmer was, and his wife was called Louise. I learned a bit of French and Chantal's English improved a lot. When Henri got better they kept me on.

'Then one day Louise went into the village; she told me when she came back that the war was over. Did I want to stay? they asked me, and I told them I'd bide my time, wait till something turned up...'

'So how did you get back—get away with it?' She fidgeted with her mug, not looking at him.

'My chance came three weeks ago. Chantal said there were a lot of soldiers —*Ingleesh Tommees,* she called them—in the village. Said they were marching and had put up tents for the night. Not three miles away, near where Chantal went to school.

'I knew I'd never have a better chance. I got out my uniform, polished my buttons and badges, and said goodbye. I set off before it was light—found the camp just about six o'clock. They'd got their tents taken down, ready to move off. There was a queue for breakfast at the field kitchen. I just joined it.'

'And you got away with it?'

'I did. Nobody took a lot of notice of me. They were all going back to Blighty for demob, I found out. There were all kinds there. Jocks, King's Own Yorkshires, Artillery lads. Nobody knew anybody and no one cared. They were going home!

'The southern regiments separated at Dover and went to Aldershot. The northerners were taken to Catterick. I needn't have worried. All I had to do was slip camp when it got dark, and walk home. Mind, I'll admit I'd been expecting all along to get found out. I had no kit with me, you see—just my rifle—so I decided if they challenged me I'd tell them my stuff was still in camp, back at Albert; that I was going home on compassionate leave because Mam was very ill.'

'And when you got home she—'

'She'd been dead two months. I felt ashamed.'

Alice pushed back her chair, walking to the window, staring out, seeing nothing. She didn't believe anything of this morning. In just sixty seconds from now, she would awaken to the sound of Tilda's knock and the pulling open of her bedroom curtains; would know it had all been a dream.

'So what will you do, Tom?'

'Do? I'm officially dead. They reckon there'll be a pardon for deserters, but not yet. I told them at home what I've just told you, then said I was coming to Rowangarth to find you. They said they hadn't heard from you in months.'

'Well, you've found me, so can I ask just one question?' She turned to face him, cheeks flushed. 'Why couldn't you have written? All the time you were on that farm you could have found a way to let me know. Andrew did it. He sent a postcard of Reims cathedral to Julia; just posted it without the Censors seeing it. You could have sent a card. The little girl would have posted it. You needn't have put your name on it, I'd have known.'

'It would have been too risky. Best I didn't go into the village, they said. If I'd been caught, Henri and Louise would have been in trouble, and I'd have been shot for desertion. And can I ask *you* one question? Why didn't you wait for me—at least till the war was over?'

'Life is full of whys and if-onlys, Tom. I can only say I'm sorry. What are we to do?' she whispered.

'*We? Do?* You and me aren't doing anything. It's too late. There's a baby—a Sutton child—between us. You won't leave your bairn and they wouldn't let you take him away. Sir Andrew, isn't he?'

'Called for Julia's husband. And that wasn't exactly what I meant. I was trying to ask how I can help you.'

'But of course! I got it wrong!' Anger showed briefly in his eyes, then he said, 'There's a job for me down south. It's a long story, but it was offered me by a bloke I met up with again at home.

582

Up north on business, he was. Hadn't been in the army—had a lame foot that kept him out. So he'd got himself started on war contracts: supplies, buying and selling. Ended up a very rich man and wanting to give jobs to ex-soldiers—ease his conscience, I reckon, because he'd done so well out of the war.

'Seems he's just bought an estate in Hampshire. There's a head keeper's job there for me. All I have to do is send him references from my past two employers. I've got one—it was given me before I came to Rowangarth; all I want is one from her ladyship. But how do I tell her I'm not dead nor ever was? How do you tell a woman who's lost both her sons to the war you are a deserter—much less ask for a reference?'

'You don't. I'll talk to Julia. She'll understand.'

'Tell her? Not likely!'

'Tom! She'll understand when she knows what made you do it. She hates that war too. Andrew was killed just days before it ended. Will you let me ask her?'

'I don't have a lot of choice, do I?'

'You don't. And Tom—say my name? Say, "I forgive you—*Alice!*"'

'Alice. Alice, bonny lass, I forgive you, though I wish you'd tell me what I'm to forgive you for; what is so enormous that

583

you can't trust me with it like I've just trusted you?'

'It isn't possible for me to tell you, Tom. I want you to forgive me for not waiting, though. There was a reason for it, but I can't tell you.'

'All right. I'll forgive you—if you'll say you understand my not writing?'

'I do. I know how it was out there. Oh, Tom.' Tears came afresh to her eyes and she hugged herself tightly against the ache inside her. 'I used to have daydreams—they kept me going—about you and me meeting. One day I'd walk in Brattocks and you'd be there—that one was my favourite. And in that dream you'd tell me the war had never happened; and always in my dreamings, you picked me a buttercup.

'I'll come back as soon as I can, and I'll bring your Testament with me. It's written inside it that your mam gave it to you when you left for the army. You'll want it back.'

'I'd like to have it, especially now she's—gone.'

'And the buttercup that's pressed inside it—do you want that too?'

For only a second he hesitated, then he said softly—said it like the Tom she knew and loved would have—'Bring me the buttercup an' all, Alice.'

'You're staying with Reuben?'

'For tonight...'

'Best Julia gives you the reference. Her handwriting is better'n mine. But if she won't, then I'll do it—on Rowangarth notepaper. You won't go? You'll wait, till morning?'

'I'll wait, Alice.'

'Then tell me just one thing more? How did you get such a job, land on your feet like that when there are men back from the army—aye, and with medals to show for it—selling bootlaces on the streets?'

'Dad knew him from way back. He owed my father a favour. And I haven't got the job. It all depends on that reference. Men like him don't give jobs without checking up, even when it's for old times' sake.'

'I'll get it,' Alice whispered wondering if he knew how much she wanted him to hold her, kiss her. 'And I'll not forget your little Bible.'

'Be careful what you say, Alice?'

He stood at the kitchen window, watching her go, wondering why he'd been such a fool; why he hadn't held her close like he'd wanted—like her eyes had begged him to. And kissed her, just the once.

He turned to the fire, raking it, laying on logs. He'd have liked to go out, take a walk in Brattocks Wood, but best he shouldn't; best no one saw him. There was no amnesty, yet, for deserters.

He sat in the fireside rocker and closed his eyes, thinking about her. He'd expected her, after what Reuben told him, to be dressed real smart, but she hadn't been. Just like she always was, in her cotton dress and pinafore; as if the war had never happened and she was sewing-maid at Rowangarth still. But those days were gone, and tomorrow, before it got light, he'd take himself off and out of her life. And regret coming here for the rest of his days—seeing her again. Because she was bonnier than ever he'd remembered, and he loved her every bit as much as when they had said goodbye that winter afternoon at the station. More, if it were possible, now that he knew he'd lost her.

25

'Thank heaven you're here!' Alice burst into the nursery, breathless from running.

'Where else do you expect me to be,' Julia demanded, 'when my sister leaves me to cope with babies and burpings and bottles and—'

'Julia! This is serious! I don't know how

to tell you.'

'What is it? Is something wrong at Keeper's?'

'No! Oh, *yes!* Put that child down, and *listen!*'

'Hold your horses and I'll take him down to Mother. And I didn't expect you back yet. Just told Cook there'd only be two for luncheon.'

'Will you *go!*'

'All right!' She snatched up a shawl, wrapping the baby in it. Something *was* wrong. 'Won't be a minute...'

'Now tell me.' Alice was pacing the floor when Julia returned.

'Well, I—' Alice drew a shuddering breath, all at once tongue-tied. How was she to tell it to Julia, whose husband would never come home? 'I—oh—it's Tom! He's at Keeper's. And I'm sorry, but there's just no other way to tell you.'

'Tom Dwerryhouse? *Your* Tom? *Alive?*'

Mutely, Alice nodded.

'But *how?* A prisoner, was he? Are you sure?'

'I'm sure.' Alice closed her eyes. She wanted to laugh, to cry. She wanted not to hurt Julia; wanted it to be exactly like in her dreamings, with the clock turned back to those blissful days before the war. She began to shake, then the tears came again, and deep, jerking sobs. 'Can you imagine it, Julia? Can you?'

'I imagine it all the time—about Andrew, that is.'

'Of course you do, and that's why it's so awful, telling you. Yet I'm glad.'

'And I'm glad for you; I truly am. But I'll ring for tea. You look as if you need a cup. And have a cigarette? They're very soothing...'

'No, thanks.' She turned to stare out of the window as Mary opened the door. Not for anything could she be seen in this state: hair disarranged, cheeks red from running, wearing an old cotton housedress and apron. Because Mary *would* notice. She always had. Straight down to the kitchen with the news, and what-did-they-make-of-that? Not that she cared. Not for herself. It was Tom she worried about.

'Tom's a deserter,' she gasped, the minute Mary closed the door behind her. 'He wasn't killed. Those special duties he was sent on...'

'Alice, go to your room! Change your dress and put your hair up properly—quickly, before Mary comes back!'

'Didn't you hear me? I said that Tom was a—'

'I heard you! But calm yourself, then you can tell me.'

In a daze, Alice went through the motions of washing her face and pinning up her hair. She was wearing a skirt and blouse when she met Mary, walking along the passage.

'Thank you. I'll take it in,' Alice smiled. She was learning never to be forward; never to be Alice of old; never to risk a snub.

'Milady...' Mary opened the nursery door for her, then closed it again softly.

'That's better,' Julia smiled. 'I'll pour. And I'm having a cigarette, if you don't mind.'

Alice shook her head, then started her pacing again, teacup ignored.

'You aren't taking this seriously, Julia. You haven't heard one word I've said.'

'Oh, but I have. And as for taking it seriously—well, it took me just the time you were out to realise we could be in quite a mess.'

'Why, for goodness' sake?'

'Because you'll be going to him, won't you—and there's Drew to think about. Legally he's yours.'

'But I'm not going anywhere! Tom made it plain he didn't want me. He mellowed a bit, but at first there was such anger in him it was as if he'd slapped me. And he was right. I should have waited for him.'

'Did you tell him why you hadn't?'

'How could I? But he told me where he had been—*he* trusted *me*. I said I'd have to tell you and he agreed that I must. He didn't do anything bad, Julia. Giles would have agreed with him, if he'd been here. Will you let me tell you? There's only you and me can help him. Will you give him a fair hearing?'

'You know I will. Just drink your tea, then begin at the beginning.'

So Alice told it; every smallest detail; every word remembered. About the special duties and the soldier condemned to die and him too young ever to have been in the fighting. Poured out every word, her eyes begging absolution for Tom.

'And that's it,' she finished, hands to her blazing cheeks, taking a gulp of tea gone cold in the cup. 'I'll give him a reference if you can't bring yourself to do it—but it would be better in your hand and, besides, I don't know what to say.'

'You would tell nothing but the truth, Alice: that Thomas Dwerryhouse was employed at Rowangarth for three years before joining the army; that he had always given satisfactory service, and could be well recommended for the position of head keeper. And then you would sign it *Alice Sutton*. Simple.

'But I'll do it for you—sign your name too. And you are right. Giles would have agreed with Tom. He hated any killing, and to have to do it in cold blood...'

'You understand, then? You don't condemn Tom for a coward?'

'A coward doesn't throw down his rifle and risk a firing squad. Your Tom was brave to do that.'

'He isn't my Tom—not any longer. We can't turn back the clock. But he's alive, and I'm thankful for that.'

'I don't understand you.' Julia stubbed out her cigarette. 'Do you imagine anything would keep me from Andrew—little Drew, even? Look, love—why don't we tell Mother? She would understand. She loved Pa just as I loved Andrew; just as I know you love Tom. She would tell you to go to him.'

'Happen she would, but what would folk think if I was to leave the child? Yet he's Rowangarth's son. Giles took him when he wed me. He isn't mine and I can't love him. I know that to your way of thinking he's the child that you and Andrew never had, and you can love him because you helped him to be born and found milk for him when he was hungry. But you aren't *me!* You weren't in the nuns' stable; didn't have to endure what I did!

'And do we tell your mother the truth, Julia—that I can leave the child because he's Elliot's? She was willing to accept the story Giles told her—could understand it, even. But to tell her now I could give up the child because I hate the man who fathered him—would she forgive the lies we'd told her?'

'But we *won't* tell her! She knows it is Tom you really loved; that it was easy to seek comfort in a moment of terrible grief. She thinks Drew was meant to be; sent to comfort *her*. To tell her the truth would be cruel. There are times when it is better to lie...'

'You're telling me to go to Tom. Will you also tell me what people would think of a woman who left her child?'

'But it's nothing to do with *people,* though we could tell them you've gone to France with Aunt Sutton because you haven't picked up as you should have done after Drew's birth. Richard James would confirm it. He's said it often enough. That would do, to be going on with. Think about it, Alice, though if I were in your shoes I'd be packing my cases now.'

'I can't believe this—not any of it. I'd expected you not to understand, to be angry about what Tom did. Is it that you want me to go? Do you want the child for yourself, Julia, and me out of the way?'

'Alice Sutton, what a goose you are! Of course I want the child. At first, I had to keep him alive—not for me, but for Mother and for Rowangarth too. And then I realised I had someone to love.

Not in the way I loved Andrew—that will never happen to me again. But there was someone who needed me—can you blame me?

'And I don't want you out of the way. You are special to me, Alice. You were there the night Andrew and I met. When you go, *if* you go, there'll be a part of me goes with you. But can't you see I want *someone* to be happy; for something good to have come out of that dreadful war!'

'You mean it, don't you? You honestly want me to be happy.' Alice took out her handkerchief, making no effort to stop the sudden tears.

'Alice! Stop your boo-hooing! I'll write that reference and you must take it at once. And while you are gone, I'll tell Mother all about it. She will agree with me—and with what Tom did, too. But tell me just one thing more? Tell me you believe me when I say I care so much for you that I want you to go? Because I do.'

'I believe you. But here we are, making plans—what are we to do if Tom is so hurt he won't ever forgive me? We're taking it for granted he wants me?'

'Don't be an idiot,' Julia flung. 'I'll go and write that reference for you. Are you *sure* you won't have a cigarette; you're shaking all over?'

Alice sped to Keeper's Cottage, the reference in her hand, Morgan straining on his lead. She wanted to laugh and cry, both at the same time. Big, lovely, happy tears. Julia had understood and so would her mother-in-law. And it were best the child be brought up amongst his own kind. Julia would be a good mother; make sure he never wanted for love. Panting for breath, she pushed open the door.

'Reuben? Tom? I'm back, and see who's with me?'

She stopped, looking around her, trying not to notice the sadness, the pity, in the old man's eyes.

'Reuben?' She snatched at her breath, running into the little front parlour, flinging wide the door. 'Where is Tom? What has happened?'

'He's gone, lass. I'm sorry. I begged him to stay, say goodbye, decent like, but he'd have none of it.'

'But I've brought his reference, his Testament.'

'He asked that I send them on. He's away down south, he says—will tell that man the reference is being sent by post. It isn't unusual for them to be sent that way.'

'Where is he, Reuben—at the station?'

'Nay, lass—he'll be half-way to York now. Had it in mind to get the afternoon train south, if he could. He had his cases with him, ready to go. You'll not catch him.'

'He didn't want me.' Alice sat heavily in the chair at the fireside, holding her hands to the warmth. 'He didn't give me a chance to explain—tell him I wanted to be with him. He only knows half the story, Reuben.'

'Aye, an' it's a shame. If I hadn't given my word, I'd have told him.'

'Maybe it's as well he never knew the truth. God knows what he might have done; blamed Elliot Sutton for coming between him and me. Knowing Tom, he'd likely have gone looking for him, done him an injury. Tom has a terrible temper on him when he's roused. Best he never knew.'

'So that's what you think, is it?' He picked up the envelope she had laid on the table, reading the words, *To Whom It May Concern*. 'That's Miss Julia's writing. Did she do it, then?'

'Yes, and gladly. I told her everything and she said I should go to Tom; leave the child with her and be damned to what people might think.'

'And so you should. Us as knows the whole truth of it would wish you well, Alice. Now you leave those things with me—I'll post them on. I said I would.'

'You know where he is? Where am I to find him?'

'Easy.' He reached behind the tea caddy. 'He left me his address. You know where he is now. Seems he decided to leave the choice to you.'

'You mean I should swallow my pride and go to him?'

'One of you has to—best it's you, Alice. Tom made the first move: let you know where he'll be. He was hurt bad. And there's no room for pride in loving. Must an old man tell you that?'

Alice met up with Jin Dobb at the stile. She was carrying the can she brought twice a day now, filled with milk for the child.

'Now then,' Jin greeted her. 'And where are you off to in such a rush? And haven't you something to tell me?'

'Tell, Jin? What about?'

'You've forgotten, haven't you; forgotten what I said that night before you went off nursing?'

'When you told my fortune, you mean? But wasn't that just a bit of fun?' Alice chose her words with care. You never knew quite where you were with Jin Dobb.

'It wasn't fun, not the way I saw it, and you'd do well to think back!'

'I remember you said I'd have two

children. Small hope of that now,' Alice admitted, warily.

'I told you there were tears for you, and I told you you'd know happiness and have two bairns. One would come in sadness; the other would bring joy. And nothing has changed. There's another bairn for you.'

'Don't, Jin! There's times I'm afraid of what you say. You said I'd have a brush with death—I remember you telling me that.'

'And you did an' all, when that babbie was born!'

'Yes,' Alice said quietly. 'But what are you trying to say? Is there something more I should know?'

'Not *know*. Remember, more like. I told you about a wood; an imaginary wood. I told you you'd walk three times through it, and twice sadly. I don't know about the crooked stick I said you'd find, an' I don't want to. But I know who the weak and frail stick was. Do you get my meaning, Alice Hawthorn?'

'I do, Jin.' They were standing at the stile, unwilling to climb over it. 'There's another walk for me?'

'You know there is. I said you'd have your straight, stout stave—if you had the courage to take that third walk, and the sense to listen to your heart...'

'You told me that, I'll not deny it.'

'Then if you won't listen to me, why aren't you listening to your heart? Where has your courage gone? Are you going to lose him a second time, just because you can't see the wood for the trees?'

'Now see here, I don't know what you are on about!' Alice swallowed hard but it did nothing to stop the wild pulse in her throat, nor calm the panic that thrashed inside her. 'Tell me? Lose him a second time? Lose *who?*'

'Tom Dwerryhouse—who else? He's here, an' you know it. I saw him this morning afore it was hardly light, going into Reuben's house. And don't try to deny it—you who looks like she don't know whether she's coming or going!'

'Jin, don't tell? He shouldn't have been here. Please, Jin...?'

'Course I won't tell if you say I'm not to. But it was him I saw, wasn't it?'

'It was, and he's gone. He just came for something.'

'He came for Alice Hawthorn, and well she knows it! Foolish woman you, to let him go!'

'He was a prisoner,' Alice gasped. 'Nobody was told.'

' 'Tis none of my business where he was, and I'll hold my tongue about seeing him, if that's what's upsetting you. But think on about what old Jin told you!'

She climbed the stile, hurrying towards the house with never a backward glance.

Think on, Jin had said, and Reuben too. And she *had* thought!

She turned on her heel, hurrying back the way she had come; past Keeper's Cottage, along the winding path to the edge of the wood where the rooks had built their nests again.

Black birds, it's Alice—Alice Hawthorn, as was—and I'm come to tell you that Tom is safe; he wasn't killed, like they said. And I want you to know I'm going to him, and nothing shall stop me! I don't know when it will be, but I'll come and see you before I go—say goodbye...

May, and the hawthorn blossom smelling bitter-sweet on the hedgerows, and the first of the buttercups flowering in the cow pasture. This was the time to go; six years on from the time of their first meeting was when it must be.

She had said her goodbye to Reuben, weeping bitterly at their parting. 'I don't want to leave you. You've always been here when I needed you—come live with me and Tom?'

'Nay, lass. The young and the old don't mix. Write me letters so I'll know how you are, and if I think you're needed here, I'll send for you—the little lad, I mean...'

'Bless you—though Julia would let me know. And it would only be if something legal cropped up—me being his mother, like. But I don't want to think this is goodbye. Come and stay with us, Reuben, for a holiday?'

'All that way? How's an old man like me to go travelling all those miles; me, that's never set foot outside the Riding?'

'But you'd be fine! I've been to France, remember, and thought nothing of it. Julia would see you on to the London train at York—you know she would—and I'd be at King's Cross to meet you. Say you'll come? Promise me hand on heart you will?'

'We-e-e-ll—happen I might. I'll think about it, though long train rides cost good money, remember!'

'But I'd send you the fare, you stubborn old thing!' Alice laughed. 'Wouldn't seeing you be worth a few shillings?'

'I'd like to think it would,' he smiled, 'but you'll need every penny you can lay your hands on, once you're wed.'

'*If* we're wed! Tom mightn't want me.'

'Happen he mightn't—but if I'm any judge, he will. A man has his pride, though, and till he knows the truth of how it was, then it's you must go to him.'

'I know that. And I *can* afford your fare, Reuben. Remember I once told you I had nearly five pounds in my penny bank when I left to go nursing? Well, they paid us twenty pounds a year when we were in France, and I hardly touched any of it. And there is Giles's money. Oh, I know that what he owned will go to the child—all of Rowangarth and the tea, in India—but when I came home he made me an allowance. My own money, he said it was, for clothes and fripperies, he said. And since I've never been one to waste money on fripperies, and needed few clothes as I was either pregnant or in black, I've got quite a lot of money. I've got enough,' she rushed on, 'to buy me a little cottage of my own, if the worst happens. If Tom doesn't want me, then I'll send to Rowangarth for my things and set up on my own, taking in sewing. I'll manage.'

'Lass, lass—he *will* want you. He's never stopped wanting you nor you him, but I'd be careful if I were you, not to let him know about all that money you have—leastways not what Sir Giles put into your pocket. Tom's so cussed proud that sometimes I could shake him—if I were young enough and daft enough to try it. Keep that brass for a rainy day, eh?'

'I will, Reuben—though now you'll be able to come to see us without having to fret overmuch about where the fare is coming from. And you *will* come? I couldn't bear it if—if...'

She threw herself into his arms, not wanting to leave him, because in leaving him she was leaving Julia, and Mother-in-law, and Brattocks Wood, and everything and everyone she had loved these years past.

'Don't take on, lovey. Old Reuben won't forget you. And when you've got saved up for a bed in the spare room, then I'll come and see you—I promise. I'm not so old I can't get myself on and off a train.'

He held her until her weeping stopped, patting her back, making little hushing sounds, telling her she'd once have given most of what was left of her life just to see Tom, yet now she was weeping because very soon she would be with him for the rest of her days.

She had walked back to Rowangarth sadly, slowly too, to give herself time to pull herself together; to tell herself how lucky she was, how easy it had been.

Mother-in-law had smoothed the way for her, letting it be known that Lady Alice was to stay for a time with Aunt Sutton, a change of air and surroundings being considered beneficial by Doctor James. It had been accepted without question too, except by Jin Dobb, who had smiled secretly because she liked knowing something others did not.

Now the time to leave had come and Julia was to drive her to the station in the pony and cart. Alice was taking just one case: the rest of her things she left behind in the little attic bedroom to be sent on later, because she was afraid to tempt Fate.

'Don't worry,' Julia had smiled. 'He'll be there, waiting.'

'I'm not so sure.' Courage it would need, Jin had said, to take a third walk through that so-to-speak wood, and courage she had in plenty, but listening to her heart, her foolish, uncertain heart, was altogether another matter.

Go! it told her most times; *stay!* it said, others. She had not heard from Tom, though Reuben seemed to know he was settled comfortably, and liking the south, though stubbornly he told her precious little else.

This then was her last walk in Brattocks Wood. She had thanked the rooks for keeping her secrets, and said goodbye, and now she must say goodbye to the child; to the bonny little boy with Sutton-fair hair, and eyes already changing from blue to grey; to the colour Sir John's had been, and Andrew's. Sad that one day he would come to realise his real mother had abandoned him, and him never to know the real truth of it. He lay in his cot in the nursery. He smiled a lot now, and gave out little chuckles when something pleased him. He looked up, smiling broadly, when she took his hand in her own.

'I'm come to say goodbye, and to wish you well, child. You have a good aunt and a fine inheritance in Rowangarth. Julia will love you always—your grandmother, too—and there will be Nathan to guide you when it's a man's advice you need. I'm sorry I couldn't love you, and that you'll always believe it was Giles who fathered you. For those things I ask your forgiveness.'

She touched his cheek gently and he smiled again, chubby arms waving. 'I'm going to Tom. This life is not for me. Once, I coveted orchids but now I know I'm a buttercup girl.

'Goodbye, little Sir Andrew. Your aunt Julia will write to me, let me know how you are. Grow up decent and true—Sutton-true—for her.'

She turned abruptly, closing the door quietly, walking down the stairs for the last time.

'Can I come in, Mother-in-law?' she whispered, standing hesitantly in the door-way of the little winter parlour.

'It's time to go already, Alice?'

'Yes. Julia has gone to get the pony and cart.'

'I would so like to come to the station with you—wave you goodbye.'

'No, dearest. We agreed it was best you shouldn't.' She was near to tears. One more kind word and she would weep like a baby. 'I want to thank you for being so good to me, so kind.'

'And I want to thank you for Drew, Alice; for letting us keep him. You must always stay in touch. You are Drew's mother—his legal guardian still. There might be decisions only you can make—you know that?'

'You shall always know where I am —even if Tom doesn't want me.'

'I don't want you to go, child. You have been such a joy to me. If ever you need a shoulder, I am here. But your Tom wants you, is waiting for you, I'm sure of it. Be happy together. You deserve to be.'

'Bless you.' Her voice was little more than a whisper. 'And will you remember me not as Alice Sutton—proud though I've been to bear the name—but as Hawthorn, who did your sewing and was glad to do it.'

She went into Helen's open arms, wanting to go, wanting to stay; wanting, all at once, to be the Alice who had come here with all she owned in a brown paper carrier bag.

Gently she laid her lips to Helen's cheek,

then walked, head high, to the door. There she paused, and turned.

'Goodbye, milady.' She made a deep, slow curtsey, head bowed, and in that moment she was a sewing-maid again.

'Goodbye, my very dear Hawthorn. God bless you and keep you.'

'I put something in your case,' Julia said as they stood on the platform at the little station. 'It's to remember me by—I want you to have it.'

'You shouldn't have. You gave me Morgan—he's enough. I'll never be far away from Rowangarth, with him to remind me.'

'Giles would have wanted you to have him.'

'Aye.' Alice wanted the train to come. If it didn't arrive soon her courage would fail her, no matter what Jinny Dobb had said. 'You'll write?' Already her eyes were bright with tears she had vowed not to shed.

'All the time.' Julia was weeping too.

'Please don't cry. And you know how I dislike being waved goodbye? Why don't you go now?' Alice pleaded. 'Give me a hug and a kiss, and promise never to forget me, then go—*please?*'

They stood, arms clasped, cheek upon cheek. 'I won't forget you.' Julia turned, then walked quickly away, head high, shoulders stiff.

Down the track, the train hooted. In just half a minute it would unload passengers and mailbags then return to York.

Alice dabbed her eyes, breathing deeply to help calm the turmoil, the awful ache inside her. The engine came to a stop, hissing and clanking and making altogether too much noise for so small and unimportant a train. She held Morgan's lead tightly, picking up her case.

Only one passenger alighted, and already a porter was piling his luggage on to a trolley. He had many cases and bags, and wore the uniform of a guards officer. He was tall, and dark, and spoke to the porter in too loud a voice.

Morgan stiffened, then gave a yelp of anger. The lead slipped from Alice's fingers.

'Come back! Come here!'

She hurried to where the spaniel crouched, teeth bared in a snarl, at the feet of the loud-mouthed man.

'Well, well, well. If it isn't the little sewing-maid,' the voice softly mocked. 'Tut! I beg your pardon. It's the young widow Sutton! Good afternoon, your ladyship!'

The dark eyes, the too-familiar smile, mocked her. The man took a step away from Morgan, still giving out low, warning growls.

Alice picked up the lead, inclining her head exactly as her ladyship would have done, clenching her hands so he wouldn't know how they shook, looking down at her shoes so he might not see the fear in her eyes.

'Mr Sutton,' she said gravely, picking up her case, walking past him as though her heart were not thudding nor her hands cold with sweat. 'Good day to you.'

She stepped on to the train, closing the compartment door, pulling on the leather strap to close the window, strangely glad she had come face to face with Elliot Sutton. Had she felt any doubts about that third walk through the wood, they were gone the instant she saw him.

Outwardly she had acquitted herself well; inside, in spite of the silent, screaming panic, she was grateful he would be the last to use her title; for where she was going, no one would ever hear of it.

The train pulled slowly away from the platform, gathering speed as it passed the far end of Brattocks Wood, where once Tom had stood to welcome her home from London.

She dabbed her eyes dry, calmer now. Alone in the compartment, she took a tiny key from her purse, and unlocked her case, curious to know what Julia had left inside for her. She lifted the tissue paper that covered it.

She remembered it well. Every stitch by hand; sewn with affection for a November bride—for a woman with love in her eyes who carried creamy white orchids, and wore a blue dress.

'Goodbye, Julia.' She lifted the silk nightdress to her cheek. They had shared too much happiness, too many tears ever to forget. 'Thank you for giving me something so precious.'

Alice rounded the bend in the lane and stopped, breath indrawn, gazing at the house standing alone in the trees. Taking in every detail with one sweeping glance, she walked nearer until she could read the words Head Keeper, painted in faded letters on the five-barred gate.

The red-brick cottage stood neglected, as if no one had passed this way for years, let alone lived there. She closed her eyes, seeing the doors brightly green again, the windows painted freshly white, and polished too—for surely they hadn't been cleaned in years!

The house stood surrounded by beech trees, their newly-opened leaves pale green and silky, bluebells growing thickly beneath them. She stood, hands possessively on the gate, loving the neglected house, wanting to clean it, care for it, live in it for ever. Timidly she lifted the iron knocker, bringing it down three times, listening to its echo inside.

It was empty. No one lived there and the realisation saddened her. She had so wanted this to be Tom's house—hers and Tom's—had seen it briefly, mentally, as it should be, could be.

Unwilling to leave just yet, she made her way to the back, for wasn't it a fact that no one in the country ever knocked on front doors. The one at the back was the one friends and visitors used; the front one was opened only for funerals, weddings and christenings—and when the vicar called.

Hope rose afresh inside her. A milk can had been left on the doorstep, a flat stone holding down the lid. Someone lived here; someone who kept labrador pups in the brick kennels to her left. They yapped excitedly as Morgan stopped, sniffed, growled a warning, then went snuffling on his way, tail wagging, nose down.

All at once she knew this was Tom's house and that his door would not be locked. She squinted through the uncurtained window at what was surely the kitchen of a man living alone; a man who piled unwashed pans and dishes into the stone sink. She knocked on the door then turned the knob, calling, 'Tom? Tom Dwerryhouse?'

A rocking chair stood to the right of a cooking range that hadn't had a shining in years, though a fire was laid in the grate with kindling and logs, ready to be lit.

She looked around her for some familiar object to finally establish that this was the house she sought. There was no rug at the hearth; the floor was in need of sweeping and scrubbing. A single chair stood beneath the whitewood table, one chair, where there ought to be a pair. It looked so lonely and alone, that tears rose in a knot in her throat. Then, as her eyes swept the walls, the mantelshelf, she knew without doubt that this was where Tom lived. She reached to take down the photograph of a smiling young girl wearing the uniform of a nurse.

To Tom with all my love. Alice.

He had not destroyed it as he might have done; he had kept it, hopefully loving her still, though his cussed pride had prevented him from writing and telling her so. And she loved him, and would tell him so; beg him not to send her away. She would even, she decided in a rush of grateful relief, tell him the truth of it all, though she had vowed never to do so. But now they had found each other again, nothing must stand in the way of their love. There must be no deceits, no suspicions, nor words left unspoken between them. She owed him the truth; best he should know so their new beginning should be free from doubt.

She looked at the mantel-clock, checking it with the watch pinned to her blouse. Soon he should return for his midday break. Taking off her hat and shawl, she laid them on the chair, then walked slowly, quietly, up the uncovered stairs.

There, she found three bedrooms; two of them small and empty; the third large and light. In it stood an unmade bed; beside it a chair with a candlestick on it. Hung on a hook behind the door was Tom's best keeping suit—the one he had been measured for in York so long ago. She touched it gently, lovingly, then returned to the bed. Turning the mattress, plumping the pillows, she quickly made it, then returned to the kitchen to wait.

The pantry door stood open, demanding her inspection. In it a rabbit hung from a hook; behind the door stood a sack of potatoes. On a plate, covered with a bowl, lay butter, margarine and cheese in small amounts; one man's rations for a week.

She closed her eyes, in her mind seeing clean-scrubbed shelves filled with jams, pickles, bottled fruit and apple pies, brown from the oven, set to cool on the slate slab.

'Tom, lad, when did you last have a decent meal?' she asked of no one in particular, checking the time again.

Suppose he didn't come home until nightfall? He could be at the far end of the estate, bread and cheese in his game bag, and a bottle of cold tea. She would wait half an hour, she decided—exactly half an hour—then return to her lodgings and unpack her case. First, though, she would leave a note to tell him where to find her—if he wanted to find her.

She opened drawers, but could find no paper on which to write; no pencil, no ink bottle, nor pen. Then all at once she remembered there was another way to tell him.

...and when I find you, my darling, I'll bring you buttercups, so you'll know I have been...

A vow made long ago to a dead lover, only he hadn't died and he still loved her—oh, please, he still loved her? She would leave something better than a pencilled note; something only she could have left there—something only he would understand.

Taking the chipped glass vase from the mantel, she filled it with water at the backyard pump, then set it on the table.

'Sorry, Morgan.' She tied the spaniel's lead to the boot scraper at the door. 'Good dog—stay!'

She heard the excited barking as she left the field, a bouquet of buttercups in her hand. The garden gate she had closed behind her stood open, and she stopped, all at once unable to move.

He was standing on the doorstep, Morgan's lead in his hand and his eyes were the blue that made you notice them, and he was every bit as tall and fair and good to look at.

'Does this creature belong to you?' He asked it gravely, softly, because his throat had gone peculiar. He could hardly say the words because she looked so beautiful; eyes big and brown and anxious, a tendril of hair trailing her cheek.

'He does,' she whispered. 'Once, he belonged to Sir Giles, but he's mine now. And he isn't a creature. He's called Morgan and I won't let him upset the game-birds.' She stood there, one hand on the gate, still wanting him, begging him silently to let her back into his heart.

'You came, Alice.'

'Did you think I wouldn't?'

'I don't know, but I wanted you to.'

He held wide his arms then, and she went into them thankfully, joyfully, letting the flowers fall, spilling them at their feet.

'Why didn't you write, Tom—tell me so?' She felt the roughness of his jacket against her cheek; the years between rolled away and they were in Brattocks Wood again, and she a slip of a lass, not old enough to wed him.

'It wouldn't have been right. That's why I left Reuben's house without saying goodbye; the choice had to be yours.' He laid his cheek to hers, loving her, needing her. 'You'll be staying?'

'Aye. I've got lodgings in the village for six weeks.' Three weeks to establish her name on the parish register; three weeks for the calling of the banns.

'I was feared you wouldn't come,' he whispered.

'Darling.' She strained closer, his nearness sending an ache of wanting tearing through her. 'Do you remember I once said there is a time and a place for everything, and that our time would come: it was the night you went away to Richmond, to the army. This isn't the place I thought it would be, but this is our day, and our time has come.

'And, Tom—I want to tell you. I said that morning at Reuben's that I never would, never could, but it's only right you should know why I didn't wait—why I married Giles. And when I tell you,

615

will you try to understand, and happen forgive me?'

He pushed her a little way from him, marvelling at the magnitude of his love for her, wondering how he had endured so long without her.

'Forgive? That I won't, bonny lass, because I took a solemn oath that if ever you came to me I would never ask. I'd take you as you were, I vowed, as the woman I loved—*love*—and wouldn't care what had come between us. Whatever it was, I don't want to know. It's you I want. Is the bairn at Rowangarth still? Do you want him here with you?'

'No, Tom. He's with her ladyship. He belongs there. He's a Sutton; Rowangarth will be his one day. Best he's with his own kind. And Julia loves him so. He's all she has now.

'But one day I *will* tell you how I could leave him behind me; explain how it was so you'll understand everything that seems not to make sense now. And since you are taking me on trust, I'll make you a promise, Tom Dwerryhouse. When I hold our firstborn in my arms, then you shall know—every last word of it. Will that satisfy you?'

'If that's the way you want it. It seems there'll be no peace till you've told it, sweetheart, so I reckon the sooner I wed you the sooner I shall know—if know I must.'

He looked down then, seeing the buttercups scattered at their feet, and he bent to gather them up, giving them to her.

'I see you've been picking flowers,' he smiled.

'For you—so you'd know who it was had left them.' She stepped inside the house, put the bouquet in the vase, then turning to him said, 'Kiss me, Tom—please?'

He tilted her chin with his forefinger, and laid his mouth gently on hers.

'I love you, Alice. Don't leave me again?'

'Never. I promise.' She reached on tiptoe, trailing her lips across his cheek, his chin, searching, eyes closed, for his mouth. And with that kiss yesterday was banished, and tomorrow as a delight still to come. 'I love you, too,' she whispered. 'I never stopped loving you.'

Through the open door a shaft of sunlight touched the buttercups and turned them into a shimmer of gold, and from the meadow a skylark flew high into the sky, trilling out a love song in notes of silver; but they did not hear it.

The publishers hope that this book has given you enjoyable reading. Large Print Books are especially designed to be as easy to see and hold as possible. If you wish a complete list of our books, please ask at your local library or write directly to: Magna Large Print Books, Long Preston, North Yorkshire, BD23 4ND, England.

This Large Print Book for the Partially sighted, who cannot read normal print, is published under the auspices of

THE ULVERSCROFT FOUNDATION

Other MAGNA General Fiction Titles In Large Print

FRANCES ANNE BOND
Return Of The Swallow

JUDY GARDINER
All On A Summer's Day

IRIS GOWER
The Sins Of Eden

HELEN MANSFIELD
Some Women Dream

ELISABETH McNEILL
The Shanghai Emerald

ELIZABETH MURPHY
To Give And To Take

JUDITH SAXTON
This Royal Breed